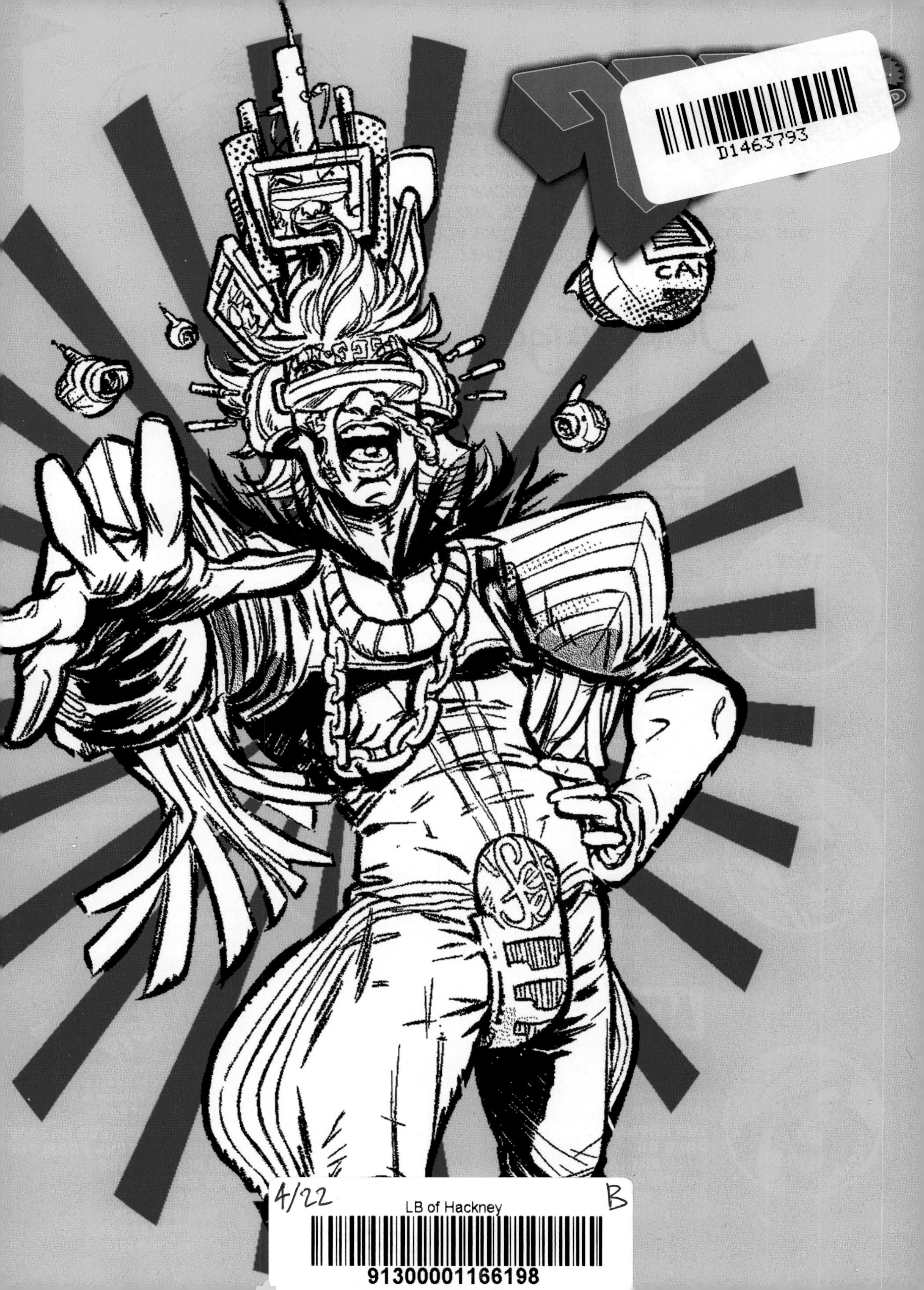

FROM ACROSS THE COSMOS I, JOKO-JARGO, HAVE GATHERED A *SIZZLING SELECTION OF SCIENCE FICTION ADVENTURES!* NOWHERE ELSE IN THE GALAXY COULD YOU FIND SUCH *PRIME PAGES* GUARANTEED TO BLOW THE FUSE OFF ANY *RUST BUCKET!* SO *STRAP IN TIGHT,* EARTHLETS, AND LET THIS ALL NEW VORTEXIN' VOLUME TAKE YOU ON A RIDE THROUGH SPACE AND TIME!

*Joko-Jargo*

## CADET DREDD

Mega-City One is a city so mean that only the very toughest cops - the Judges - can keep it in order. Cadet Dredd is training to be one of those Judges.

## HARLEM HEROES

Gem's a Justice Academy Drop Out with only one thing on their mind - Aeroball! But can Gem and friends succeed in the fastest, dirtiest sport in Mega-City One?

## ANDERSON PSI DIVISION

Anderson is a Judge in Mega-City One's Psi Division. She's a psychic, which means she reads minds to fight crimes!

## ACTION PACT

Plucked from their time and their eras, a group of soldiers led by Commander Drake must do endless tasks in order to find their way back home!

## VIVA Forever

She's fabulous, fashionable and - to Mega-City One's richest citizens - an utter fiend! Viva Forever is about to pull off the heist of her life!

# ROLL CALL

## MAYFLIES

The Mayflies are genetic infantry - specially recreated super-soldiers - from Nu-Earth, a planet caught in an endless war between the Norts and the Southers.

## FUTURE SHOCKS

Future Shocks are mindbending, out of this world tales, with twists that will leave you vortexed!

# THRILL ZONE

A HAZARDOUS COLLECTION OF JOKES, PUZZLES AND FACT FILES - WELCOME TO THE THRILL ZONE!

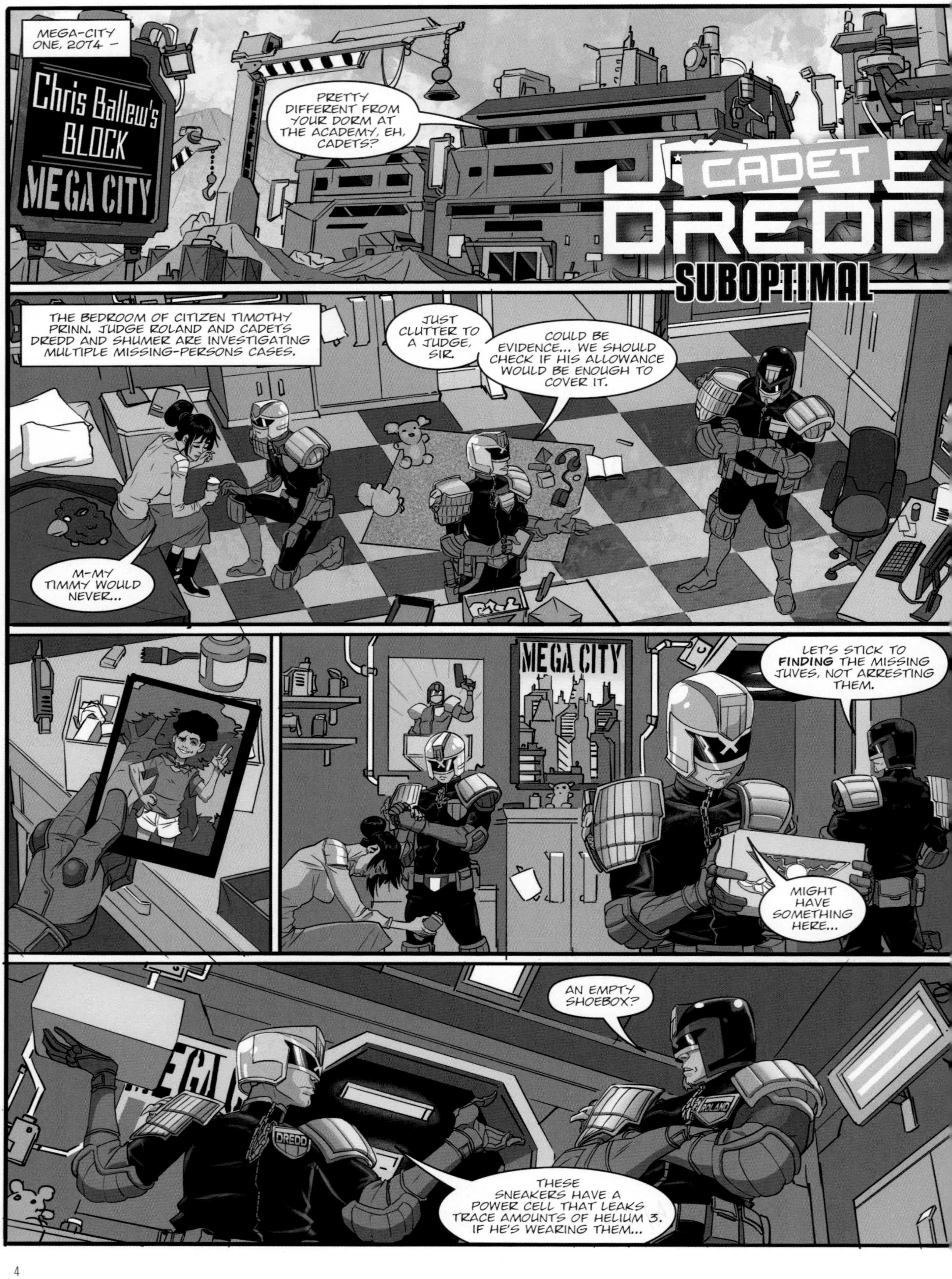
MEGA-CITY ONE, 2074 –
Chris Ballew's BLOCK
MEGA CITY
PRETTY DIFFERENT FROM YOUR DORM AT THE ACADEMY, EH, CADETS?
CADET
DREDD
SUBOPTIMAL
THE BEDROOM OF CITIZEN TIMOTHY PRINN. JUDGE ROLAND AND CADETS DREDD AND SHUMER ARE INVESTIGATING MULTIPLE MISSING-PERSONS CASES.
JUST CLUTTER TO A JUDGE, SIR.
COULD BE EVIDENCE... WE SHOULD CHECK IF HIS ALLOWANCE WOULD BE ENOUGH TO COVER IT.
M-MY TIMMY WOULD NEVER...
MEGA CITY
LET'S STICK TO **FINDING** THE MISSING JUVES, NOT ARRESTING THEM.
MIGHT HAVE SOMETHING HERE...
AN EMPTY SHOEBOX?
DREDD
ROLAND
THESE SNEAKERS HAVE A POWER CELL THAT LEAKS TRACE AMOUNTS OF HELIUM 3. IF HE'S WEARING THEM...

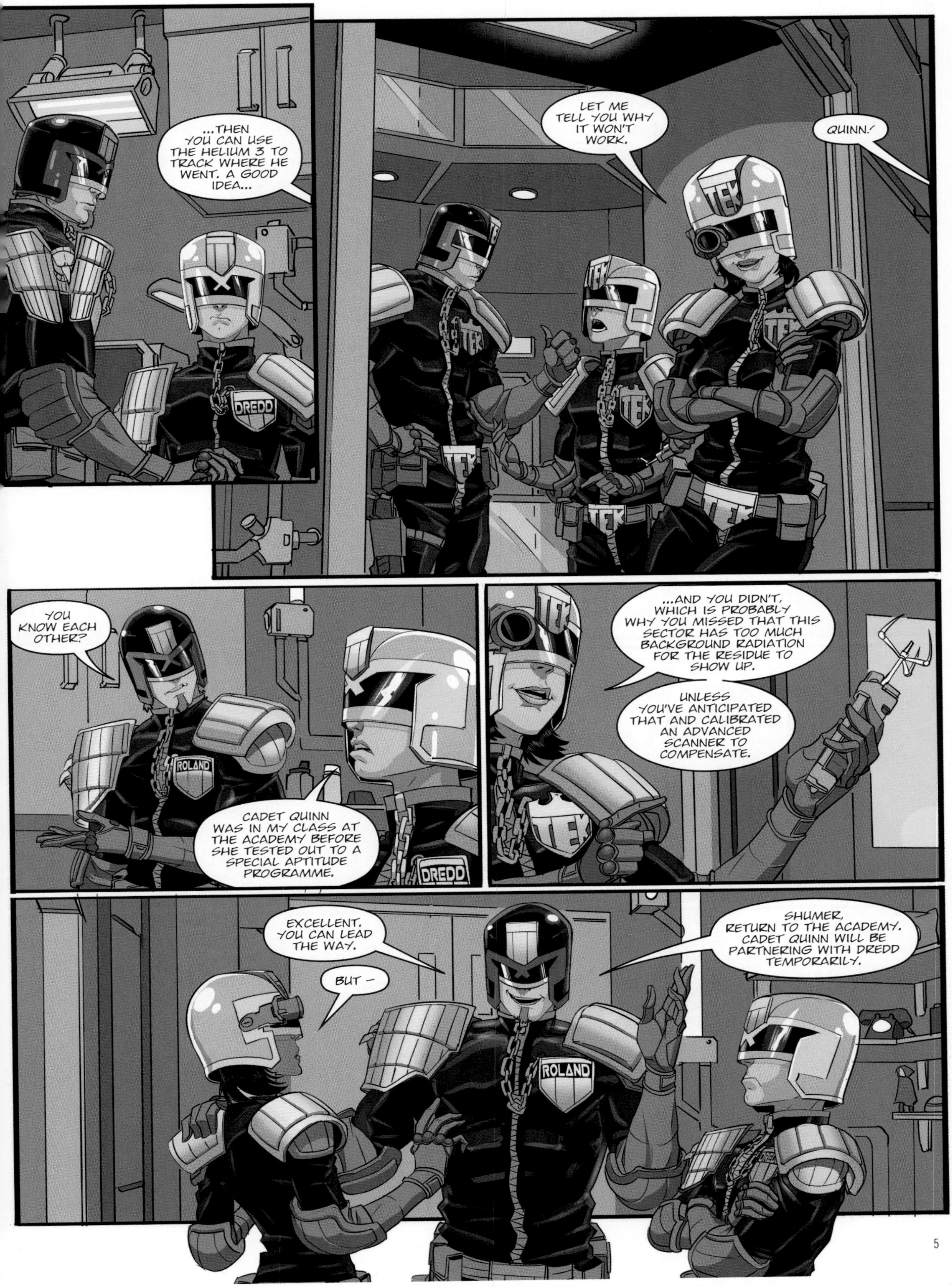
...THEN YOU CAN USE THE HELIUM 3 TO TRACK WHERE HE WENT. A GOOD IDEA...
LET ME TELL YOU WHY IT WON'T WORK.
QUINN!
YOU KNOW EACH OTHER?
CADET QUINN WAS IN MY CLASS AT THE ACADEMY BEFORE SHE TESTED OUT TO A SPECIAL APTITUDE PROGRAMME.
...AND YOU DIDN'T, WHICH IS PROBABLY WHY YOU MISSED THAT THIS SECTOR HAS TOO MUCH BACKGROUND RADIATION FOR THE RESIDUE TO SHOW UP.
UNLESS YOU'VE ANTICIPATED THAT AND CALIBRATED AN ADVANCED SCANNER TO COMPENSATE.
EXCELLENT. YOU CAN LEAD THE WAY.
BUT –
SHUMER, RETURN TO THE ACADEMY. CADET QUINN WILL BE PARTNERING WITH DREDD TEMPORARILY.

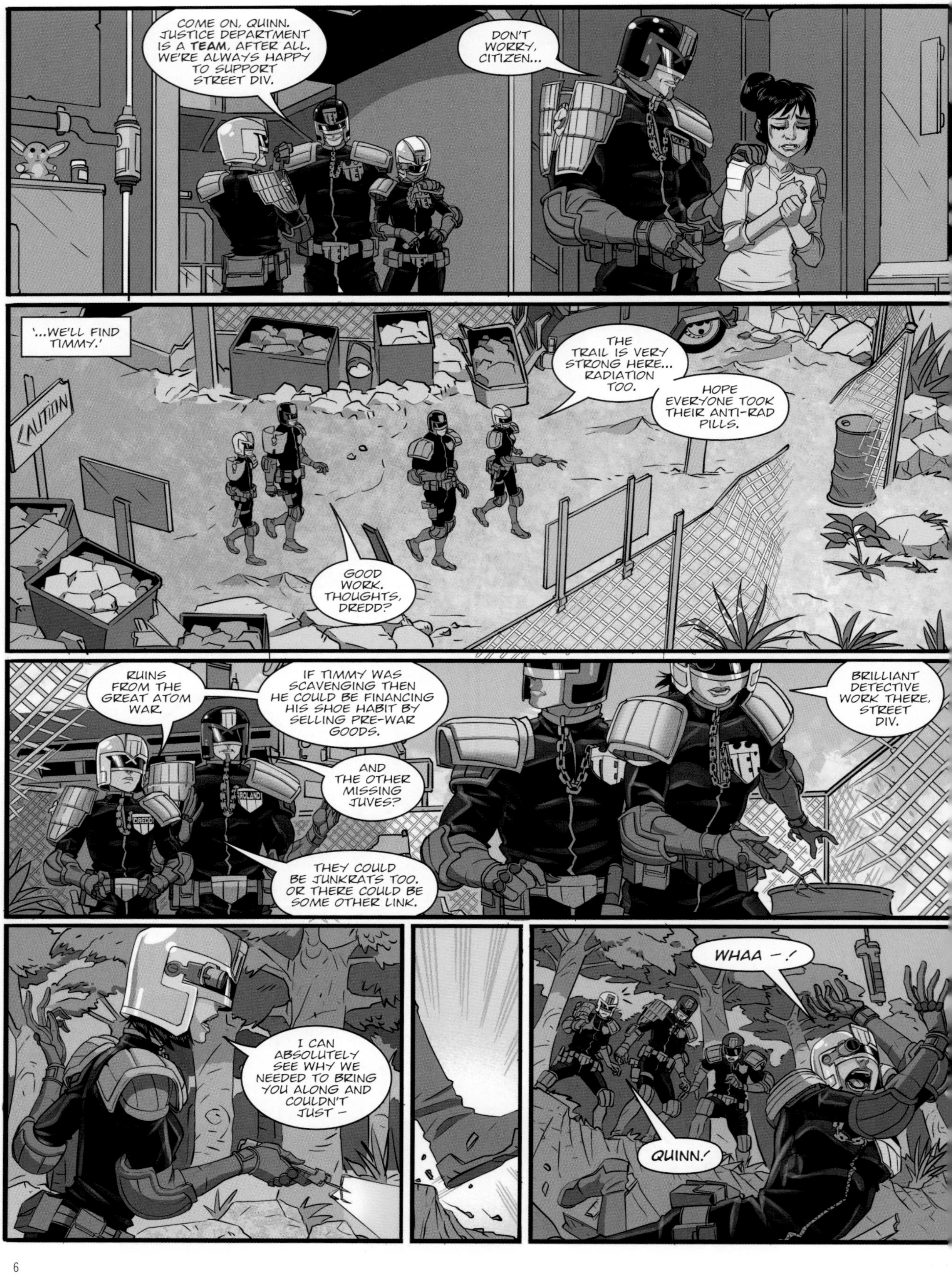
COME ON, QUINN. JUSTICE DEPARTMENT IS A TEAM, AFTER ALL. WE'RE ALWAYS HAPPY TO SUPPORT STREET DIV.
DON'T WORRY, CITIZEN...
'...WE'LL FIND TIMMY.'
CAUTION
THE TRAIL IS VERY STRONG HERE... RADIATION TOO.
HOPE EVERYONE TOOK THEIR ANTI-RAD PILLS.
GOOD WORK. THOUGHTS, DREDD?
RUINS FROM THE GREAT ATOM WAR.
IF TIMMY WAS SCAVENGING THEN HE COULD BE FINANCING HIS SHOE HABIT BY SELLING PRE-WAR GOODS.
AND THE OTHER MISSING JUVES?
THEY COULD BE JUNKRATS TOO. OR THERE COULD BE SOME OTHER LINK.
BRILLIANT DETECTIVE WORK THERE, STREET DIV.
I CAN ABSOLUTELY SEE WHY WE NEEDED TO BRING YOU ALONG AND COULDN'T JUST –
WHAA –!
QUINN!

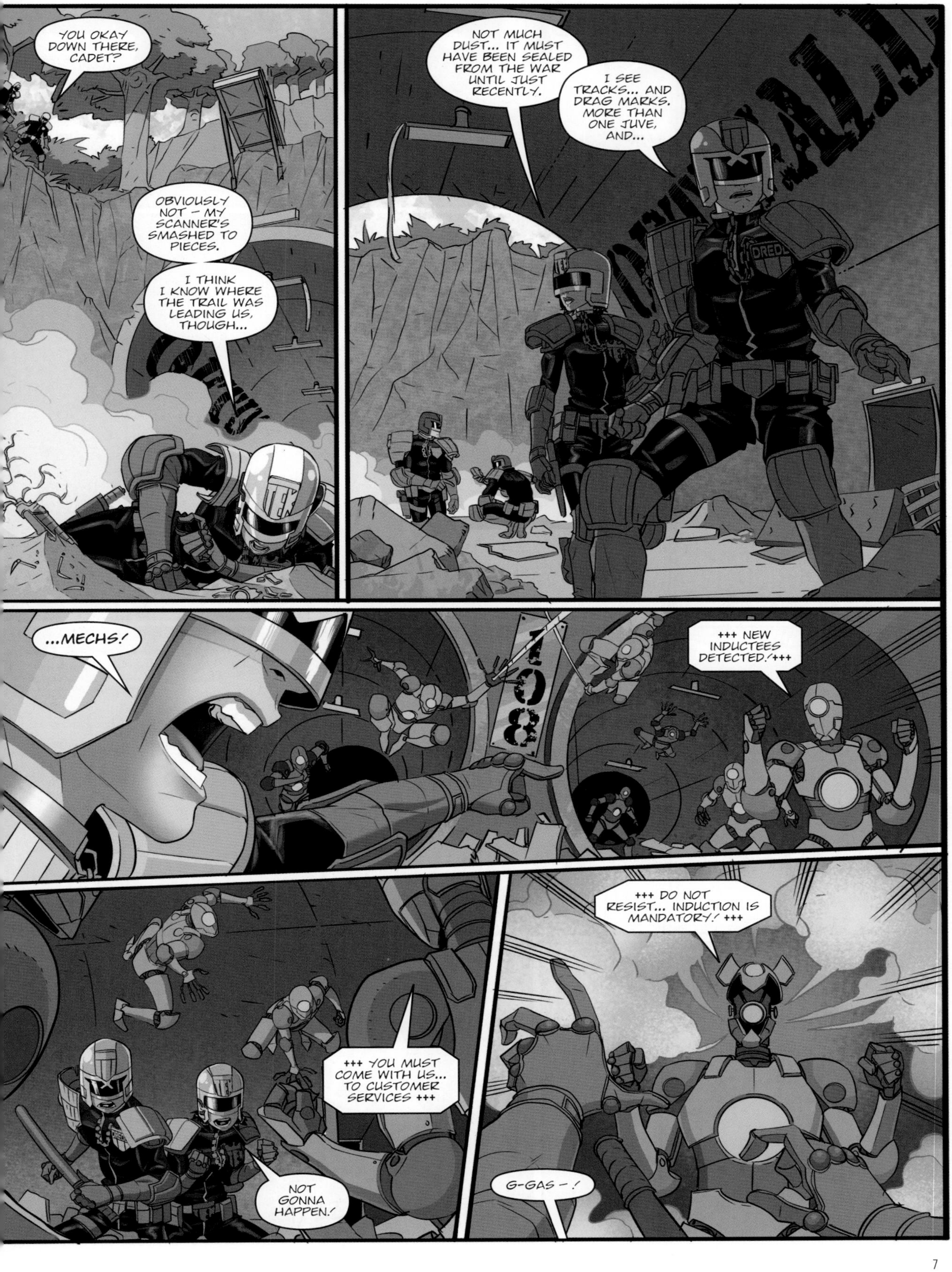
YOU OKAY DOWN THERE, CADET?
OBVIOUSLY NOT – MY SCANNER'S SMASHED TO PIECES.
I THINK I KNOW WHERE THE TRAIL WAS LEADING US, THOUGH...
NOT MUCH DUST... IT MUST HAVE BEEN SEALED FROM THE WAR UNTIL JUST RECENTLY.
I SEE TRACKS... AND DRAG MARKS. MORE THAN ONE JUVE, AND...
...MECHS!
+++ NEW INDUCTEES DETECTED! +++
+++ YOU MUST COME WITH US... TO CUSTOMER SERVICES +++
NOT GONNA HAPPEN!
+++ DO NOT RESIST... INDUCTION IS MANDATORY! +++
G-GAS –!

WHU – ?

WELCOME, NEW INDUCTEES, TO **OPTI-MALL**, WHERE YOUR CONVENIENCE, COMPLIANCE AND SAFETY ARE OUR KEY TO SUCCESS!

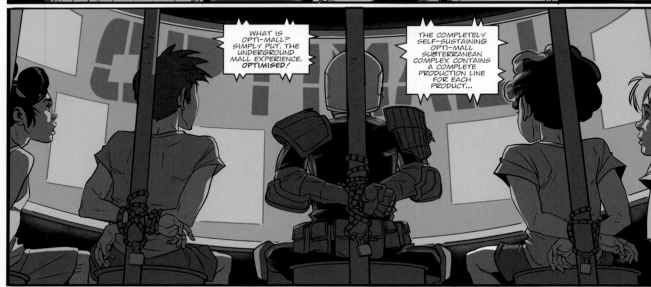

WHAT IS OPTI-MALL? SIMPLY PUT, THE UNDERGROUND MALL EXPERIENCE, OPTIMISED!

THE COMPLETELY SELF-SUSTAINING OPTI-MALL SUBTERRANEAN COMPLEX CONTAINS A COMPLETE PRODUCTION LINE FOR EACH PRODUCT...

...FULLY AUTOMATED AND STOCKED TO KEEP RUNNING FOR DECADES.

TIMMY...

BUT WHERE DO YOU COME INTO THIS?

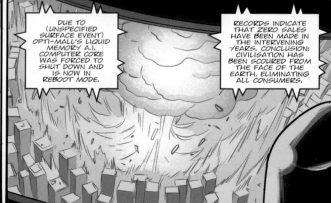

DUE TO (UNSPECIFIED SURFACE EVENT) OPTI-MALL'S LIQUID MEMORY A.I. COMPUTER CORE WAS FORCED TO SHUT DOWN AND IS NOW IN REBOOT MODE.

RECORDS INDICATE THAT ZERO SALES HAVE BEEN MADE IN THE INTERVENING YEARS. CONCLUSION: CIVILISATION HAS BEEN SCOURED FROM THE FACE OF THE EARTH, ELIMINATING ALL CONSUMERS.

FURTHER CONCLUSION: NEW CONSUMERS MUST BE RECRUITED FROM THE SURVIVORS OF (UNSPECIFIED SURFACE EVENT) – YOU!

NNNGH!

HOLD ON, LET ME GET THAT FOR YOU.

THEY TOOK OUR LAWGIVERS BUT THEY MISSED MY TOOLS.

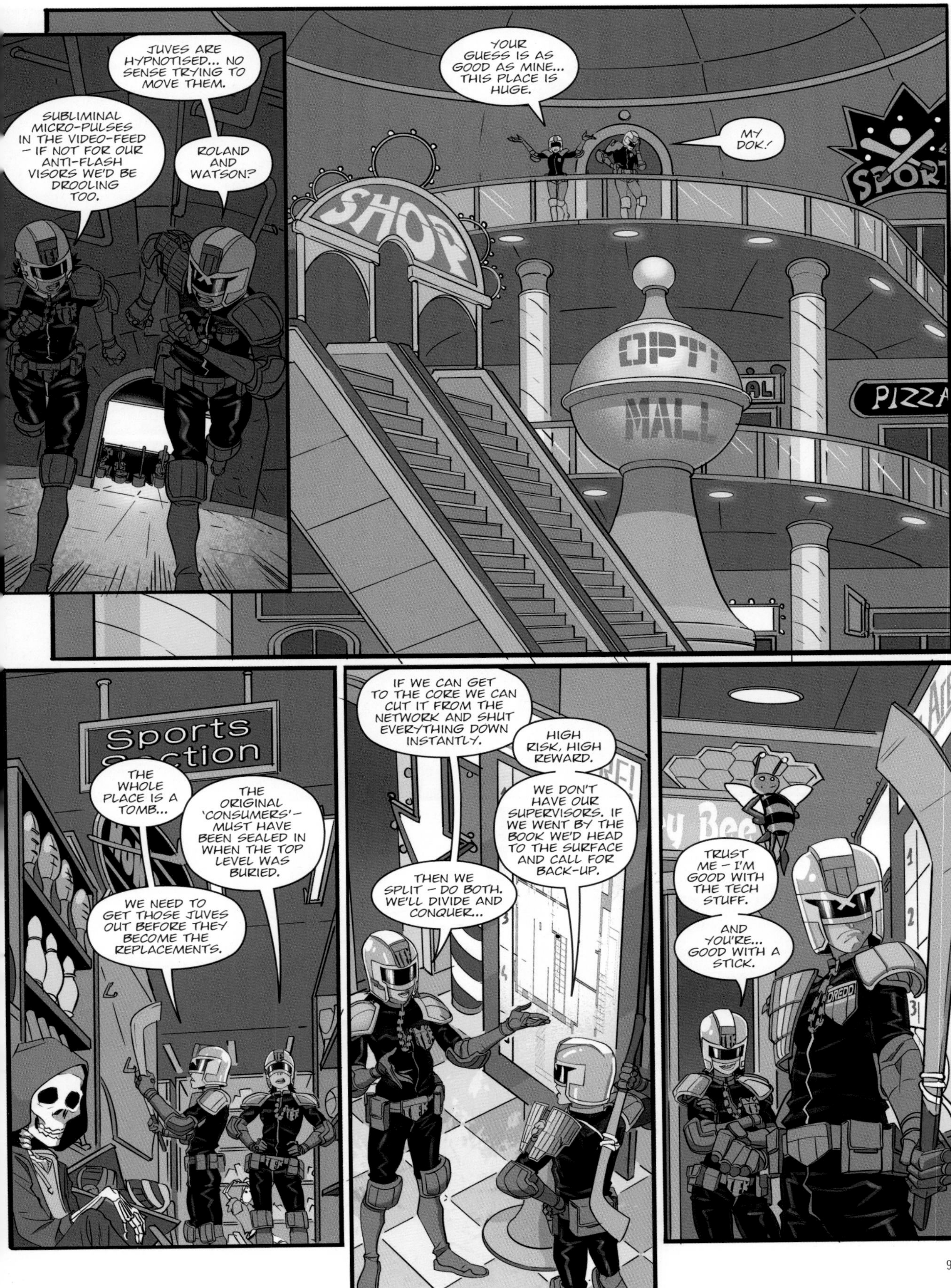

JUVES ARE HYPNOTISED... NO SENSE TRYING TO MOVE THEM.
SUBLIMINAL MICRO-PULSES IN THE VIDEO-FEED – IF NOT FOR OUR ANTI-FLASH VISORS WE'D BE DROOLING TOO.
ROLAND AND WATSON?
YOUR GUESS IS AS GOOD AS MINE... THIS PLACE IS HUGE.
MY DOK!
SHOP
OPTI MALL
PIZZA
Sports Section
THE WHOLE PLACE IS A TOMB...
THE ORIGINAL 'CONSUMERS'– MUST HAVE BEEN SEALED IN WHEN THE TOP LEVEL WAS BURIED.
WE NEED TO GET THOSE JUVES OUT BEFORE THEY BECOME THE REPLACEMENTS.
IF WE CAN GET TO THE CORE WE CAN CUT IT FROM THE NETWORK AND SHUT EVERYTHING DOWN INSTANTLY.
HIGH RISK, HIGH REWARD.
WE DON'T HAVE OUR SUPERVISORS. IF WE WENT BY THE BOOK WE'D HEAD TO THE SURFACE AND CALL FOR BACK-UP.
THEN WE SPLIT – DO BOTH. WE'LL DIVIDE AND CONQUER...
TRUST ME – I'M GOOD WITH THE TECH STUFF.
AND YOU'RE... GOOD WITH A STICK.

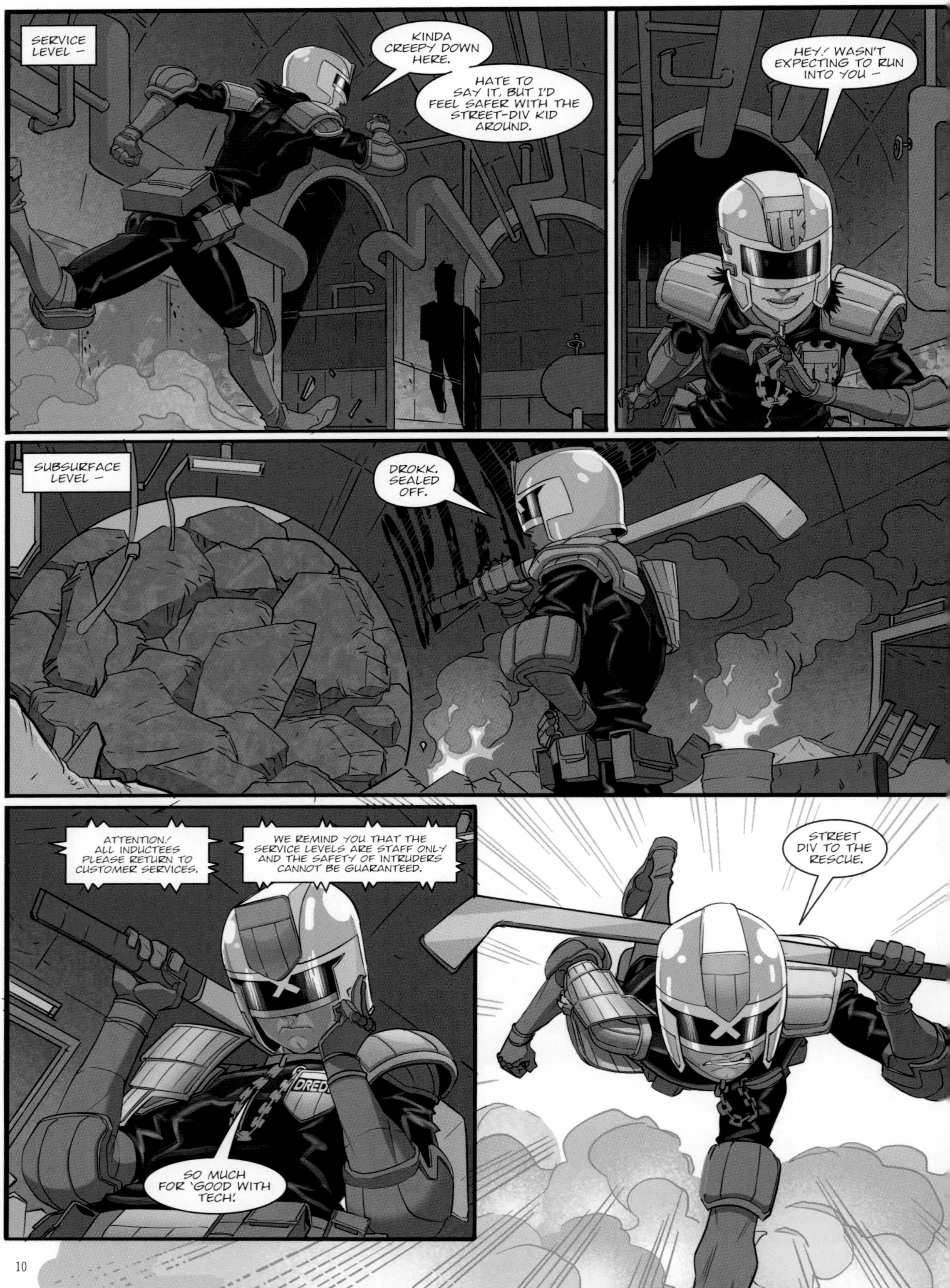
SERVICE LEVEL –
KINDA CREEPY DOWN HERE.
HATE TO SAY IT, BUT I'D FEEL SAFER WITH THE STREET-DIV KID AROUND.
HEY! WASN'T EXPECTING TO RUN INTO YOU –
SUBSURFACE LEVEL –
DROKK. SEALED OFF.
ATTENTION! ALL INDUCTEES PLEASE RETURN TO CUSTOMER SERVICES.
WE REMIND YOU THAT THE SERVICE LEVELS ARE STAFF ONLY AND THE SAFETY OF INTRUDERS CANNOT BE GUARANTEED.
SO MUCH FOR 'GOOD WITH TECH.'
STREET DIV TO THE RESCUE.

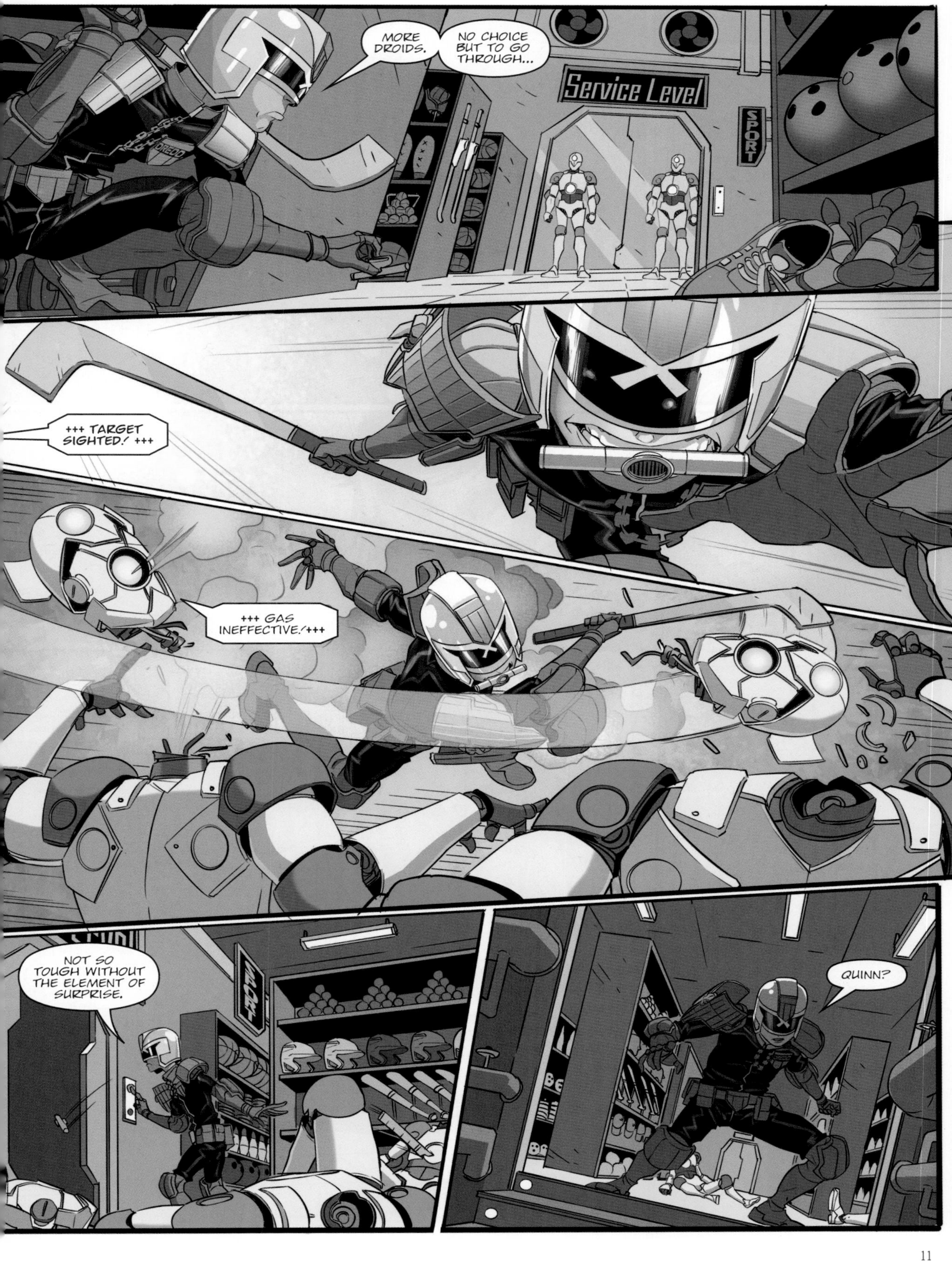
MORE DROIDS.
NO CHOICE BUT TO GO THROUGH...
Service Level
SPORT
+++ TARGET SIGHTED! +++
+++ GAS INEFFECTIVE! +++
NOT SO TOUGH WITHOUT THE ELEMENT OF SURPRISE.
SPORT
QUINN?

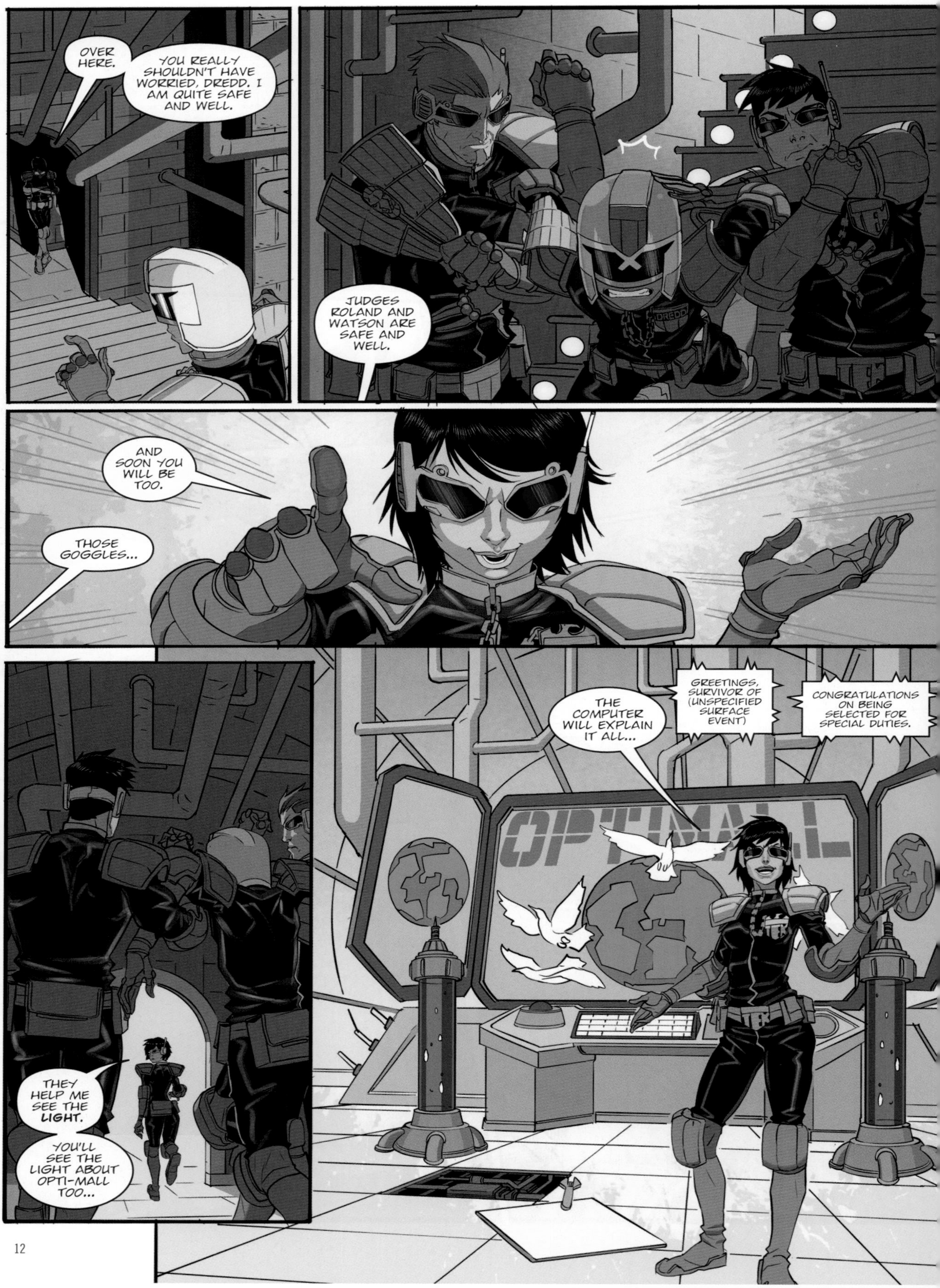
OVER HERE.
YOU REALLY SHOULDN'T HAVE WORRIED, DREDD. I AM QUITE SAFE AND WELL.
JUDGES ROLAND AND WATSON ARE SAFE AND WELL.
AND SOON YOU WILL BE TOO.
THOSE GOGGLES...
THEY HELP ME SEE THE LIGHT.
YOU'LL SEE THE LIGHT ABOUT OPTI-MALL TOO...
THE COMPUTER WILL EXPLAIN IT ALL...
GREETINGS, SURVIVOR OF (UNSPECIFIED SURFACE EVENT)
CONGRATULATIONS ON BEING SELECTED FOR SPECIAL DUTIES.
OPTIMALL

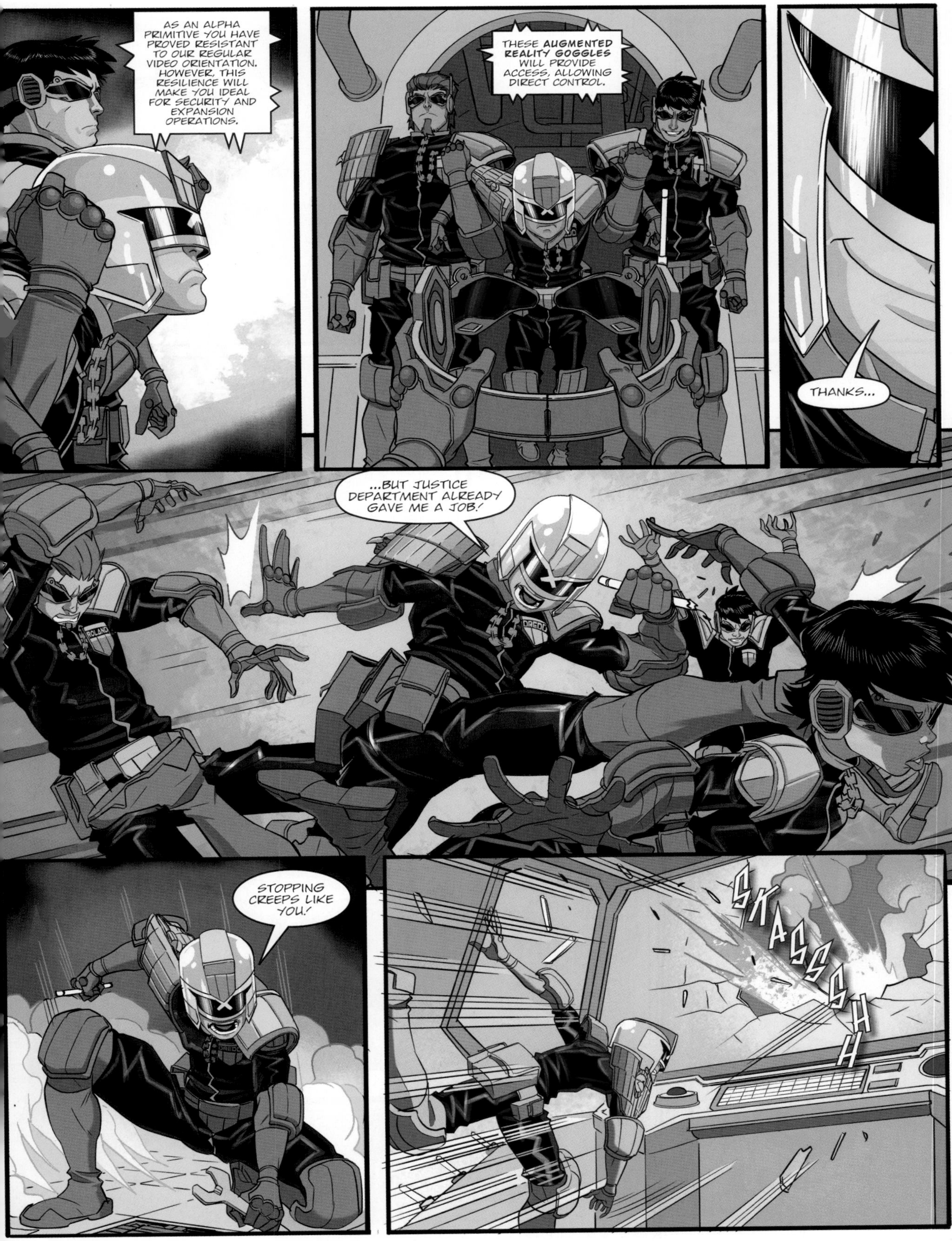
AS AN ALPHA PRIMITIVE YOU HAVE PROVED RESISTANT TO OUR REGULAR VIDEO ORIENTATION. HOWEVER, THIS RESILIENCE WILL MAKE YOU IDEAL FOR SECURITY AND EXPANSION OPERATIONS.
THESE **AUGMENTED REALITY GOGGLES** WILL PROVIDE ACCESS, ALLOWING DIRECT CONTROL.
THANKS...
...BUT JUSTICE DEPARTMENT ALREADY GAVE ME A JOB!
ROLAND
DREDD
STOPPING CREEPS LIKE YOU!
SKASSSHH

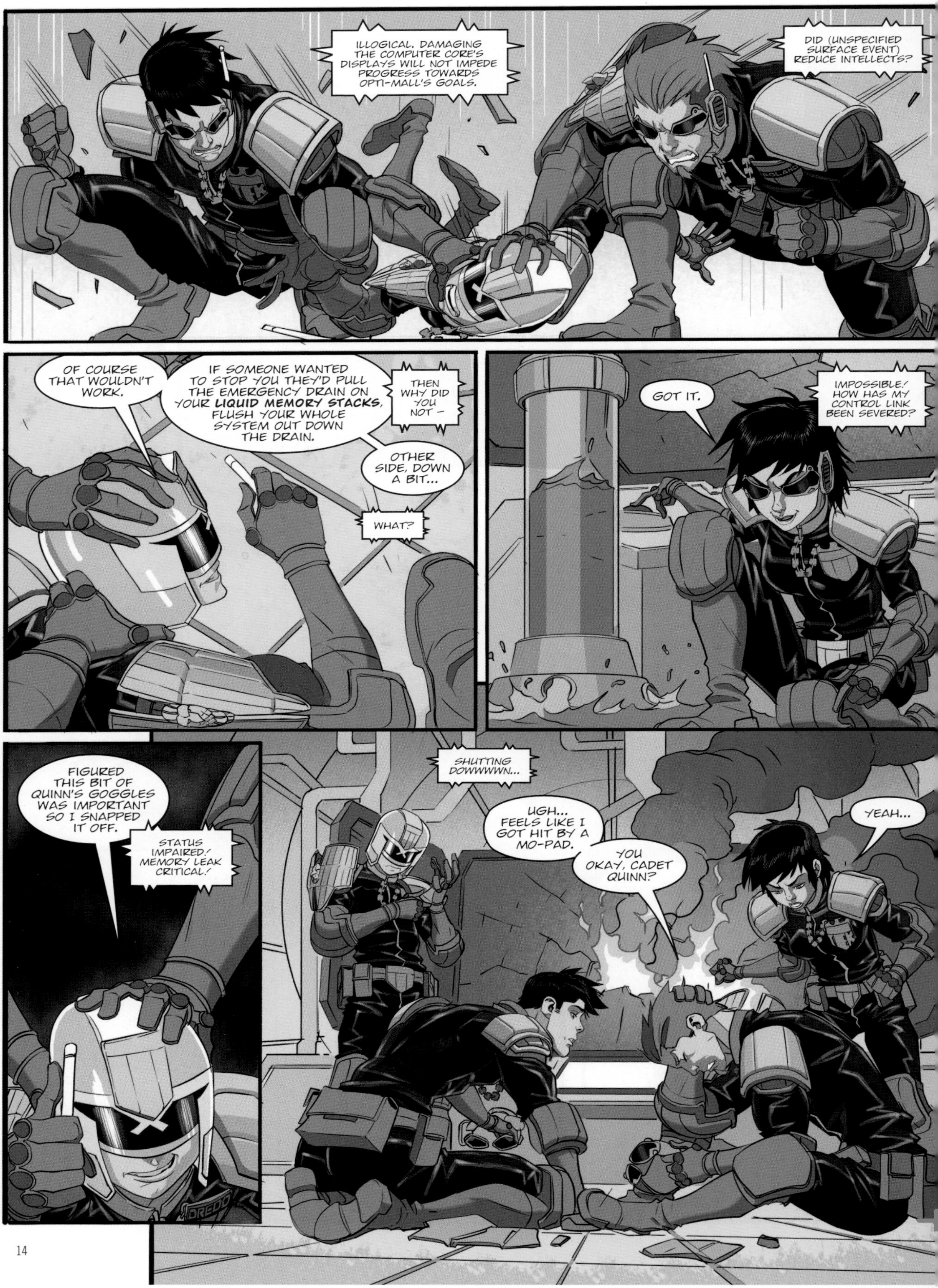
ILLOGICAL. DAMAGING THE COMPUTER CORE'S DISPLAYS WILL NOT IMPEDE PROGRESS TOWARDS OPTI-MALL'S GOALS.
DID (UNSPECIFIED SURFACE EVENT) REDUCE INTELLECTS?
OF COURSE THAT WOULDN'T WORK.
IF SOMEONE WANTED TO STOP YOU THEY'D PULL THE EMERGENCY DRAIN ON YOUR **LIQUID MEMORY STACKS**, FLUSH YOUR WHOLE SYSTEM OUT DOWN THE DRAIN.
THEN WHY DID YOU NOT –
OTHER SIDE, DOWN A BIT...
WHAT?
GOT IT.
IMPOSSIBLE! HOW HAS MY CONTROL LINK BEEN SEVERED?
FIGURED THIS BIT OF QUINN'S GOGGLES WAS IMPORTANT SO I SNAPPED IT OFF.
STATUS IMPAIRED! MEMORY LEAK CRITICAL!
SHUTTING DOWWWWN...
UGH... FEELS LIKE I GOT HIT BY A MO-PAD.
YOU OKAY, CADET QUINN?
YEAH...

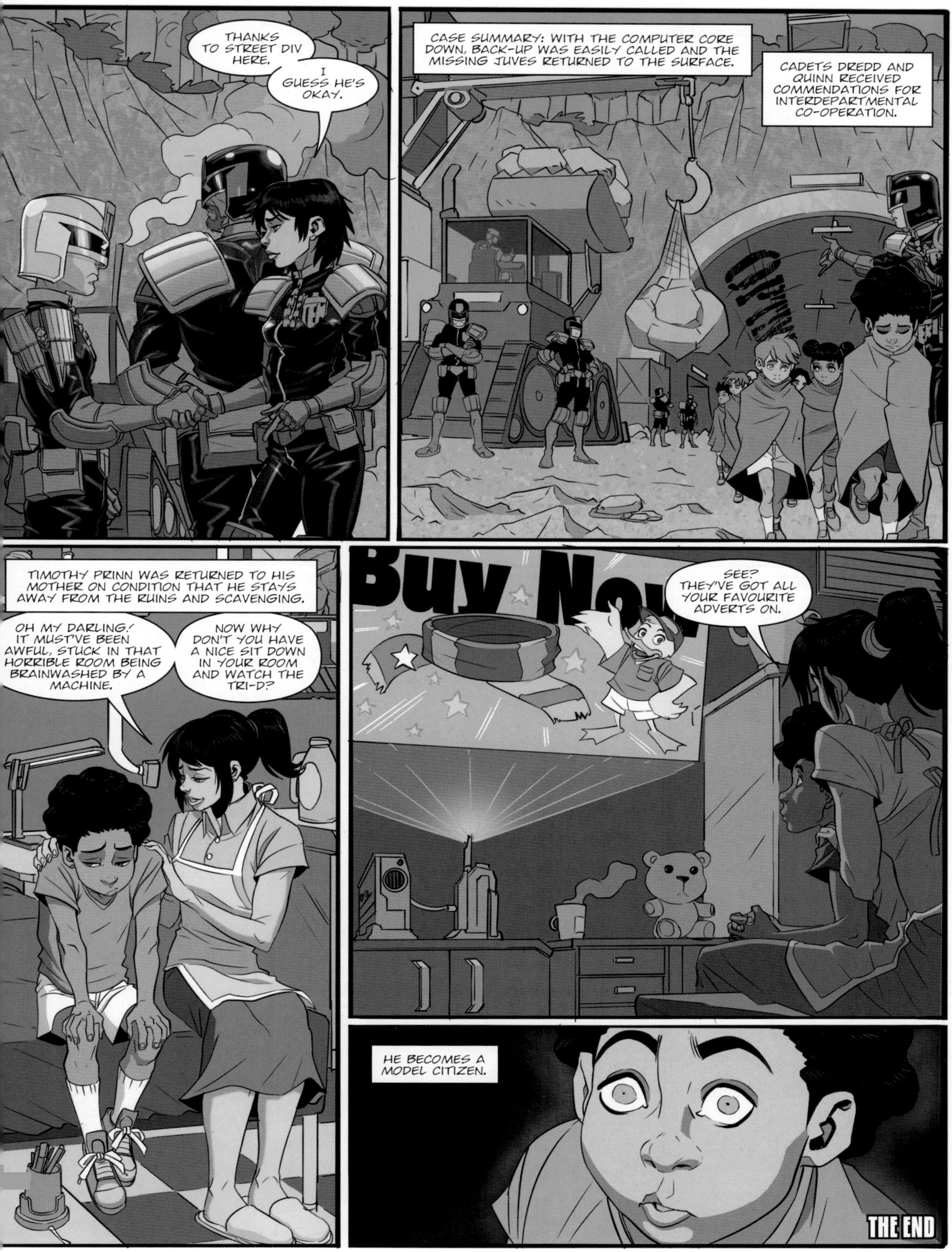
THANKS TO STREET DIV HERE.
I GUESS HE'S OKAY.
CASE SUMMARY: WITH THE COMPUTER CORE DOWN, BACK-UP WAS EASILY CALLED AND THE MISSING JUVES RETURNED TO THE SURFACE.
CADETS DREDD AND QUINN RECEIVED COMMENDATIONS FOR INTERDEPARTMENTAL CO-OPERATION.
TIMOTHY PRINN WAS RETURNED TO HIS MOTHER ON CONDITION THAT HE STAYS AWAY FROM THE RUINS AND SCAVENGING.
OH MY DARLING! IT MUST'VE BEEN AWFUL, STUCK IN THAT HORRIBLE ROOM BEING BRAINWASHED BY A MACHINE.
NOW WHY DON'T YOU HAVE A NICE SIT DOWN IN YOUR ROOM AND WATCH THE TRI-D?
Buy Now
SEE? THEY'VE GOT ALL YOUR FAVOURITE ADVERTS ON.
HE BECOMES A MODEL CITIZEN.
THE END

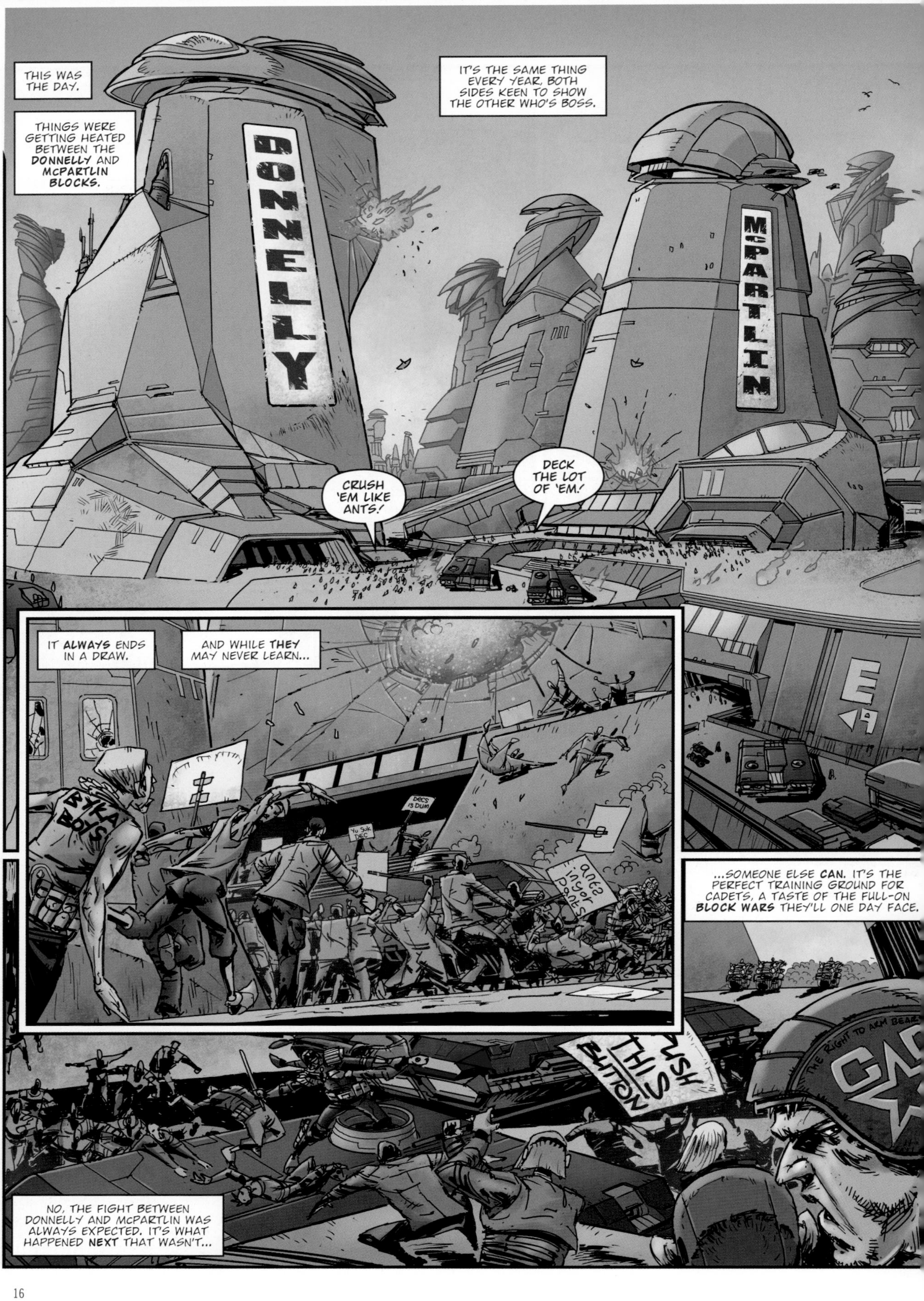
THIS WAS THE DAY.
THINGS WERE GETTING HEATED BETWEEN THE DONNELLY AND McPARTLIN BLOCKS.
IT'S THE SAME THING EVERY YEAR, BOTH SIDES KEEN TO SHOW THE OTHER WHO'S BOSS.
DONNELLY
McPARTLIN
CRUSH 'EM LIKE ANTS!
DECK THE LOT OF 'EM!
IT ALWAYS ENDS IN A DRAW.
AND WHILE THEY MAY NEVER LEARN...
BYKA BOYS
DECS IS DUM
YU SUK DEC
...SOMEONE ELSE CAN. IT'S THE PERFECT TRAINING GROUND FOR CADETS, A TASTE OF THE FULL-ON BLOCK WARS THEY'LL ONE DAY FACE.
THIS BUTTON
NO, THE FIGHT BETWEEN DONNELLY AND McPARTLIN WAS ALWAYS EXPECTED. IT'S WHAT HAPPENED NEXT THAT WASN'T...

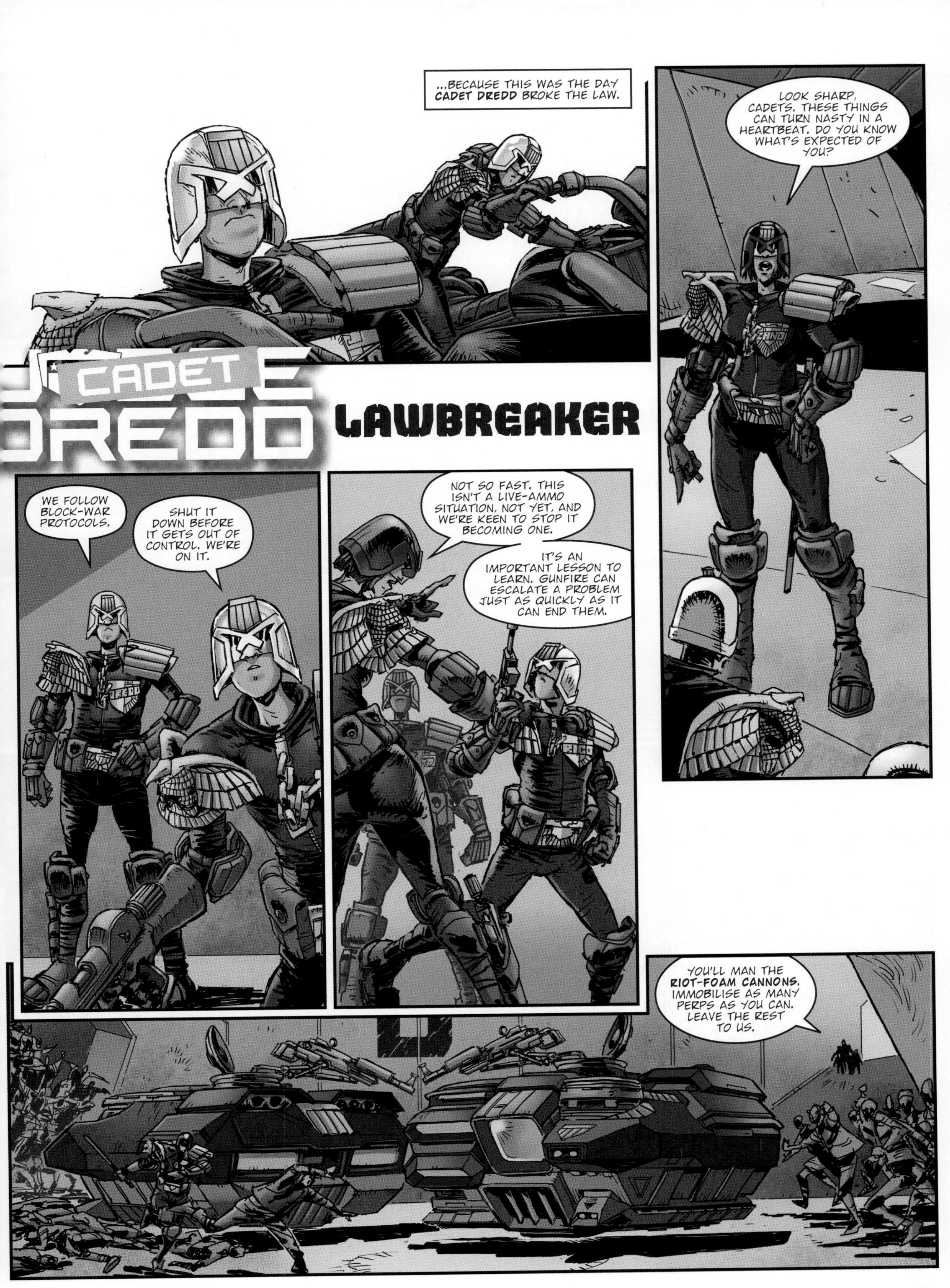

...BECAUSE THIS WAS THE DAY CADET DREDD BROKE THE LAW.
LOOK SHARP, CADETS. THESE THINGS CAN TURN NASTY IN A HEARTBEAT. DO YOU KNOW WHAT'S EXPECTED OF YOU?
CADET DREDD
LAWBREAKER
WE FOLLOW BLOCK-WAR PROTOCOLS.
SHUT IT DOWN BEFORE IT GETS OUT OF CONTROL. WE'RE ON IT.
NOT SO FAST. THIS ISN'T A LIVE-AMMO SITUATION, NOT YET, AND WE'RE KEEN TO STOP IT BECOMING ONE.
IT'S AN IMPORTANT LESSON TO LEARN. GUNFIRE CAN ESCALATE A PROBLEM JUST AS QUICKLY AS IT CAN END THEM.
YOU'LL MAN THE RIOT-FOAM CANNONS. IMMOBILISE AS MANY PERPS AS YOU CAN. LEAVE THE REST TO US.

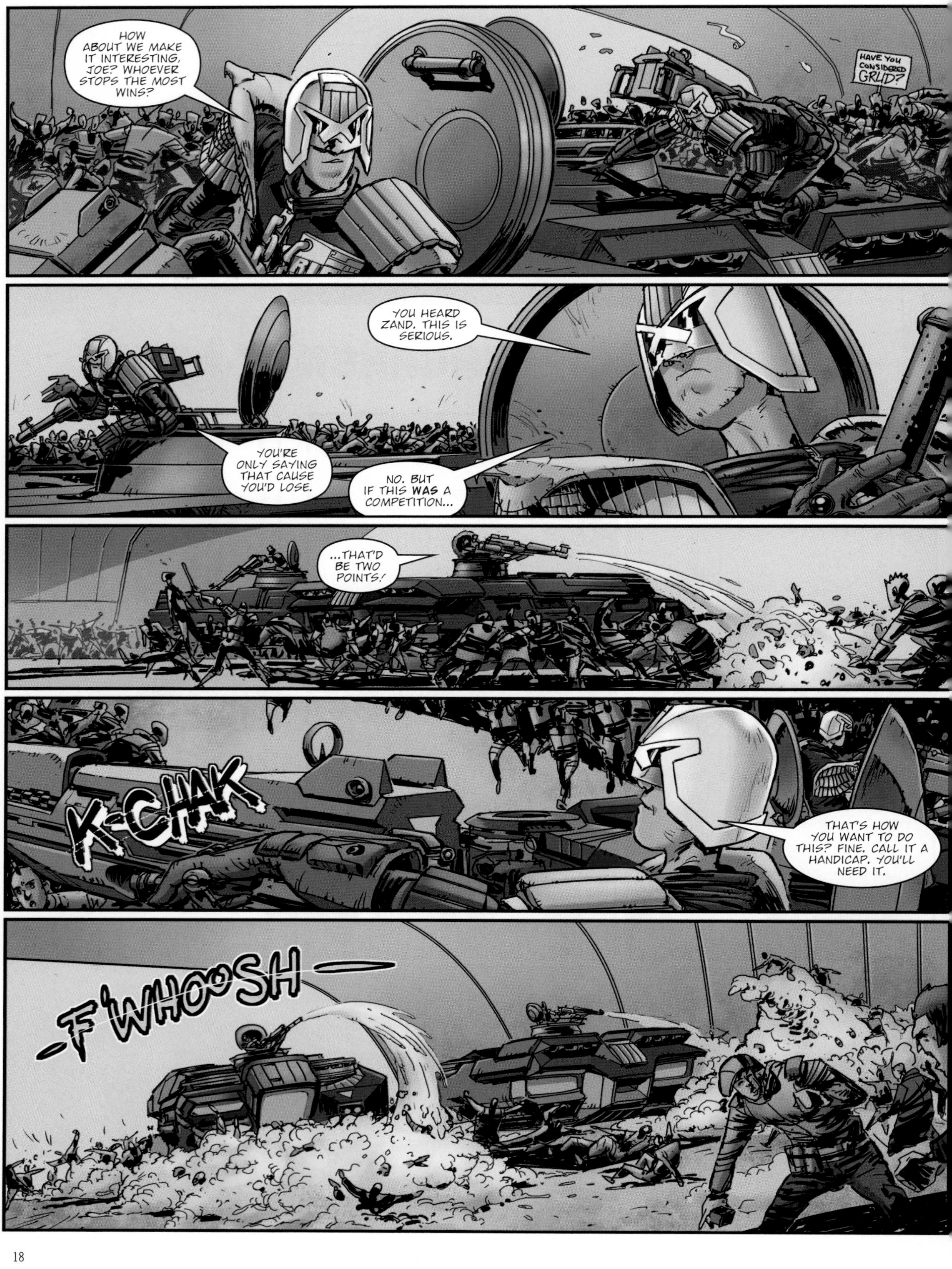
HOW ABOUT WE MAKE IT INTERESTING, JOE? WHOEVER STOPS THE MOST WINS?
HAVE YOU CONSIDERED GRUD?
YOU HEARD ZAND. THIS IS SERIOUS.
YOU'RE ONLY SAYING THAT CAUSE YOU'D LOSE.
NO. BUT IF THIS **WAS** A COMPETITION...
...THAT'D BE TWO POINTS!
K-CHAK
THAT'S HOW YOU WANT TO DO THIS? FINE. CALL IT A HANDICAP. YOU'LL NEED IT.
-F'WHOOSH-

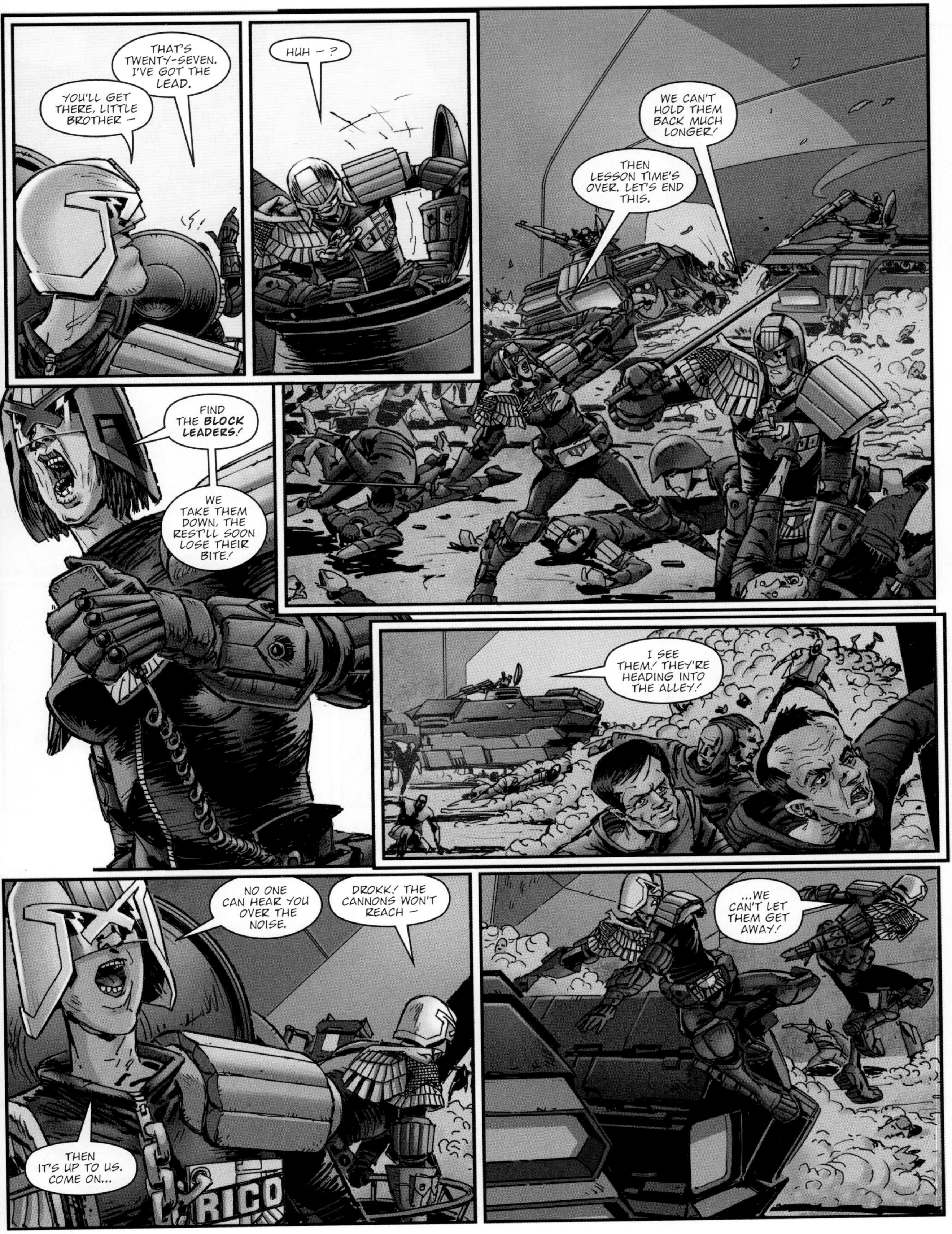
THAT'S TWENTY-SEVEN. I'VE GOT THE LEAD.
YOU'LL GET THERE, LITTLE BROTHER –
HUH – ?
WE CAN'T HOLD THEM BACK MUCH LONGER!
THEN LESSON TIME'S OVER. LET'S END THIS.
FIND THE **BLOCK LEADERS!**
WE TAKE THEM DOWN, THE REST'LL SOON LOSE THEIR BITE!
I SEE THEM! THEY'RE HEADING INTO THE ALLEY!
NO ONE CAN HEAR YOU OVER THE NOISE.
DROKK! THE CANNONS WON'T REACH –
THEN IT'S UP TO US. COME ON...
RICO
...WE CAN'T LET THEM GET AWAY!

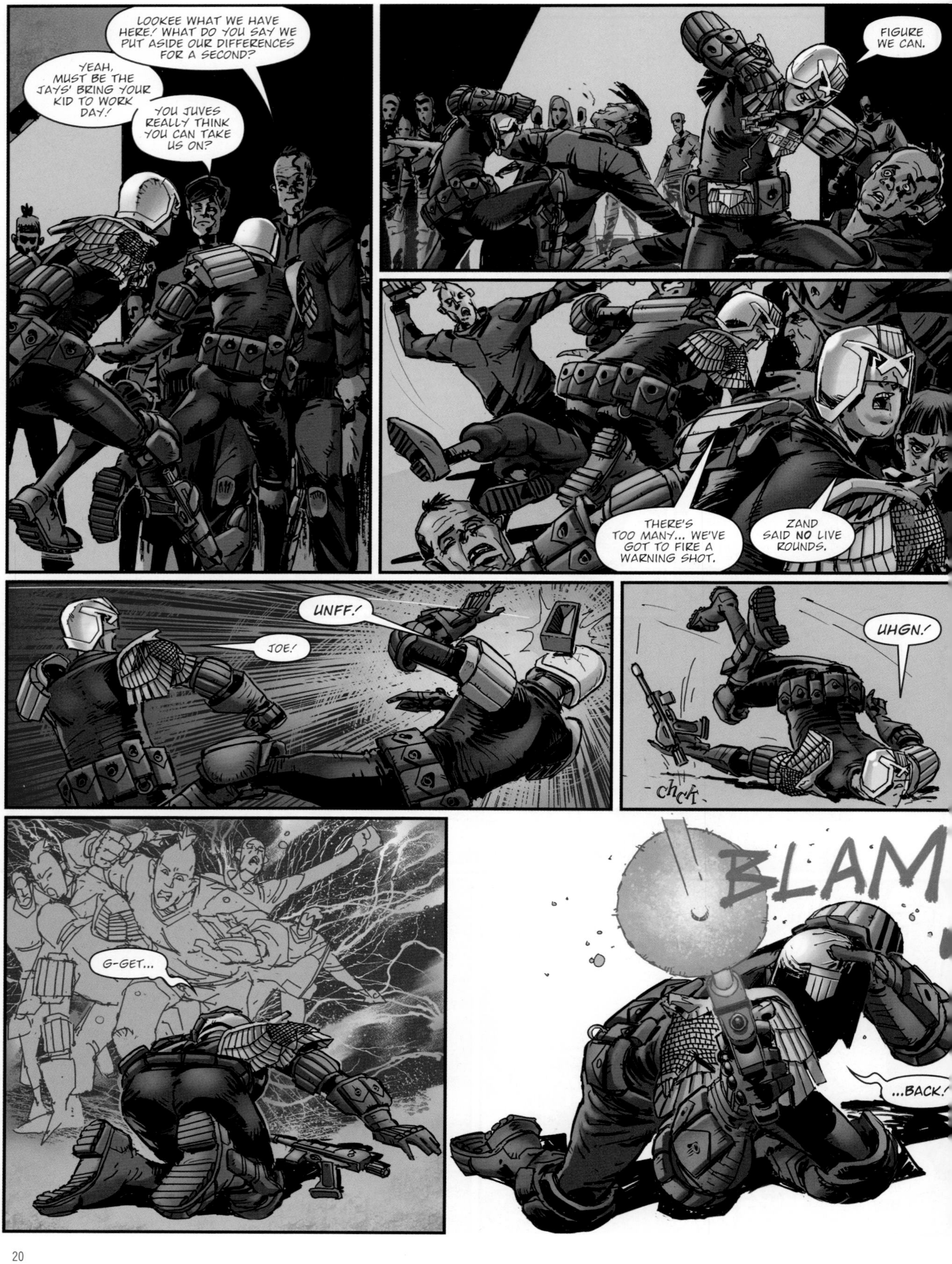
LOOKEE WHAT WE HAVE HERE! WHAT DO YOU SAY WE PUT ASIDE OUR DIFFERENCES FOR A SECOND?
YEAH, MUST BE THE JAYS' BRING YOUR KID TO WORK DAY!
YOU JUVES REALLY THINK YOU CAN TAKE US ON?
FIGURE WE CAN.
THERE'S TOO MANY... WE'VE GOT TO FIRE A WARNING SHOT.
ZAND SAID NO LIVE ROUNDS.
UNFF!
JOE!
UHGN!
chck
G-GET...
BLAM
...BACK!

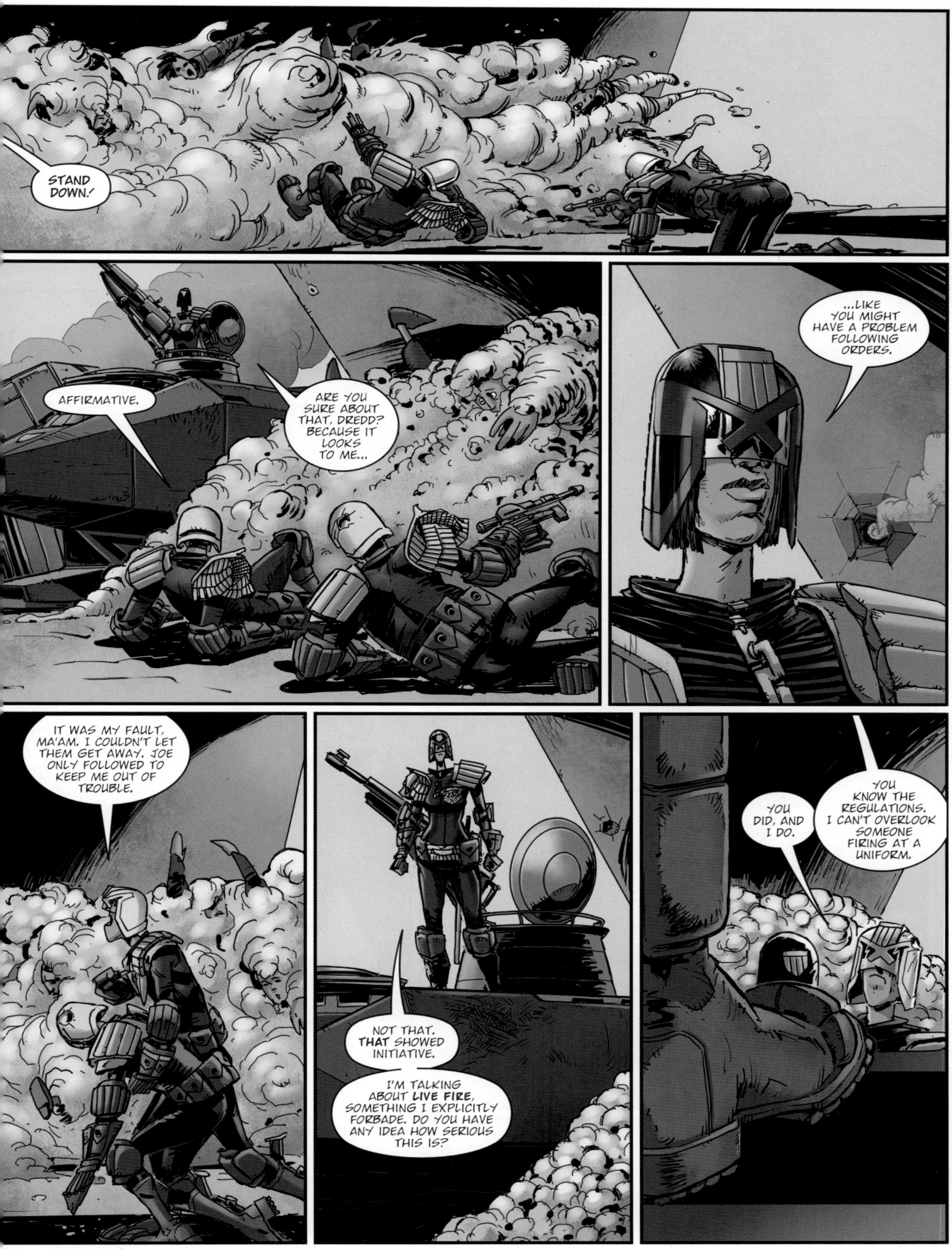
STAND DOWN!
AFFIRMATIVE.
ARE YOU SURE ABOUT THAT, DREDD? BECAUSE IT LOOKS TO ME...
...LIKE YOU MIGHT HAVE A PROBLEM FOLLOWING ORDERS.
IT WAS MY FAULT, MA'AM. I COULDN'T LET THEM GET AWAY. JOE ONLY FOLLOWED TO KEEP ME OUT OF TROUBLE.
NOT THAT. **THAT** SHOWED INITIATIVE.
I'M TALKING ABOUT **LIVE FIRE**, SOMETHING I EXPLICITLY FORBADE. DO YOU HAVE ANY IDEA HOW SERIOUS THIS IS?
YOU DID, AND I DO.
YOU KNOW THE REGULATIONS. I CAN'T OVERLOOK SOMEONE FIRING AT A UNIFORM.

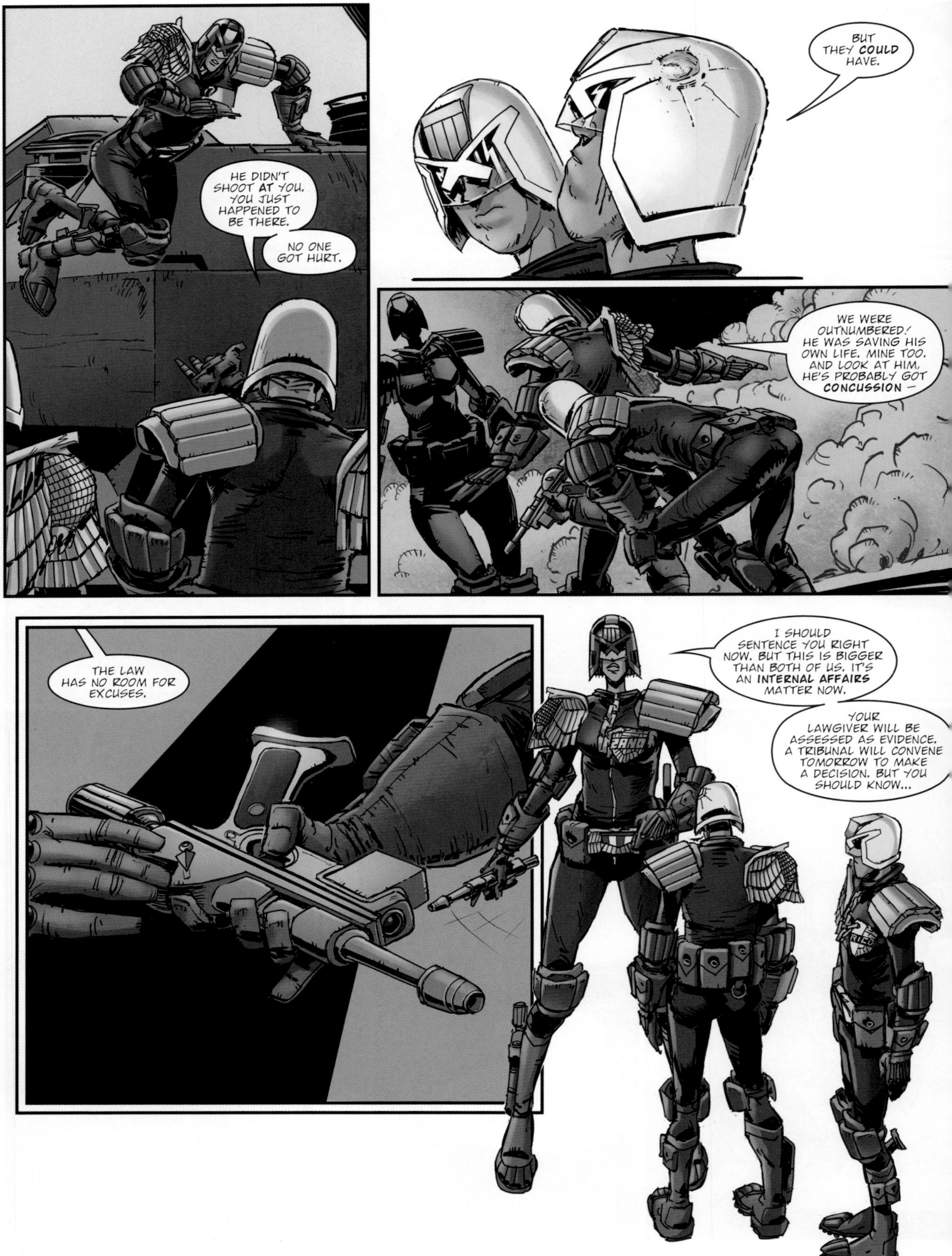

HE DIDN'T SHOOT AT YOU. YOU JUST HAPPENED TO BE THERE.
NO ONE GOT HURT.
BUT THEY COULD HAVE.
WE WERE OUTNUMBERED! HE WAS SAVING HIS OWN LIFE. MINE TOO. AND LOOK AT HIM, HE'S PROBABLY GOT CONCUSSION –
THE LAW HAS NO ROOM FOR EXCUSES.
I SHOULD SENTENCE YOU RIGHT NOW. BUT THIS IS BIGGER THAN BOTH OF US. IT'S AN INTERNAL AFFAIRS MATTER NOW.
YOUR LAWGIVER WILL BE ASSESSED AS EVIDENCE. A TRIBUNAL WILL CONVENE TOMORROW TO MAKE A DECISION. BUT YOU SHOULD KNOW...

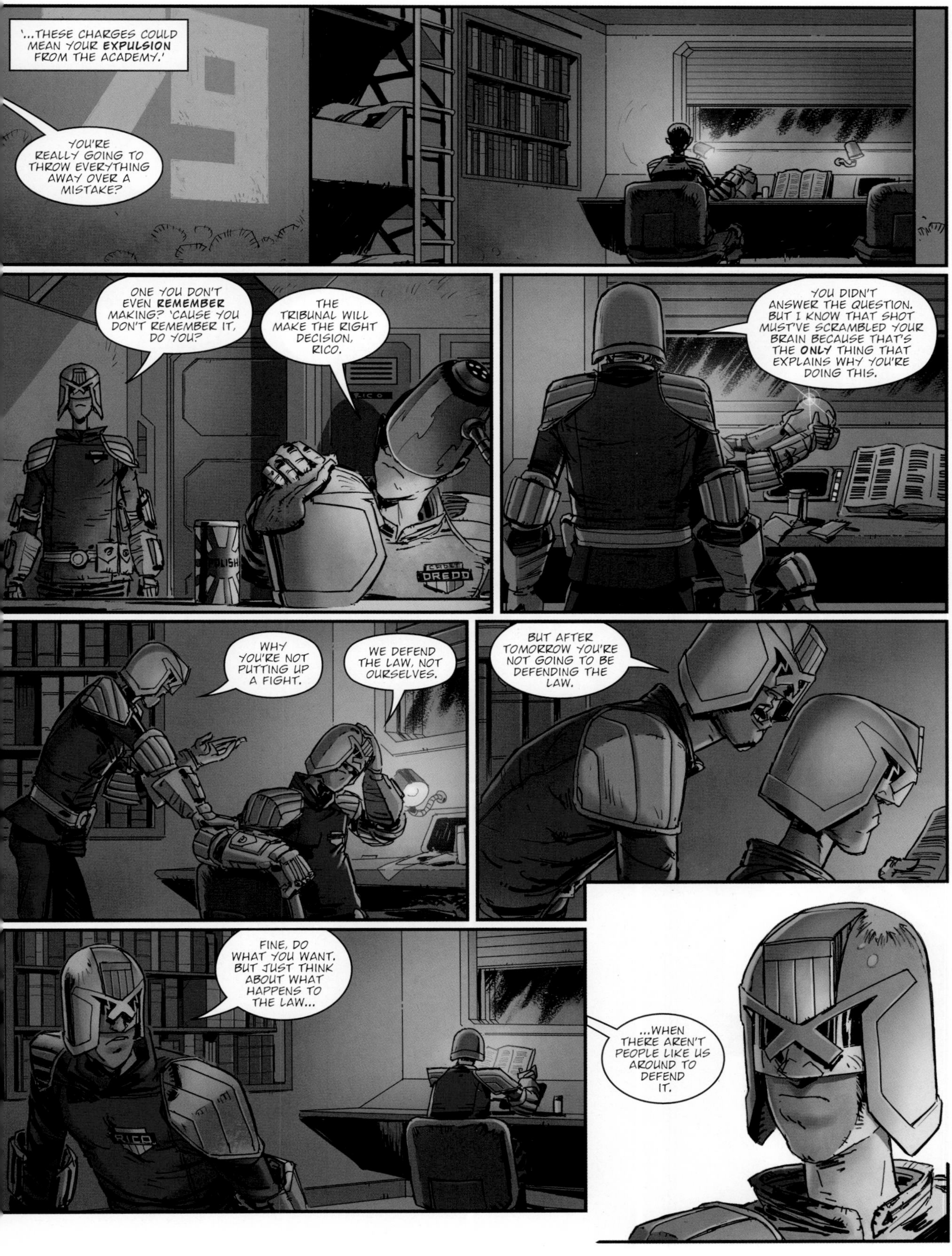
'...THESE CHARGES COULD MEAN YOUR EXPULSION FROM THE ACADEMY.'
YOU'RE REALLY GOING TO THROW EVERYTHING AWAY OVER A MISTAKE?
ONE YOU DON'T EVEN REMEMBER MAKING? 'CAUSE YOU DON'T REMEMBER IT, DO YOU?
THE TRIBUNAL WILL MAKE THE RIGHT DECISION, RICO.
POLISH
CADET DREDD
YOU DIDN'T ANSWER THE QUESTION. BUT I KNOW THAT SHOT MUST'VE SCRAMBLED YOUR BRAIN BECAUSE THAT'S THE ONLY THING THAT EXPLAINS WHY YOU'RE DOING THIS.
WHY YOU'RE NOT PUTTING UP A FIGHT.
WE DEFEND THE LAW, NOT OURSELVES.
BUT AFTER TOMORROW YOU'RE NOT GOING TO BE DEFENDING THE LAW.
FINE, DO WHAT YOU WANT. BUT JUST THINK ABOUT WHAT HAPPENS TO THE LAW...
RICO
...WHEN THERE AREN'T PEOPLE LIKE US AROUND TO DEFEND IT.

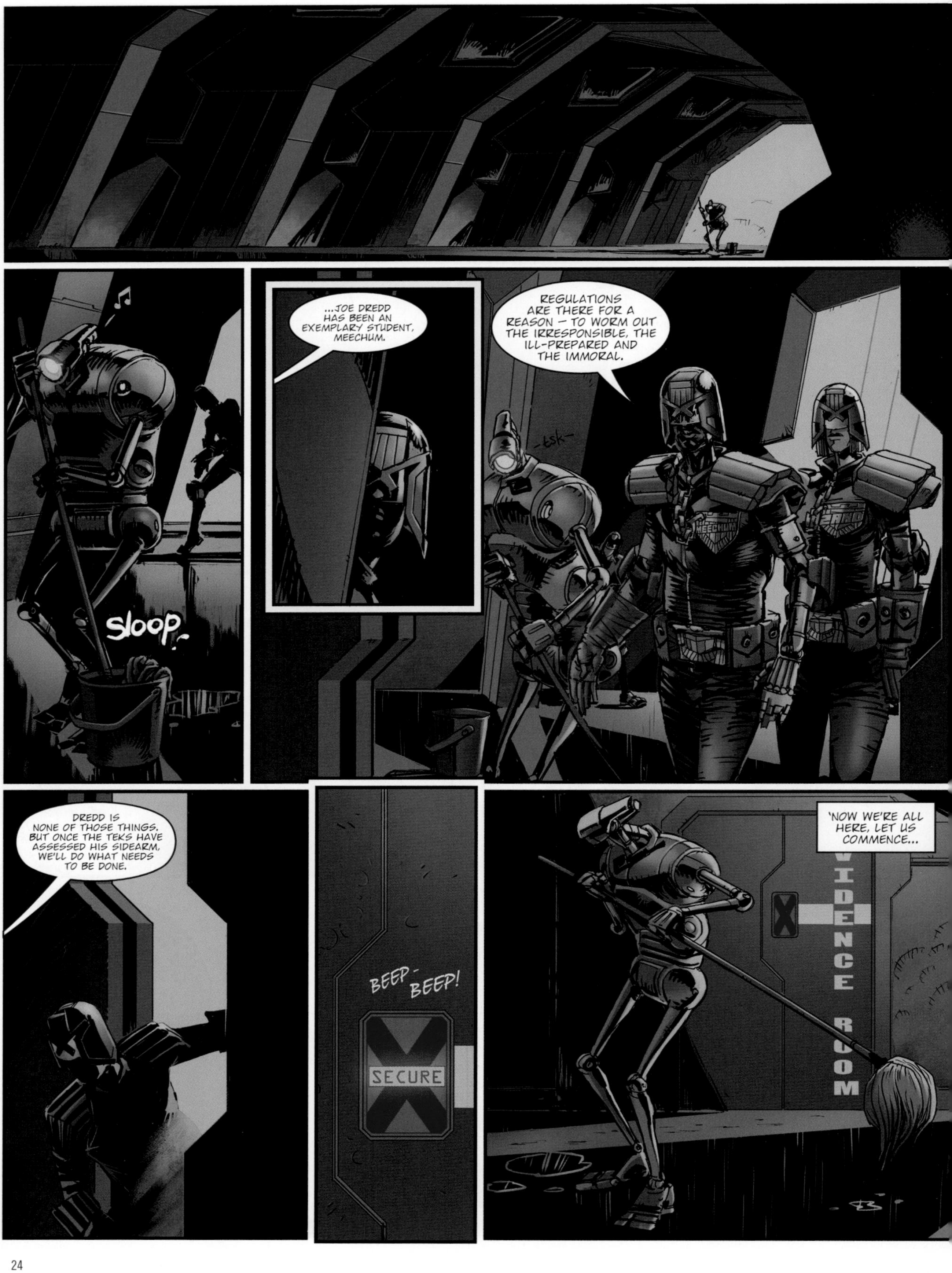
SLOOP
...JOE DREDD HAS BEEN AN EXEMPLARY STUDENT, MEECHUM.
REGULATIONS ARE THERE FOR A REASON — TO WORM OUT THE IRRESPONSIBLE, THE ILL-PREPARED AND THE IMMORAL.
-tsk-
MEECHUM
DREDD IS NONE OF THOSE THINGS. BUT ONCE THE TEKS HAVE ASSESSED HIS SIDEARM, WE'LL DO WHAT NEEDS TO BE DONE.
BEEP-BEEP!
SECURE
'NOW WE'RE ALL HERE, LET US COMMENCE...
VIDENCE ROOM

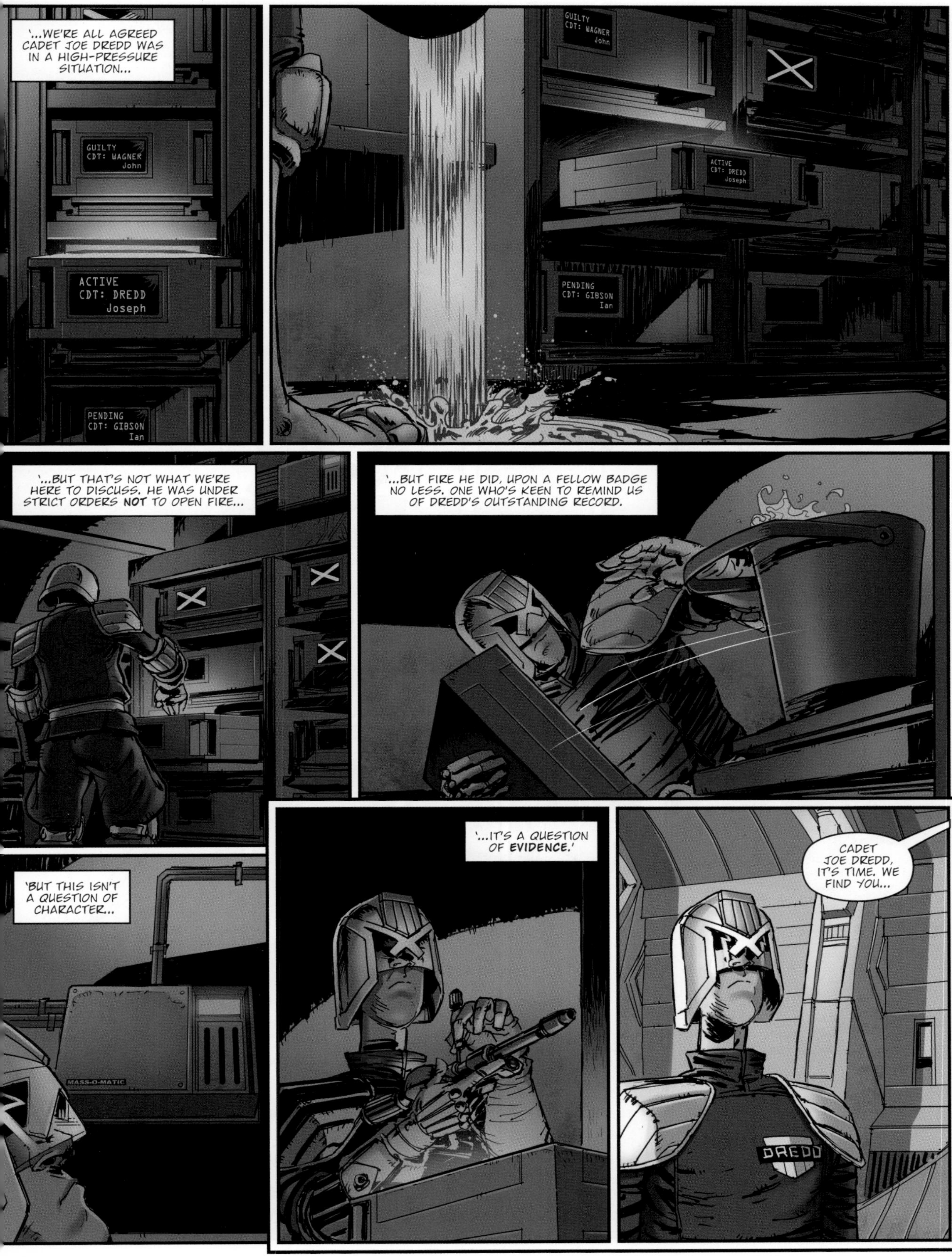
'...WE'RE ALL AGREED CADET JOE DREDD WAS IN A HIGH-PRESSURE SITUATION...
GUILTY CDT: WAGNER John
ACTIVE CDT: DREDD Joseph
PENDING CDT: GIBSON Ian
GUILTY CDT: WAGNER John
ACTIVE CDT: DREDD Joseph
PENDING CDT: GIBSON Ian
'...BUT THAT'S NOT WHAT WE'RE HERE TO DISCUSS. HE WAS UNDER STRICT ORDERS **NOT** TO OPEN FIRE...
'...BUT FIRE HE DID, UPON A FELLOW BADGE NO LESS. ONE WHO'S KEEN TO REMIND US OF DREDD'S OUTSTANDING RECORD.
'BUT THIS ISN'T A QUESTION OF CHARACTER...
MASS-O-MATIC
'...IT'S A QUESTION OF **EVIDENCE**.'
CADET JOE DREDD, IT'S TIME. WE FIND YOU...
DREDD

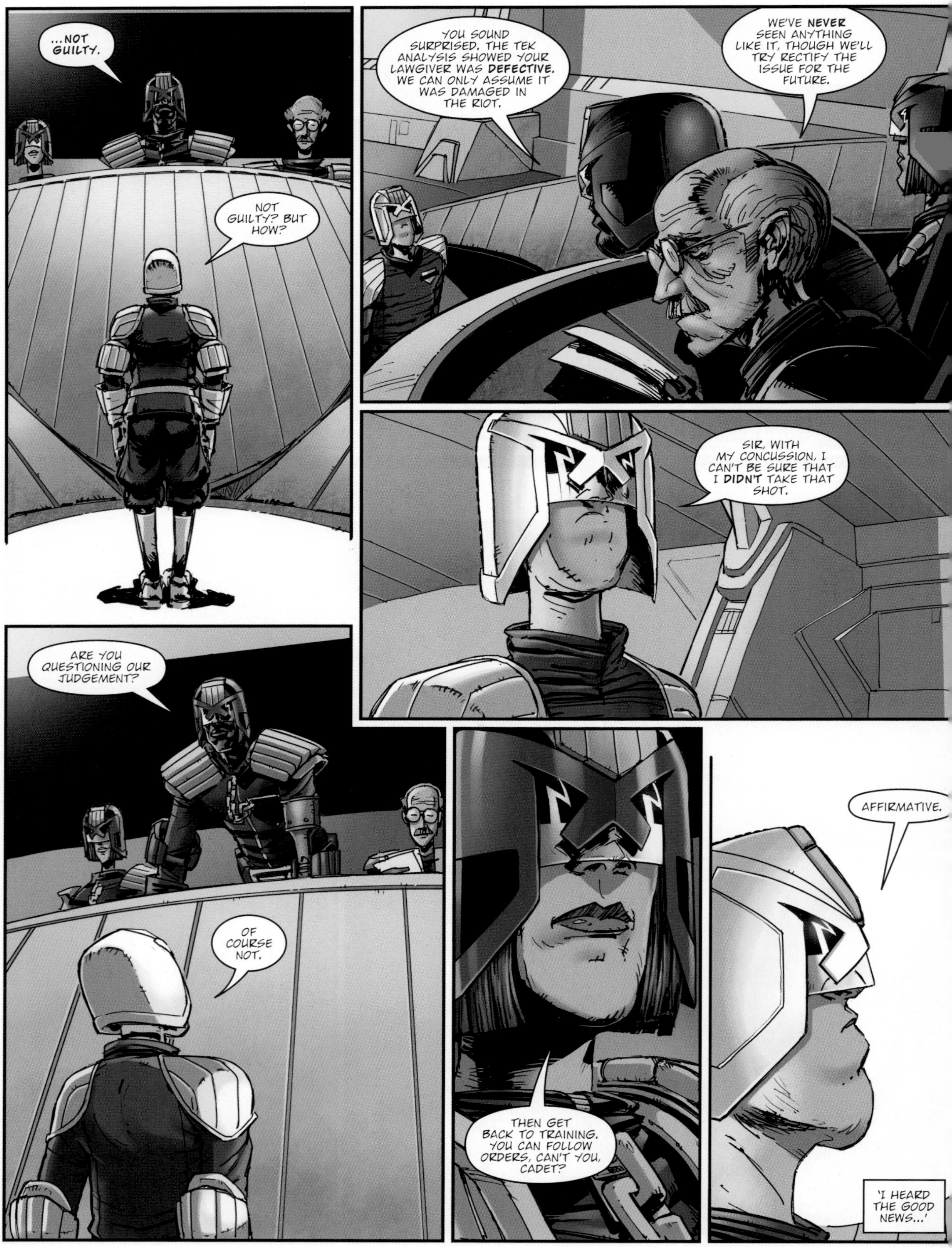

...NOT GUILTY.
NOT GUILTY? BUT HOW?
YOU SOUND SURPRISED. THE TEK ANALYSIS SHOWED YOUR LAWGIVER WAS DEFECTIVE. WE CAN ONLY ASSUME IT WAS DAMAGED IN THE RIOT.
WE'VE NEVER SEEN ANYTHING LIKE IT, THOUGH WE'LL TRY RECTIFY THE ISSUE FOR THE FUTURE.
SIR, WITH MY CONCUSSION, I CAN'T BE SURE THAT I DIDN'T TAKE THAT SHOT.
ARE YOU QUESTIONING OUR JUDGEMENT?
OF COURSE NOT.
THEN GET BACK TO TRAINING. YOU CAN FOLLOW ORDERS, CAN'T YOU, CADET?
AFFIRMATIVE.
'I HEARD THE GOOD NEWS...'

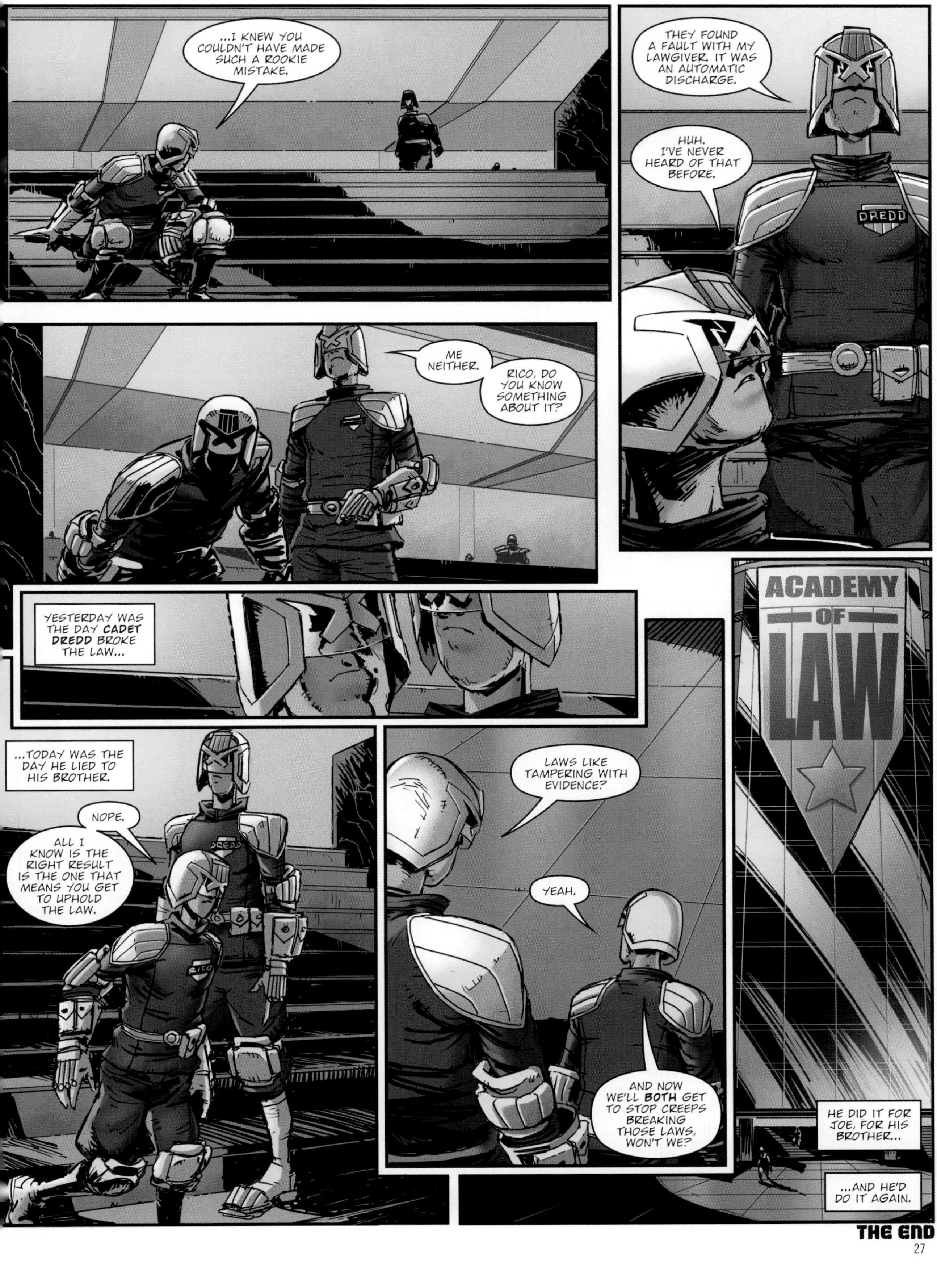

...I KNEW YOU COULDN'T HAVE MADE SUCH A ROOKIE MISTAKE.
THEY FOUND A FAULT WITH MY LAWGIVER. IT WAS AN AUTOMATIC DISCHARGE.
HUH. I'VE NEVER HEARD OF THAT BEFORE.
DREDD
ME NEITHER.
RICO, DO YOU KNOW SOMETHING ABOUT IT?
YESTERDAY WAS THE DAY CADET DREDD BROKE THE LAW...
ACADEMY OF LAW
...TODAY WAS THE DAY HE LIED TO HIS BROTHER.
NOPE.
ALL I KNOW IS THE RIGHT RESULT IS THE ONE THAT MEANS YOU GET TO UPHOLD THE LAW.
DREDD
RICO
LAWS LIKE TAMPERING WITH EVIDENCE?
YEAH.
AND NOW WE'LL BOTH GET TO STOP CREEPS BREAKING THOSE LAWS, WON'T WE?
HE DID IT FOR JOE, FOR HIS BROTHER...
...AND HE'D DO IT AGAIN.


THE END

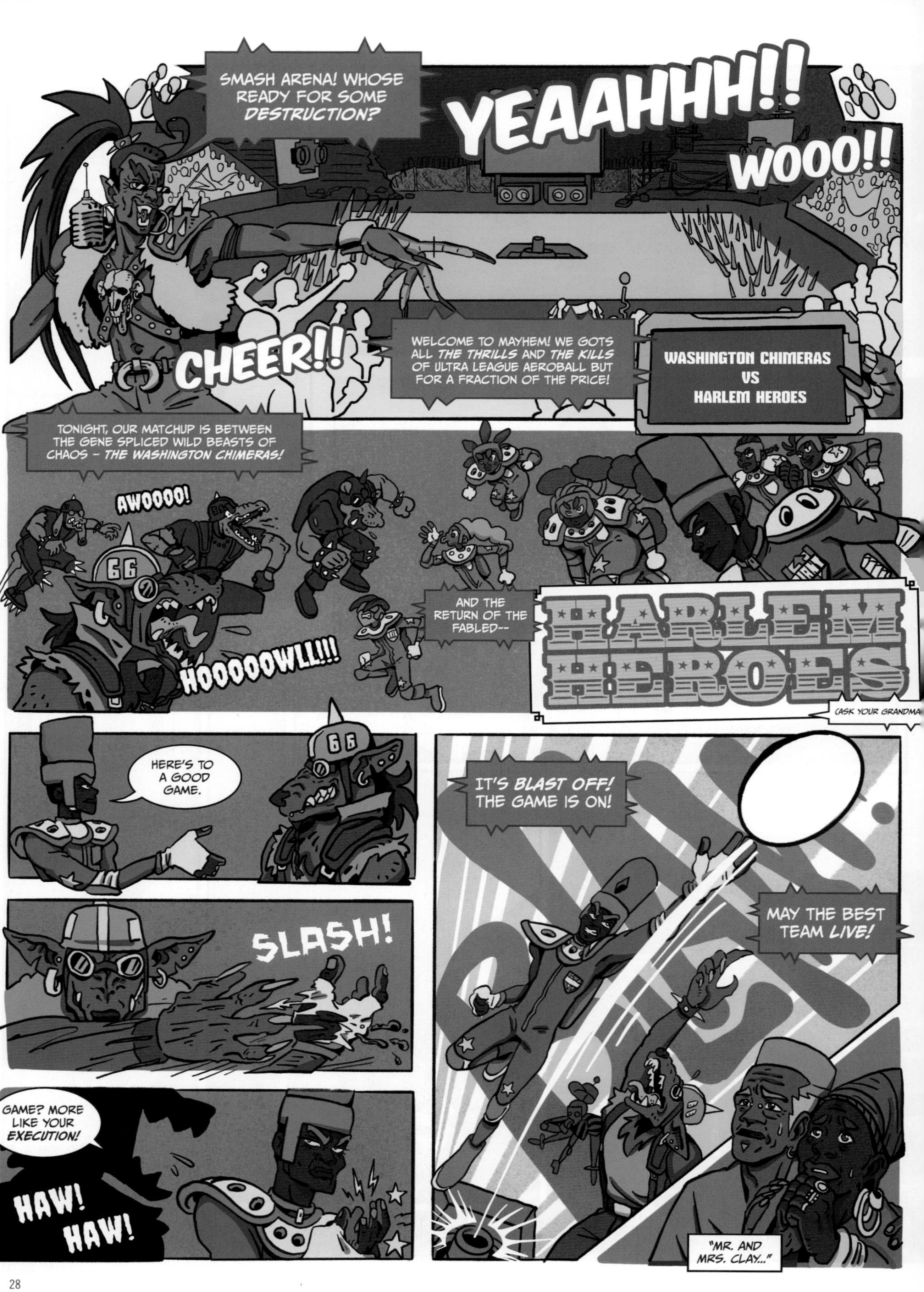
SMASH ARENA! WHOSE READY FOR SOME DESTRUCTION?
YEAAHHH!!
WOOO!!
CHEER!!
WELCOME TO MAYHEM! WE GOTS ALL THE THRILLS AND THE KILLS OF ULTRA LEAGUE AEROBALL BUT FOR A FRACTION OF THE PRICE!
WASHINGTON CHIMERAS VS HARLEM HEROES
TONIGHT, OUR MATCHUP IS BETWEEN THE GENE SPLICED WILD BEASTS OF CHAOS – THE WASHINGTON CHIMERAS!
AWOOOO!
HOOOOOWLL!!!
AND THE RETURN OF THE FABLED--
HARLEM HEROES
(ASK YOUR GRANDMA
HERE'S TO A GOOD GAME.
SLASH!
GAME? MORE LIKE YOUR EXECUTION!
HAW! HAW!
IT'S BLAST OFF! THE GAME IS ON!
MAY THE BEST TEAM LIVE!
"MR. AND MRS. CLAY..."

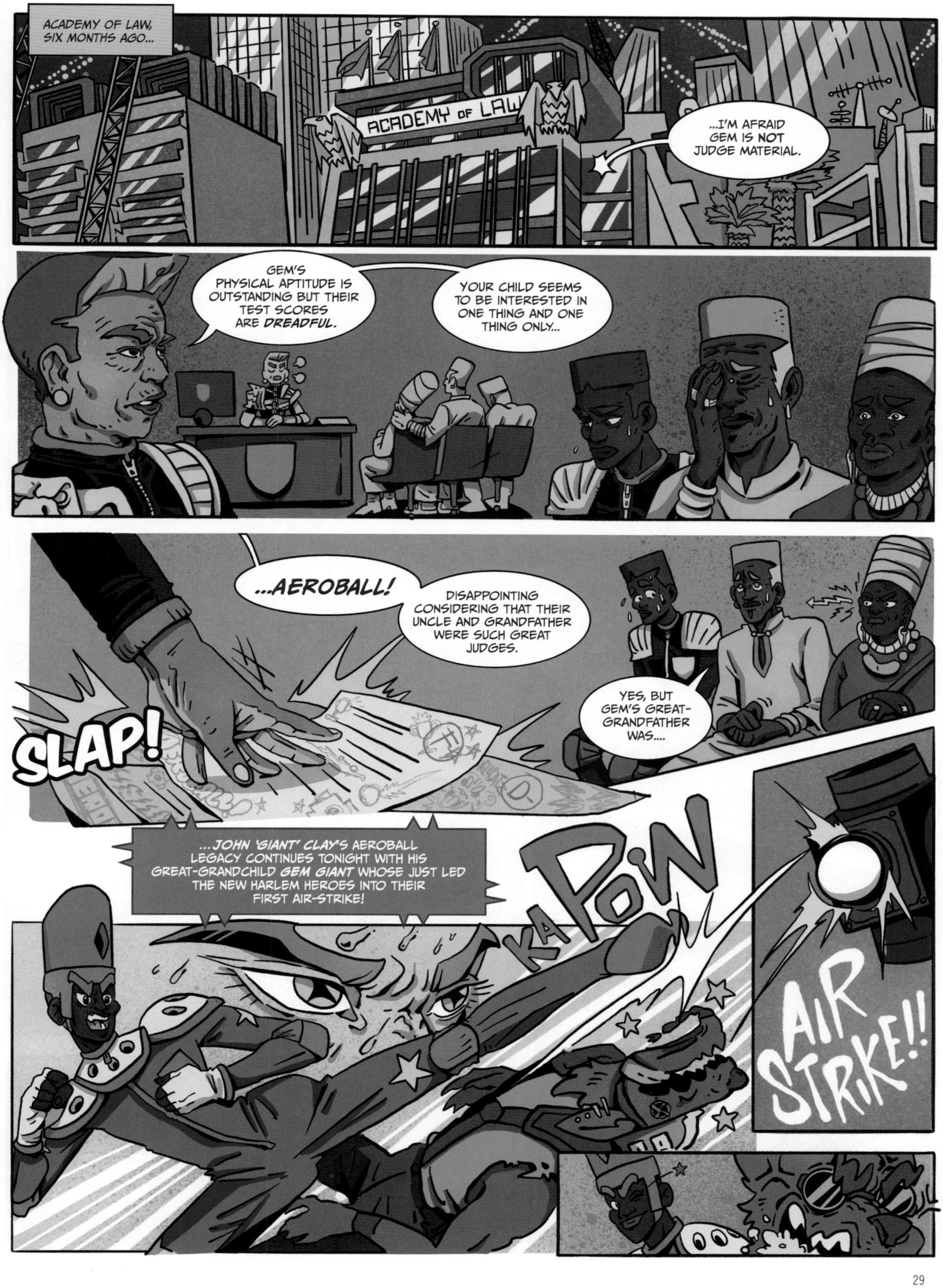
ACADEMY OF LAW, SIX MONTHS AGO...
ACADEMY OF LAW
...I'M AFRAID GEM IS NOT JUDGE MATERIAL.
GEM'S PHYSICAL APTITUDE IS OUTSTANDING BUT THEIR TEST SCORES ARE DREADFUL.
YOUR CHILD SEEMS TO BE INTERESTED IN ONE THING AND ONE THING ONLY...
...AEROBALL!
DISAPPOINTING CONSIDERING THAT THEIR UNCLE AND GRANDFATHER WERE SUCH GREAT JUDGES.
SLAP!
YES, BUT GEM'S GREAT-GRANDFATHER WAS....
...JOHN 'GIANT' CLAY'S AEROBALL LEGACY CONTINUES TONIGHT WITH HIS GREAT-GRANDCHILD GEM GIANT WHOSE JUST LED THE NEW HARLEM HEROES INTO THEIR FIRST AIR-STRIKE!
KA POW
AIR STRIKE!!

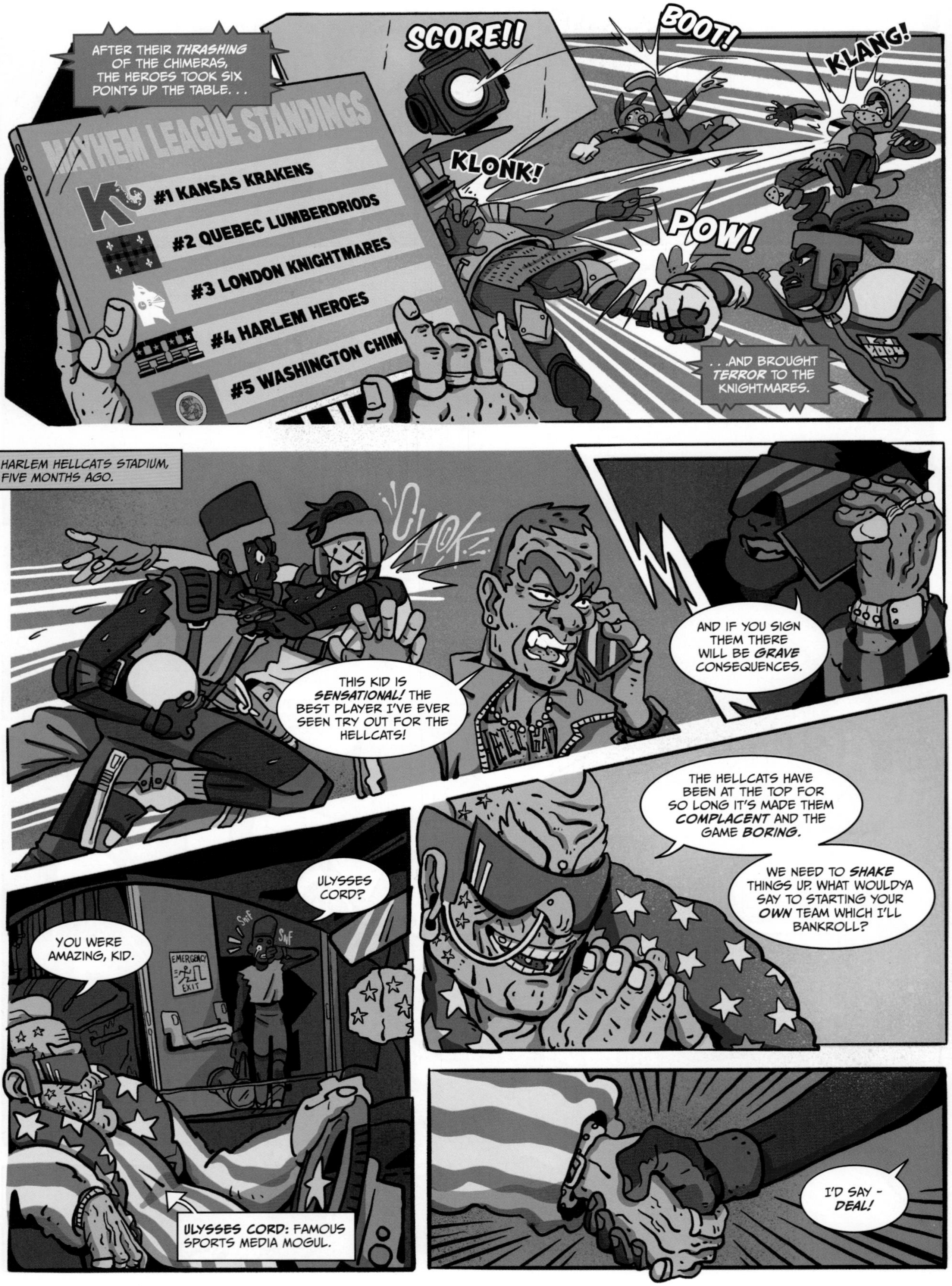

AFTER THEIR THRASHING OF THE CHIMERAS, THE HEROES TOOK SIX POINTS UP THE TABLE. . .
MAYHEM LEAGUE STANDINGS
#1 KANSAS KRAKENS
#2 QUEBEC LUMBERDRIODS
#3 LONDON KNIGHTMARES
#4 HARLEM HEROES
#5 WASHINGTON CHIM
SCORE!!
BOOT!
KLANG!
KLONK!
POW!
. . .AND BROUGHT TERROR TO THE KNIGHTMARES.
HARLEM HELLCATS STADIUM, FIVE MONTHS AGO.
CHOK
THIS KID IS SENSATIONAL! THE BEST PLAYER I'VE EVER SEEN TRY OUT FOR THE HELLCATS!
AND IF YOU SIGN THEM THERE WILL BE GRAVE CONSEQUENCES.
ULYSSES CORD?
YOU WERE AMAZING, KID.
EMERGENCY EXIT
ULYSSES CORD: FAMOUS SPORTS MEDIA MOGUL.
THE HELLCATS HAVE BEEN AT THE TOP FOR SO LONG IT'S MADE THEM COMPLACENT AND THE GAME BORING.
WE NEED TO SHAKE THINGS UP. WHAT WOULDYA SAY TO STARTING YOUR OWN TEAM WHICH I'LL BANKROLL?
I'D SAY - DEAL!

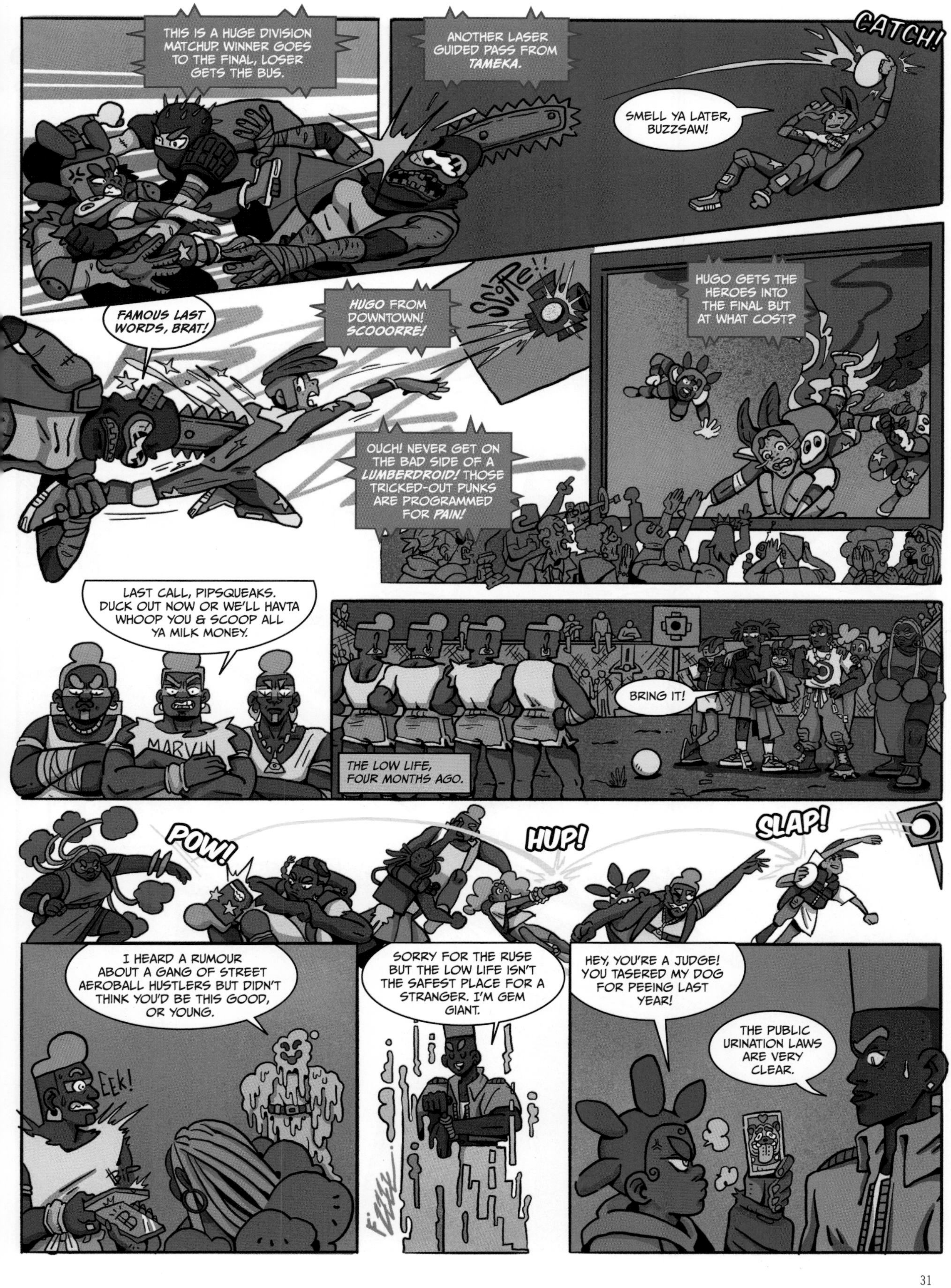
THIS IS A HUGE DIVISION MATCHUP. WINNER GOES TO THE FINAL, LOSER GETS THE BUS.
ANOTHER LASER GUIDED PASS FROM TAMEKA.
CATCH!
SMELL YA LATER, BUZZSAW!
FAMOUS LAST WORDS, BRAT!
HUGO FROM DOWNTOWN! SCOOORRE!
SCORE!!
HUGO GETS THE HEROES INTO THE FINAL BUT AT WHAT COST?
OUCH! NEVER GET ON THE BAD SIDE OF A LUMBERDROID! THOSE TRICKED-OUT PUNKS ARE PROGRAMMED FOR PAIN!
LAST CALL, PIPSQUEAKS. DUCK OUT NOW OR WE'LL HAVTA WHOOP YOU & SCOOP ALL YA MILK MONEY.
MARVIN
BRING IT!
THE LOW LIFE, FOUR MONTHS AGO.
POW!
HUP!
SLAP!
I HEARD A RUMOUR ABOUT A GANG OF STREET AEROBALL HUSTLERS BUT DIDN'T THINK YOU'D BE THIS GOOD, OR YOUNG.
EEK!
SORRY FOR THE RUSE BUT THE LOW LIFE ISN'T THE SAFEST PLACE FOR A STRANGER. I'M GEM GIANT.
HEY, YOU'RE A JUDGE! YOU TASERED MY DOG FOR PEEING LAST YEAR!
THE PUBLIC URINATION LAWS ARE VERY CLEAR.

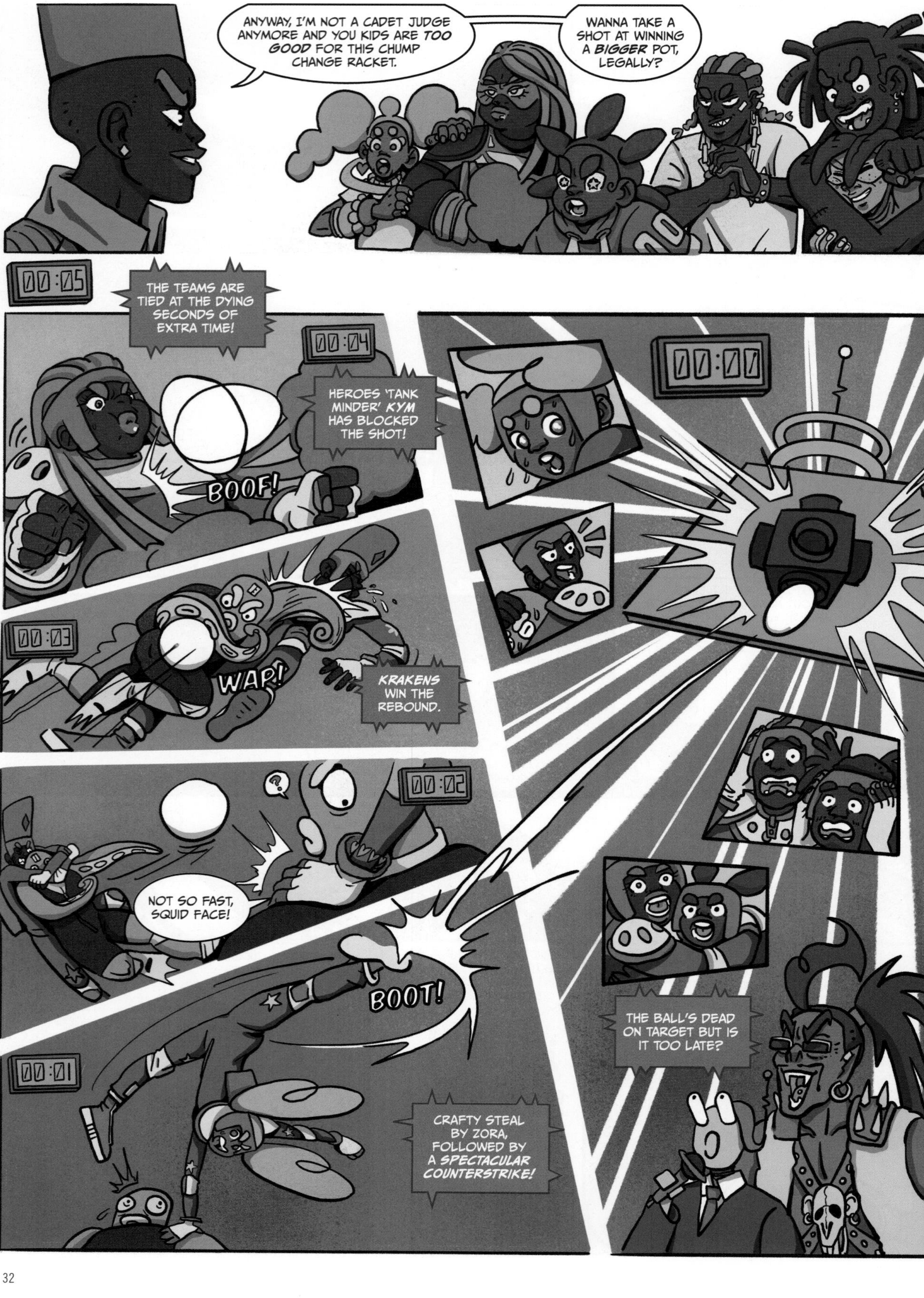
ANYWAY, I'M NOT A CADET JUDGE ANYMORE AND YOU KIDS ARE *TOO GOOD* FOR THIS CHUMP CHANGE RACKET.
WANNA TAKE A SHOT AT WINNING A *BIGGER* POT, LEGALLY?
00:05
THE TEAMS ARE TIED AT THE DYING SECONDS OF EXTRA TIME!
00:04
HEROES 'TANK MINDER' *KYM* HAS BLOCKED THE SHOT!
BOOF!
00:03
WAP!
*KRAKENS* WIN THE REBOUND.
00:02
NOT SO FAST, SQUID FACE!
BOOT!
00:01
CRAFTY STEAL BY ZORA, FOLLOWED BY A *SPECTACULAR COUNTERSTRIKE!*
00:00
THE BALL'S DEAD ON TARGET BUT IS IT TOO LATE?

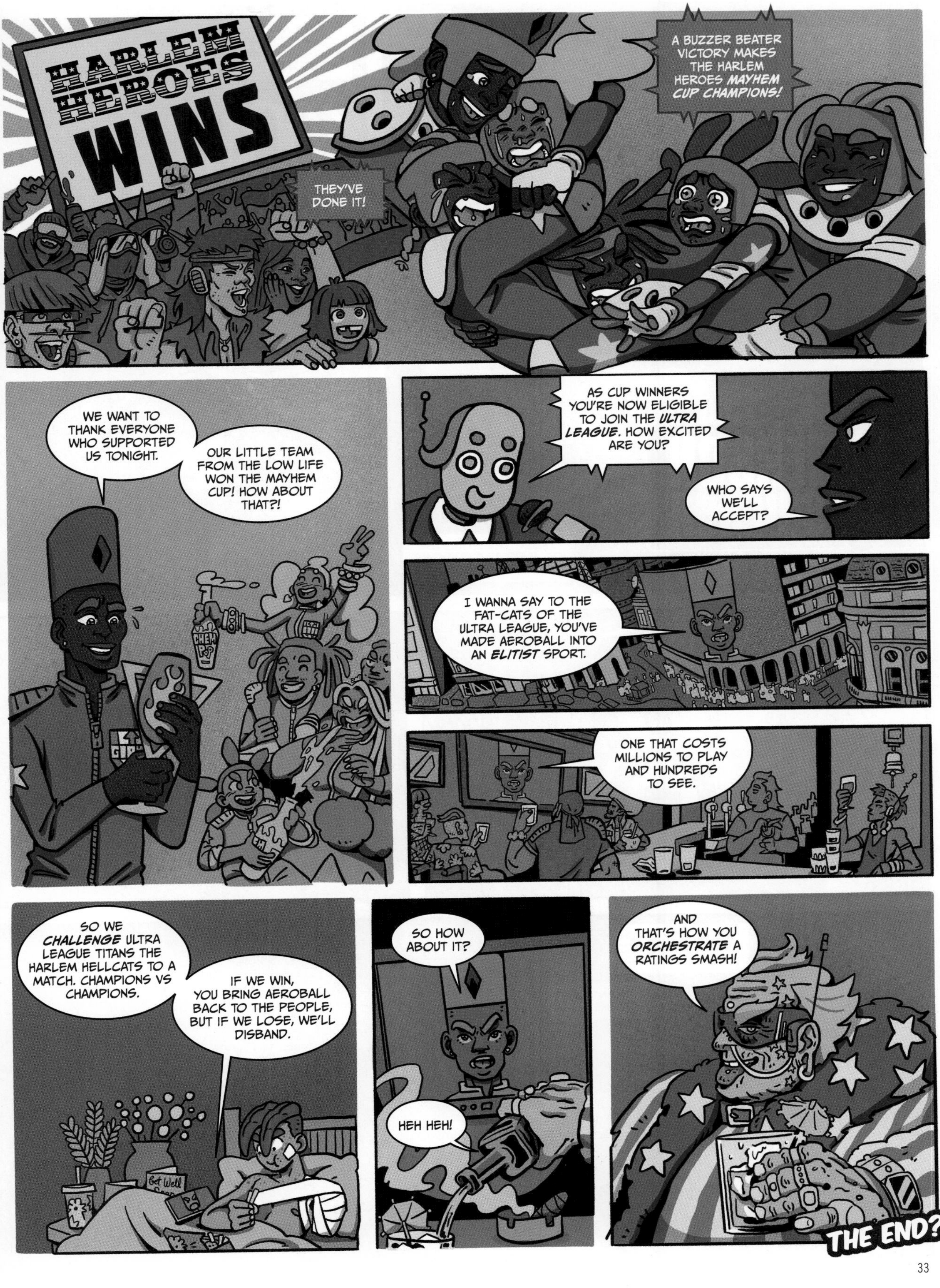
HARLEM HEROES WINS
THEY'VE DONE IT!
A BUZZER BEATER VICTORY MAKES THE HARLEM HEROES MAYHEM CUP CHAMPIONS!
WE WANT TO THANK EVERYONE WHO SUPPORTED US TONIGHT.
OUR LITTLE TEAM FROM THE LOW LIFE WON THE MAYHEM CUP! HOW ABOUT THAT?!
CHEM POP
AS CUP WINNERS YOU'RE NOW ELIGIBLE TO JOIN THE ULTRA LEAGUE. HOW EXCITED ARE YOU?
WHO SAYS WE'LL ACCEPT?
I WANNA SAY TO THE FAT-CATS OF THE ULTRA LEAGUE, YOU'VE MADE AEROBALL INTO AN ELITIST SPORT.
ONE THAT COSTS MILLIONS TO PLAY AND HUNDREDS TO SEE.
SO WE CHALLENGE ULTRA LEAGUE TITANS THE HARLEM HELLCATS TO A MATCH. CHAMPIONS VS CHAMPIONS.
IF WE WIN, YOU BRING AEROBALL BACK TO THE PEOPLE, BUT IF WE LOSE, WE'LL DISBAND.
SO HOW ABOUT IT?
HEH HEH!
AND THAT'S HOW YOU ORCHESTRATE A RATINGS SMASH!
THE END?

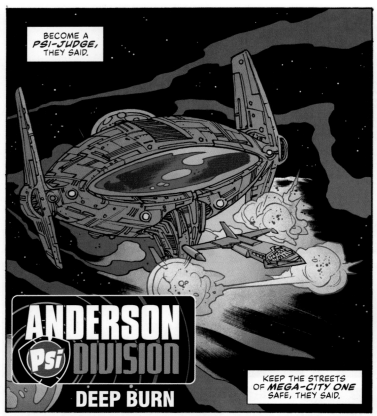

BECOME A *PSI-JUDGE*, THEY SAID.

# ANDERSON Psi DIVISION
## DEEP BURN

KEEP THE STREETS OF *MEGA-CITY ONE* SAFE, THEY SAID.

THEY NEVER SAID I'LL BE DOING IT IN *DEEP SPACE!*

FOOM

DROKK! THEY'RE LOCKING ON!

SOME KIND OF TRACTOR BEAM!

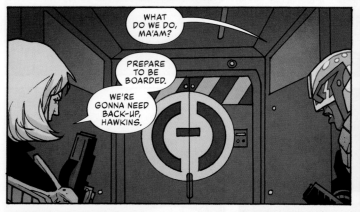

WHAT DO WE DO, MA'AM?

PREPARE TO BE BOARDED.

WE'RE GONNA NEED BACK-UP, HAWKINS.

ON IT.

MY ABILITY IS TO CREATE *PSYCHIC PROJECTIONS.*

PHANTOMS OF THE MIND.

READY?

READY.

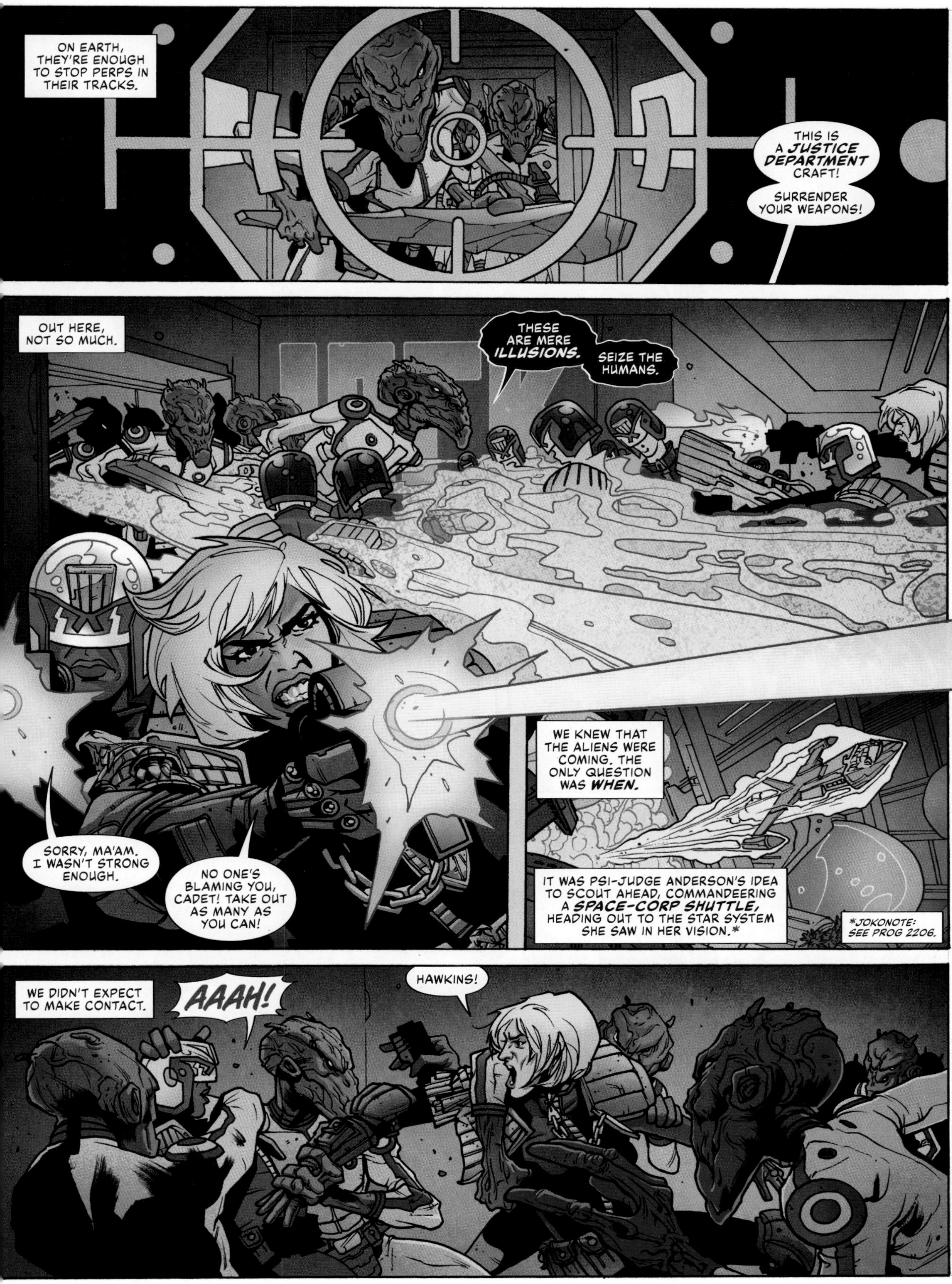

ON EARTH, THEY'RE ENOUGH TO STOP PERPS IN THEIR TRACKS.
THIS IS A JUSTICE DEPARTMENT CRAFT!
SURRENDER YOUR WEAPONS!
OUT HERE, NOT SO MUCH.
THESE ARE MERE ILLUSIONS.
SEIZE THE HUMANS.
SORRY, MA'AM. I WASN'T STRONG ENOUGH.
NO ONE'S BLAMING YOU, CADET! TAKE OUT AS MANY AS YOU CAN!
WE KNEW THAT THE ALIENS WERE COMING. THE ONLY QUESTION WAS WHEN.
IT WAS PSI-JUDGE ANDERSON'S IDEA TO SCOUT AHEAD, COMMANDEERING A SPACE-CORP SHUTTLE, HEADING OUT TO THE STAR SYSTEM SHE SAW IN HER VISION.*
*JOKONOTE: SEE PROG 2206.
WE DIDN'T EXPECT TO MAKE CONTACT.
AAAH!
HAWKINS!

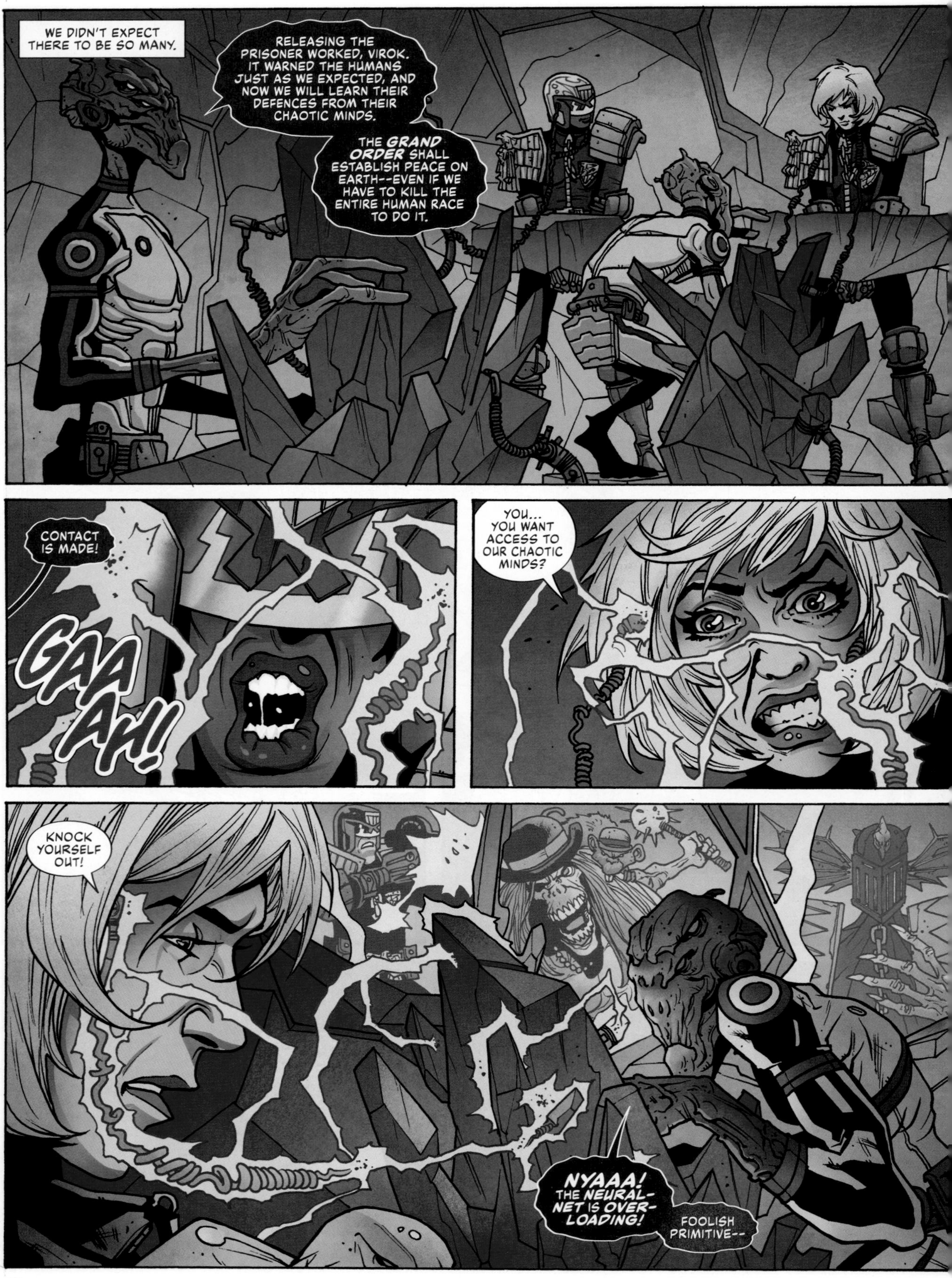

WE DIDN'T EXPECT THERE TO BE SO MANY.
RELEASING THE PRISONER WORKED, VIROK. IT WARNED THE HUMANS JUST AS WE EXPECTED, AND NOW WE WILL LEARN THEIR DEFENCES FROM THEIR CHAOTIC MINDS.
THE GRAND ORDER SHALL ESTABLISH PEACE ON EARTH--EVEN IF WE HAVE TO KILL THE ENTIRE HUMAN RACE TO DO IT.
CONTACT IS MADE!
GAAAAH!
YOU... YOU WANT ACCESS TO OUR CHAOTIC MINDS?
KNOCK YOURSELF OUT!
NYAAA! THE NEURAL-NET IS OVER-LOADING!
FOOLISH PRIMITIVE--

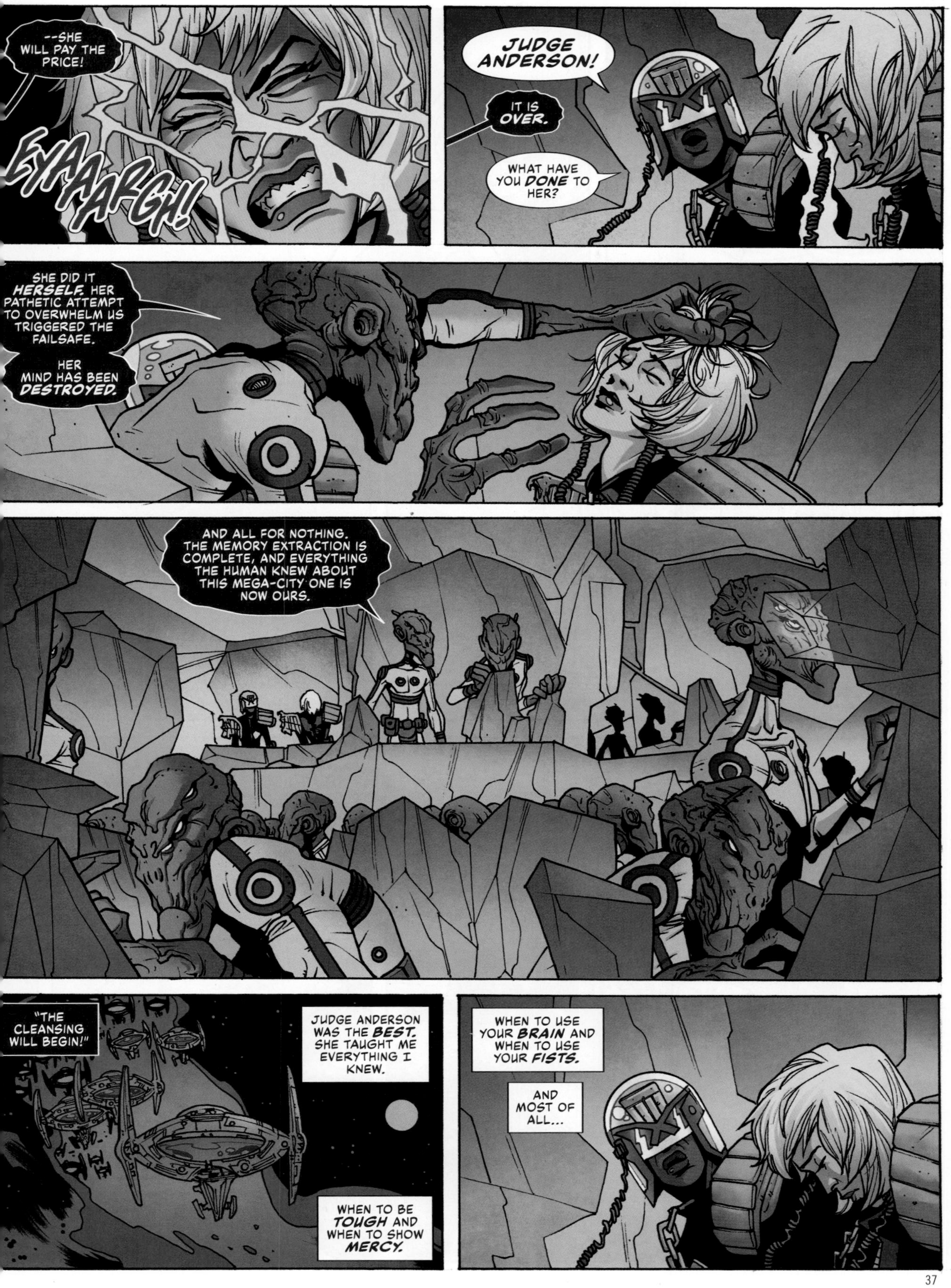
--SHE WILL PAY THE PRICE!
EYAAAARGH!
JUDGE ANDERSON!
IT IS OVER.
WHAT HAVE YOU DONE TO HER?
SHE DID IT HERSELF. HER PATHETIC ATTEMPT TO OVERWHELM US TRIGGERED THE FAILSAFE.
HER MIND HAS BEEN DESTROYED.
AND ALL FOR NOTHING. THE MEMORY EXTRACTION IS COMPLETE, AND EVERYTHING THE HUMAN KNEW ABOUT THIS MEGA-CITY ONE IS NOW OURS.
"THE CLEANSING WILL BEGIN!"
JUDGE ANDERSON WAS THE BEST. SHE TAUGHT ME EVERYTHING I KNEW.
WHEN TO BE TOUGH AND WHEN TO SHOW MERCY.
WHEN TO USE YOUR BRAIN AND WHEN TO USE YOUR FISTS.
AND MOST OF ALL...

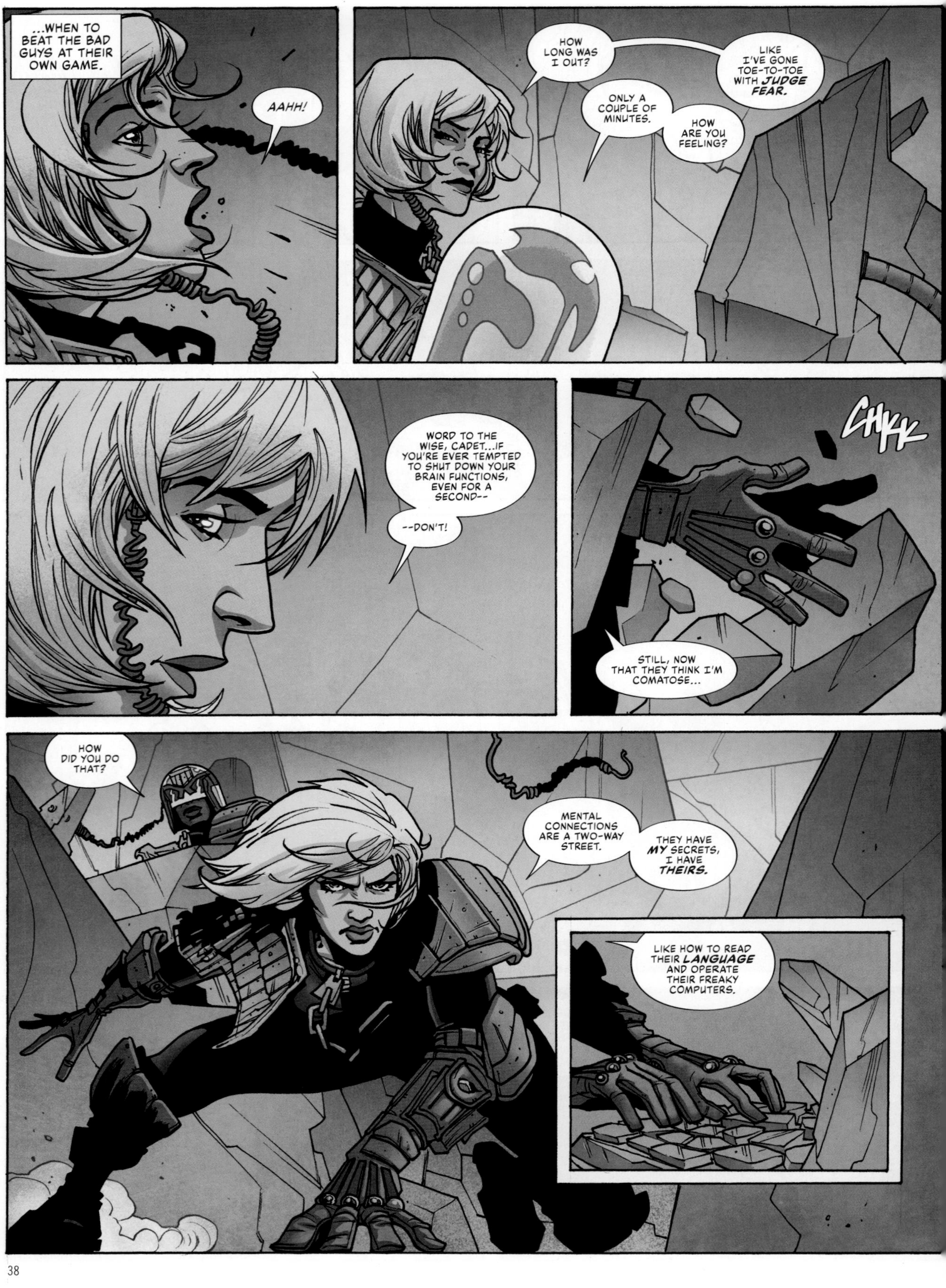
...WHEN TO BEAT THE BAD GUYS AT THEIR OWN GAME.
AAHH!
HOW LONG WAS I OUT?
ONLY A COUPLE OF MINUTES.
HOW ARE YOU FEELING?
LIKE I'VE GONE TOE-TO-TOE WITH JUDGE FEAR.
WORD TO THE WISE, CADET...IF YOU'RE EVER TEMPTED TO SHUT DOWN YOUR BRAIN FUNCTIONS, EVEN FOR A SECOND--
--DON'T!
CHKK
STILL, NOW THAT THEY THINK I'M COMATOSE...
HOW DID YOU DO THAT?
MENTAL CONNECTIONS ARE A TWO-WAY STREET.
THEY HAVE MY SECRETS, I HAVE THEIRS.
LIKE HOW TO READ THEIR LANGUAGE AND OPERATE THEIR FREAKY COMPUTERS.

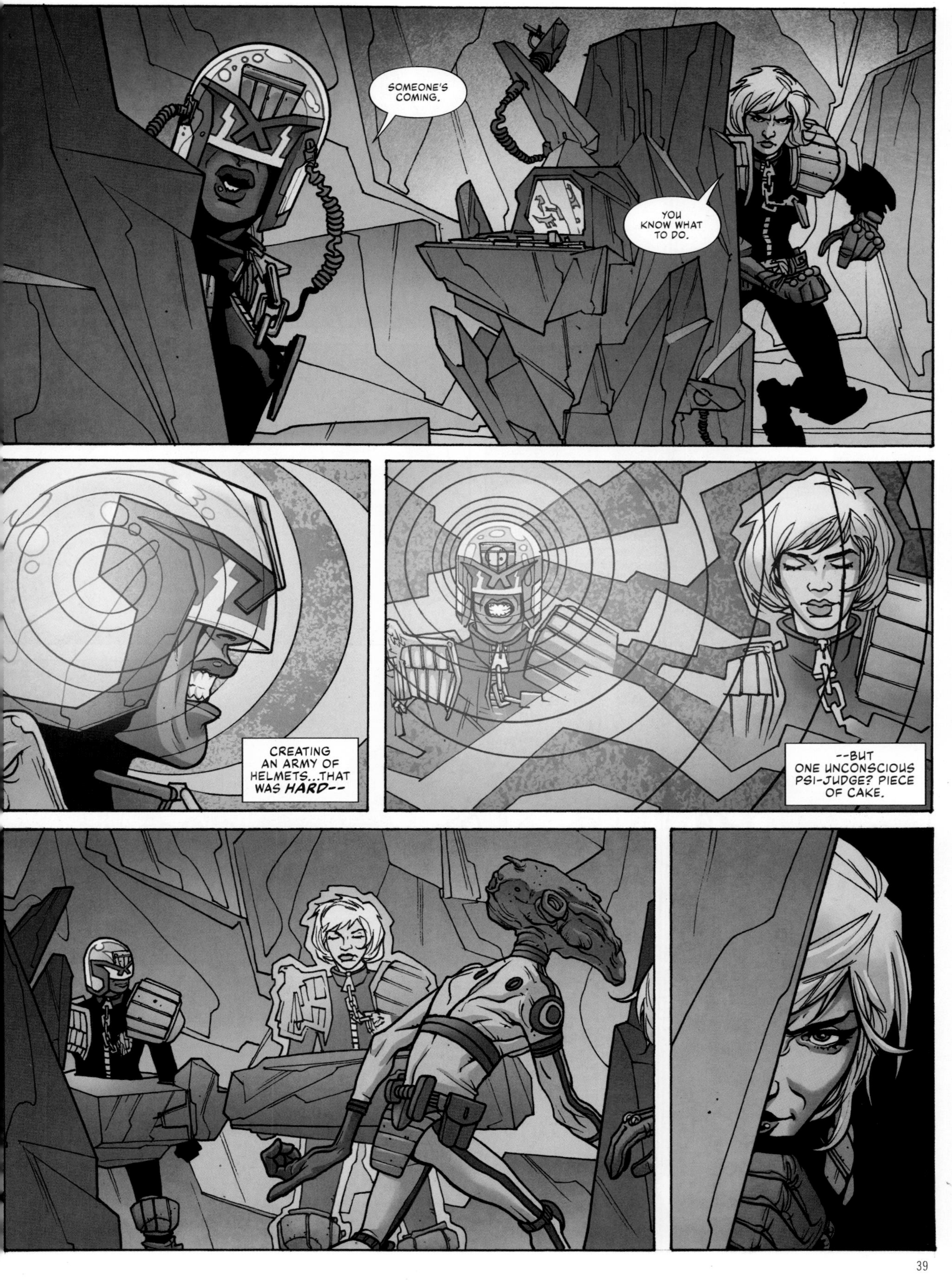
SOMEONE'S COMING.
YOU KNOW WHAT TO DO.
CREATING AN ARMY OF HELMETS...THAT WAS HARD--
--BUT ONE UNCONSCIOUS PSI-JUDGE? PIECE OF CAKE.

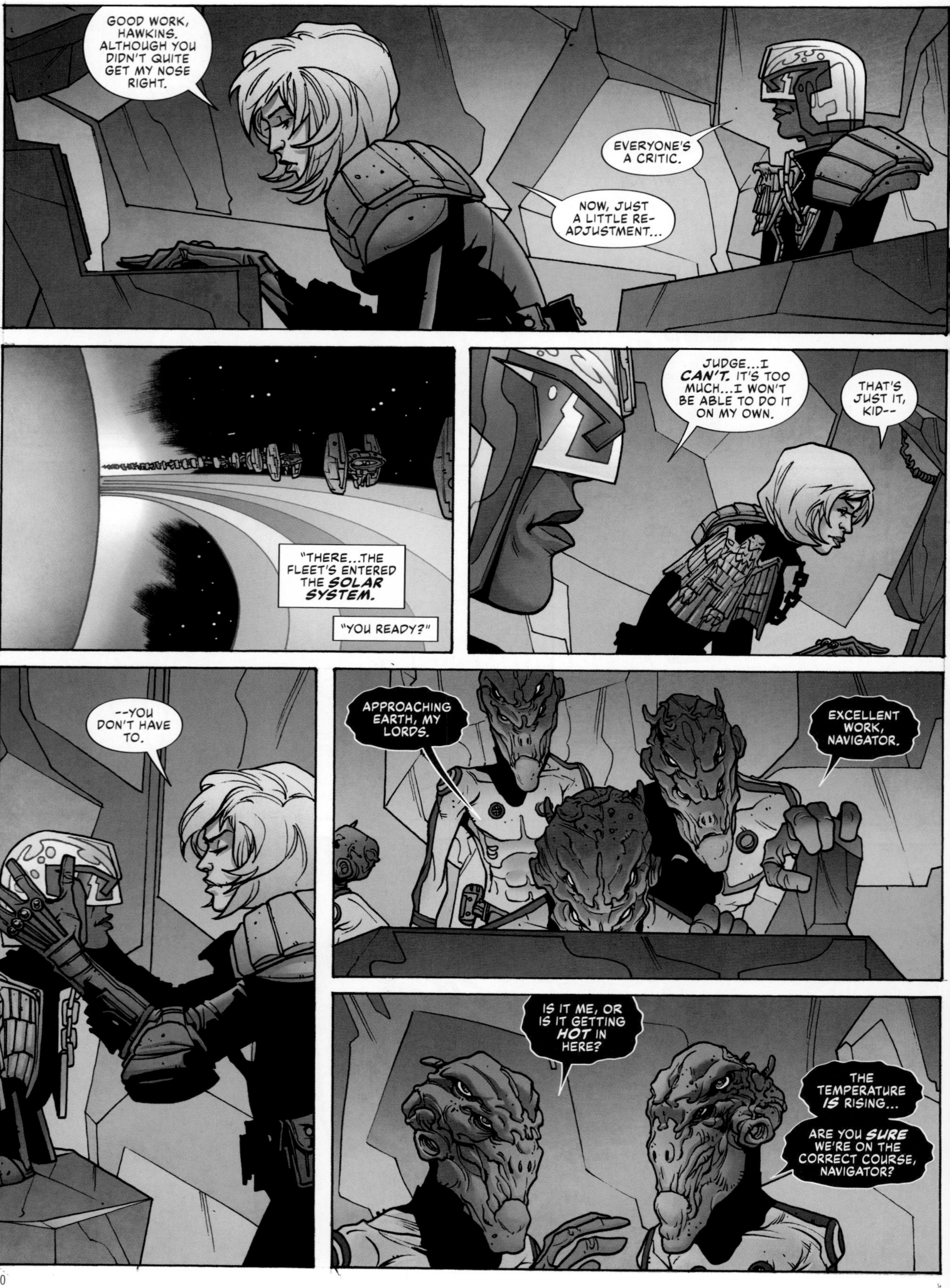
GOOD WORK, HAWKINS. ALTHOUGH YOU DIDN'T QUITE GET MY NOSE RIGHT.
EVERYONE'S A CRITIC.
NOW, JUST A LITTLE RE-ADJUSTMENT...
"THERE...THE FLEET'S ENTERED THE SOLAR SYSTEM.
"YOU READY?"
JUDGE...I CAN'T. IT'S TOO MUCH...I WON'T BE ABLE TO DO IT ON MY OWN.
THAT'S JUST IT, KID--
--YOU DON'T HAVE TO.
APPROACHING EARTH, MY LORDS.
EXCELLENT WORK, NAVIGATOR.
IS IT ME, OR IS IT GETTING HOT IN HERE?
THE TEMPERATURE IS RISING...
ARE YOU SURE WE'RE ON THE CORRECT COURSE, NAVIGATOR?

OF COURSE. IT'S RIGHT AHEAD, RIPE FOR THE CLEANSING.

ITS BIGGER THAN I EXPECTED.

NO MATTER. PREPARE TO LAND. SET US DOWN ON TOP OF MEGA-CITY ONE--

VWOOOP
VWOOOP
VWOOOP

WH-WHAT IS HAPPENING?

HEAT-SHIELDS ARE *FAILING!* WE'RE BURNING UP!

BURNING UP? FROM ENTERING EARTH'S ATMOSPHERE?

NOT EXACTLY.

*NNN!* I'M NOT SURE I CAN HANG ON MUCH LONGER...

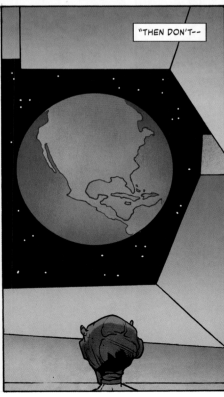

"THEN DON'T--

"--LET THEM SEE WHERE THEY *REALLY* ARE!"

NO!

41

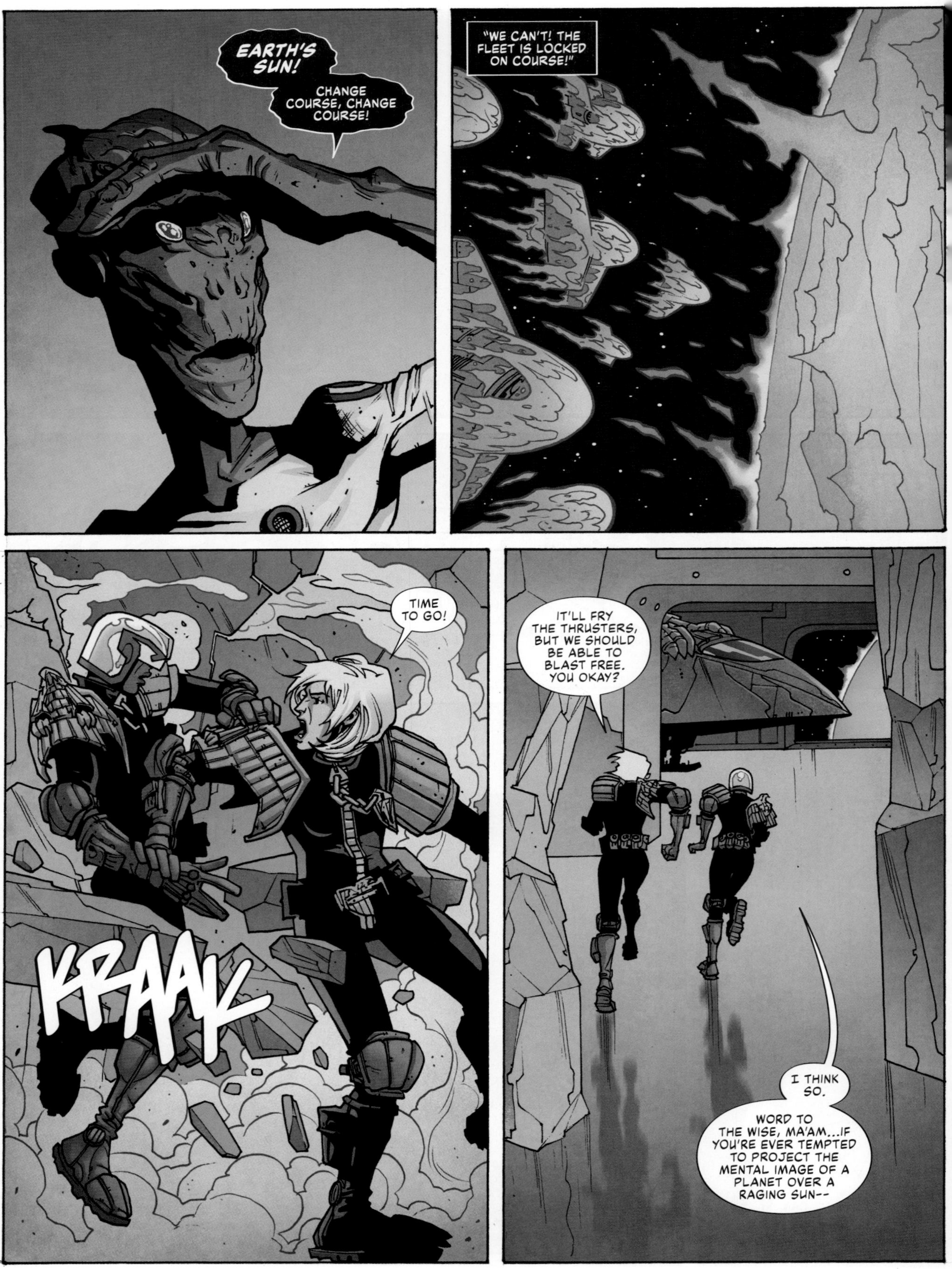
EARTH'S SUN!
CHANGE COURSE, CHANGE COURSE!
"WE CAN'T! THE FLEET IS LOCKED ON COURSE!"
TIME TO GO!
KRAAK
IT'LL FRY THE THRUSTERS, BUT WE SHOULD BE ABLE TO BLAST FREE. YOU OKAY?
I THINK SO.
WORD TO THE WISE, MA'AM...IF YOU'RE EVER TEMPTED TO PROJECT THE MENTAL IMAGE OF A PLANET OVER A RAGING SUN--

--DON'T!

BUT THAT'S JUST IT.

SHE *DID* PROJECT THE IMAGE...WITH ME, MY TALENT. HER STRENGTH.

JUDGE ANDERSON, THE BEST MENTOR A CADET COULD EVER HAVE...

BUT IF YOU EVER THREATEN HER PLANET...

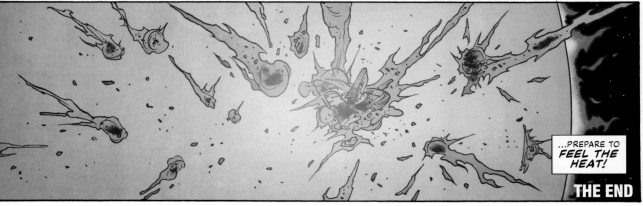

...PREPARE TO *FEEL THE HEAT!*

**THE END**

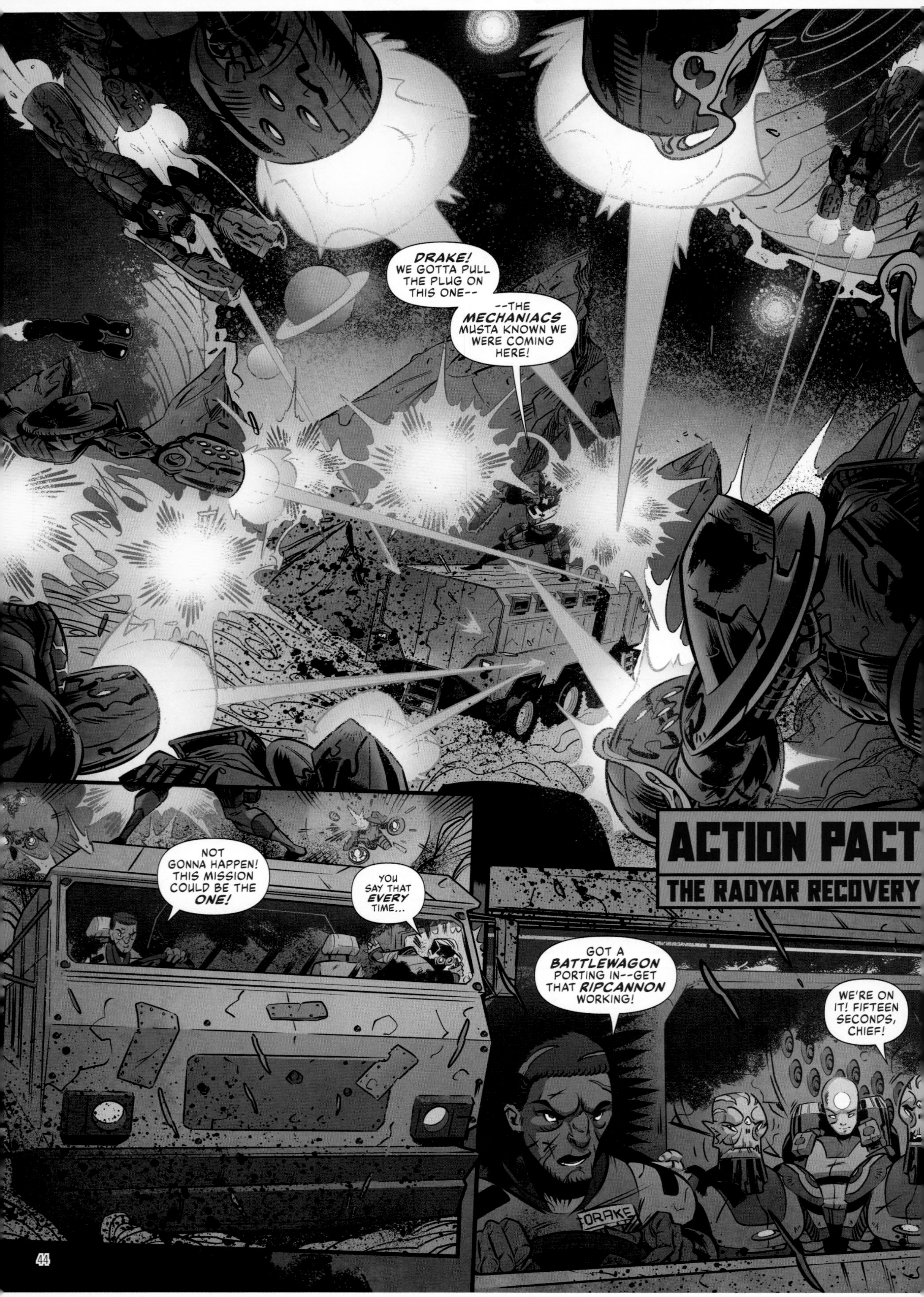
DRAKE! WE GOTTA PULL THE PLUG ON THIS ONE--
--THE MECHANIACS MUSTA KNOWN WE WERE COMING HERE!
ACTION PACT
THE RADYAR RECOVERY
NOT GONNA HAPPEN! THIS MISSION COULD BE THE ONE!
YOU SAY THAT EVERY TIME...
GOT A BATTLEWAGON PORTING IN--GET THAT RIPCANNON WORKING!
WE'RE ON IT! FIFTEEN SECONDS, CHIEF!
DRAKE

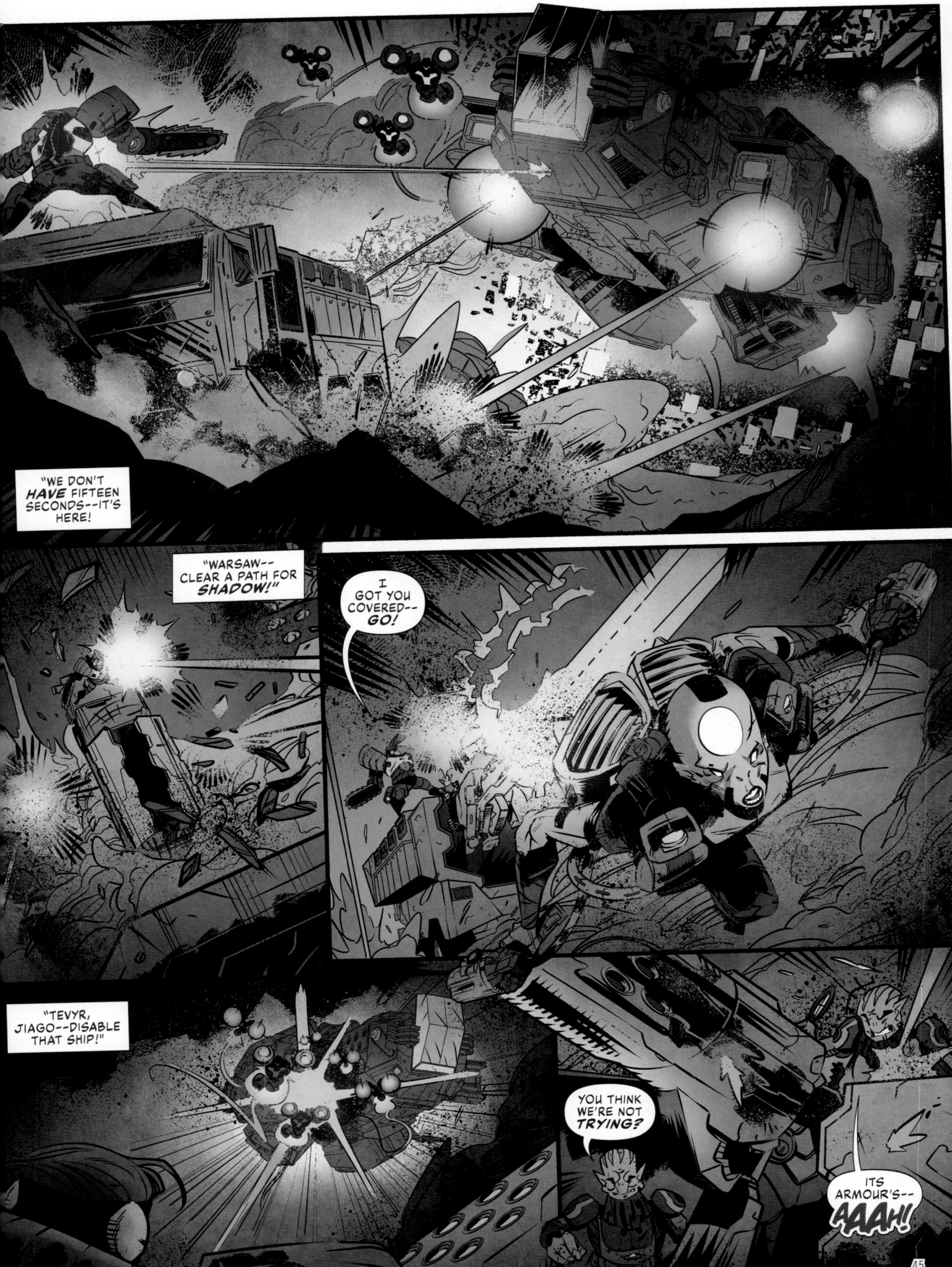
"WE DON'T HAVE FIFTEEN SECONDS--IT'S HERE!
"WARSAW--CLEAR A PATH FOR SHADOW!"
I GOT YOU COVERED--GO!
"TEVYR, JIAGO--DISABLE THAT SHIP!"
YOU THINK WE'RE NOT TRYING?
ITS ARMOUR'S--
AAAH!

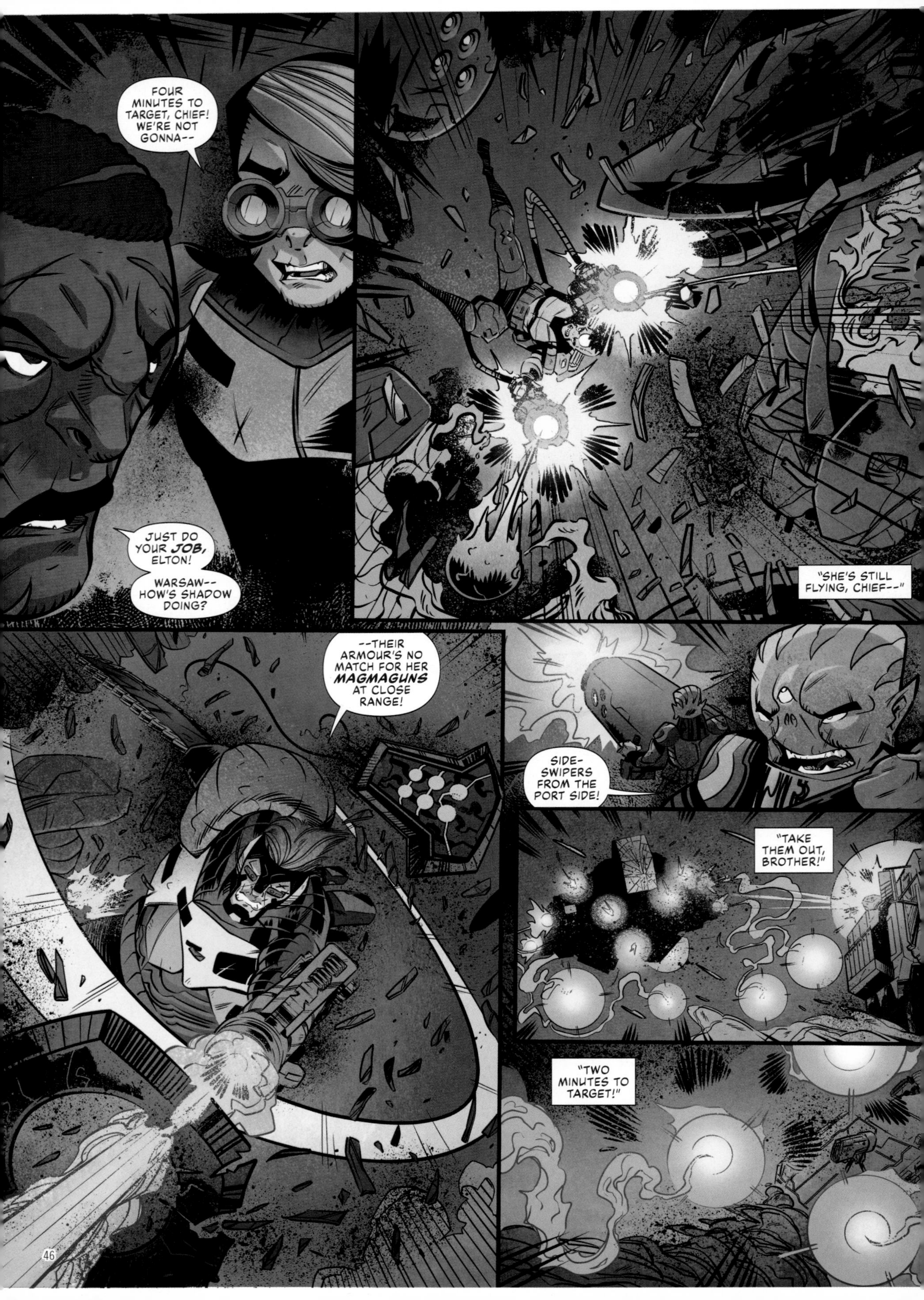
FOUR MINUTES TO TARGET, CHIEF! WE'RE NOT GONNA--
JUST DO YOUR JOB, ELTON!
WARSAW-- HOW'S SHADOW DOING?
"SHE'S STILL FLYING, CHIEF--"
--THEIR ARMOUR'S NO MATCH FOR HER MAGMAGUNS AT CLOSE RANGE!
SIDE-SWIPERS FROM THE PORT SIDE!
"TAKE THEM OUT, BROTHER!"
"TWO MINUTES TO TARGET!"

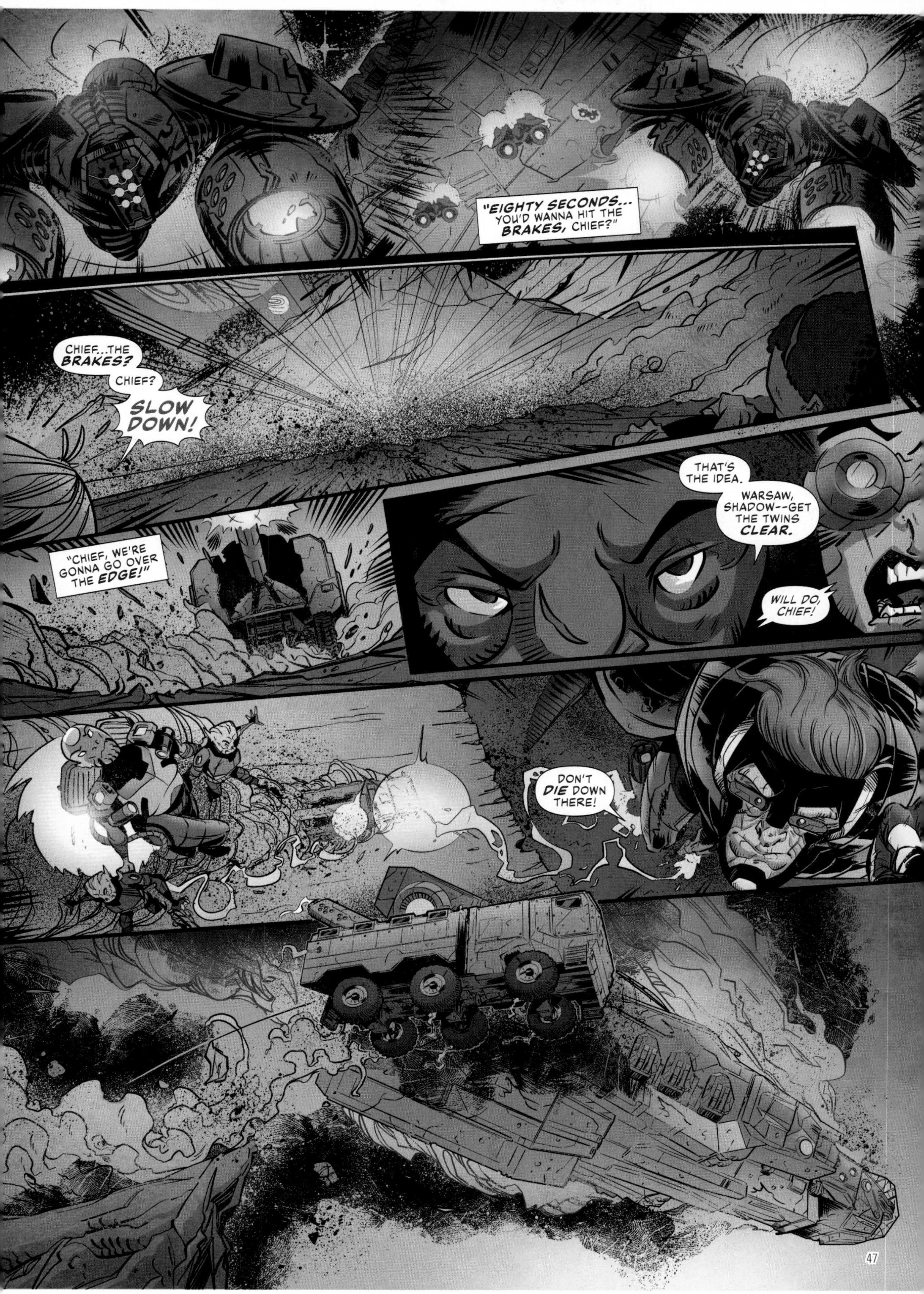
"EIGHTY SECONDS... YOU'D WANNA HIT THE BRAKES, CHIEF?"
CHIEF...THE BRAKES?
CHIEF?
SLOW DOWN!
"CHIEF, WE'RE GONNA GO OVER THE EDGE!"
THAT'S THE IDEA.
WARSAW, SHADOW--GET THE TWINS CLEAR.
WILL DO, CHIEF!
DON'T DIE DOWN THERE!

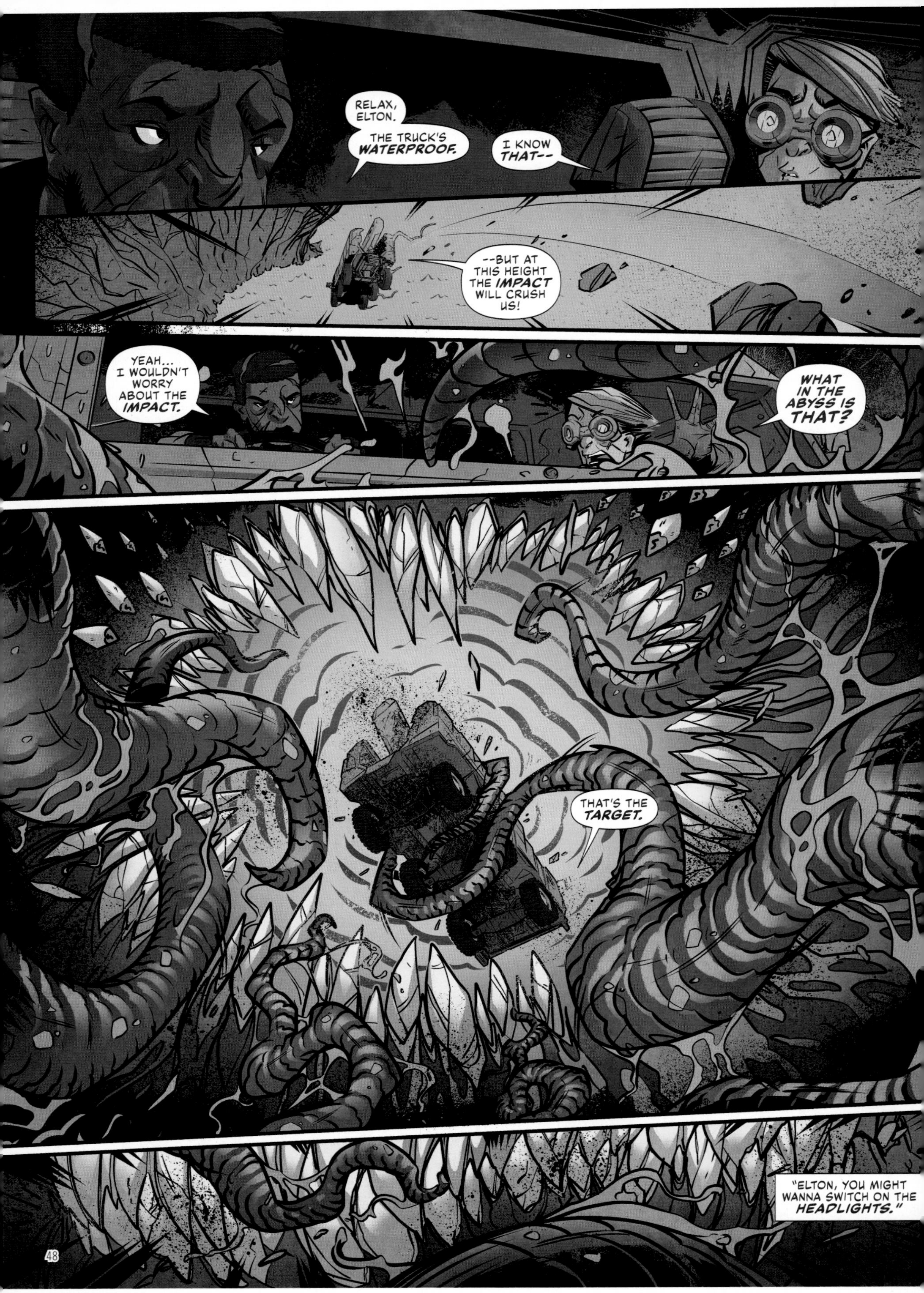
RELAX, ELTON.
THE TRUCK'S *WATERPROOF.*
I KNOW *THAT*--
--BUT AT THIS HEIGHT THE *IMPACT* WILL CRUSH US!
YEAH... I WOULDN'T WORRY ABOUT THE *IMPACT.*
*WHAT IN THE ABYSS IS THAT?*
THAT'S THE *TARGET.*
"ELTON, YOU MIGHT WANNA SWITCH ON THE *HEADLIGHTS.*"

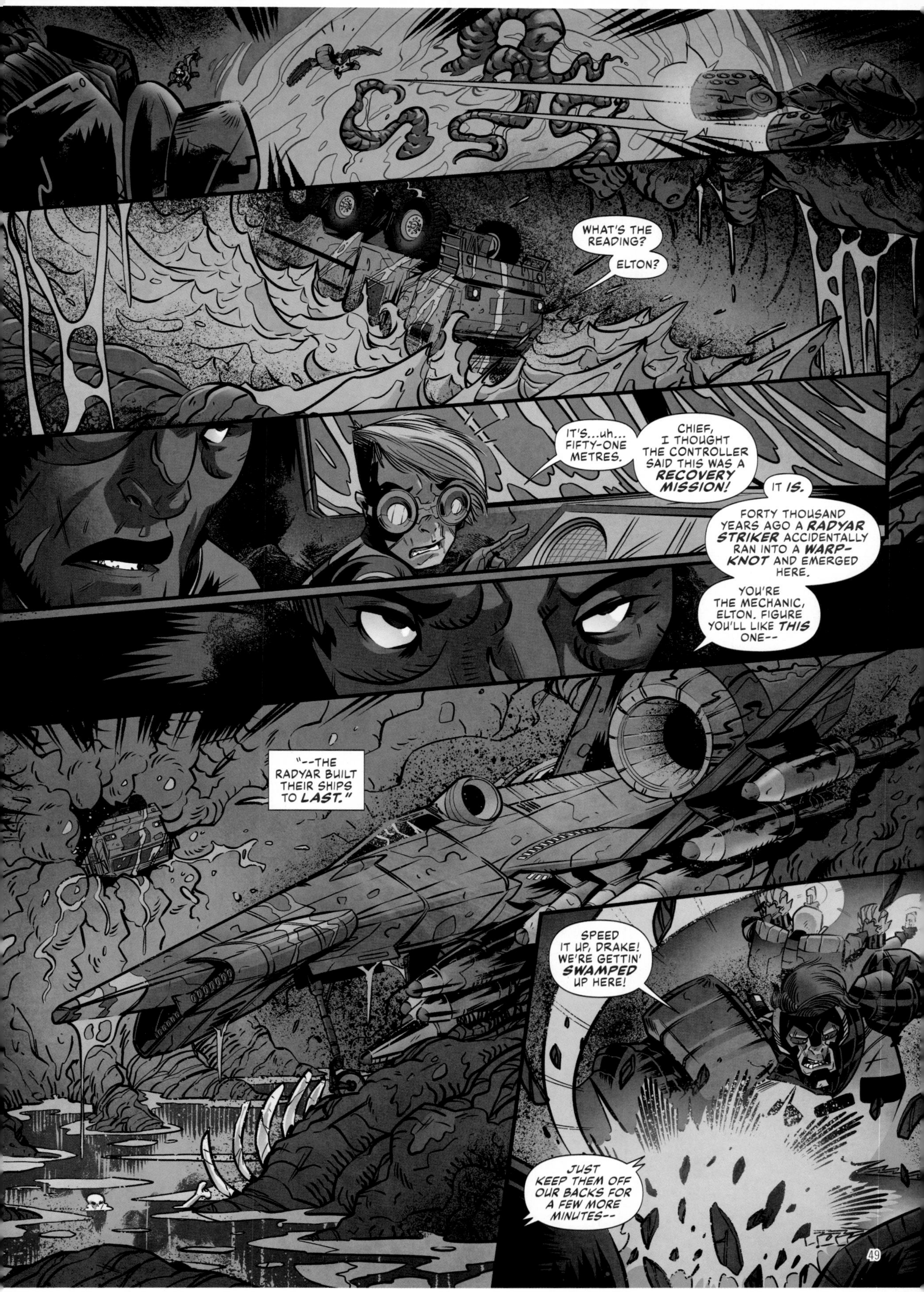
WHAT'S THE READING?
ELTON?
IT'S...uh... FIFTY-ONE METRES.
CHIEF, I THOUGHT THE CONTROLLER SAID THIS WAS A RECOVERY MISSION!
IT IS.
FORTY THOUSAND YEARS AGO A RADYAR STRIKER ACCIDENTALLY RAN INTO A WARP-KNOT AND EMERGED HERE.
YOU'RE THE MECHANIC, ELTON. FIGURE YOU'LL LIKE THIS ONE--
"--THE RADYAR BUILT THEIR SHIPS TO LAST."
SPEED IT UP, DRAKE! WE'RE GETTIN' SWAMPED UP HERE!
JUST KEEP THEM OFF OUR BACKS FOR A FEW MORE MINUTES--

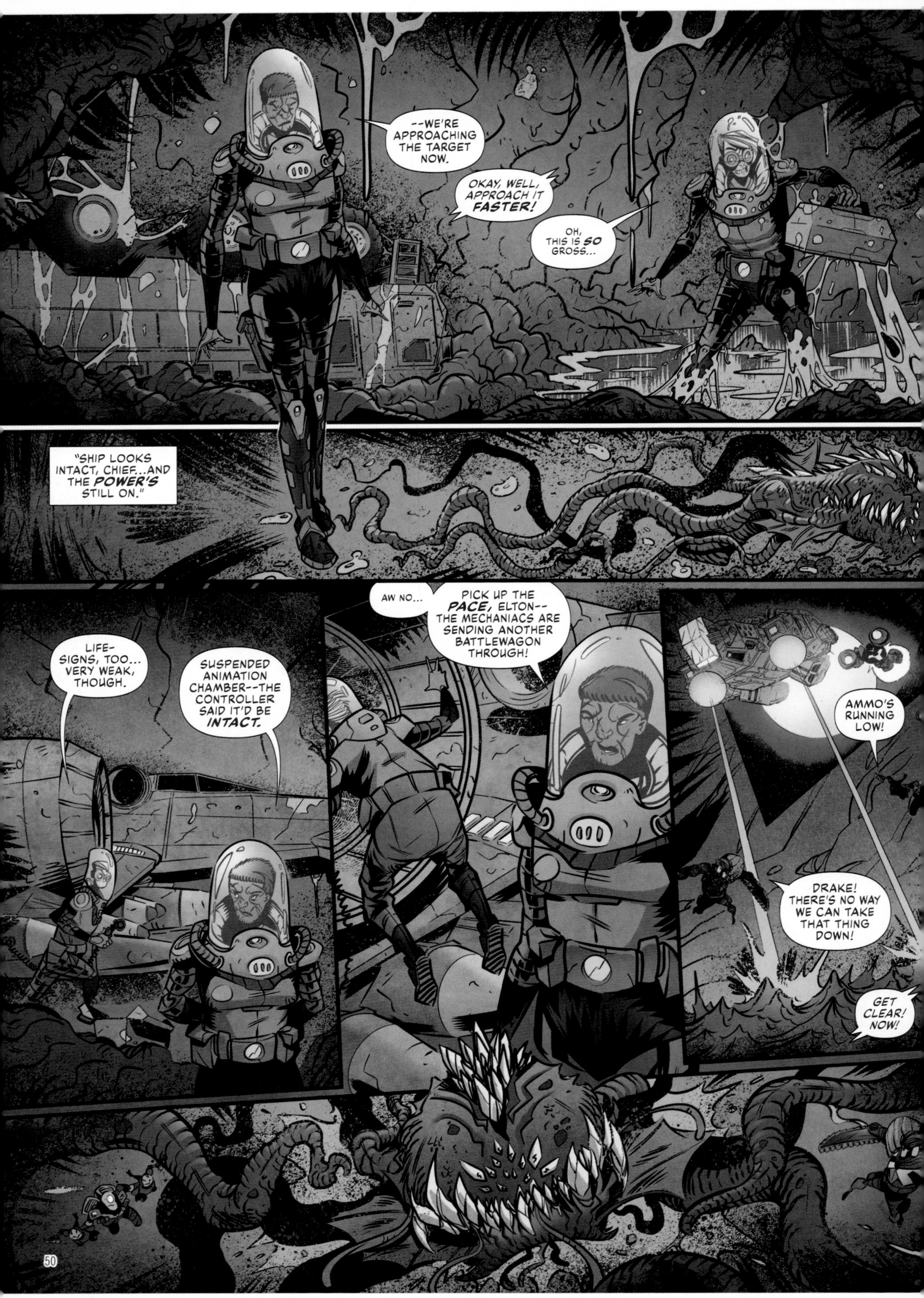
--WE'RE APPROACHING THE TARGET NOW.
OKAY, WELL, APPROACH IT FASTER!
OH, THIS IS SO GROSS...
"SHIP LOOKS INTACT, CHIEF...AND THE POWER'S STILL ON."
LIFE-SIGNS, TOO... VERY WEAK, THOUGH.
SUSPENDED ANIMATION CHAMBER--THE CONTROLLER SAID IT'D BE INTACT.
AW NO...
PICK UP THE PACE, ELTON--THE MECHANIACS ARE SENDING ANOTHER BATTLEWAGON THROUGH!
AMMO'S RUNNING LOW!
DRAKE! THERE'S NO WAY WE CAN TAKE THAT THING DOWN!
GET CLEAR! NOW!

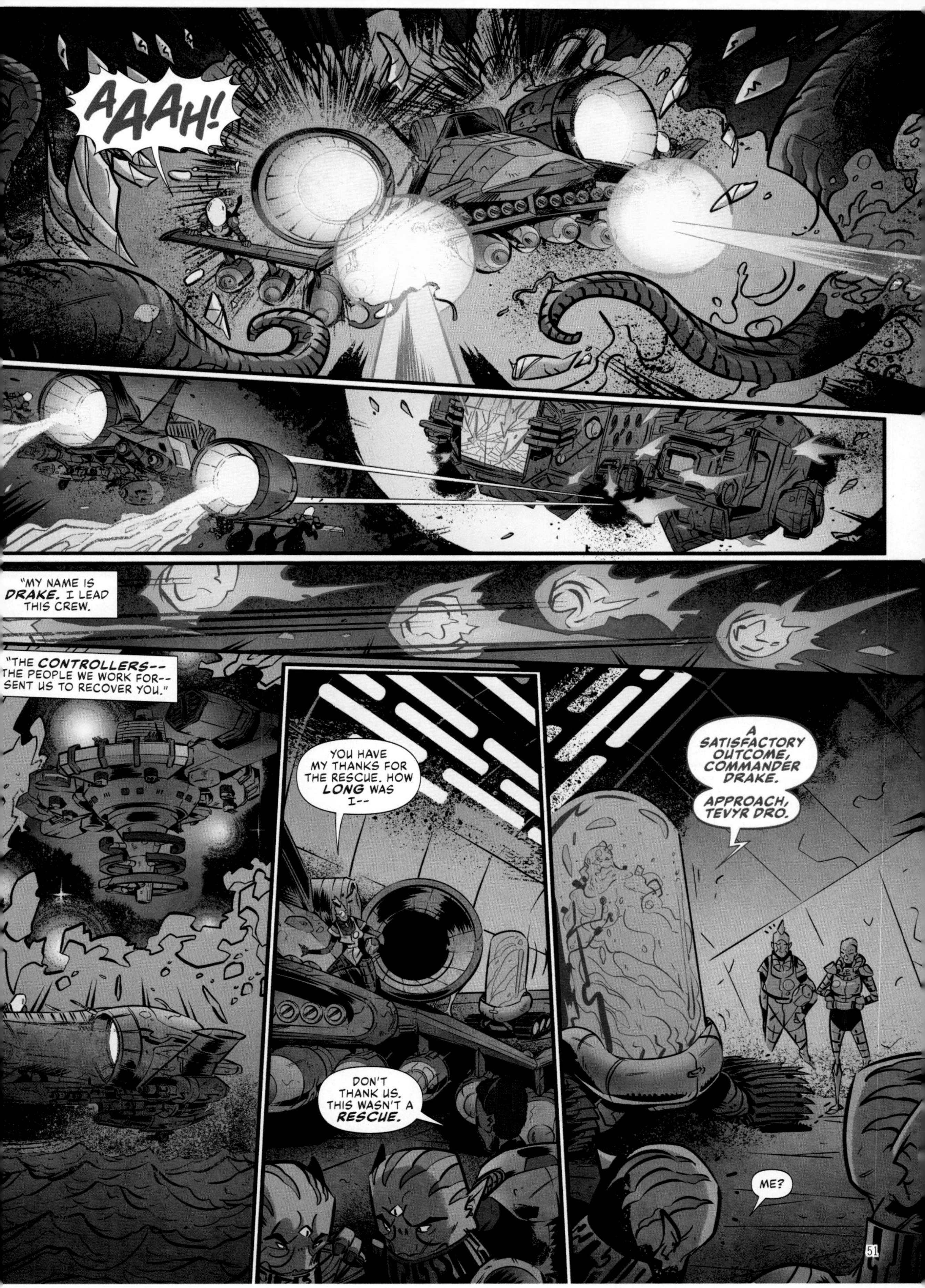
AAAH!
"MY NAME IS DRAKE. I LEAD THIS CREW.
"THE CONTROLLERS-- THE PEOPLE WE WORK FOR-- SENT US TO RECOVER YOU."
YOU HAVE MY THANKS FOR THE RESCUE. HOW LONG WAS I--
DON'T THANK US. THIS WASN'T A RESCUE.
A SATISFACTORY OUTCOME, COMMANDER DRAKE.
APPROACH, TEVYR DRO.
ME?

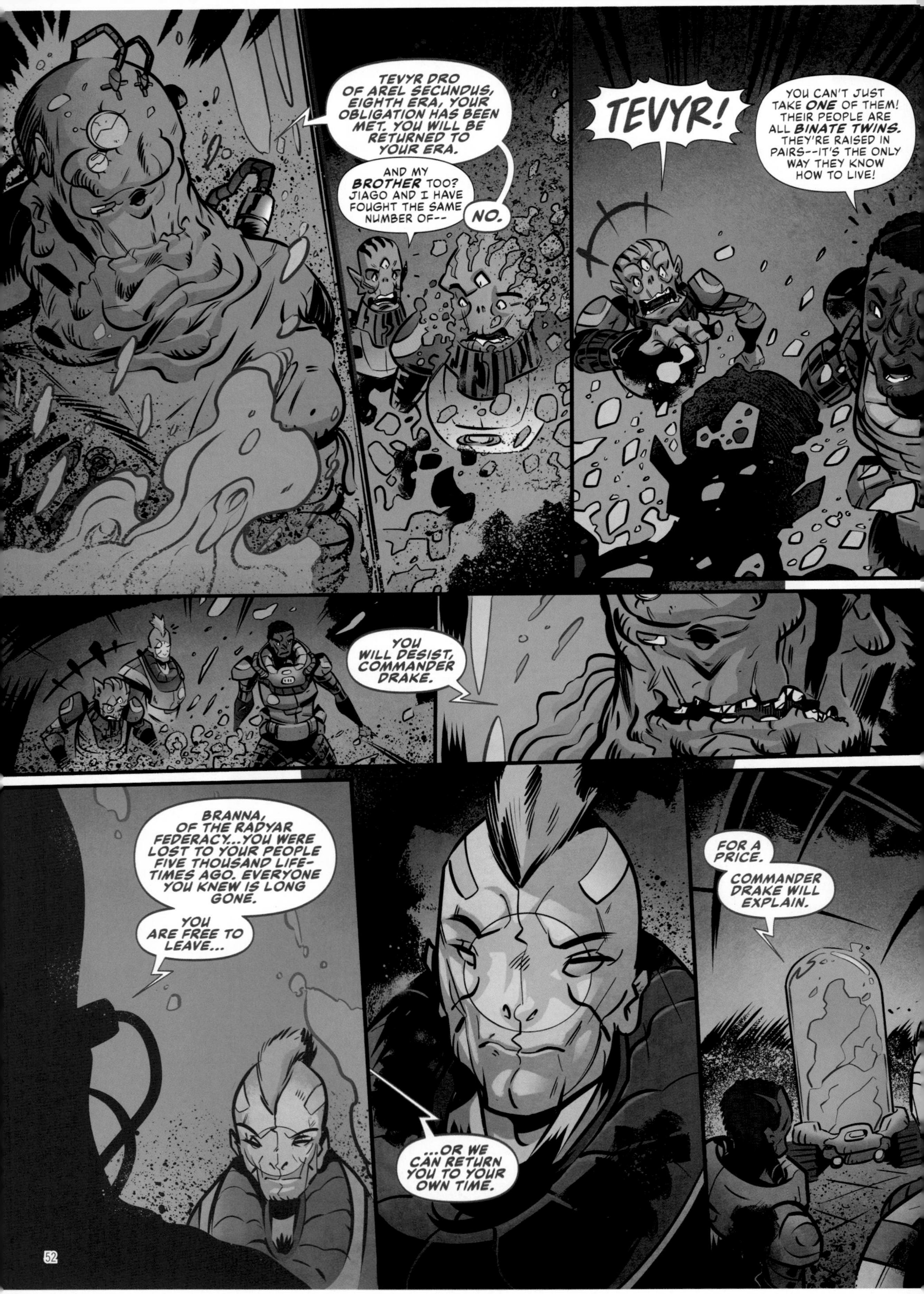

TEVYR DRO OF AREL SECUNDUS, EIGHTH ERA, YOUR OBLIGATION HAS BEEN MET. YOU WILL BE RETURNED TO YOUR ERA.
AND MY BROTHER TOO? JIAGO AND I HAVE FOUGHT THE SAME NUMBER OF--
NO.
TEVYR!
YOU CAN'T JUST TAKE ONE OF THEM! THEIR PEOPLE ARE ALL BINATE TWINS. THEY'RE RAISED IN PAIRS--IT'S THE ONLY WAY THEY KNOW HOW TO LIVE!
YOU WILL DESIST, COMMANDER DRAKE.
BRANNA, OF THE RADYAR FEDERACY...YOU WERE LOST TO YOUR PEOPLE FIVE THOUSAND LIFE-TIMES AGO. EVERYONE YOU KNEW IS LONG GONE.
YOU ARE FREE TO LEAVE...
...OR WE CAN RETURN YOU TO YOUR OWN TIME.
FOR A PRICE.
COMMANDER DRAKE WILL EXPLAIN.

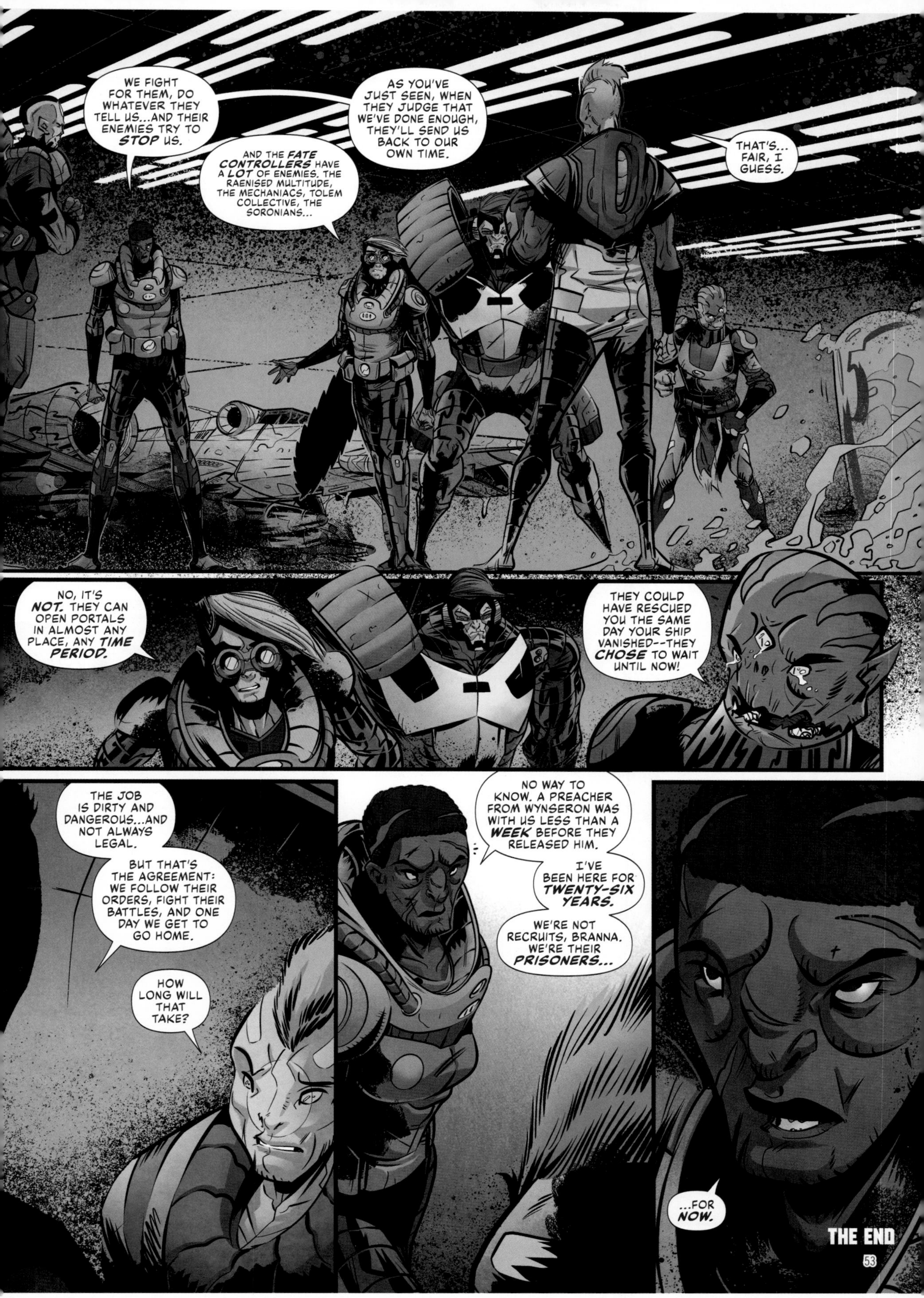
WE FIGHT FOR THEM, DO WHATEVER THEY TELL US...AND THEIR ENEMIES TRY TO STOP US.
AND THE FATE CONTROLLERS HAVE A LOT OF ENEMIES. THE RAENISED MULTITUDE, THE MECHANIACS, TOLEM COLLECTIVE, THE SORONIANS...
AS YOU'VE JUST SEEN, WHEN THEY JUDGE THAT WE'VE DONE ENOUGH, THEY'LL SEND US BACK TO OUR OWN TIME.
THAT'S... FAIR, I GUESS.
NO, IT'S NOT. THEY CAN OPEN PORTALS IN ALMOST ANY PLACE, ANY TIME PERIOD.
THEY COULD HAVE RESCUED YOU THE SAME DAY YOUR SHIP VANISHED--THEY CHOSE TO WAIT UNTIL NOW!
THE JOB IS DIRTY AND DANGEROUS...AND NOT ALWAYS LEGAL.
BUT THAT'S THE AGREEMENT: WE FOLLOW THEIR ORDERS, FIGHT THEIR BATTLES, AND ONE DAY WE GET TO GO HOME.
HOW LONG WILL THAT TAKE?
NO WAY TO KNOW. A PREACHER FROM WYNSERON WAS WITH US LESS THAN A WEEK BEFORE THEY RELEASED HIM.
I'VE BEEN HERE FOR TWENTY-SIX YEARS.
WE'RE NOT RECRUITS, BRANNA. WE'RE THEIR PRISONERS...
...FOR NOW.
THE END

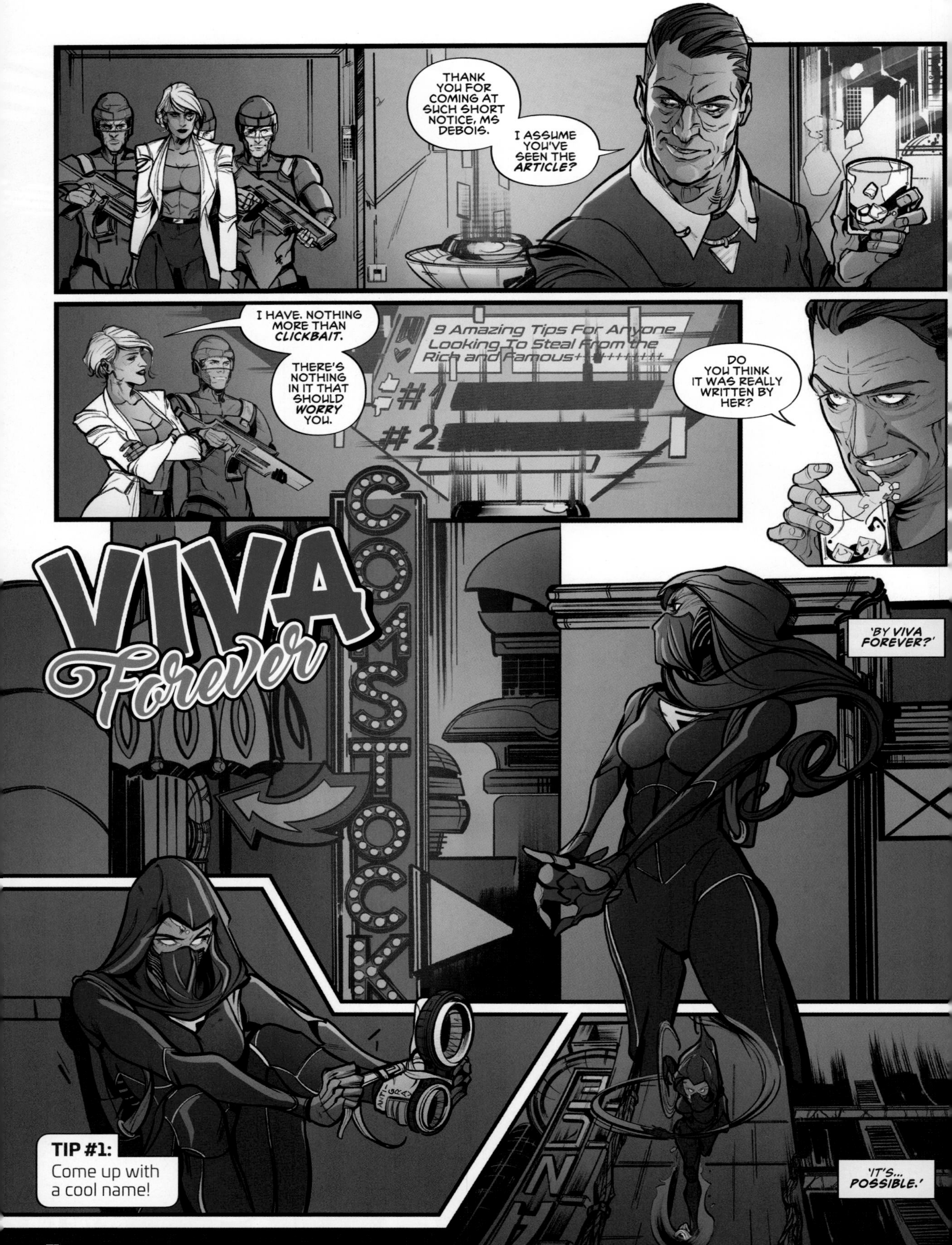
THANK YOU FOR COMING AT SUCH SHORT NOTICE, MS DEBOIS.
I ASSUME YOU'VE SEEN THE ARTICLE?
I HAVE. NOTHING MORE THAN CLICKBAIT.
THERE'S NOTHING IN IT THAT SHOULD WORRY YOU.
9 Amazing Tips For Anyone Looking To Steal From the Rich and Famous
#1 [redacted]
#2 [redacted]
DO YOU THINK IT WAS REALLY WRITTEN BY HER?
VIVA Forever
COMSTOCK
'BY VIVA FOREVER?'
TIP #1:
Come up with a cool name!
'IT'S... POSSIBLE.'

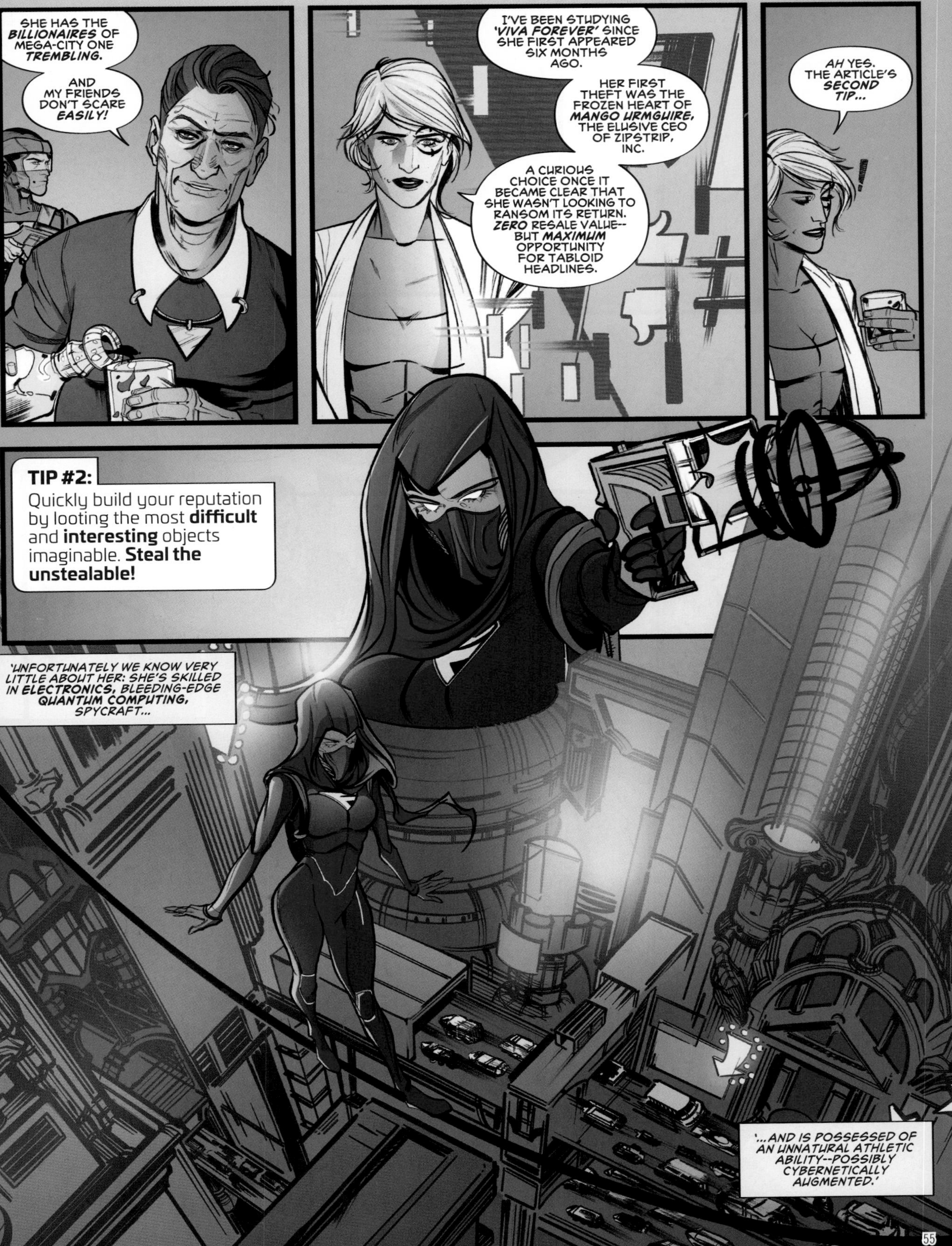
SHE HAS THE *BILLIONAIRES* OF MEGA-CITY ONE *TREMBLING.*
AND MY FRIENDS DON'T SCARE *EASILY!*
I'VE BEEN STUDYING *'VIVA FOREVER'* SINCE SHE FIRST APPEARED SIX MONTHS AGO.
HER FIRST THEFT WAS THE FROZEN HEART OF *MANGO URMGUIRE,* THE ELUSIVE CEO OF ZIPSTRIP, INC.
A CURIOUS CHOICE ONCE IT BECAME CLEAR THAT SHE WASN'T LOOKING TO RANSOM ITS RETURN. *ZERO* RESALE VALUE-- BUT *MAXIMUM* OPPORTUNITY FOR TABLOID HEADLINES.
*AH YES. THE ARTICLE'S* ***SECOND TIP...***
**TIP #2:**
Quickly build your reputation by looting the most **difficult** and **interesting** objects imaginable. **Steal the unstealable!**
*'UNFORTUNATELY WE KNOW VERY LITTLE ABOUT HER: SHE'S SKILLED IN* ***ELECTRONICS,*** *BLEEDING-EDGE* ***QUANTUM COMPUTING,*** *SPYCRAFT...*
*'...AND IS POSSESSED OF AN UNNATURAL ATHLETIC ABILITY--POSSIBLY CYBERNETICALLY AUGMENTED.'*

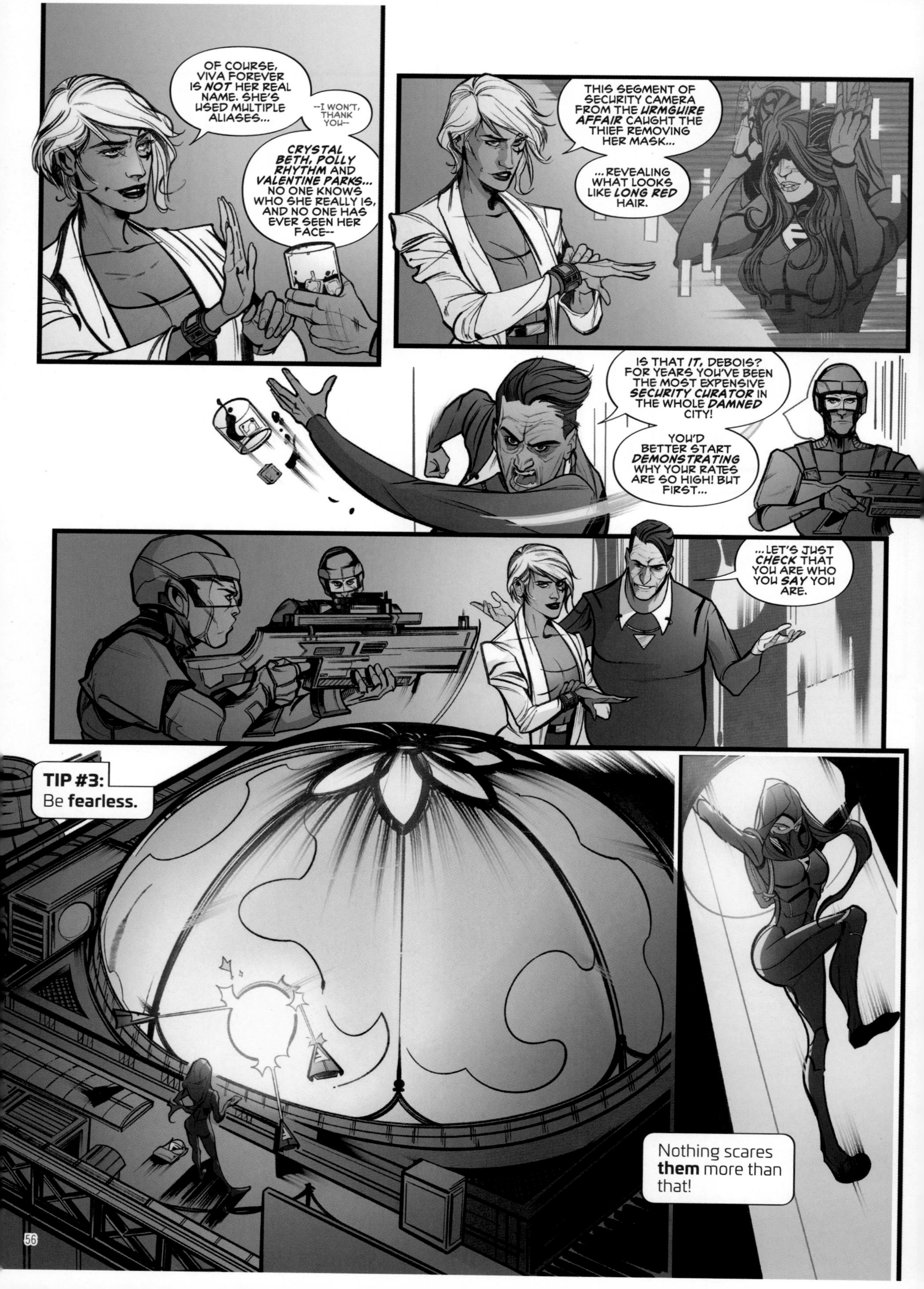
OF COURSE, VIVA FOREVER IS NOT HER REAL NAME. SHE'S USED MULTIPLE ALIASES...
--I WON'T, THANK YOU--
CRYSTAL BETH, POLLY RHYTHM AND VALENTINE PARKS... NO ONE KNOWS WHO SHE REALLY IS, AND NO ONE HAS EVER SEEN HER FACE--
THIS SEGMENT OF SECURITY CAMERA FROM THE URMGUIRE AFFAIR CAUGHT THE THIEF REMOVING HER MASK...
...REVEALING WHAT LOOKS LIKE LONG RED HAIR.
IS THAT IT, DEBOIS? FOR YEARS YOU'VE BEEN THE MOST EXPENSIVE SECURITY CURATOR IN THE WHOLE DAMNED CITY!
YOU'D BETTER START DEMONSTRATING WHY YOUR RATES ARE SO HIGH! BUT FIRST...
...LET'S JUST CHECK THAT YOU ARE WHO YOU SAY YOU ARE.
TIP #3:
Be fearless.
Nothing scares them more than that!

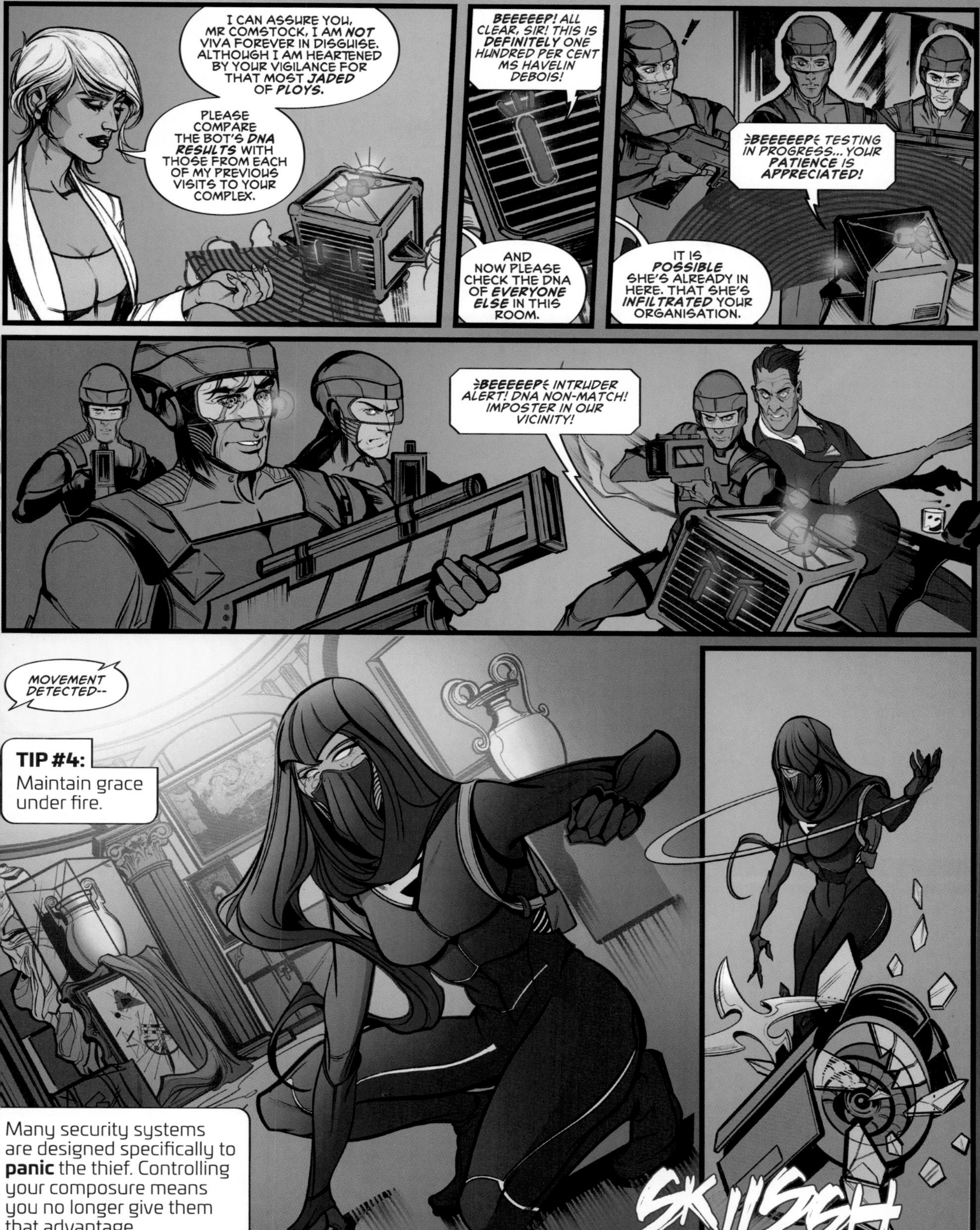

I CAN ASSURE YOU, MR COMSTOCK, I AM NOT VIVA FOREVER IN DISGUISE. ALTHOUGH I AM HEARTENED BY YOUR VIGILANCE FOR THAT MOST JADED OF PLOYS.
PLEASE COMPARE THE BOT'S DNA RESULTS WITH THOSE FROM EACH OF MY PREVIOUS VISITS TO YOUR COMPLEX.
BEEEEEP! ALL CLEAR, SIR! THIS IS DEFINITELY ONE HUNDRED PER CENT MS HAVELIN DEBOIS!
AND NOW PLEASE CHECK THE DNA OF EVERYONE ELSE IN THIS ROOM.
!
>BEEEEEP< TESTING IN PROGRESS... YOUR PATIENCE IS APPRECIATED!
IT IS POSSIBLE SHE'S ALREADY IN HERE. THAT SHE'S INFILTRATED YOUR ORGANISATION.
>BEEEEEP< INTRUDER ALERT! DNA NON-MATCH! IMPOSTER IN OUR VICINITY!
MOVEMENT DETECTED--
SKIISSH


**TIP #4:**
Maintain grace under fire.

Many security systems are designed specifically to **panic** the thief. Controlling your composure means you no longer give them that advantage.

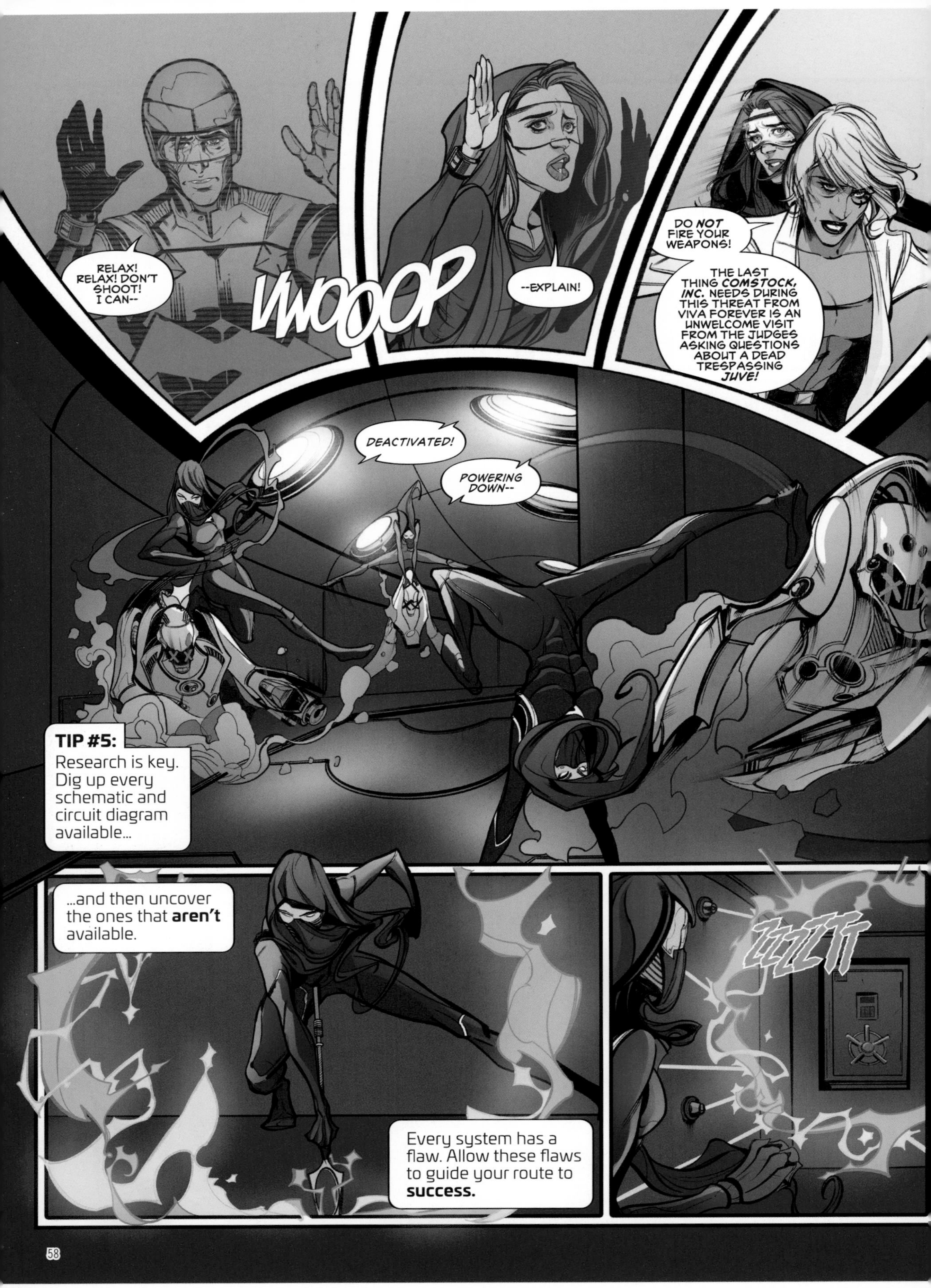
RELAX! RELAX! DON'T SHOOT! I CAN--
VWOOOP
--EXPLAIN!
DO NOT FIRE YOUR WEAPONS!
THE LAST THING COMSTOCK, INC. NEEDS DURING THIS THREAT FROM VIVA FOREVER IS AN UNWELCOME VISIT FROM THE JUDGES ASKING QUESTIONS ABOUT A DEAD TRESPASSING JUVE!
DEACTIVATED!
POWERING DOWN--
TIP #5:
Research is key. Dig up every schematic and circuit diagram available...
...and then uncover the ones that aren't available.
Every system has a flaw. Allow these flaws to guide your route to success.
ZZZZTT

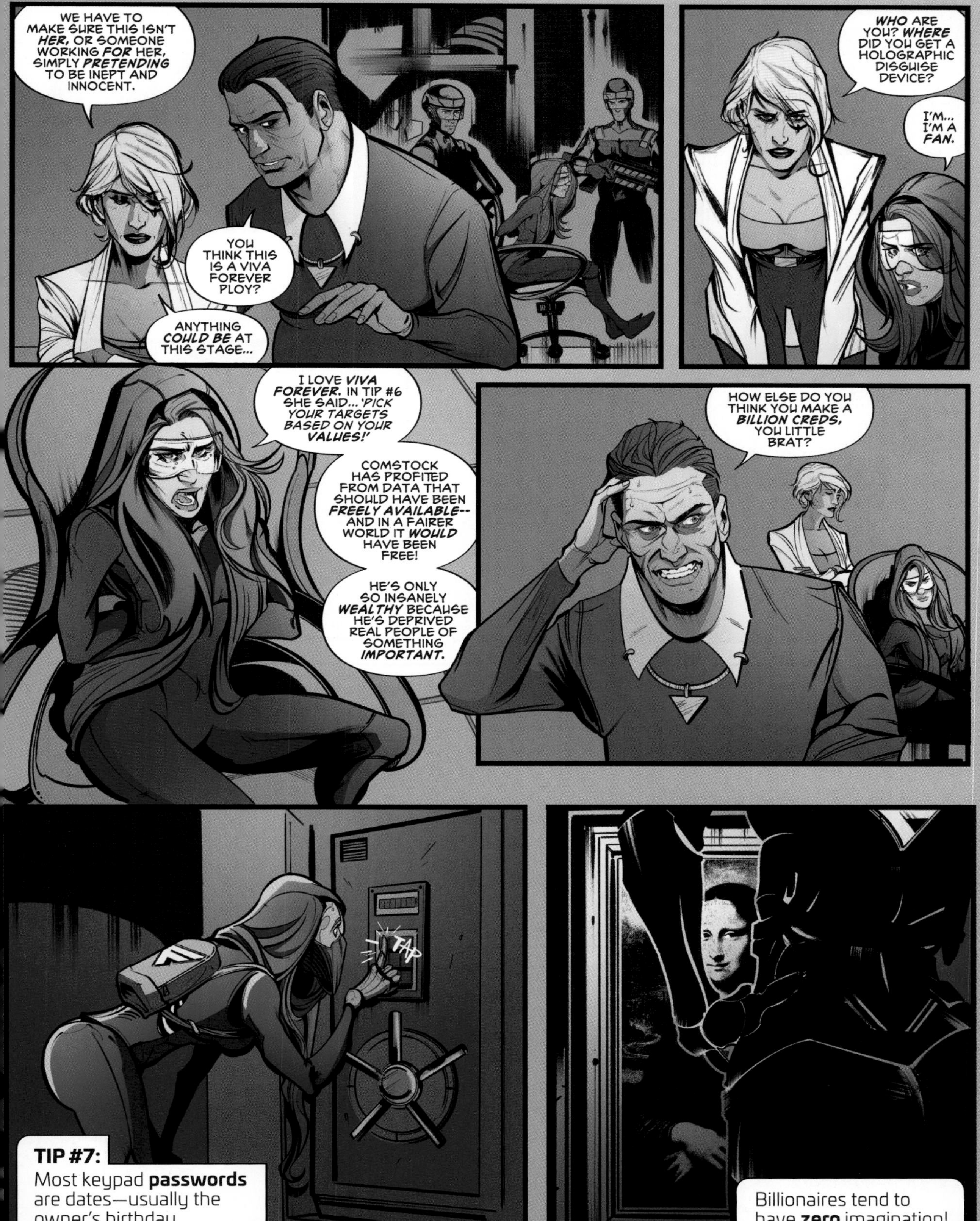

WE HAVE TO MAKE SURE THIS ISN'T HER, OR SOMEONE WORKING FOR HER, SIMPLY PRETENDING TO BE INEPT AND INNOCENT.
YOU THINK THIS IS A VIVA FOREVER PLOY?
ANYTHING COULD BE AT THIS STAGE...
WHO ARE YOU? WHERE DID YOU GET A HOLOGRAPHIC DISGUISE DEVICE?
I'M... I'M A FAN.
I LOVE VIVA FOREVER. IN TIP #6 SHE SAID... 'PICK YOUR TARGETS BASED ON YOUR VALUES!'
COMSTOCK HAS PROFITED FROM DATA THAT SHOULD HAVE BEEN FREELY AVAILABLE-- AND IN A FAIRER WORLD IT WOULD HAVE BEEN FREE!
HE'S ONLY SO INSANELY WEALTHY BECAUSE HE'S DEPRIVED REAL PEOPLE OF SOMETHING IMPORTANT.
HOW ELSE DO YOU THINK YOU MAKE A BILLION CREDS, YOU LITTLE BRAT?
TAP
TIP #7:
Most keypad passwords are dates—usually the owner's birthday.
Billionaires tend to have zero imagination!

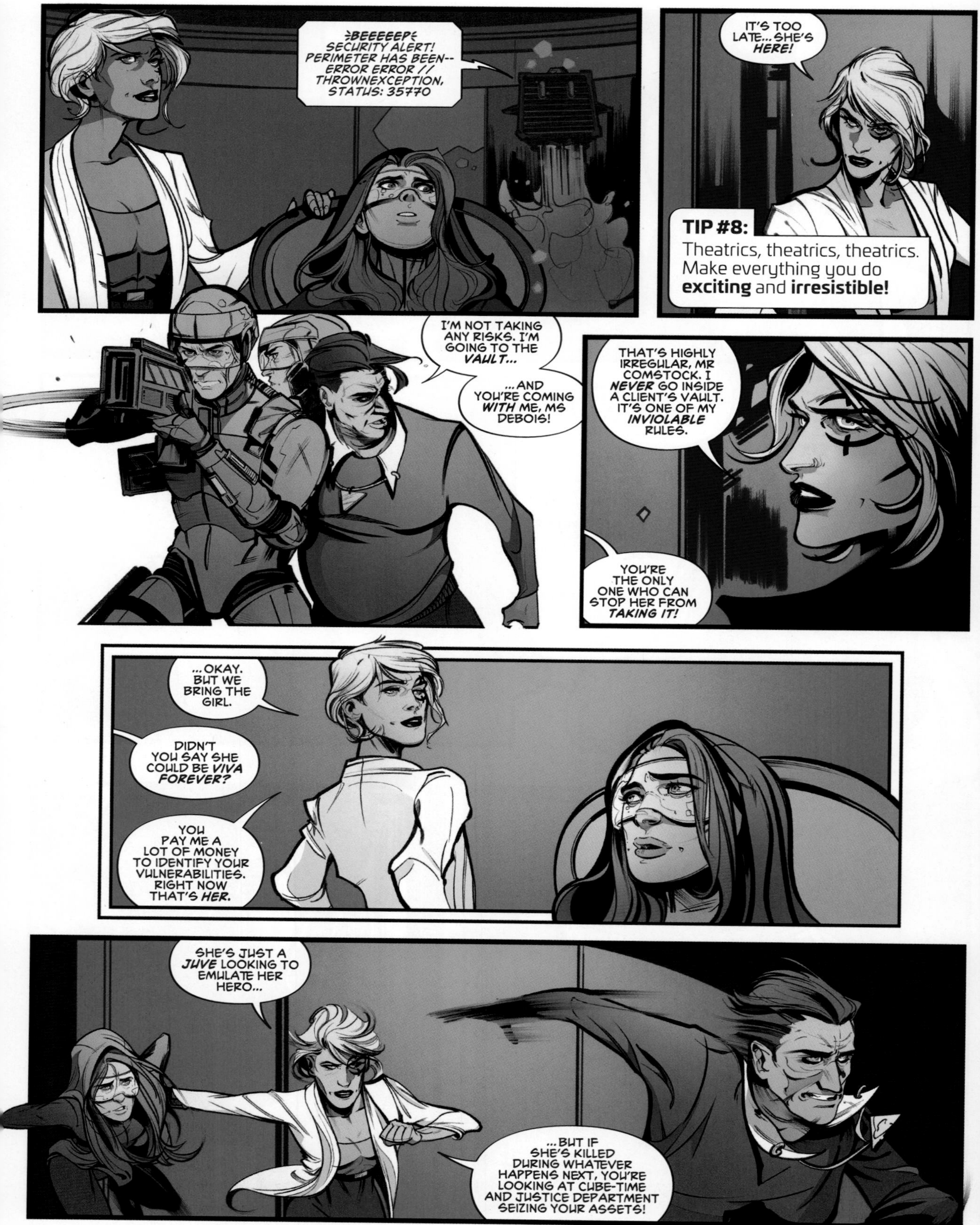

≥BEEEEEP≤ SECURITY ALERT! PERIMETER HAS BEEN-- ERROR ERROR // THROWNEXCEPTION, STATUS: 35770
IT'S TOO LATE... SHE'S HERE!
TIP #8:
Theatrics, theatrics, theatrics. Make everything you do **exciting** and **irresistible!**
I'M NOT TAKING ANY RISKS. I'M GOING TO THE VAULT...
...AND YOU'RE COMING WITH ME, MS DEBOIS!
THAT'S HIGHLY IRREGULAR, MR COMSTOCK. I NEVER GO INSIDE A CLIENT'S VAULT. IT'S ONE OF MY INVIOLABLE RULES.
YOU'RE THE ONLY ONE WHO CAN STOP HER FROM TAKING IT!
...OKAY. BUT WE BRING THE GIRL.
DIDN'T YOU SAY SHE COULD BE VIVA FOREVER?
YOU PAY ME A LOT OF MONEY TO IDENTIFY YOUR VULNERABILITIES. RIGHT NOW THAT'S HER.
SHE'S JUST A JUVE LOOKING TO EMULATE HER HERO...
...BUT IF SHE'S KILLED DURING WHATEVER HAPPENS NEXT, YOU'RE LOOKING AT CUBE-TIME AND JUSTICE DEPARTMENT SEIZING YOUR ASSETS!

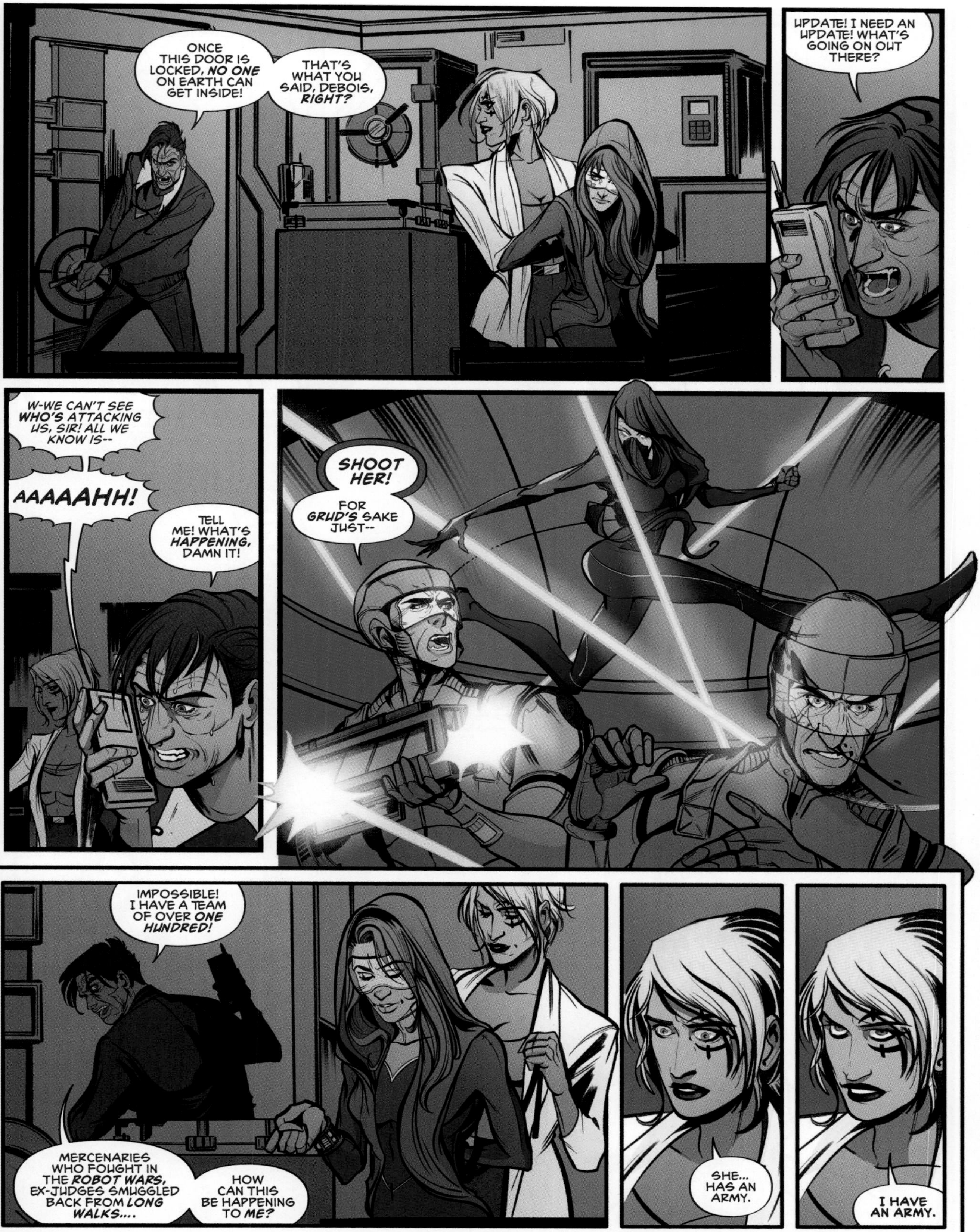

ONCE THIS DOOR IS LOCKED, NO ONE ON EARTH CAN GET INSIDE!
THAT'S WHAT YOU SAID, DEBOIS, RIGHT?
UPDATE! I NEED AN UPDATE! WHAT'S GOING ON OUT THERE?
W-WE CAN'T SEE WHO'S ATTACKING US, SIR! ALL WE KNOW IS--
AAAAAHH!
TELL ME! WHAT'S HAPPENING, DAMN IT!
SHOOT HER!
FOR GRUD'S SAKE JUST--
IMPOSSIBLE! I HAVE A TEAM OF OVER ONE HUNDRED!
MERCENARIES WHO FOUGHT IN THE ROBOT WARS, EX-JUDGES SMUGGLED BACK FROM LONG WALKS....
HOW CAN THIS BE HAPPENING TO ME?
SHE... HAS AN ARMY.
I HAVE AN ARMY.

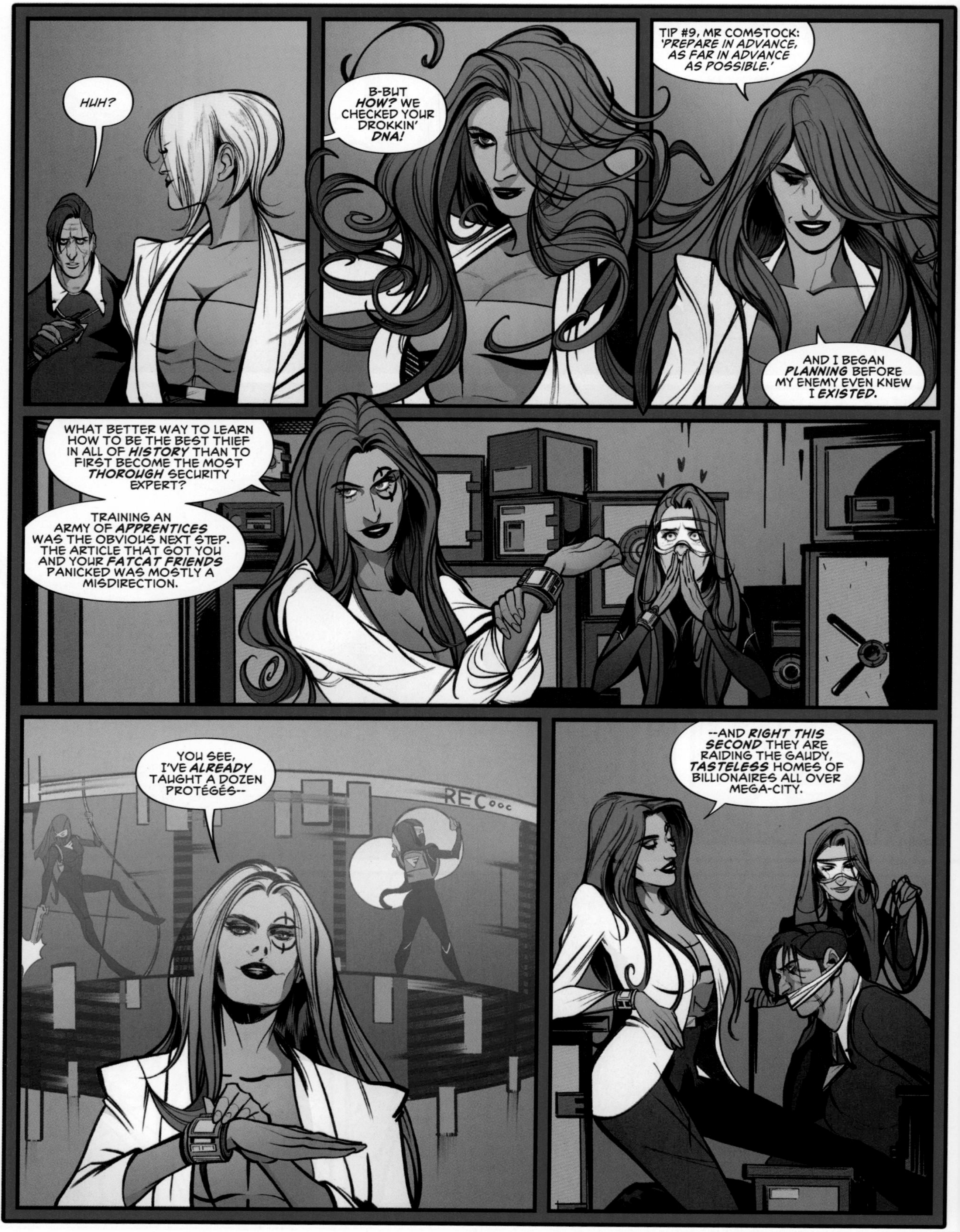

HUH?
B-BUT HOW? WE CHECKED YOUR DROKKIN' DNA!
TIP #9, MR COMSTOCK: 'PREPARE IN ADVANCE, AS FAR IN ADVANCE AS POSSIBLE.'
AND I BEGAN PLANNING BEFORE MY ENEMY EVEN KNEW I EXISTED.
WHAT BETTER WAY TO LEARN HOW TO BE THE BEST THIEF IN ALL OF HISTORY THAN TO FIRST BECOME THE MOST THOROUGH SECURITY EXPERT?
TRAINING AN ARMY OF APPRENTICES WAS THE OBVIOUS NEXT STEP. THE ARTICLE THAT GOT YOU AND YOUR FATCAT FRIENDS PANICKED WAS MOSTLY A MISDIRECTION.
YOU SEE, I'VE ALREADY TAUGHT A DOZEN PROTÉGÉS--
REC
--AND RIGHT THIS SECOND THEY ARE RAIDING THE GAUDY, TASTELESS HOMES OF BILLIONAIRES ALL OVER MEGA-CITY.

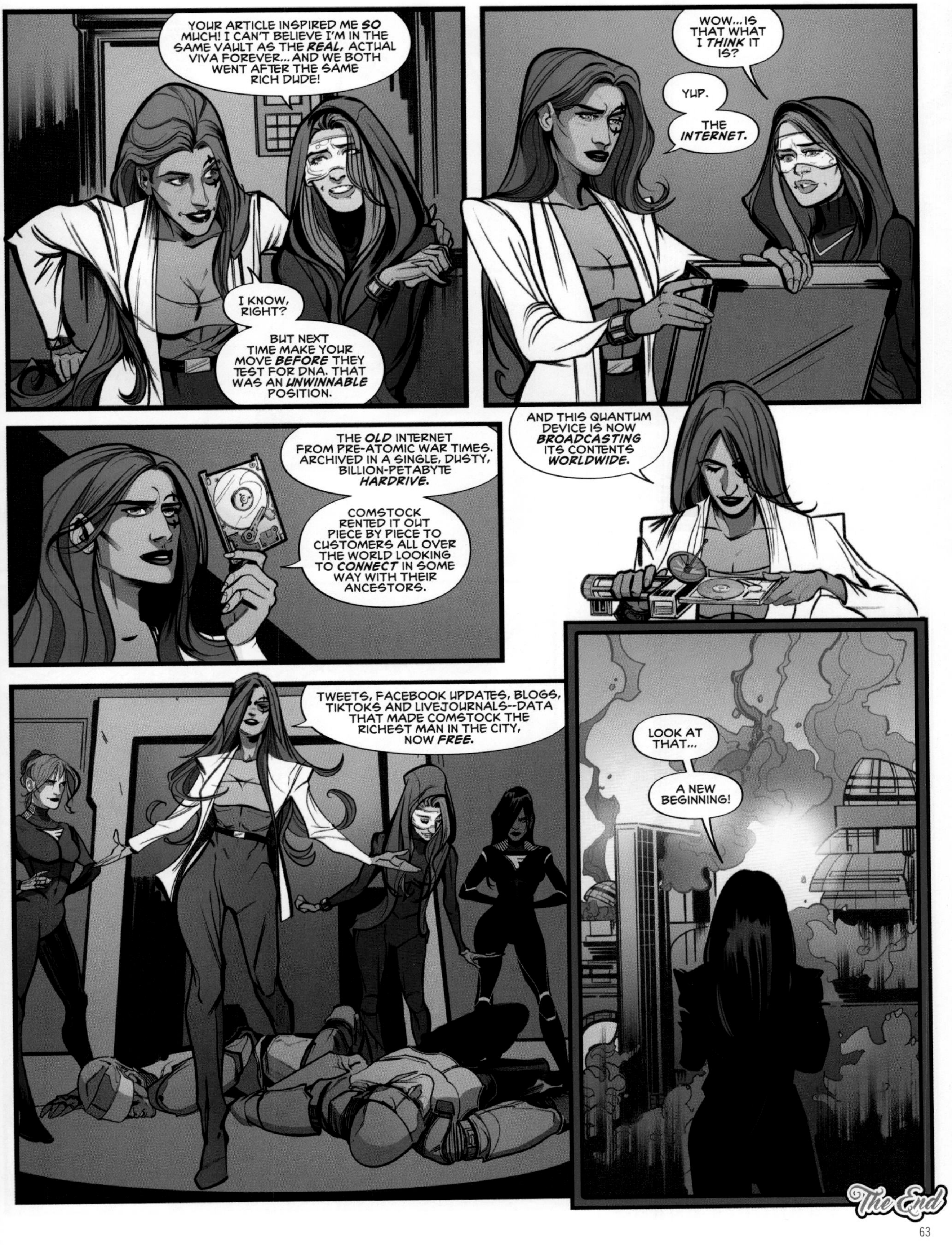

YOUR ARTICLE INSPIRED ME SO MUCH! I CAN'T BELIEVE I'M IN THE SAME VAULT AS THE REAL, ACTUAL VIVA FOREVER... AND WE BOTH WENT AFTER THE SAME RICH DUDE!
I KNOW, RIGHT?
BUT NEXT TIME MAKE YOUR MOVE BEFORE THEY TEST FOR DNA. THAT WAS AN UNWINNABLE POSITION.
WOW... IS THAT WHAT I THINK IT IS?
YUP.
THE INTERNET.
THE OLD INTERNET FROM PRE-ATOMIC WAR TIMES. ARCHIVED IN A SINGLE, DUSTY, BILLION-PETABYTE HARDRIVE.
COMSTOCK RENTED IT OUT PIECE BY PIECE TO CUSTOMERS ALL OVER THE WORLD LOOKING TO CONNECT IN SOME WAY WITH THEIR ANCESTORS.
AND THIS QUANTUM DEVICE IS NOW BROADCASTING ITS CONTENTS WORLDWIDE.
TWEETS, FACEBOOK UPDATES, BLOGS, TIKTOKS AND LIVEJOURNALS--DATA THAT MADE COMSTOCK THE RICHEST MAN IN THE CITY, NOW FREE.
LOOK AT THAT...
A NEW BEGINNING!
The End

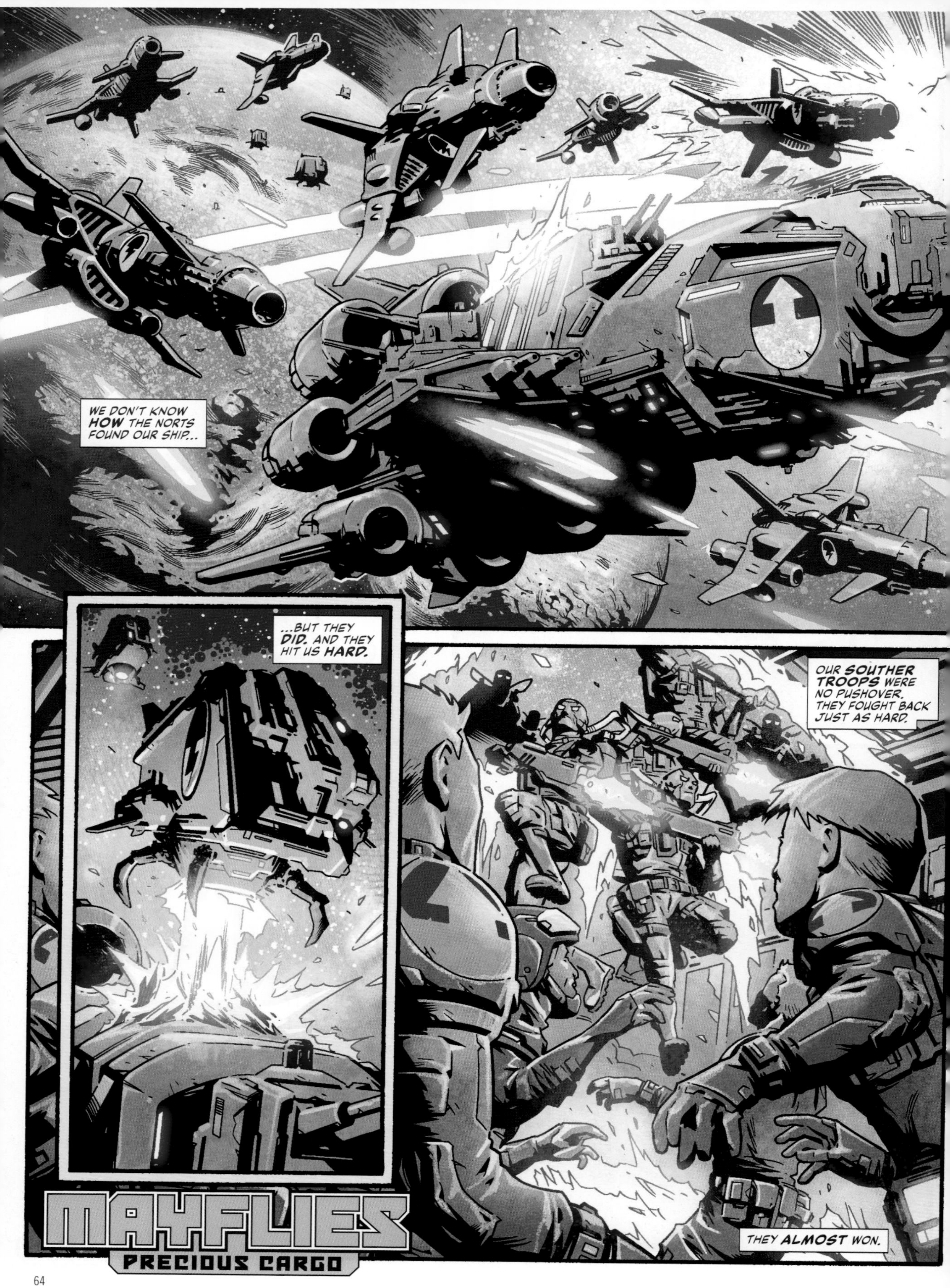
WE DON'T KNOW **HOW** THE NORTS FOUND OUR SHIP...
...BUT THEY **DID.** AND THEY HIT US **HARD.**
OUR **SOUTHER TROOPS** WERE NO PUSHOVER. THEY FOUGHT BACK JUST AS HARD.
MAYFLIES
PRECIOUS CARGO
THEY **ALMOST** WON.

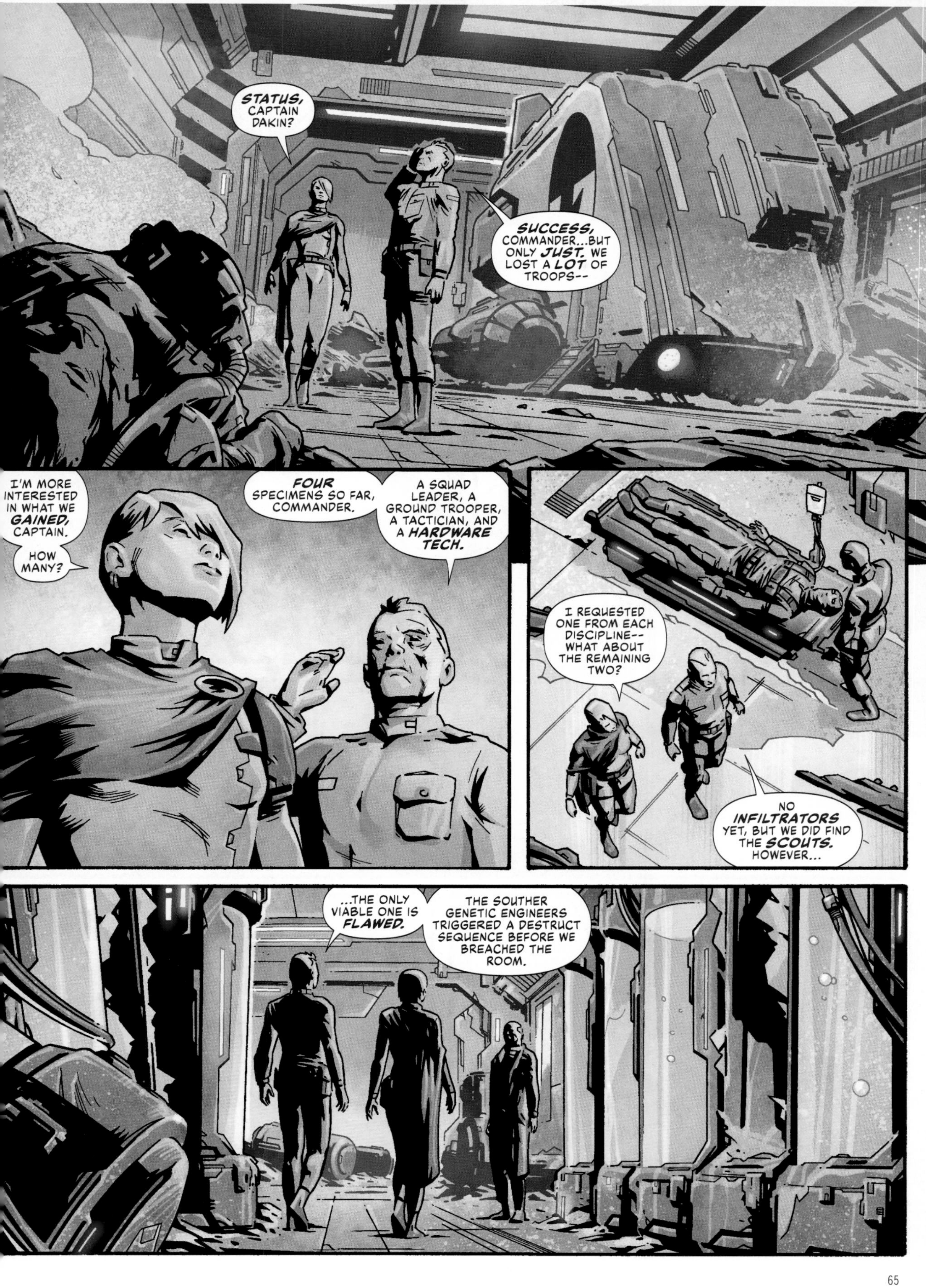

STATUS, CAPTAIN DAKIN?
SUCCESS, COMMANDER...BUT ONLY JUST. WE LOST A LOT OF TROOPS--
I'M MORE INTERESTED IN WHAT WE GAINED, CAPTAIN.
HOW MANY?
FOUR SPECIMENS SO FAR, COMMANDER.
A SQUAD LEADER, A GROUND TROOPER, A TACTICIAN, AND A HARDWARE TECH.
I REQUESTED ONE FROM EACH DISCIPLINE-- WHAT ABOUT THE REMAINING TWO?
NO INFILTRATORS YET, BUT WE DID FIND THE SCOUTS. HOWEVER...
...THE ONLY VIABLE ONE IS FLAWED.
THE SOUTHER GENETIC ENGINEERS TRIGGERED A DESTRUCT SEQUENCE BEFORE WE BREACHED THE ROOM.

IT'S A *CHILD*, DOCTOR VIETT. DISCONNECT IT.

DISCONNECT IT.

COMMANDER NIGHTINGALE, THE SCOUT COULD *WAKE* IF WE UNPLUG HER FROM THE--

THE SOUTHERS HAD HER ISOLATED FROM HER FELLOW SCOUTS. THAT'S WHY SHE WASN'T DESTROYED WITH THE OTHERS.

SHE'D BEEN MARKED FOR *DISPOSAL* BECAUSE OF THE PIGMENTATION FLAW--

--BUT SHE SHOWED TREMENDOUS APTITUDE SO THEY KEPT HER AROUND FOR *STUDY.*

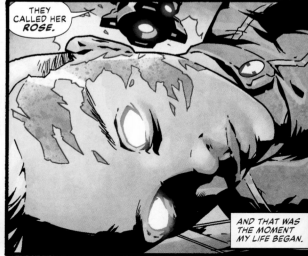

THEY CALLED HER *ROSE.*

AND THAT WAS THE MOMENT MY LIFE BEGAN.

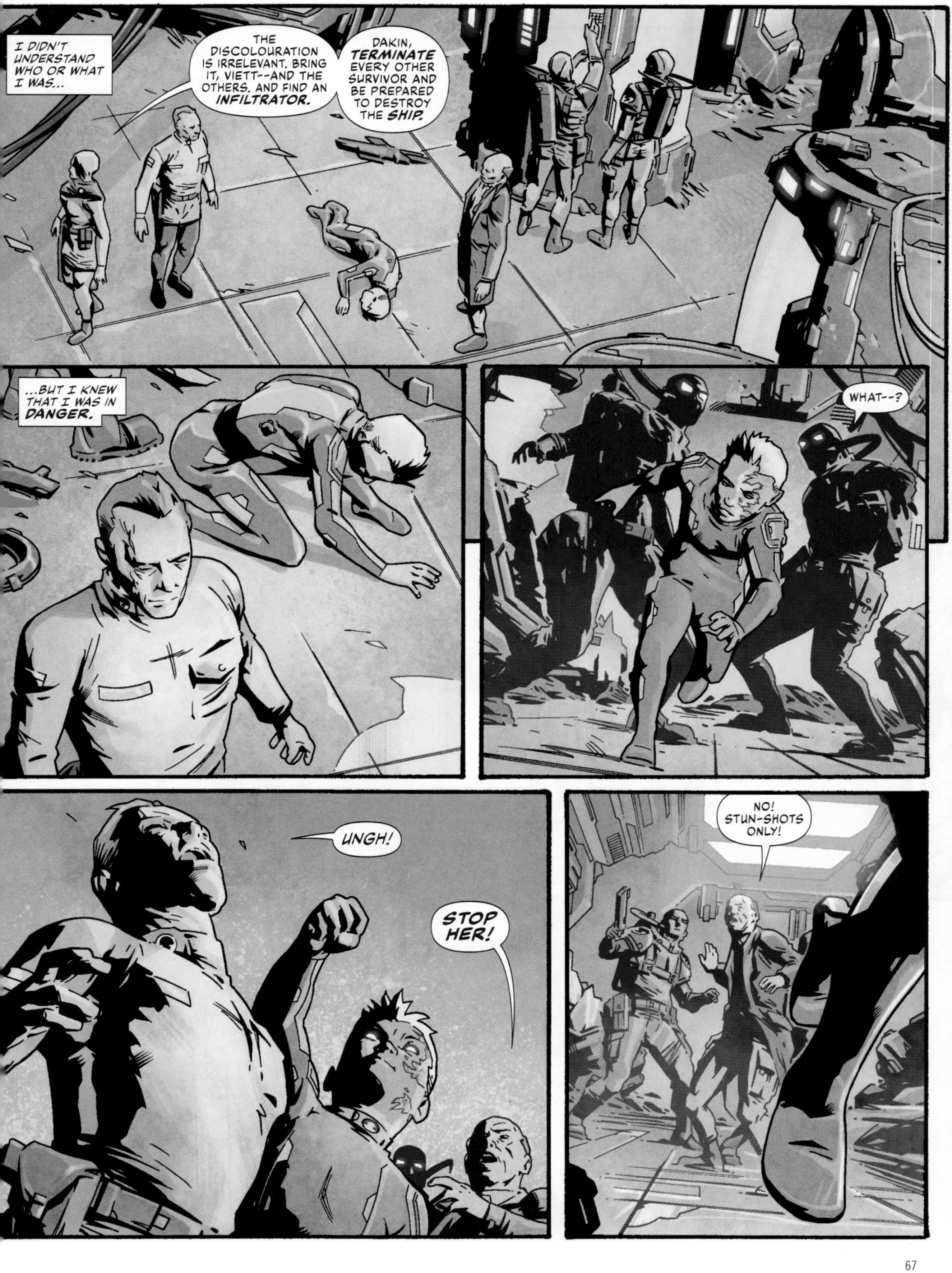
I DIDN'T UNDERSTAND WHO OR WHAT I WAS...
THE DISCOLOURATION IS IRRELEVANT. BRING IT, VIETT--AND THE OTHERS. AND FIND AN INFILTRATOR.
DAKIN, TERMINATE EVERY OTHER SURVIVOR AND BE PREPARED TO DESTROY THE SHIP.
...BUT I KNEW THAT I WAS IN DANGER.
WHAT--?
UNGH!
STOP HER!
NO! STUN-SHOTS ONLY!

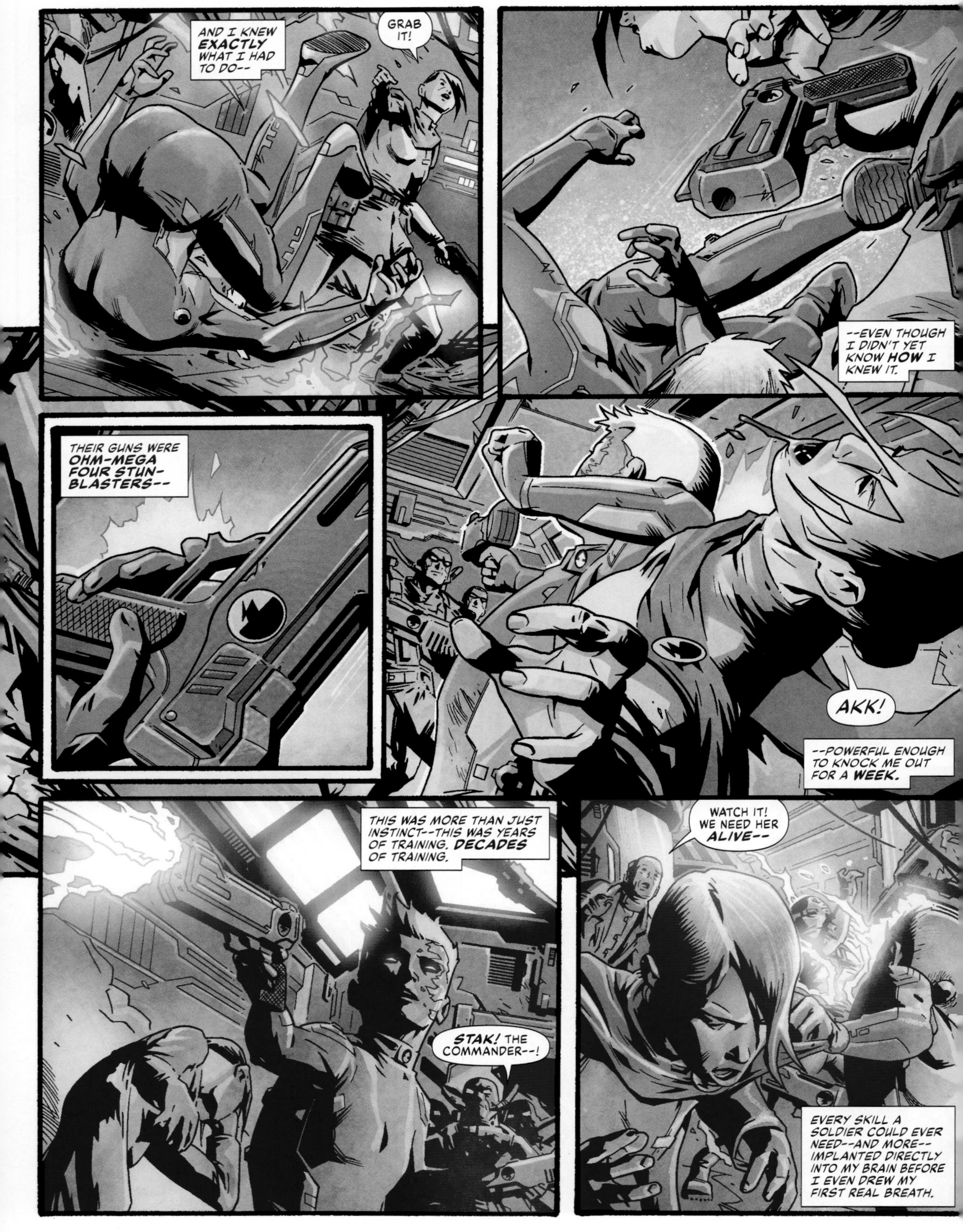
AND I KNEW EXACTLY WHAT I HAD TO DO--
GRAB IT!
--EVEN THOUGH I DIDN'T YET KNOW HOW I KNEW IT.
THEIR GUNS WERE OHM-MEGA FOUR STUN-BLASTERS--
AKK!
--POWERFUL ENOUGH TO KNOCK ME OUT FOR A WEEK.
THIS WAS MORE THAN JUST INSTINCT--THIS WAS YEARS OF TRAINING. DECADES OF TRAINING.
STAK! THE COMMANDER--!
WATCH IT! WE NEED HER ALIVE--
EVERY SKILL A SOLDIER COULD EVER NEED--AND MORE--IMPLANTED DIRECTLY INTO MY BRAIN BEFORE I EVEN DREW MY FIRST REAL BREATH.

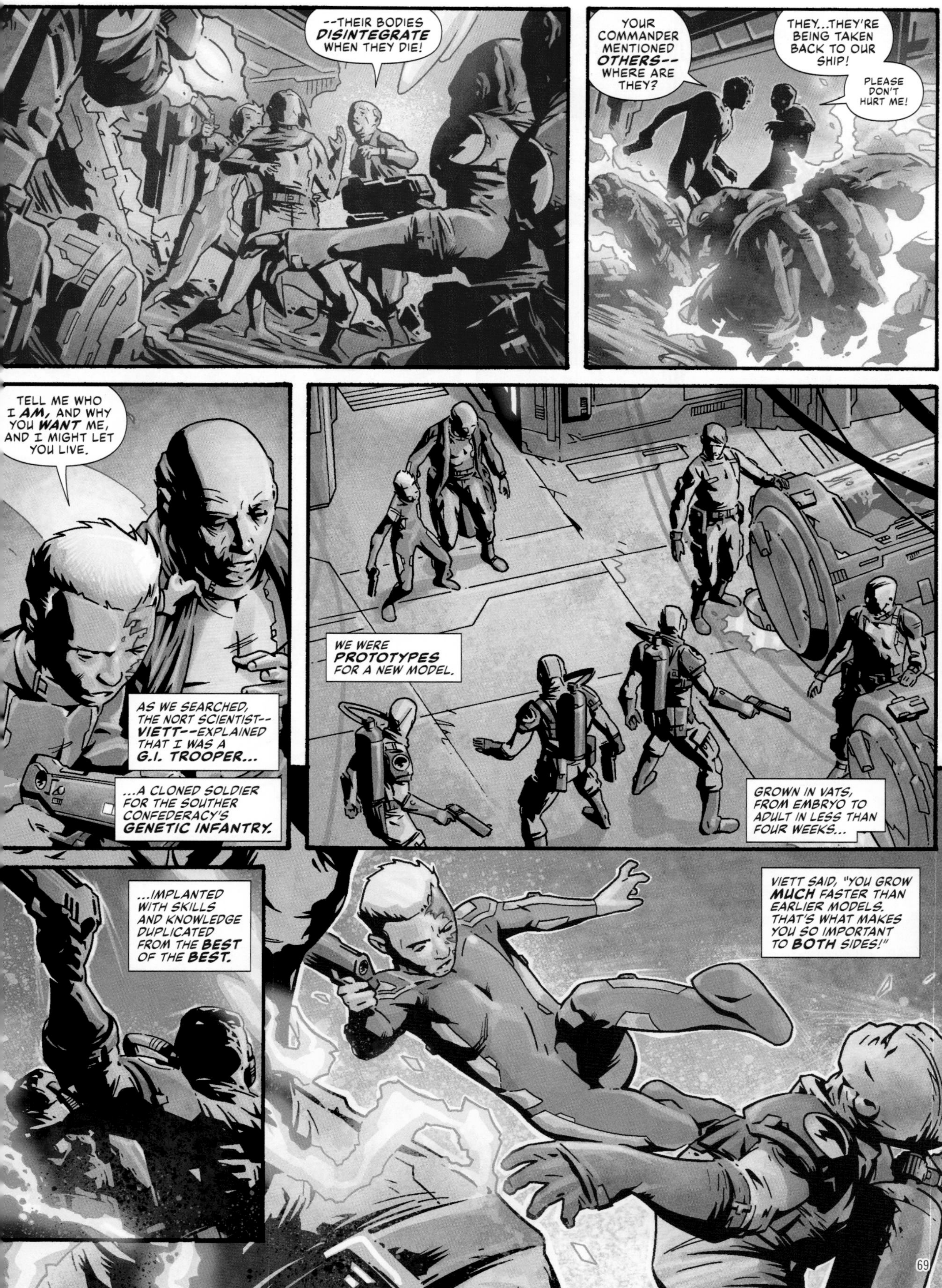
--THEIR BODIES DISINTEGRATE WHEN THEY DIE!
YOUR COMMANDER MENTIONED OTHERS-- WHERE ARE THEY?
THEY...THEY'RE BEING TAKEN BACK TO OUR SHIP!
PLEASE DON'T HURT ME!
TELL ME WHO I AM, AND WHY YOU WANT ME, AND I MIGHT LET YOU LIVE.
AS WE SEARCHED, THE NORT SCIENTIST--VIETT--EXPLAINED THAT I WAS A G.I. TROOPER...
...A CLONED SOLDIER FOR THE SOUTHER CONFEDERACY'S GENETIC INFANTRY.
WE WERE PROTOTYPES FOR A NEW MODEL.
GROWN IN VATS, FROM EMBRYO TO ADULT IN LESS THAN FOUR WEEKS...
...IMPLANTED WITH SKILLS AND KNOWLEDGE DUPLICATED FROM THE BEST OF THE BEST.
VIETT SAID, "YOU GROW MUCH FASTER THAN EARLIER MODELS. THAT'S WHAT MAKES YOU SO IMPORTANT TO BOTH SIDES!"

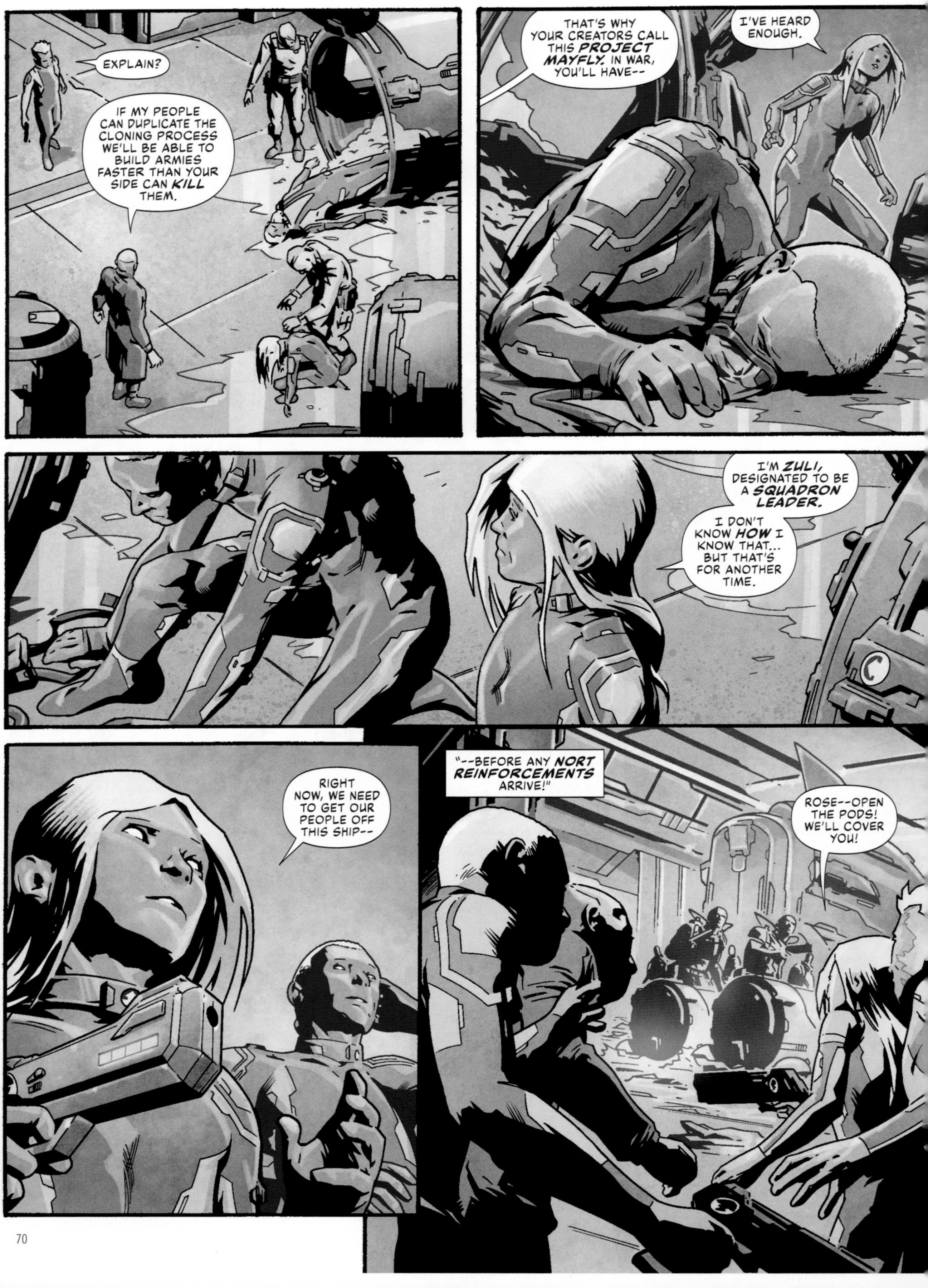

EXPLAIN?
IF MY PEOPLE CAN DUPLICATE THE CLONING PROCESS WE'LL BE ABLE TO BUILD ARMIES FASTER THAN YOUR SIDE CAN KILL THEM.
THAT'S WHY YOUR CREATORS CALL THIS PROJECT MAYFLY. IN WAR, YOU'LL HAVE--
I'VE HEARD ENOUGH.
I'M ZULI, DESIGNATED TO BE A SQUADRON LEADER.
I DON'T KNOW HOW I KNOW THAT... BUT THAT'S FOR ANOTHER TIME.
RIGHT NOW, WE NEED TO GET OUR PEOPLE OFF THIS SHIP--
"--BEFORE ANY NORT REINFORCEMENTS ARRIVE!"
ROSE--OPEN THE PODS! WE'LL COVER YOU!

THE BIG GUY--THE GROUND TROOPER-- HAD BEEN NICKNAMED **WRECKS** BY THE GENETICISTS BECAUSE HE'D BROKEN TWO **GESTATION PODS.**

LIKE THE REST OF US, WRECKS WAS A **PROTOTYPE**--BUT IN HIS CASE THEY'D NUDGED THE **STRENGTH** DIAL A LITTLE TOO HIGH.

HOW MANY MORE?

J-JUST THESE TWO-- AND...THERE WAS A **GLITCH.**

GLITCH?

A POD THAT WAS ALREADY **EMPTY.**

IT SHOULD HAVE HELD AN **INFILTRATOR.**

WATCH THAT NORT! WE **NEED** HIM!

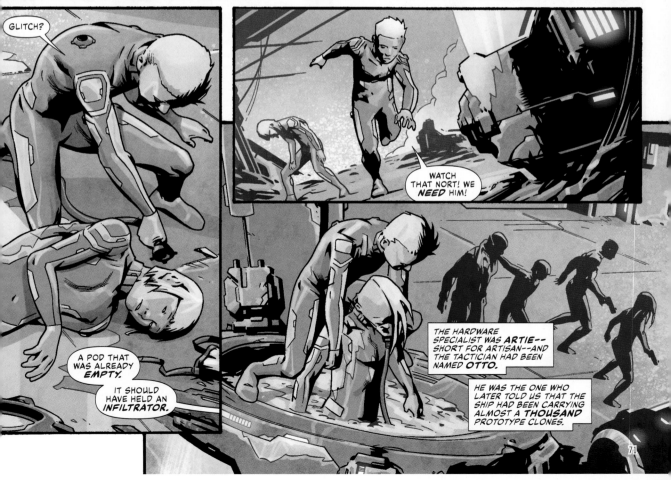

THE HARDWARE SPECIALIST WAS **ARTIE**-- SHORT FOR ARTISAN--AND THE TACTICIAN HAD BEEN NAMED **OTTO.**

HE WAS THE ONE WHO LATER TOLD US THAT THE SHIP HAD BEEN CARRYING ALMOST A **THOUSAND** PROTOTYPE CLONES.

71

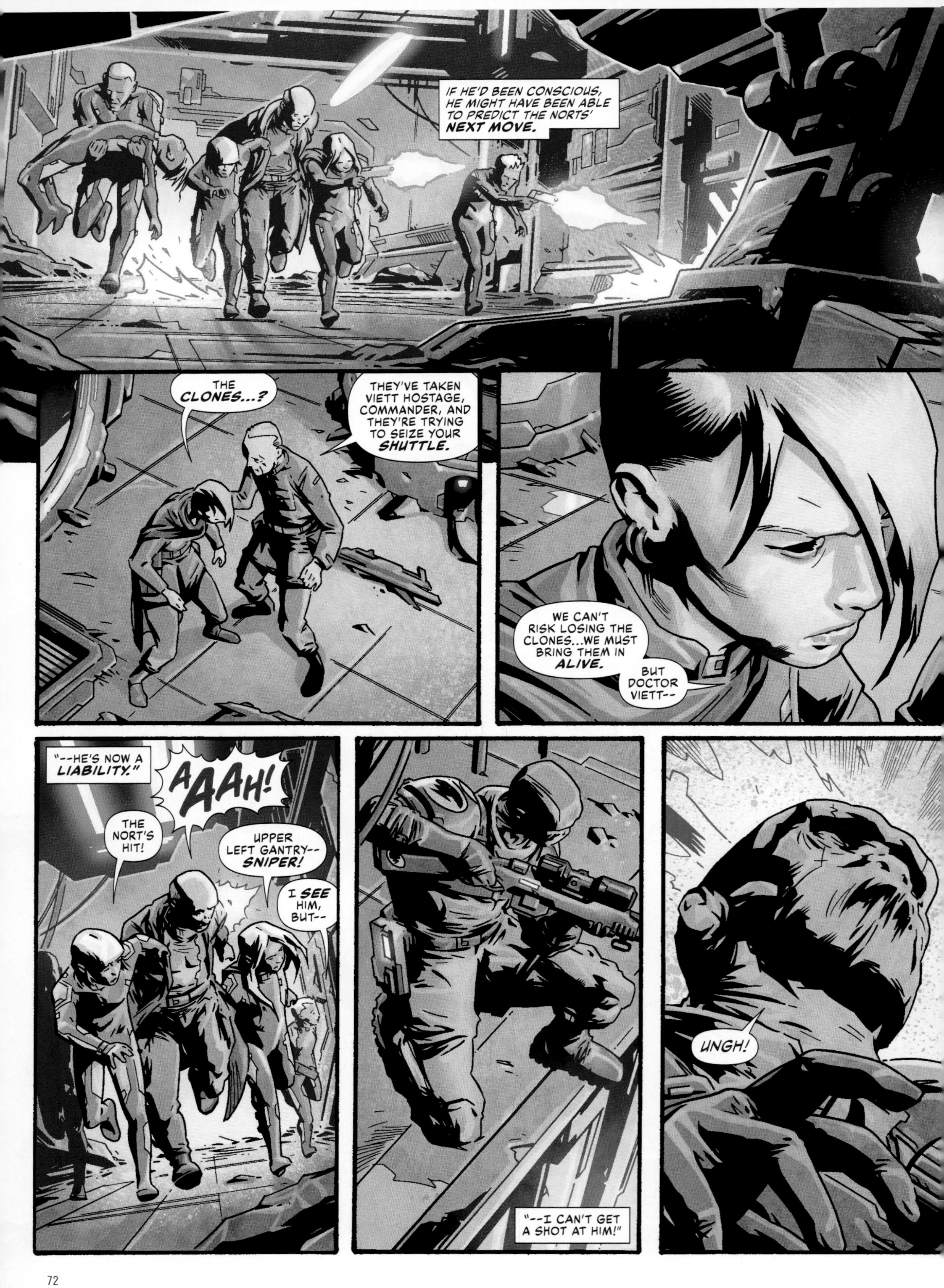
IF HE'D BEEN CONSCIOUS, HE MIGHT HAVE BEEN ABLE TO PREDICT THE NORTS' NEXT MOVE.
THE CLONES...?
THEY'VE TAKEN VIETT HOSTAGE, COMMANDER, AND THEY'RE TRYING TO SEIZE YOUR SHUTTLE.
WE CAN'T RISK LOSING THE CLONES...WE MUST BRING THEM IN ALIVE.
BUT DOCTOR VIETT--
"--HE'S NOW A LIABILITY."
AAAH!
THE NORT'S HIT!
UPPER LEFT GANTRY-- SNIPER!
I SEE HIM, BUT--
"--I CAN'T GET A SHOT AT HIM!"
UNGH!

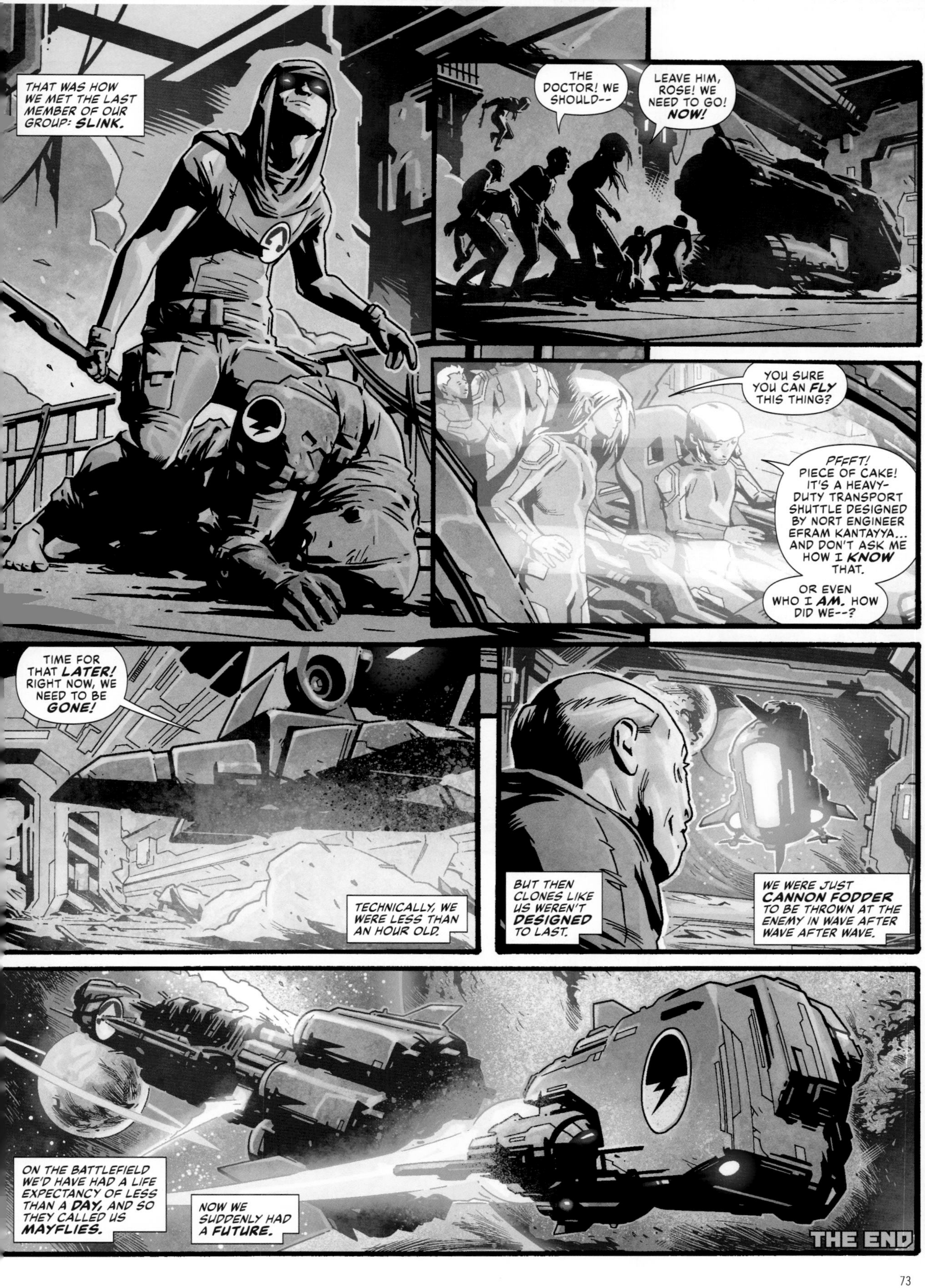
THAT WAS HOW WE MET THE LAST MEMBER OF OUR GROUP: SLINK.
THE DOCTOR! WE SHOULD--
LEAVE HIM, ROSE! WE NEED TO GO! NOW!
YOU SURE YOU CAN FLY THIS THING?
PFFFT! PIECE OF CAKE! IT'S A HEAVY-DUTY TRANSPORT SHUTTLE DESIGNED BY NORT ENGINEER EFRAM KANTAYYA... AND DON'T ASK ME HOW I KNOW THAT.
OR EVEN WHO I AM. HOW DID WE--?
TIME FOR THAT LATER! RIGHT NOW, WE NEED TO BE GONE!
TECHNICALLY, WE WERE LESS THAN AN HOUR OLD.
BUT THEN CLONES LIKE US WEREN'T DESIGNED TO LAST.
WE WERE JUST CANNON FODDER TO BE THROWN AT THE ENEMY IN WAVE AFTER WAVE AFTER WAVE.
ON THE BATTLEFIELD WE'D HAVE HAD A LIFE EXPECTANCY OF LESS THAN A DAY, AND SO THEY CALLED US MAYFLIES.
NOW WE SUDDENLY HAD A FUTURE.
THE END

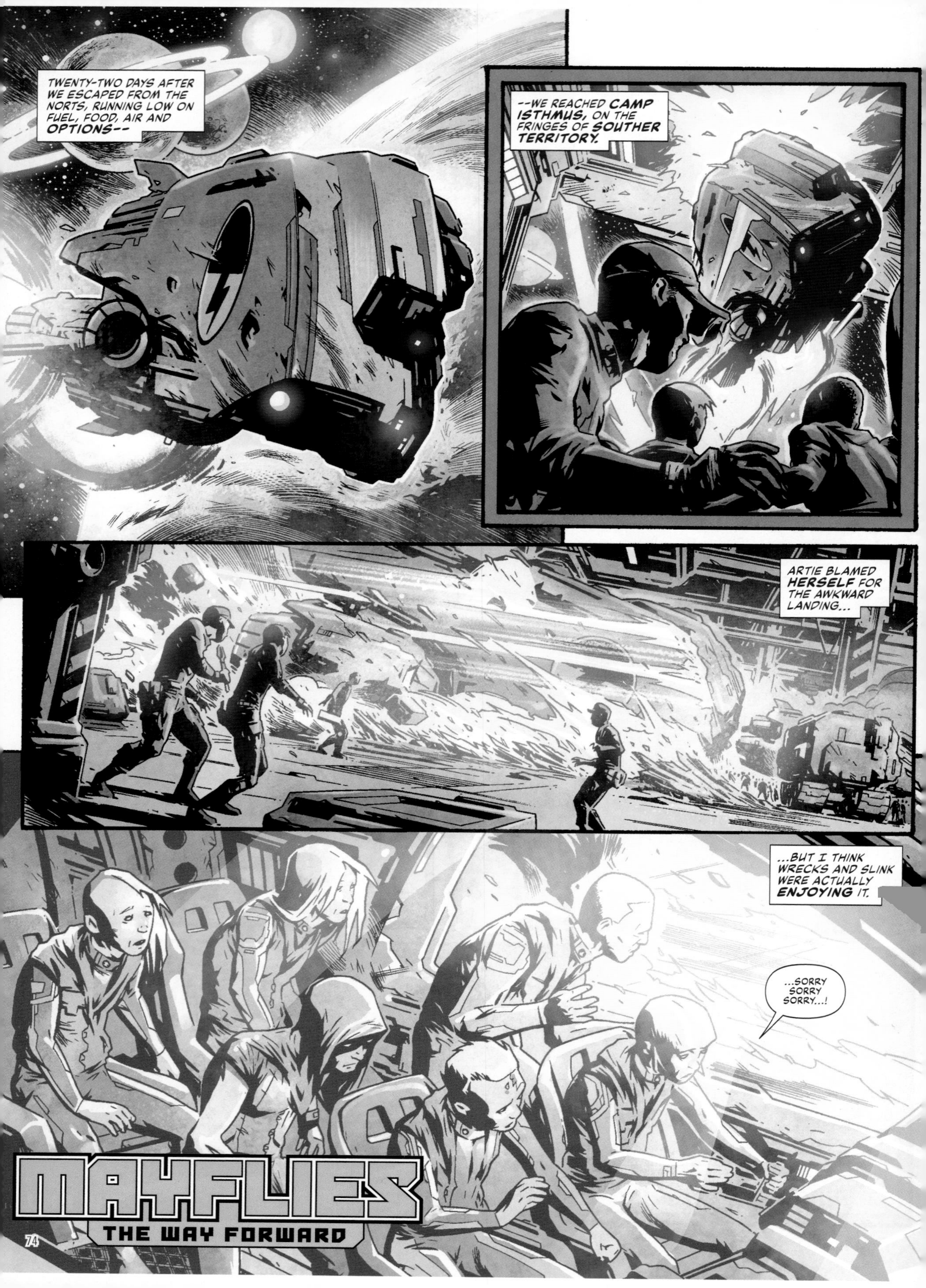

TWENTY-TWO DAYS AFTER WE ESCAPED FROM THE NORTS, RUNNING LOW ON FUEL, FOOD, AIR AND OPTIONS--
--WE REACHED CAMP ISTHMUS, ON THE FRINGES OF SOUTHER TERRITORY.
ARTIE BLAMED HERSELF FOR THE AWKWARD LANDING...
...BUT I THINK WRECKS AND SLINK WERE ACTUALLY ENJOYING IT.
...SORRY SORRY SORRY...!
MAYFLIES
THE WAY FORWARD

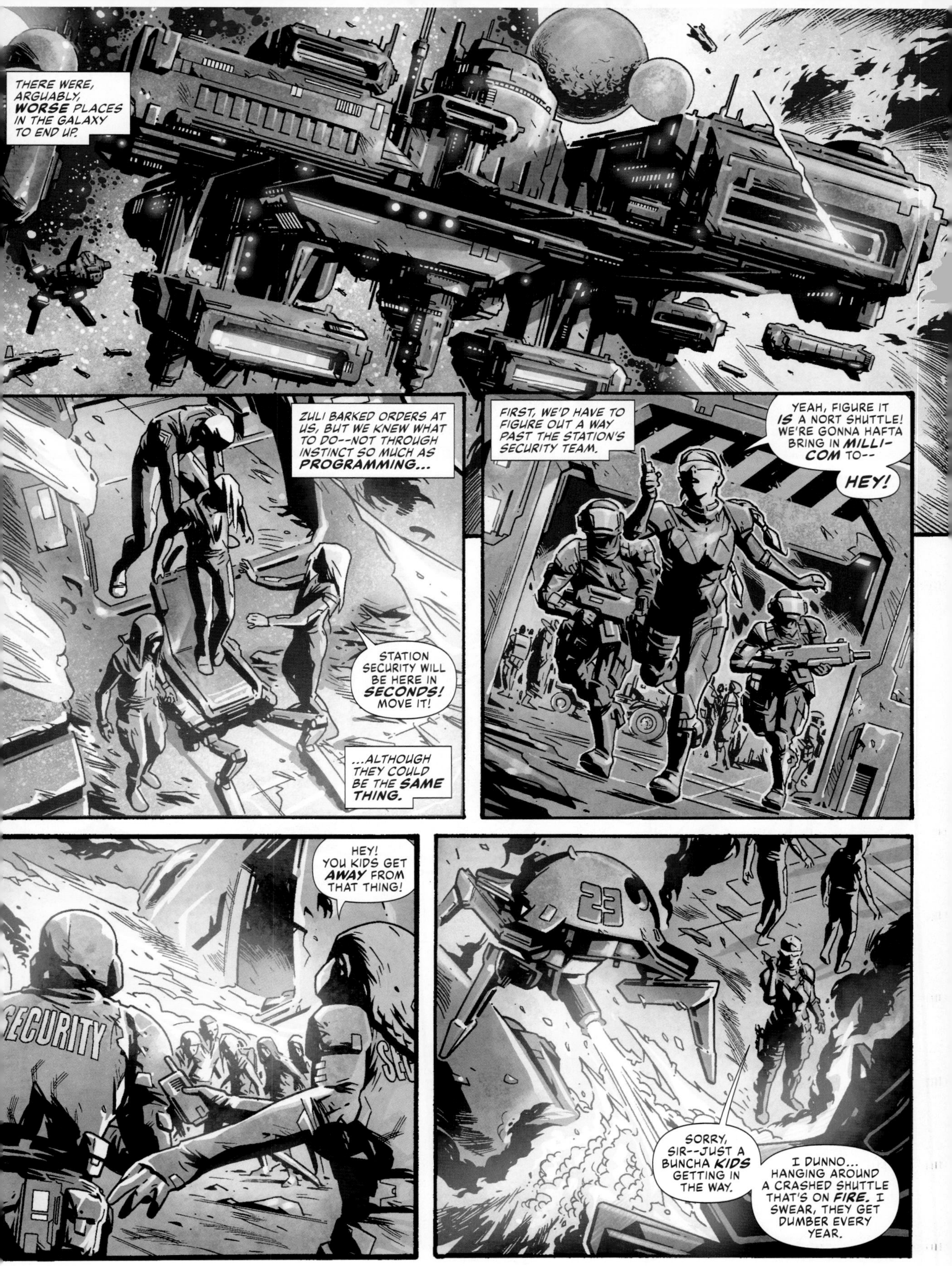
THERE WERE, ARGUABLY, WORSE PLACES IN THE GALAXY TO END UP.
ZULI BARKED ORDERS AT US, BUT WE KNEW WHAT TO DO--NOT THROUGH INSTINCT SO MUCH AS PROGRAMMING...
STATION SECURITY WILL BE HERE IN SECONDS! MOVE IT!
...ALTHOUGH THEY COULD BE THE SAME THING.
FIRST, WE'D HAVE TO FIGURE OUT A WAY PAST THE STATION'S SECURITY TEAM.
YEAH, FIGURE IT IS A NORT SHUTTLE! WE'RE GONNA HAFTA BRING IN MILLI-COM TO--
HEY!
HEY! YOU KIDS GET AWAY FROM THAT THING!
SECURITY
23
SORRY, SIR--JUST A BUNCHA KIDS GETTING IN THE WAY.
I DUNNO... HANGING AROUND A CRASHED SHUTTLE THAT'S ON FIRE. I SWEAR, THEY GET DUMBER EVERY YEAR.

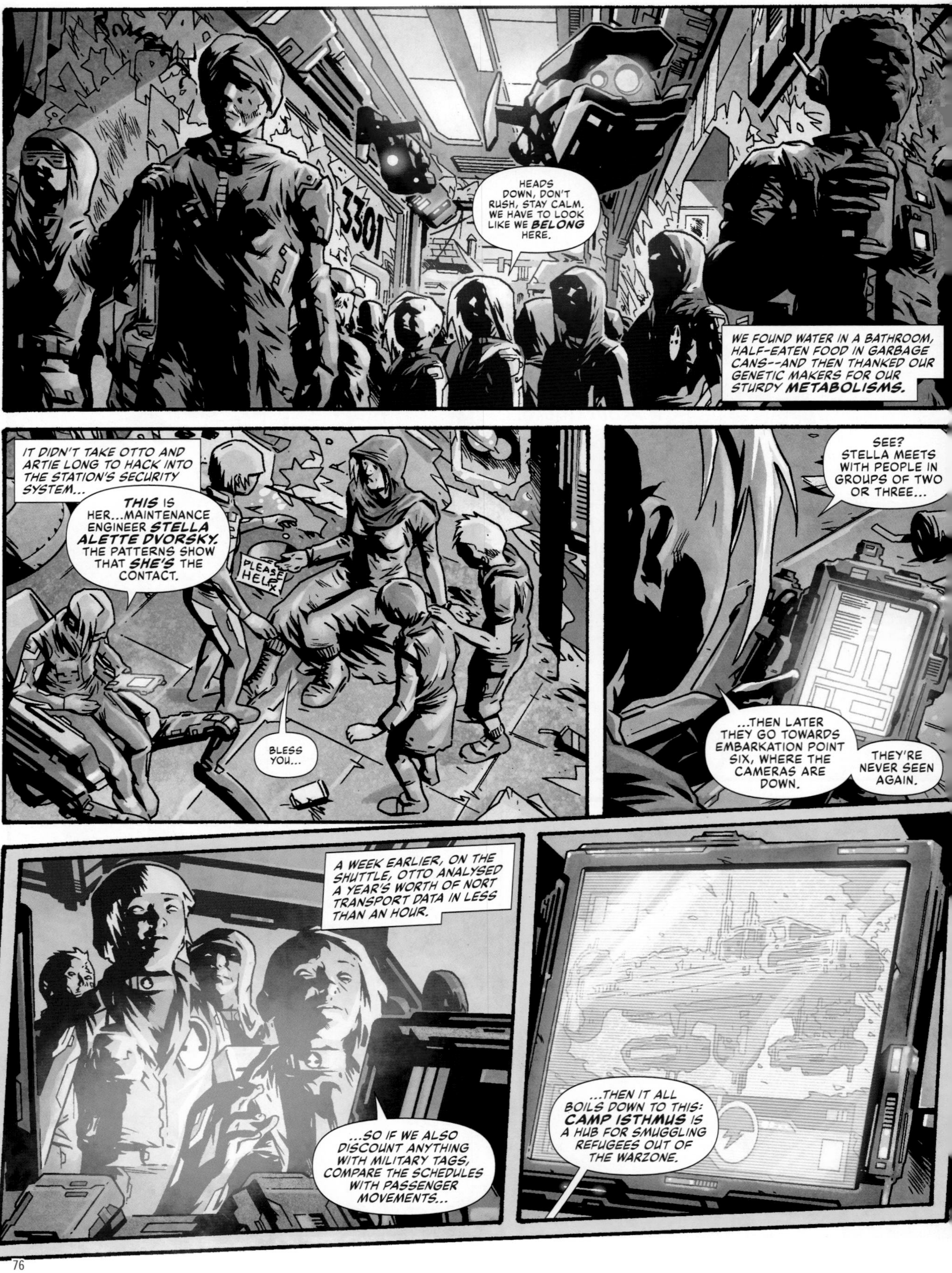
HEADS DOWN, DON'T RUSH, STAY CALM. WE HAVE TO LOOK LIKE WE BELONG HERE.
3301
WE FOUND WATER IN A BATHROOM, HALF-EATEN FOOD IN GARBAGE CANS--AND THEN THANKED OUR GENETIC MAKERS FOR OUR STURDY METABOLISMS.
IT DIDN'T TAKE OTTO AND ARTIE LONG TO HACK INTO THE STATION'S SECURITY SYSTEM...
THIS IS HER...MAINTENANCE ENGINEER STELLA ALETTE DVORSKY. THE PATTERNS SHOW THAT SHE'S THE CONTACT.
PLEASE HELP
BLESS YOU...
SEE? STELLA MEETS WITH PEOPLE IN GROUPS OF TWO OR THREE...
...THEN LATER THEY GO TOWARDS EMBARKATION POINT SIX, WHERE THE CAMERAS ARE DOWN.
THEY'RE NEVER SEEN AGAIN.
A WEEK EARLIER, ON THE SHUTTLE, OTTO ANALYSED A YEAR'S WORTH OF NORT TRANSPORT DATA IN LESS THAN AN HOUR.
...SO IF WE ALSO DISCOUNT ANYTHING WITH MILITARY TAGS, COMPARE THE SCHEDULES WITH PASSENGER MOVEMENTS...
...THEN IT ALL BOILS DOWN TO THIS: CAMP ISTHMUS IS A HUB FOR SMUGGLING REFUGEES OUT OF THE WARZONE.

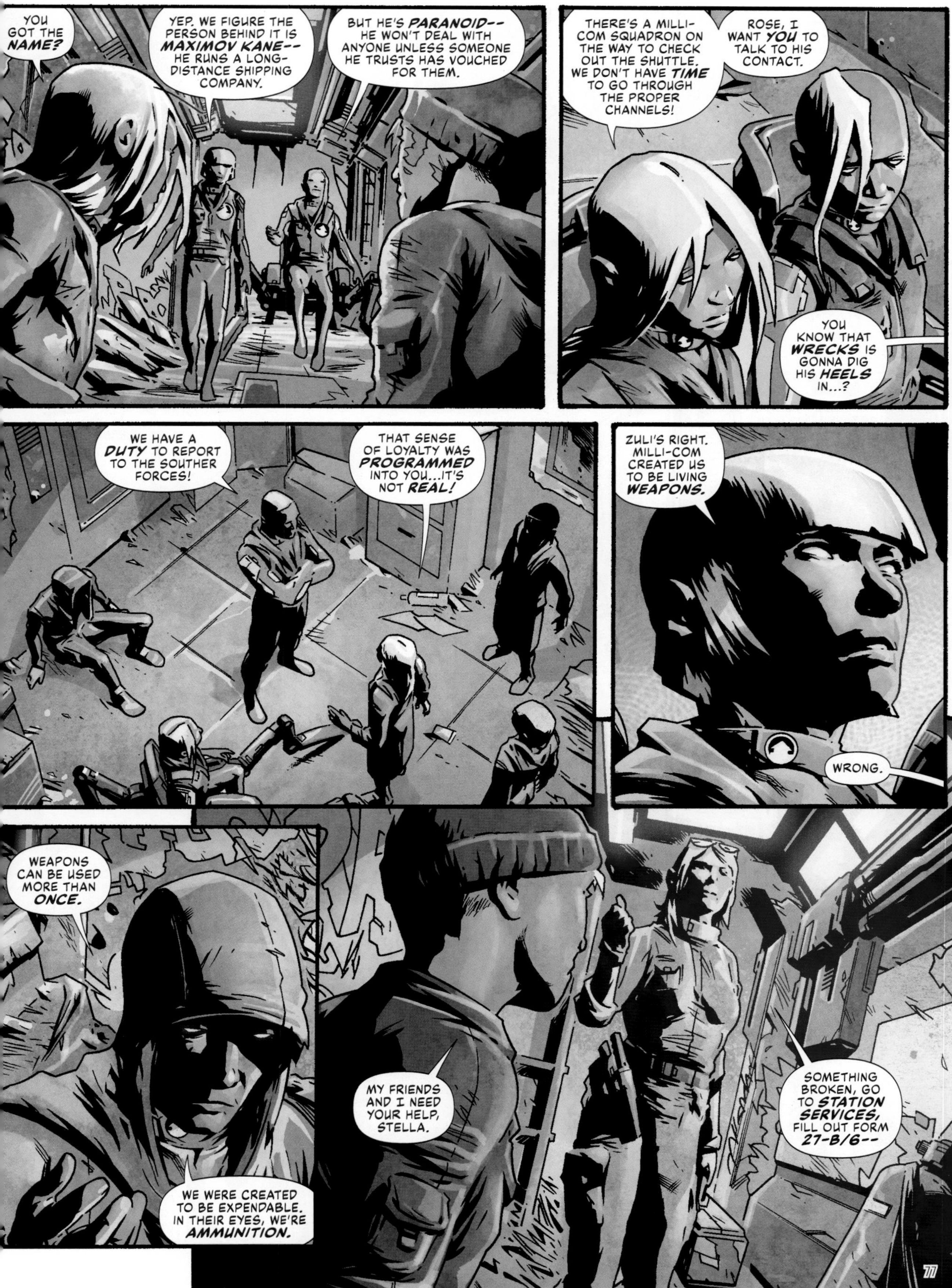

YOU GOT THE NAME?
YEP. WE FIGURE THE PERSON BEHIND IT IS MAXIMOV KANE-- HE RUNS A LONG-DISTANCE SHIPPING COMPANY.
BUT HE'S PARANOID-- HE WON'T DEAL WITH ANYONE UNLESS SOMEONE HE TRUSTS HAS VOUCHED FOR THEM.
THERE'S A MILLI-COM SQUADRON ON THE WAY TO CHECK OUT THE SHUTTLE. WE DON'T HAVE TIME TO GO THROUGH THE PROPER CHANNELS!
ROSE, I WANT YOU TO TALK TO HIS CONTACT.
YOU KNOW THAT WRECKS IS GONNA DIG HIS HEELS IN...?
WE HAVE A DUTY TO REPORT TO THE SOUTHER FORCES!
THAT SENSE OF LOYALTY WAS PROGRAMMED INTO YOU...IT'S NOT REAL!
ZULI'S RIGHT. MILLI-COM CREATED US TO BE LIVING WEAPONS.
WRONG.
WEAPONS CAN BE USED MORE THAN ONCE.
WE WERE CREATED TO BE EXPENDABLE. IN THEIR EYES, WE'RE AMMUNITION.
MY FRIENDS AND I NEED YOUR HELP, STELLA.
SOMETHING BROKEN, GO TO STATION SERVICES, FILL OUT FORM 27-B/6--

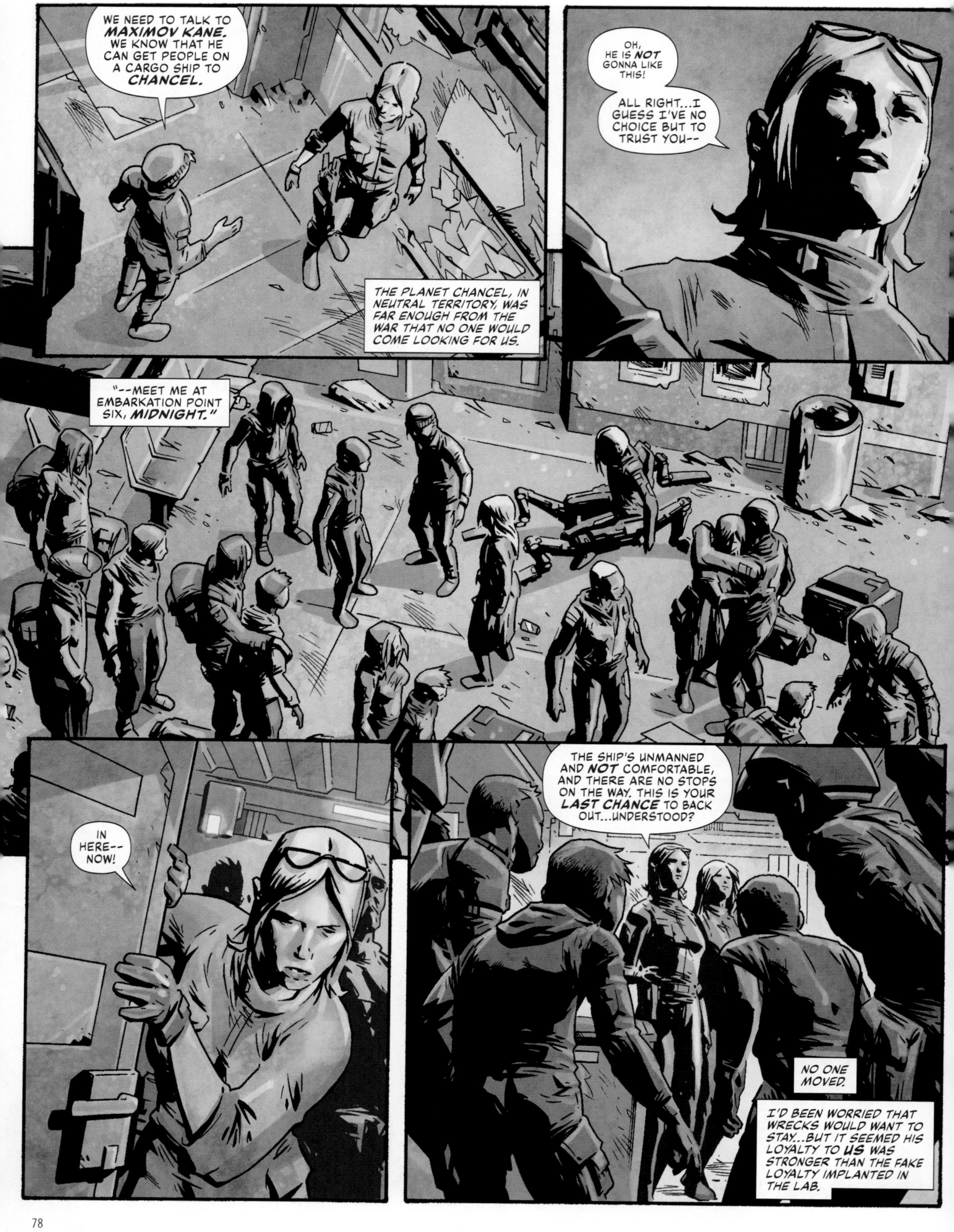
WE NEED TO TALK TO MAXIMOV KANE. WE KNOW THAT HE CAN GET PEOPLE ON A CARGO SHIP TO CHANCEL.
THE PLANET CHANCEL, IN NEUTRAL TERRITORY, WAS FAR ENOUGH FROM THE WAR THAT NO ONE WOULD COME LOOKING FOR US.
OH, HE IS NOT GONNA LIKE THIS!
ALL RIGHT...I GUESS I'VE NO CHOICE BUT TO TRUST YOU--
"--MEET ME AT EMBARKATION POINT SIX, MIDNIGHT."
IN HERE--NOW!
THE SHIP'S UNMANNED AND NOT COMFORTABLE, AND THERE ARE NO STOPS ON THE WAY. THIS IS YOUR LAST CHANCE TO BACK OUT...UNDERSTOOD?
NO ONE MOVED.
I'D BEEN WORRIED THAT WRECKS WOULD WANT TO STAY...BUT IT SEEMED HIS LOYALTY TO US WAS STRONGER THAN THE FAKE LOYALTY IMPLANTED IN THE LAB.

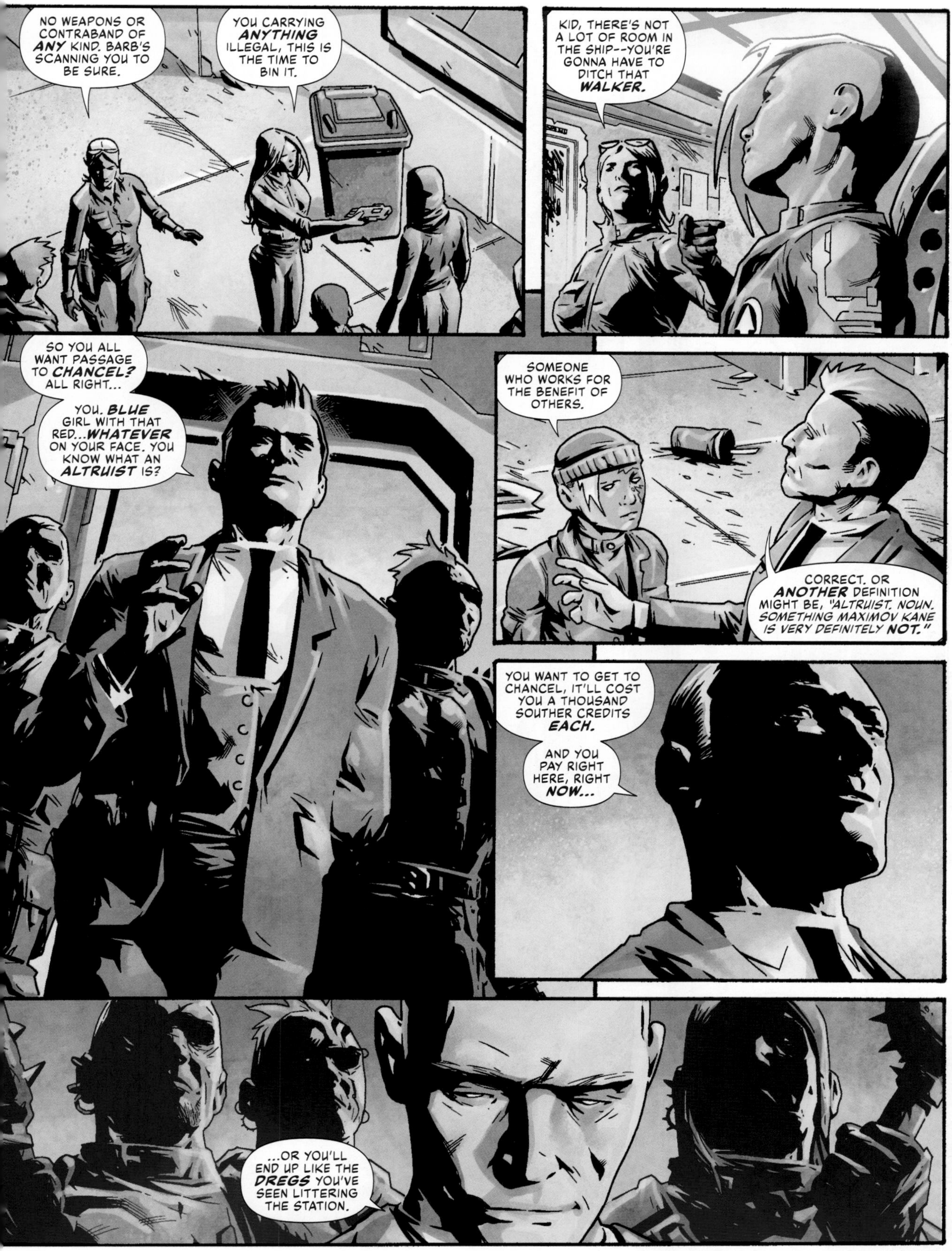
NO WEAPONS OR CONTRABAND OF ANY KIND. BARB'S SCANNING YOU TO BE SURE.
YOU CARRYING ANYTHING ILLEGAL, THIS IS THE TIME TO BIN IT.
KID, THERE'S NOT A LOT OF ROOM IN THE SHIP--YOU'RE GONNA HAVE TO DITCH THAT WALKER.
SO YOU ALL WANT PASSAGE TO CHANCEL? ALL RIGHT...
YOU. BLUE GIRL WITH THAT RED...WHATEVER ON YOUR FACE. YOU KNOW WHAT AN ALTRUIST IS?
SOMEONE WHO WORKS FOR THE BENEFIT OF OTHERS.
CORRECT. OR ANOTHER DEFINITION MIGHT BE, "ALTRUIST. NOUN. SOMETHING MAXIMOV KANE IS VERY DEFINITELY NOT."
YOU WANT TO GET TO CHANCEL, IT'LL COST YOU A THOUSAND SOUTHER CREDITS EACH.
AND YOU PAY RIGHT HERE, RIGHT NOW...
...OR YOU'LL END UP LIKE THE DREGS YOU'VE SEEN LITTERING THE STATION.

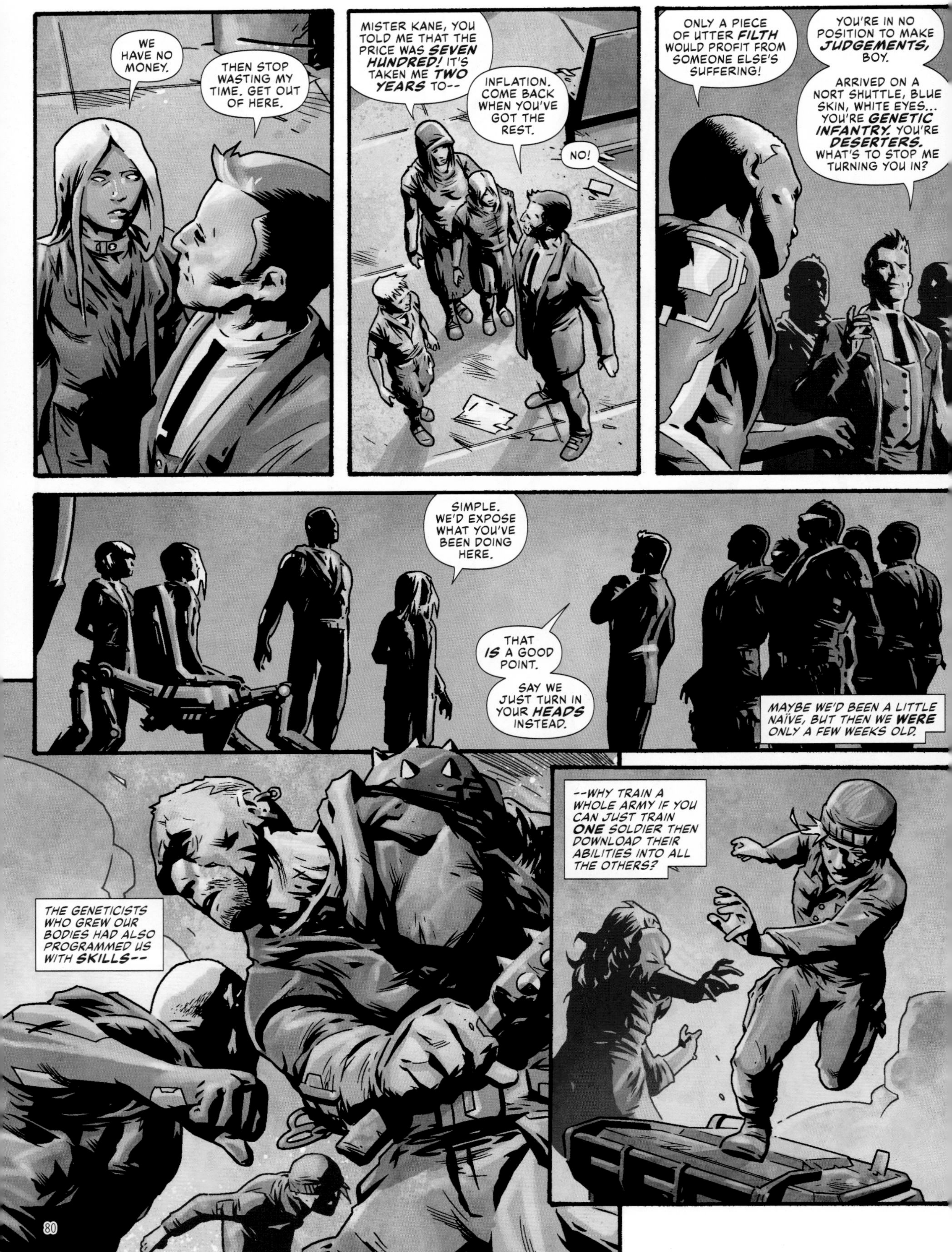

WE HAVE NO MONEY.
THEN STOP WASTING MY TIME. GET OUT OF HERE.
MISTER KANE, YOU TOLD ME THAT THE PRICE WAS SEVEN HUNDRED! IT'S TAKEN ME TWO YEARS TO--
INFLATION. COME BACK WHEN YOU'VE GOT THE REST.
NO!
ONLY A PIECE OF UTTER FILTH WOULD PROFIT FROM SOMEONE ELSE'S SUFFERING!
YOU'RE IN NO POSITION TO MAKE JUDGEMENTS, BOY.
ARRIVED ON A NORT SHUTTLE, BLUE SKIN, WHITE EYES... YOU'RE GENETIC INFANTRY. YOU'RE DESERTERS. WHAT'S TO STOP ME TURNING YOU IN?
SIMPLE. WE'D EXPOSE WHAT YOU'VE BEEN DOING HERE.
THAT IS A GOOD POINT.
SAY WE JUST TURN IN YOUR HEADS INSTEAD.
MAYBE WE'D BEEN A LITTLE NAÏVE, BUT THEN WE WERE ONLY A FEW WEEKS OLD.
THE GENETICISTS WHO GREW OUR BODIES HAD ALSO PROGRAMMED US WITH SKILLS--
--WHY TRAIN A WHOLE ARMY IF YOU CAN JUST TRAIN ONE SOLDIER THEN DOWNLOAD THEIR ABILITIES INTO ALL THE OTHERS?

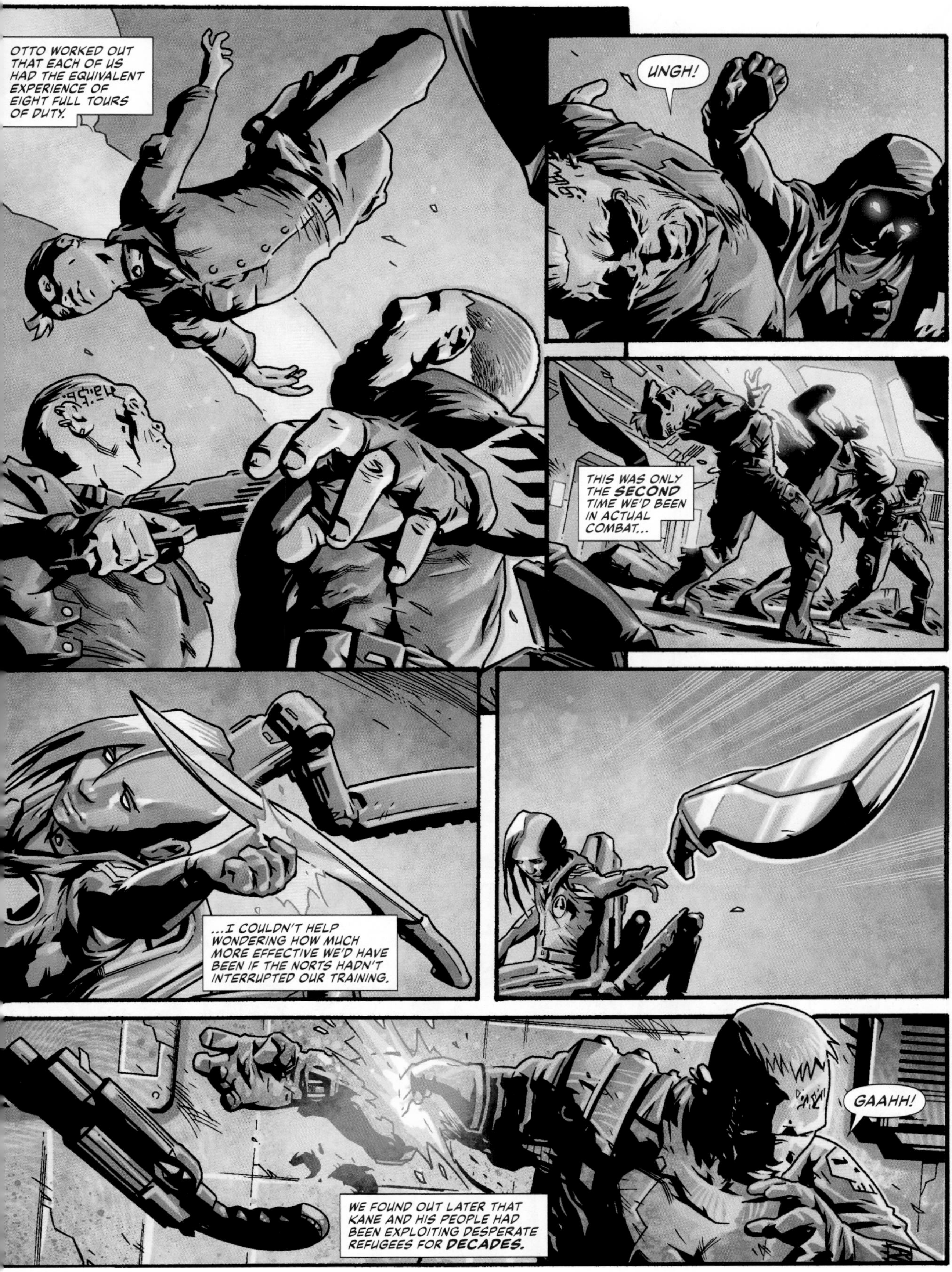

OTTO WORKED OUT THAT EACH OF US HAD THE EQUIVALENT EXPERIENCE OF EIGHT FULL TOURS OF DUTY.
UNGH!
THIS WAS ONLY THE SECOND TIME WE'D BEEN IN ACTUAL COMBAT...
...I COULDN'T HELP WONDERING HOW MUCH MORE EFFECTIVE WE'D HAVE BEEN IF THE NORTS HADN'T INTERRUPTED OUR TRAINING.
GAAHH!
WE FOUND OUT LATER THAT KANE AND HIS PEOPLE HAD BEEN EXPLOITING DESPERATE REFUGEES FOR DECADES.

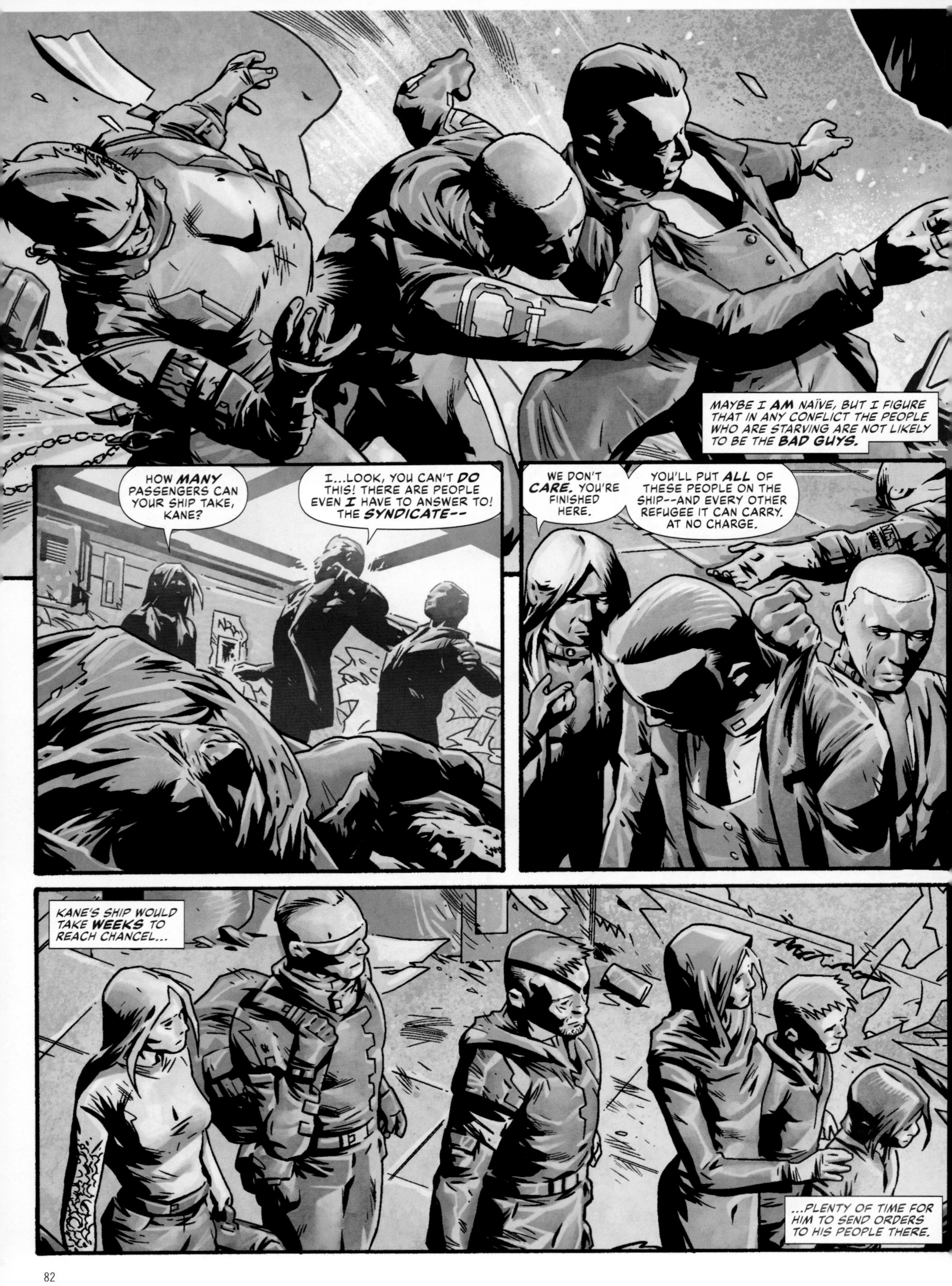

MAYBE I AM NAÏVE, BUT I FIGURE THAT IN ANY CONFLICT THE PEOPLE WHO ARE STARVING ARE NOT LIKELY TO BE THE BAD GUYS.
HOW MANY PASSENGERS CAN YOUR SHIP TAKE, KANE?
I...LOOK, YOU CAN'T DO THIS! THERE ARE PEOPLE EVEN I HAVE TO ANSWER TO! THE SYNDICATE--
WE DON'T CARE. YOU'RE FINISHED HERE.
YOU'LL PUT ALL OF THESE PEOPLE ON THE SHIP--AND EVERY OTHER REFUGEE IT CAN CARRY. AT NO CHARGE.
KANE'S SHIP WOULD TAKE WEEKS TO REACH CHANCEL...
...PLENTY OF TIME FOR HIM TO SEND ORDERS TO HIS PEOPLE THERE.

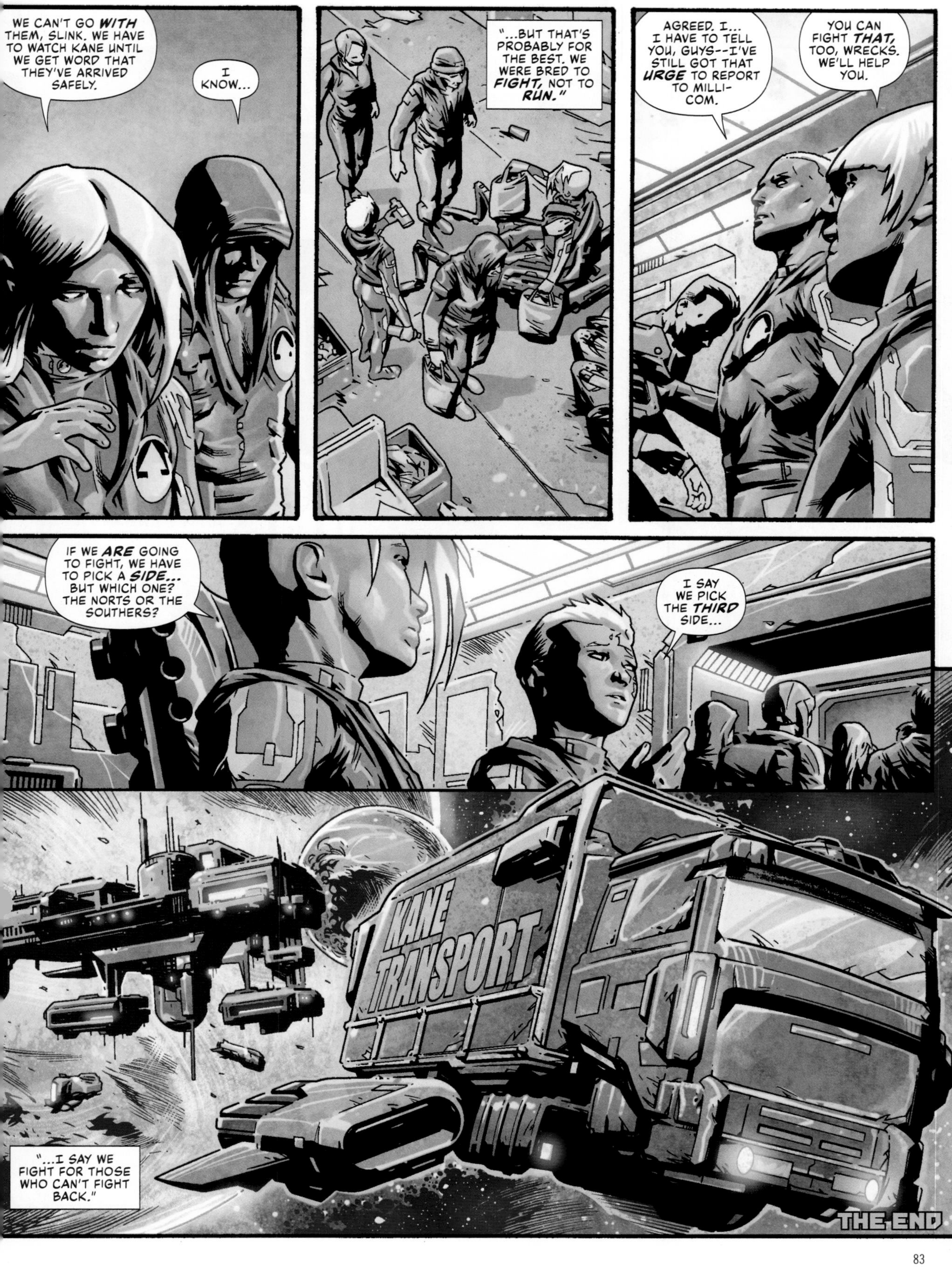
WE CAN'T GO WITH THEM, SLINK. WE HAVE TO WATCH KANE UNTIL WE GET WORD THAT THEY'VE ARRIVED SAFELY.
I KNOW...
"...BUT THAT'S PROBABLY FOR THE BEST. WE WERE BRED TO FIGHT, NOT TO RUN."
AGREED. I... I HAVE TO TELL YOU, GUYS--I'VE STILL GOT THAT URGE TO REPORT TO MILLI-COM.
YOU CAN FIGHT THAT, TOO, WRECKS. WE'LL HELP YOU.
IF WE ARE GOING TO FIGHT, WE HAVE TO PICK A SIDE... BUT WHICH ONE? THE NORTS OR THE SOUTHERS?
I SAY WE PICK THE THIRD SIDE...
KANE TRANSPORT
"...I SAY WE FIGHT FOR THOSE WHO CAN'T FIGHT BACK."
THE END

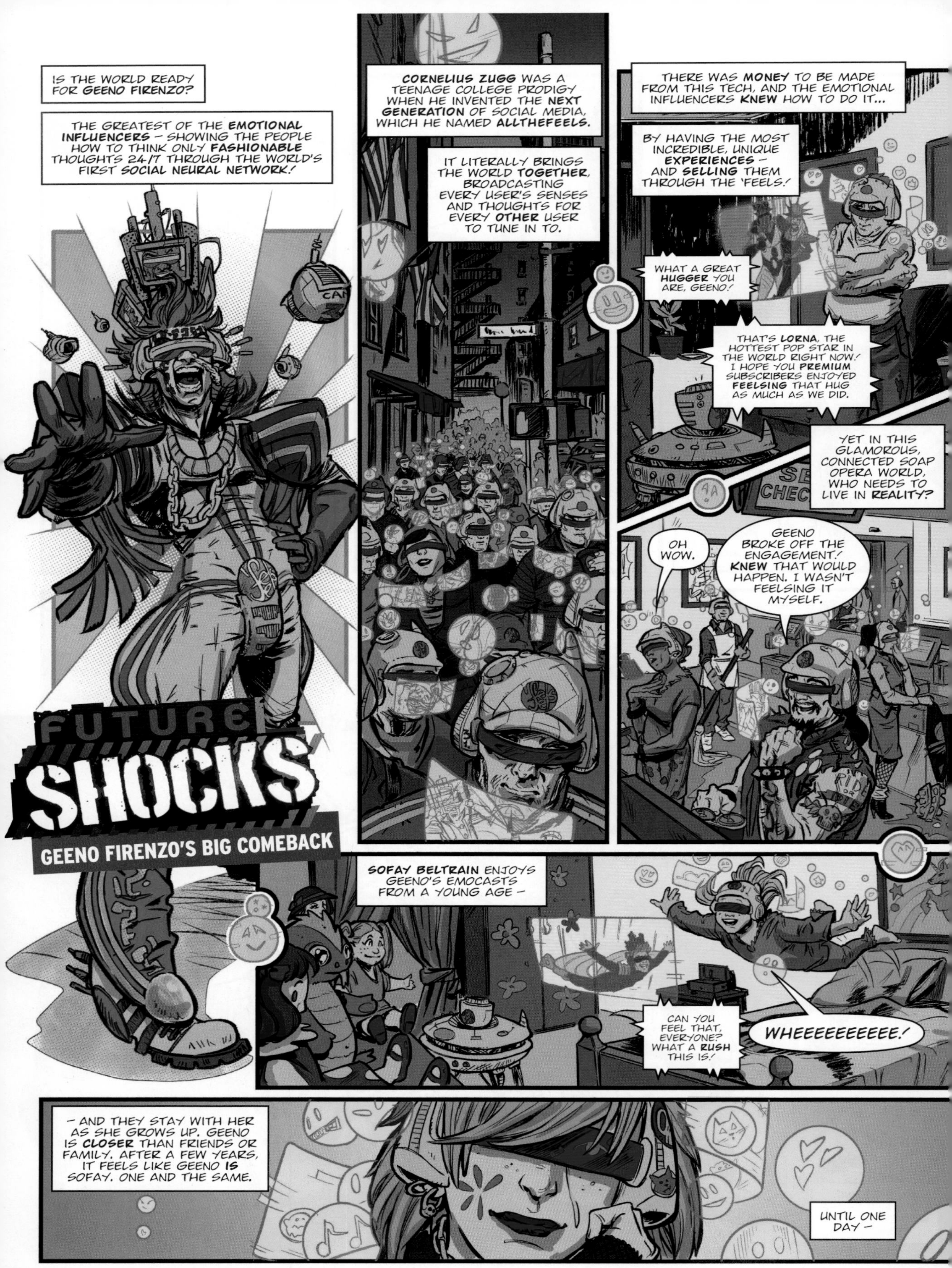
IS THE WORLD READY FOR GEENO FIRENZO?
THE GREATEST OF THE EMOTIONAL INFLUENCERS – SHOWING THE PEOPLE HOW TO THINK ONLY FASHIONABLE THOUGHTS 24/7 THROUGH THE WORLD'S FIRST SOCIAL NEURAL NETWORK!
FUTURE SHOCKS
GEENO FIRENZO'S BIG COMEBACK
CORNELIUS ZUGG WAS A TEENAGE COLLEGE PRODIGY WHEN HE INVENTED THE NEXT GENERATION OF SOCIAL MEDIA, WHICH HE NAMED ALLTHEFEELS.
IT LITERALLY BRINGS THE WORLD TOGETHER, BROADCASTING EVERY USER'S SENSES AND THOUGHTS FOR EVERY OTHER USER TO TUNE IN TO.
THERE WAS MONEY TO BE MADE FROM THIS TECH, AND THE EMOTIONAL INFLUENCERS KNEW HOW TO DO IT...
BY HAVING THE MOST INCREDIBLE, UNIQUE EXPERIENCES – AND SELLING THEM THROUGH THE 'FEELS.'
WHAT A GREAT HUGGER YOU ARE, GEENO!
THAT'S LORNA, THE HOTTEST POP STAR IN THE WORLD RIGHT NOW! I HOPE YOU PREMIUM SUBSCRIBERS ENJOYED FEELSING THAT HUG AS MUCH AS WE DID.
YET IN THIS GLAMOROUS, CONNECTED SOAP OPERA WORLD, WHO NEEDS TO LIVE IN REALITY?
OH WOW.
GEENO BROKE OFF THE ENGAGEMENT! KNEW THAT WOULD HAPPEN. I WASN'T FEELSING IT MYSELF.
SOFAY BELTRAIN ENJOYS GEENO'S EMOCASTS FROM A YOUNG AGE –
CAN YOU FEEL THAT, EVERYONE? WHAT A RUSH THIS IS!
WHEEEEEEEEEE!
– AND THEY STAY WITH HER AS SHE GROWS UP. GEENO IS CLOSER THAN FRIENDS OR FAMILY. AFTER A FEW YEARS, IT FEELS LIKE GEENO IS SOFAY. ONE AND THE SAME.
UNTIL ONE DAY –

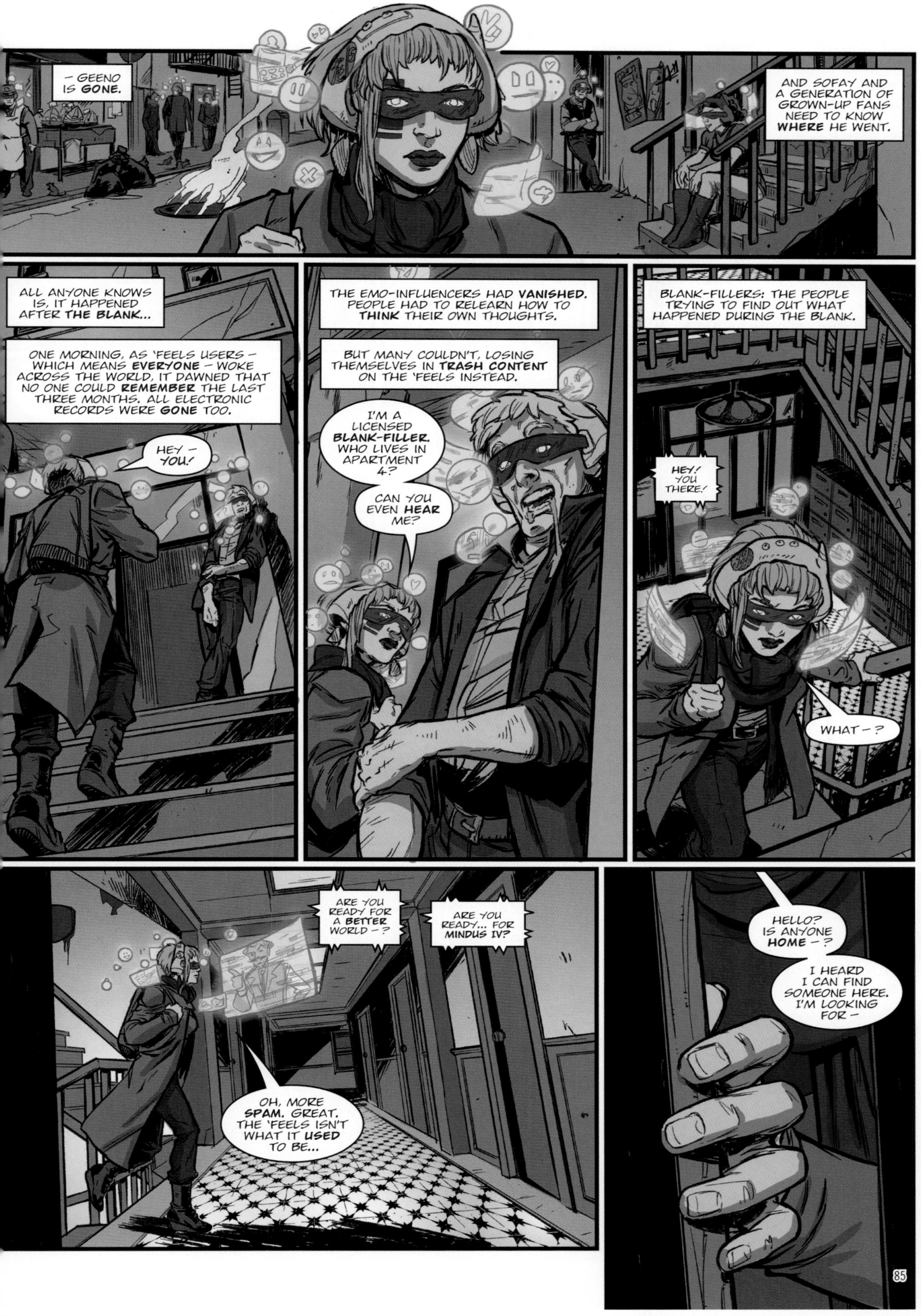
– GEENO IS GONE.
AND SOFAY AND A GENERATION OF GROWN-UP FANS NEED TO KNOW WHERE HE WENT.
ALL ANYONE KNOWS IS, IT HAPPENED AFTER THE BLANK...
ONE MORNING, AS 'FEELS USERS – WHICH MEANS EVERYONE – WOKE ACROSS THE WORLD, IT DAWNED THAT NO ONE COULD REMEMBER THE LAST THREE MONTHS. ALL ELECTRONIC RECORDS WERE GONE TOO.
HEY – YOU!
THE EMO-INFLUENCERS HAD VANISHED. PEOPLE HAD TO RELEARN HOW TO THINK THEIR OWN THOUGHTS.
BUT MANY COULDN'T, LOSING THEMSELVES IN TRASH CONTENT ON THE 'FEELS INSTEAD.
I'M A LICENSED BLANK-FILLER. WHO LIVES IN APARTMENT 4?
CAN YOU EVEN HEAR ME?
BLANK-FILLERS: THE PEOPLE TRYING TO FIND OUT WHAT HAPPENED DURING THE BLANK.
HEY! YOU THERE!
WHAT – ?
ARE YOU READY FOR A BETTER WORLD – ?
ARE YOU READY... FOR MINDUS IV?
OH, MORE SPAM. GREAT. THE 'FEELS ISN'T WHAT IT USED TO BE...
HELLO? IS ANYONE HOME – ?
I HEARD I CAN FIND SOMEONE HERE. I'M LOOKING FOR –

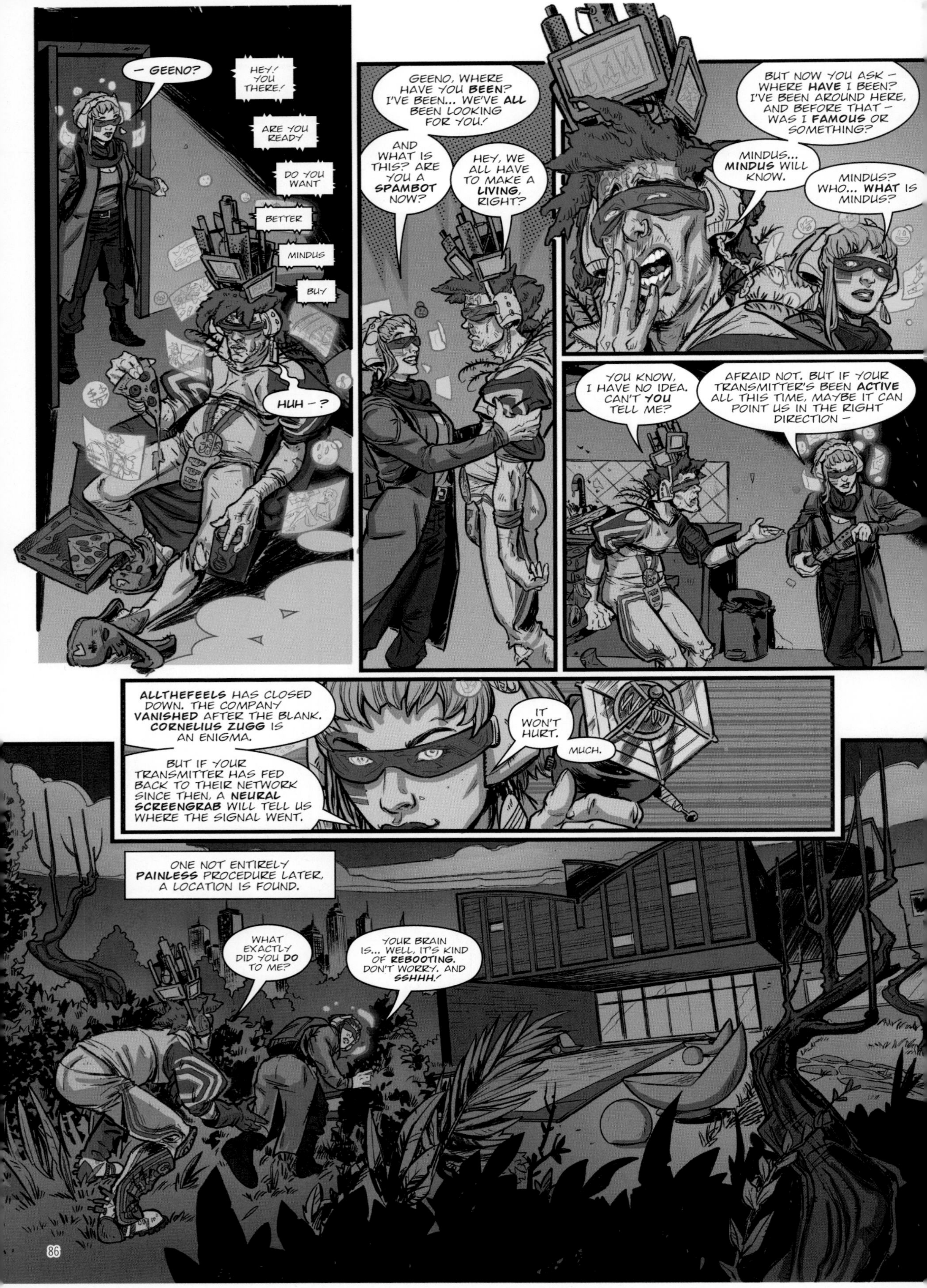

– GEENO?
HEY! YOU THERE!
ARE YOU READY
DO YOU WANT
BETTER
MINDUS
BUY
HUH – ?
GEENO, WHERE HAVE YOU BEEN? I'VE BEEN... WE'VE ALL BEEN LOOKING FOR YOU!
AND WHAT IS THIS? ARE YOU A SPAMBOT NOW?
HEY, WE ALL HAVE TO MAKE A LIVING, RIGHT?
BUT NOW YOU ASK – WHERE HAVE I BEEN? I'VE BEEN AROUND HERE, AND BEFORE THAT – WAS I FAMOUS OR SOMETHING?
MINDUS... MINDUS WILL KNOW.
MINDUS? WHO... WHAT IS MINDUS?
YOU KNOW, I HAVE NO IDEA. CAN'T YOU TELL ME?
AFRAID NOT. BUT IF YOUR TRANSMITTER'S BEEN ACTIVE ALL THIS TIME, MAYBE IT CAN POINT US IN THE RIGHT DIRECTION –
ALLTHEFEELS HAS CLOSED DOWN. THE COMPANY VANISHED AFTER THE BLANK. CORNELIUS ZUGG IS AN ENIGMA.
BUT IF YOUR TRANSMITTER HAS FED BACK TO THEIR NETWORK SINCE THEN, A NEURAL SCREENGRAB WILL TELL US WHERE THE SIGNAL WENT.
IT WON'T HURT.
MUCH.
ONE NOT ENTIRELY PAINLESS PROCEDURE LATER, A LOCATION IS FOUND.
WHAT EXACTLY DID YOU DO TO ME?
YOUR BRAIN IS... WELL, IT'S KIND OF REBOOTING. DON'T WORRY. AND SSHHH!

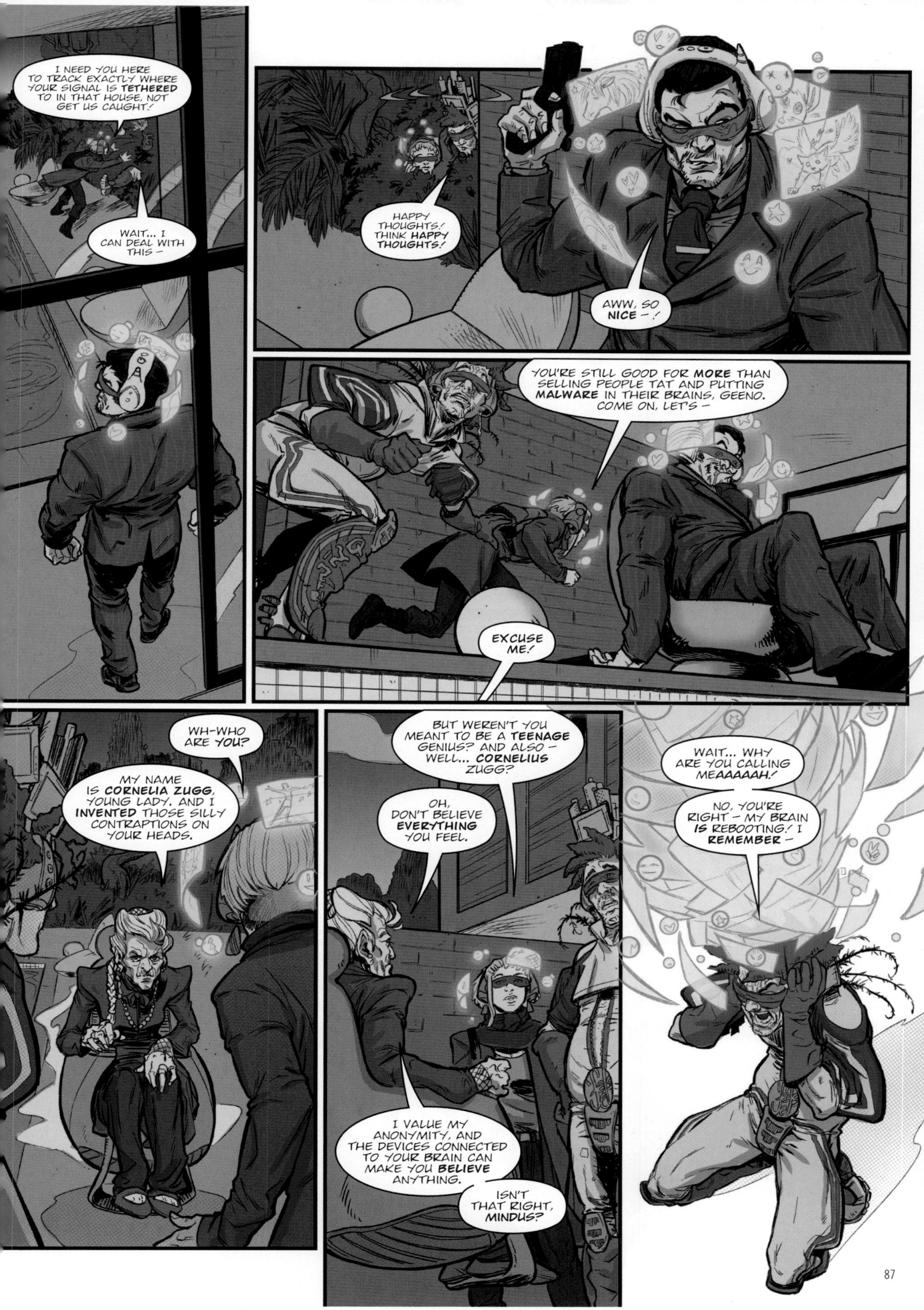
I NEED YOU HERE TO TRACK EXACTLY WHERE YOUR SIGNAL IS **TETHERED** TO IN THAT HOUSE, NOT GET US CAUGHT!
WAIT... I CAN DEAL WITH THIS –
HAPPY THOUGHTS! THINK **HAPPY THOUGHTS!**
AWW, SO **NICE** –!
YOU'RE STILL GOOD FOR **MORE** THAN SELLING PEOPLE TAT AND PUTTING **MALWARE** IN THEIR BRAINS, GEENO. COME ON, LET'S –
**EXCUSE ME!**
WH-WHO ARE **YOU?**
MY NAME IS **CORNELIA ZUGG**, YOUNG LADY. AND I **INVENTED** THOSE SILLY CONTRAPTIONS ON YOUR HEADS.
BUT WEREN'T YOU MEANT TO BE A **TEENAGE** GENIUS? AND ALSO – WELL... **CORNELIUS** ZUGG?
OH, DON'T BELIEVE **EVERYTHING** YOU FEEL.
I VALUE MY ANONYMITY, AND THE DEVICES CONNECTED TO YOUR BRAIN CAN MAKE YOU **BELIEVE** ANYTHING.
ISN'T THAT RIGHT, **MINDUS?**
WAIT... WHY ARE YOU CALLING MEAAAAAH!
NO, YOU'RE RIGHT – MY BRAIN **IS** REBOOTING! I **REMEMBER** –

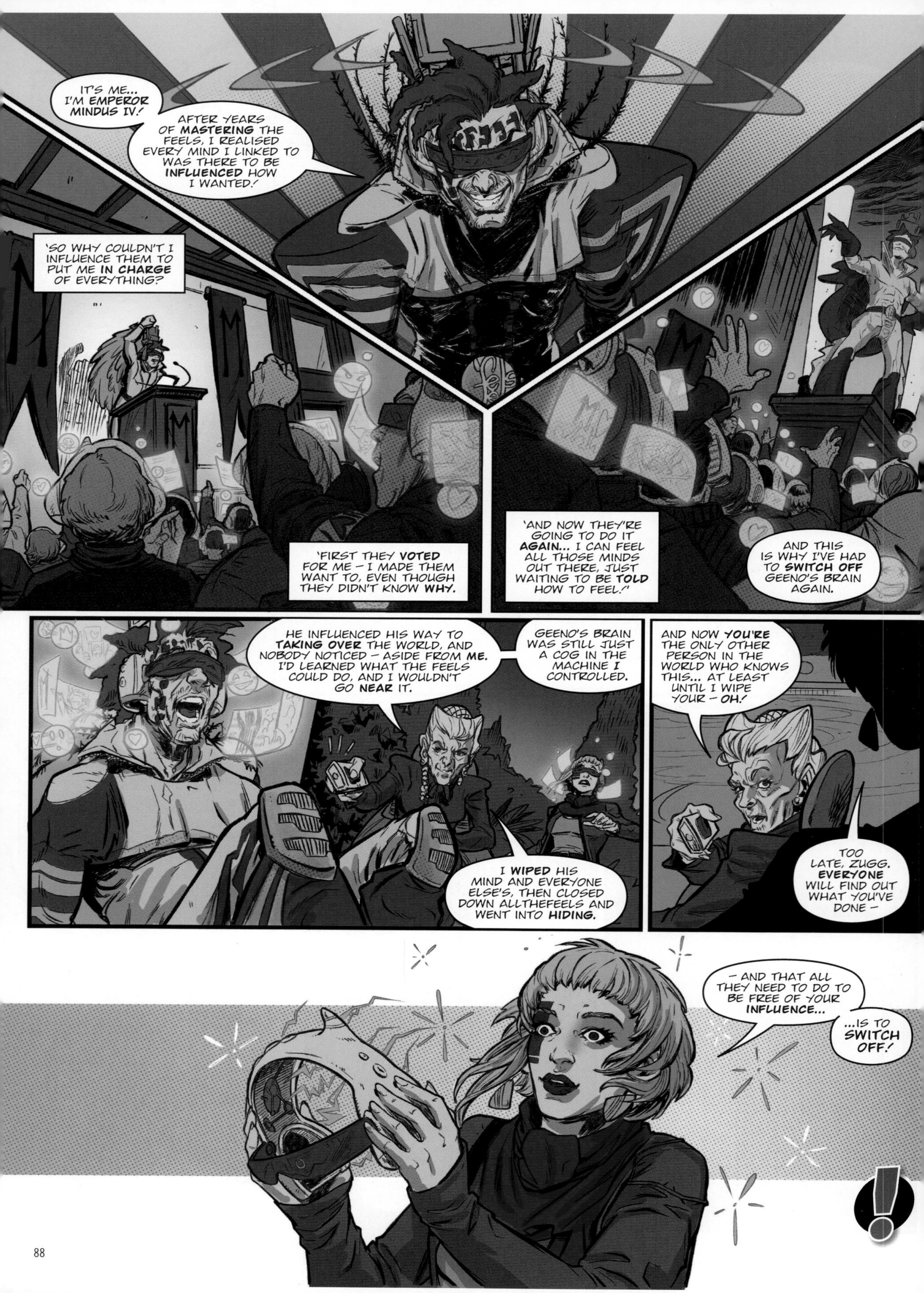
IT'S ME... I'M EMPEROR MINDUS IV!
AFTER YEARS OF MASTERING THE FEELS, I REALISED EVERY MIND I LINKED TO WAS THERE TO BE INFLUENCED HOW I WANTED!
'SO WHY COULDN'T I INFLUENCE THEM TO PUT ME IN CHARGE OF EVERYTHING?
'FIRST THEY VOTED FOR ME – I MADE THEM WANT TO, EVEN THOUGH THEY DIDN'T KNOW WHY.
'AND NOW THEY'RE GOING TO DO IT AGAIN... I CAN FEEL ALL THOSE MINDS OUT THERE, JUST WAITING TO BE TOLD HOW TO FEEL.'
AND THIS IS WHY I'VE HAD TO SWITCH OFF GEENO'S BRAIN AGAIN.
HE INFLUENCED HIS WAY TO TAKING OVER THE WORLD, AND NOBODY NOTICED – ASIDE FROM ME. I'D LEARNED WHAT THE FEELS COULD DO, AND I WOULDN'T GO NEAR IT.
GEENO'S BRAIN WAS STILL JUST A COG IN THE MACHINE I CONTROLLED.
I WIPED HIS MIND AND EVERYONE ELSE'S, THEN CLOSED DOWN ALLTHEFEELS AND WENT INTO HIDING.
AND NOW YOU'RE THE ONLY OTHER PERSON IN THE WORLD WHO KNOWS THIS... AT LEAST UNTIL I WIPE YOUR – OH!
TOO LATE, ZUGG. EVERYONE WILL FIND OUT WHAT YOU'VE DONE –
– AND THAT ALL THEY NEED TO DO TO BE FREE OF YOUR INFLUENCE...
...IS TO SWITCH OFF!

IMAGINE BEING **ALONE** IN THE UNIVERSE. IMAGINE HOW **TERRIBLE** THAT WOULD BE.

# FUTURE! SHOCKS

## SPACE EXPECTATIONS

TROUBLE IS, WE'VE LOOKED **EVERYWHERE** FOR **LIFE** AND WE CAN'T FIND **ANYTHING**.

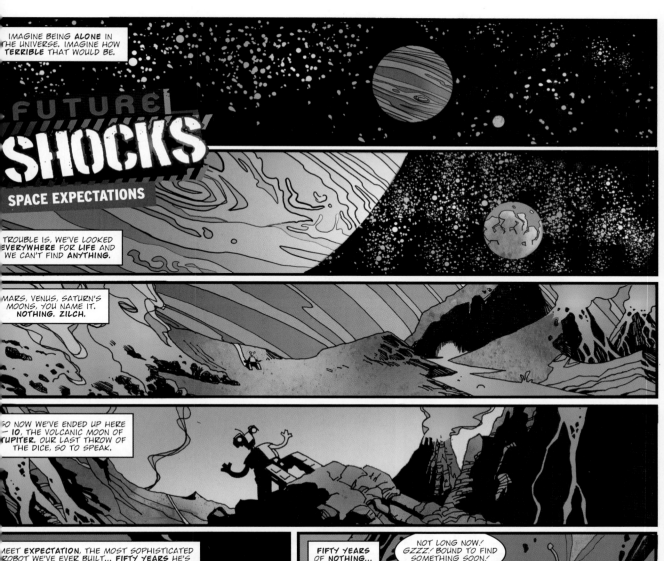

MARS, VENUS, SATURN'S MOONS, YOU NAME IT. **NOTHING. ZILCH.**

SO NOW WE'VE ENDED UP HERE — **IO**, THE VOLCANIC MOON OF **JUPITER**. OUR LAST THROW OF THE DICE, SO TO SPEAK.

MEET EXPECTATION, THE MOST SOPHISTICATED ROBOT WE'VE EVER BUILT... **FIFTY YEARS** HE'S BEEN **SEARCHING** THIS DESOLATE PLACE.

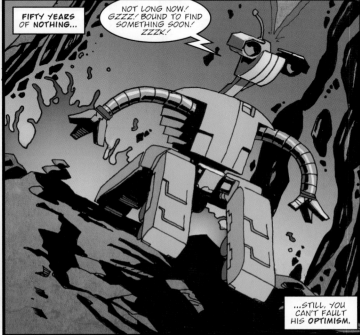

**FIFTY YEARS** OF **NOTHING**...

NOT LONG NOW! GZZZ! BOUND TO FIND SOMETHING SOON! ZZZK!

...STILL, YOU CAN'T FAULT HIS **OPTIMISM**.

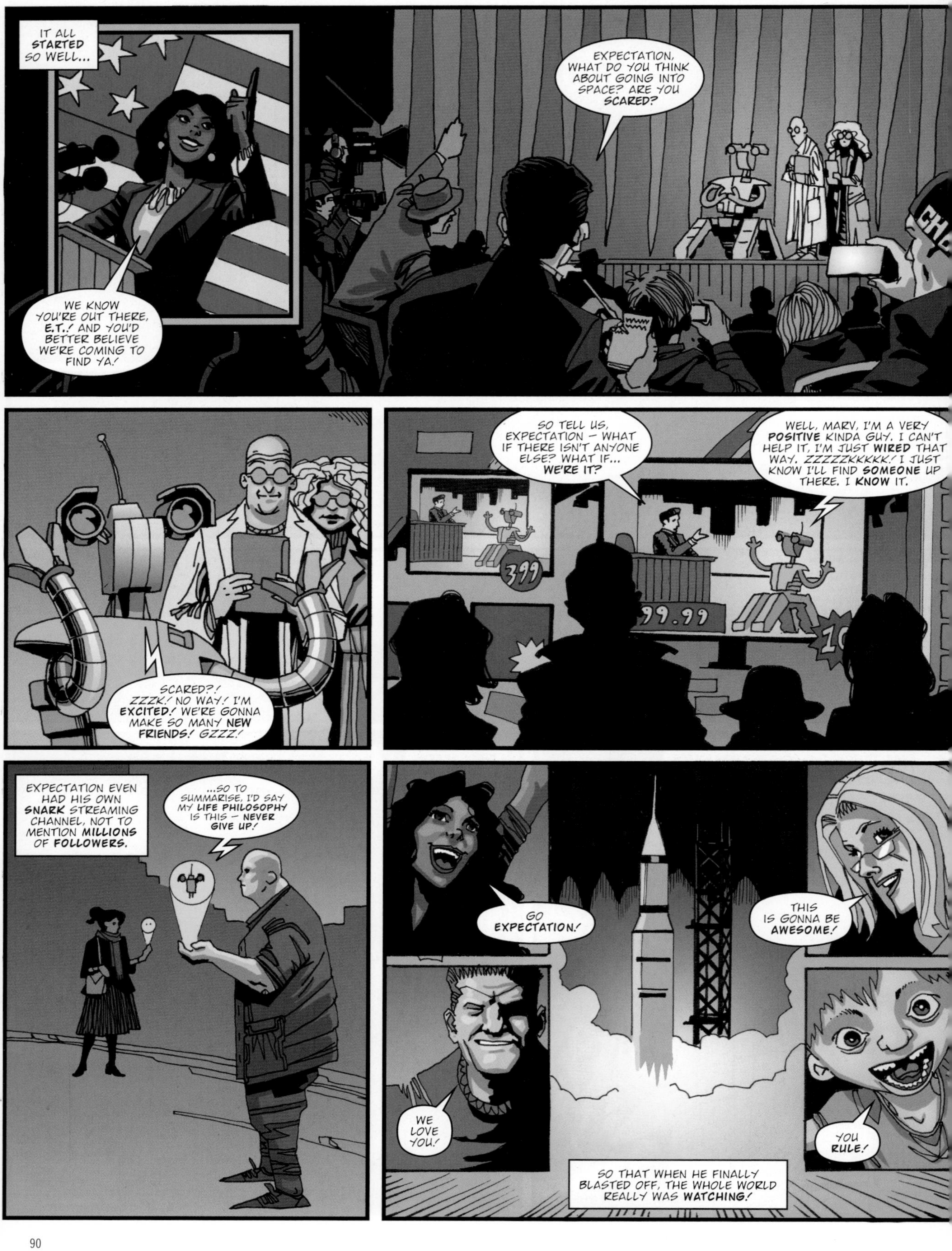
IT ALL STARTED SO WELL...
WE KNOW YOU'RE OUT THERE, E.T.! AND YOU'D BETTER BELIEVE WE'RE COMING TO FIND YA!
EXPECTATION, WHAT DO YOU THINK ABOUT GOING INTO SPACE? ARE YOU SCARED?
SCARED?! ZZZK! NO WAY! I'M EXCITED! WE'RE GONNA MAKE SO MANY NEW FRIENDS! GZZZ!
SO TELL US, EXPECTATION – WHAT IF THERE ISN'T ANYONE ELSE? WHAT IF... WE'RE IT?
WELL, MARV, I'M A VERY POSITIVE KINDA GUY. I CAN'T HELP IT, I'M JUST WIRED THAT WAY. ZZZZZKKKKK! I JUST KNOW I'LL FIND SOMEONE UP THERE. I KNOW IT.
399
99.99
EXPECTATION EVEN HAD HIS OWN SNARK STREAMING CHANNEL, NOT TO MENTION MILLIONS OF FOLLOWERS.
...SO TO SUMMARISE, I'D SAY MY LIFE PHILOSOPHY IS THIS – NEVER GIVE UP!
GO EXPECTATION!
THIS IS GONNA BE AWESOME!
WE LOVE YOU!
YOU RULE!
SO THAT WHEN HE FINALLY BLASTED OFF, THE WHOLE WORLD REALLY WAS WATCHING!

BUT THAT WAS A **HALF A CENTURY** AGO AND **866.96 MILLION KILOMETRES** AWAY. NO ONE REMEMBERS EXPECTATION NOW...

HE KNOWS BECAUSE HE STILL CHECKS HIS **SNARK** ACCOUNT...

BLOG

54

OF COURSE HE COULD SIMPLY CHOOSE TO **FINISH HIS MISSION.** HE COULD JUST SEND THE MESSAGE — '**NO LIFE HERE!**'..

ANY MOMENT NOW I'M GONNA FIND SOMETHING! ZZZK! I CAN SENSE IT!

...BUT THAT ISN'T HOW EXPECTATION IS **WIRED.**

HMM, I DON'T LIKE THESE **TREMORS...** ZZZK! THIS IS THE WORST **MOONQUAKE** YET —

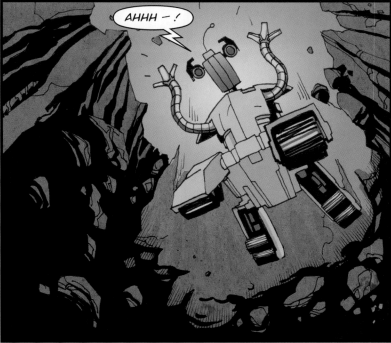

AHHH — !

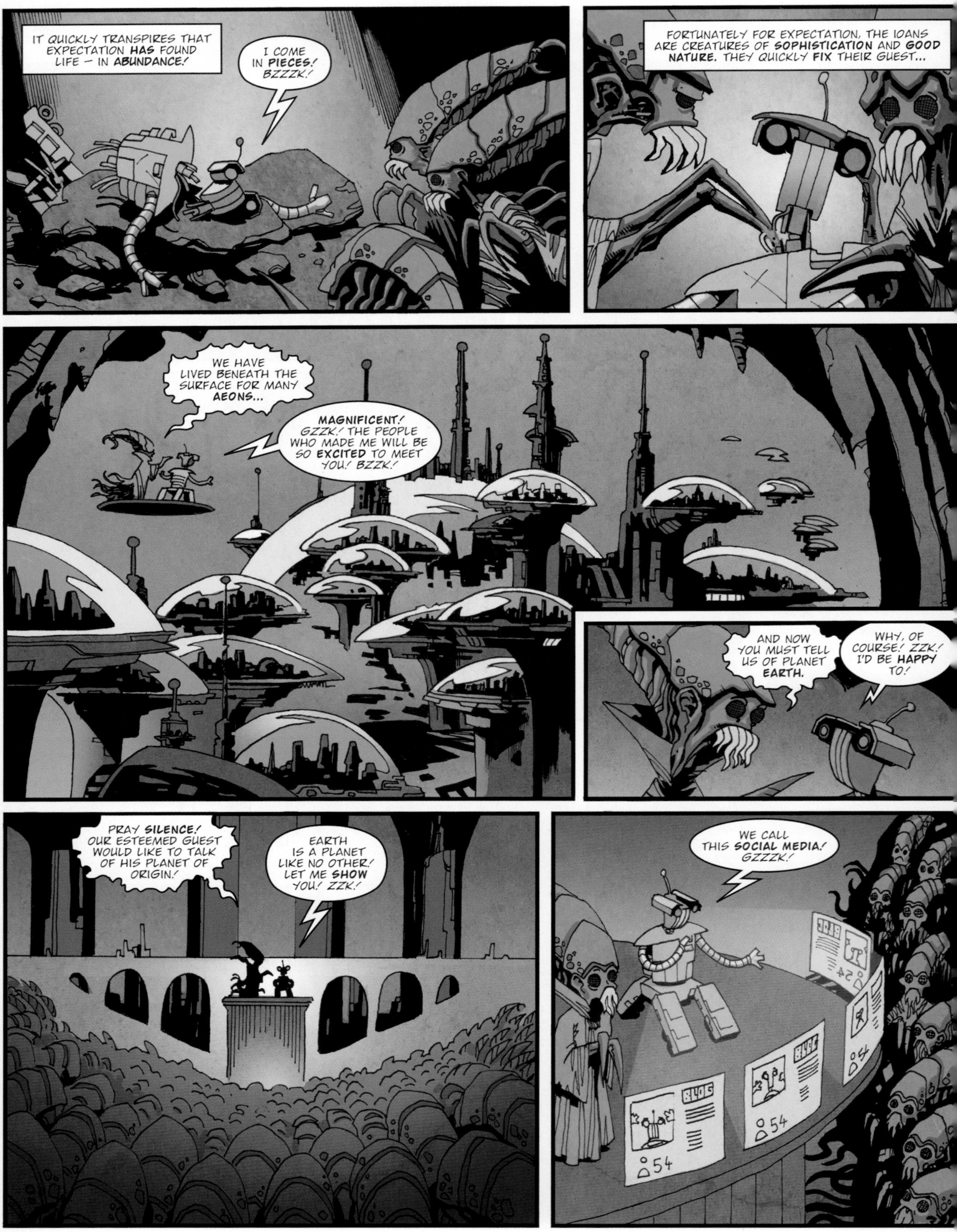

IT QUICKLY TRANSPIRES THAT EXPECTATION HAS FOUND LIFE – IN ABUNDANCE!
I COME IN PIECES! BZZZK!
FORTUNATELY FOR EXPECTATION, THE IOANS ARE CREATURES OF SOPHISTICATION AND GOOD NATURE. THEY QUICKLY FIX THEIR GUEST...
WE HAVE LIVED BENEATH THE SURFACE FOR MANY AEONS...
MAGNIFICENT! GZZK! THE PEOPLE WHO MADE ME WILL BE SO EXCITED TO MEET YOU! BZZK!
AND NOW YOU MUST TELL US OF PLANET EARTH.
WHY, OF COURSE! ZZK! I'D BE HAPPY TO!
PRAY SILENCE! OUR ESTEEMED GUEST WOULD LIKE TO TALK OF HIS PLANET OF ORIGIN!
EARTH IS A PLANET LIKE NO OTHER! LET ME SHOW YOU! ZZK!
WE CALL THIS SOCIAL MEDIA! GZZZK!
BLOG
54
BLOG
54
BLOG
54
54

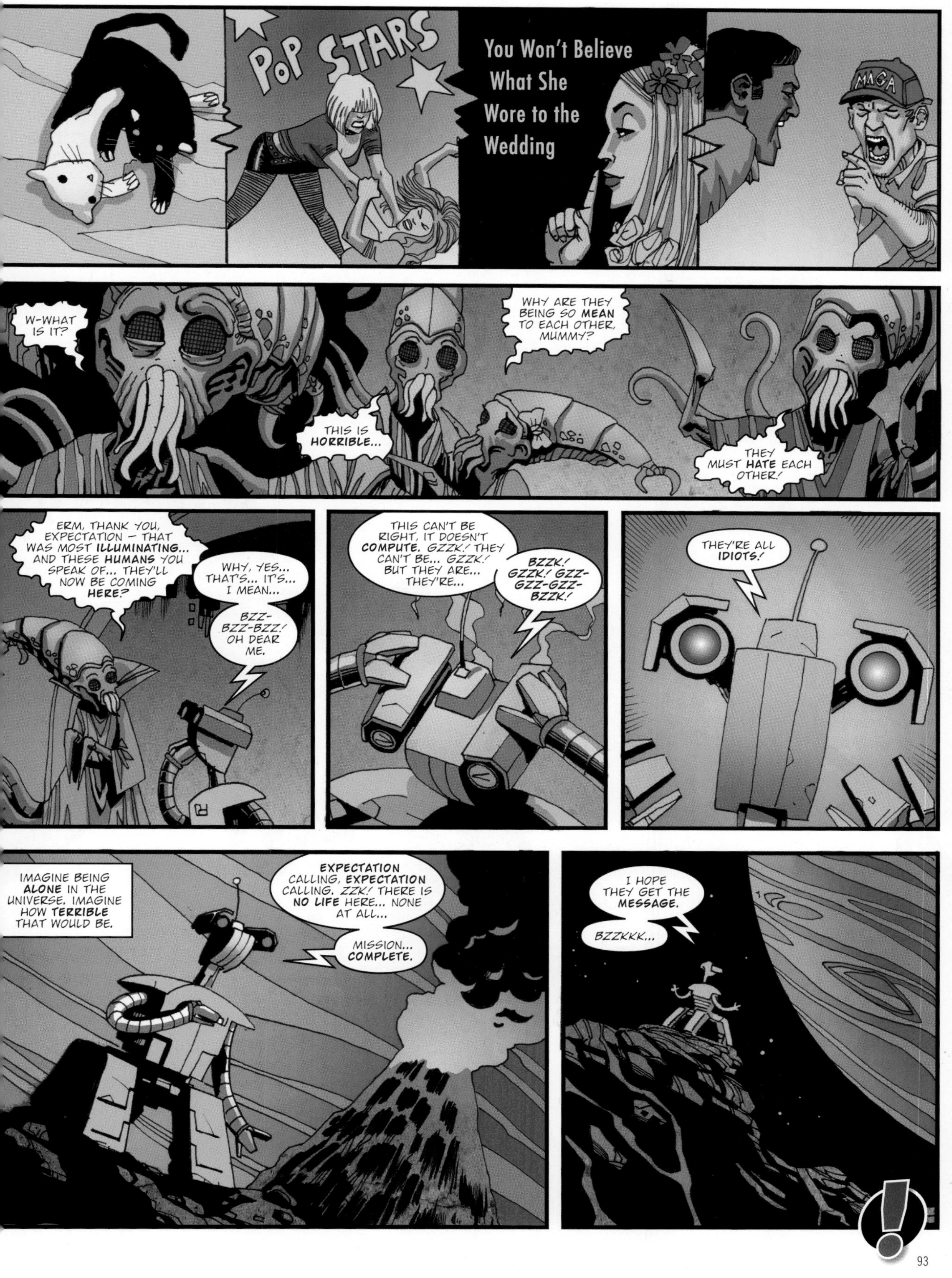

POP STARS
You Won't Believe What She Wore to the Wedding
MAGA
W-WHAT IS IT?
WHY ARE THEY BEING SO MEAN TO EACH OTHER, MUMMY?
THIS IS HORRIBLE...
THEY MUST HATE EACH OTHER!
ERM, THANK YOU, EXPECTATION – THAT WAS MOST ILLUMINATING... AND THESE HUMANS YOU SPEAK OF... THEY'LL NOW BE COMING HERE?
WHY, YES... THAT'S... IT'S... I MEAN...
BZZ-BZZ-BZZ! OH DEAR ME.
THIS CAN'T BE RIGHT, IT DOESN'T COMPUTE. GZZK! THEY CAN'T BE... GZZK! BUT THEY ARE... THEY'RE...
BZZK! GZZK! GZZ-GZZ-GZZ-BZZK!
THEY'RE ALL IDIOTS!
IMAGINE BEING ALONE IN THE UNIVERSE. IMAGINE HOW TERRIBLE THAT WOULD BE.
EXPECTATION CALLING, EXPECTATION CALLING. ZZK! THERE IS NO LIFE HERE... NONE AT ALL...
MISSION... COMPLETE.
I HOPE THEY GET THE MESSAGE.
BZZKKK...

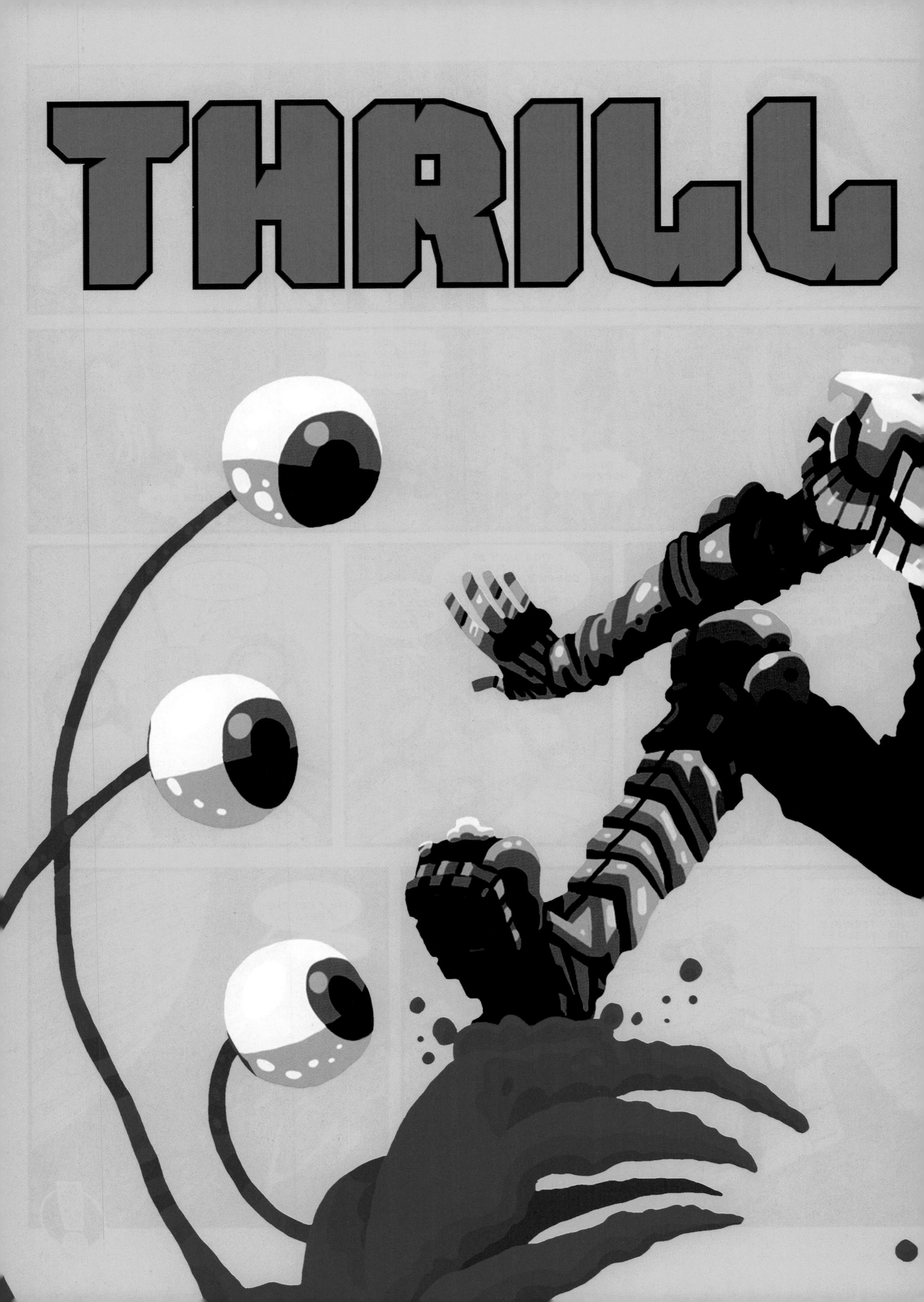
THRILL

# ZONE

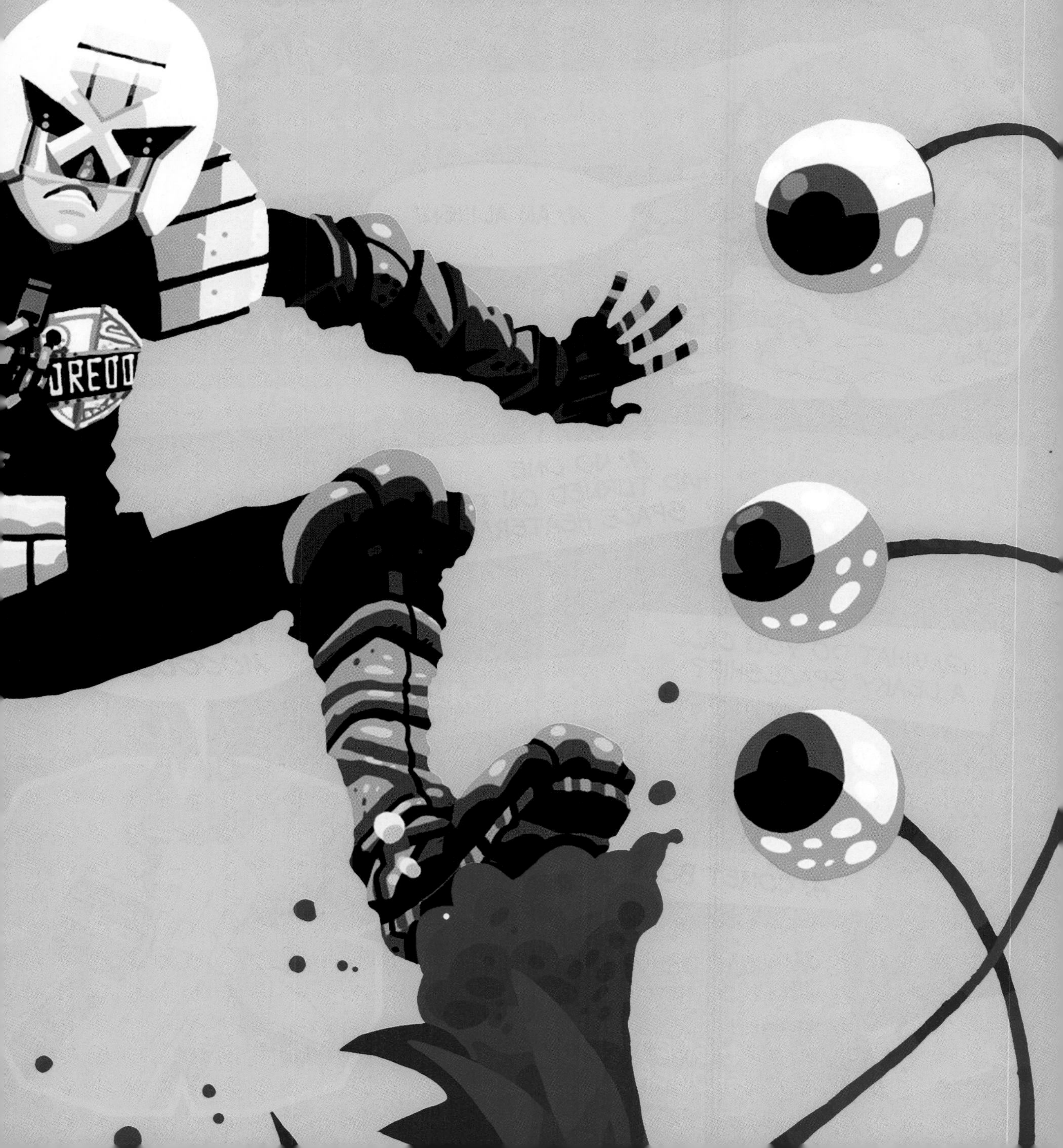

# JOKO'S JOKES

WELCOME NERBLORBS TO THE FUNNIEST PAGES IN THE GALAXY! CAN YOUR INSIDES HANDLE THE *EXTREME TUMMY BUSTIN'* THAT'S ABOUT TO COMMENCE?

HA!

HA!

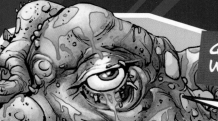

**Q:** WHAT DO YOU CALL AN ALIEN WITH THREE EYES?

**A:** AN ALIIIEN!

**Q:** WHAT'S THE BEST SONG TO SING ON A SPACESHIP?

**A:** AN ASTEROID-BELTER!

**Q:** WHY WERE THE STARS COLD?

**A:** NO ONE HAD TURNED ON THE SPACE HEATER!

**Q:** WHY DO COWS BECOME ASTRONAUTS?

**A:** THEY WANT TO SEE THE MOOOOON!

**Q:** WHAT DO YOU CALL A LEAKY SPACESHIP?

**A:** A CRYING SAUCER!

**Q:** WHAT DO D.R. AND QUINCH LIKE TO READ?

**A:** COMET BOOKS!

**Q:** WHAT DO YOU DO WITH A DIRTY STAR?

**A:** GIVE IT A METEOR SHOWER!

HA!

Q: WHAT IS AN ASTRONAUT'S FAVOURITE MUSIC?

A: ROCKET ROLL!

HA!

Q: HOW DID THE PLANET CRUSH THE ALIEN?

A: HE SATURN IT!

Q: WHAT'S AN ALIEN'S FAVOURITE GAME?

A: ASTRONAUTS AND CROSSES!

HA!

Q: WHO FLIES A SPACESHIP MADE OF PASTRY?

A: A PIE-LOT!

Q: WHAT'S THE HEAVIEST DRINK IN THE GALAXY?

A: GRAVI-TEA!

A: WHAT DID THE ALIENS SAY WHEN THEY CRASHED THEIR SPACESHIP?

A: U.F-D'OH!

Q: WHAT'S THE SMELLIEST PLANET?

A: POO-TO!

HA! HA!

# THRILL-SEARCH

CAN YOU FIND THESE AWESOME 2000 AD REGENED CHARACTERS AND SERIES IN THE GRID?

INTESTINAUTS
ACTION PACT
FINDER
KEEPER
FULL TILT BOOGIE
ROGUE TROOPER
CADET DREDD

ANDERSON
THE GRONK
PANDORA PERFECT
ABELARD SNAZZ
STRONTIUM DOG
DEPARTMENT K
VENUS BLUEGENES

THERE ARE 1
IN TOTAL –
HAPPY HUNTIN
JOKO-JARG

```
X F U L L T I L T B O O G I E D V
A R O G U E T R O O P E R A D I E
C I C O F V I B L U B N A K U N N
T U A M I B A N D E R S O N O T U
I H D Y N Z Q U I O T I K B E E S
O U E A D E P A R T M E N T K S B
N N T G E B L O O G E R U P I T L
P I D O R W I G U P P Y T E G I U
A G R O G O A T E S I Z B U G N E
C B E L U S N R R C L E M A Q A G
T A D I D E N K T I G R C A T U E
U T D A B E L A R D S N A Z Z T N
T C E F R E P A R O D N A P A S E
Z S T R O N T I U M D O G I G J S
```

# ANDERSON'S BRAIN BUSTERS!

UH-OH! SOMEONE'S BROKEN INTO THE GRAND HALL OF JUSTICE EVIDENCE ROOM! BUT WHO WAS IT? WHAT DID THEY STEAL? AND WHERE DID THEY GO? JUDGE ANDERSON (PSI DIVISION) IS ON THE CASE!

## CASE ONE

YIKES, IT'S LIKE A JUNGLE IN HERE! THERE'S PSYCHIC IMPRINTS EVERYWHERE FROM ALL THE OBJECTS WHICH HAVE BEEN PUT HERE OVER THE YEARS. SORT THE PSYCHIC OBJECTS BY SPELLING THEM OUT INTO THE GRID BELOW TO FIND OUT MORE ABOUT WHAT'S BEEN TAKEN!

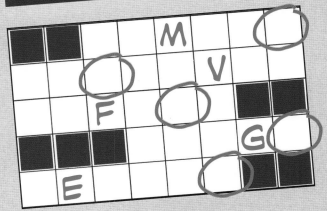

*HINTS!*
- SOMETHING FUN TO READ!

- SOMETHING THE CADETS USE TO SHOOT BAD GUYS!

- SOMETHING YOU DRINK IN THE MORNING FOR ENERGY!

- SOMETHING CADET DREDD WEARS ON HIS UNIFORM!

- SOMETHING TO PROTECT YOUR HEAD!

# CASE TWO

S... W... E... E... T...
WHATEVER THE CREEPS TOOK, ITS DANG DELICIOUS!
LET'S CONJURE A PSYCHIC IMAGE OF WHAT IT COULD BE!

JOIN THE DOTS TO HELP ANDERSON!

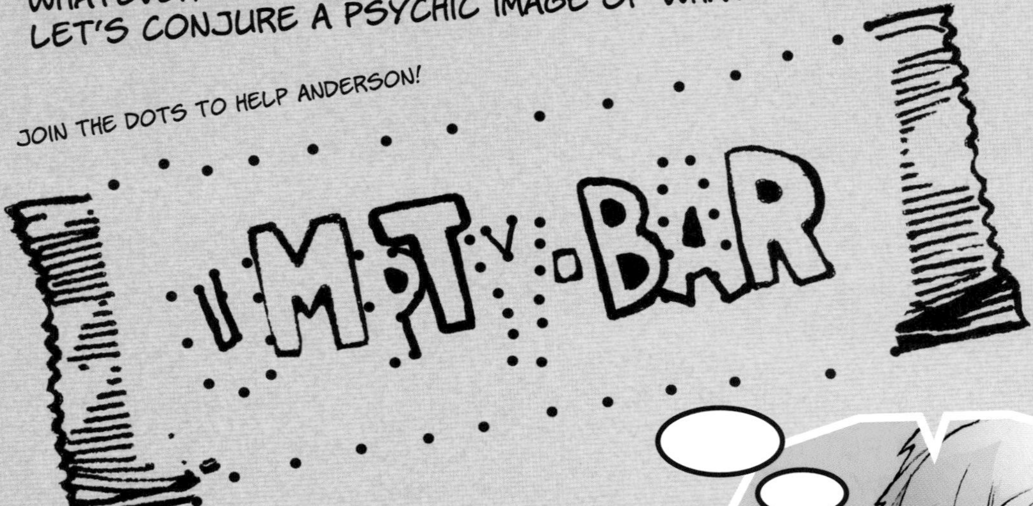

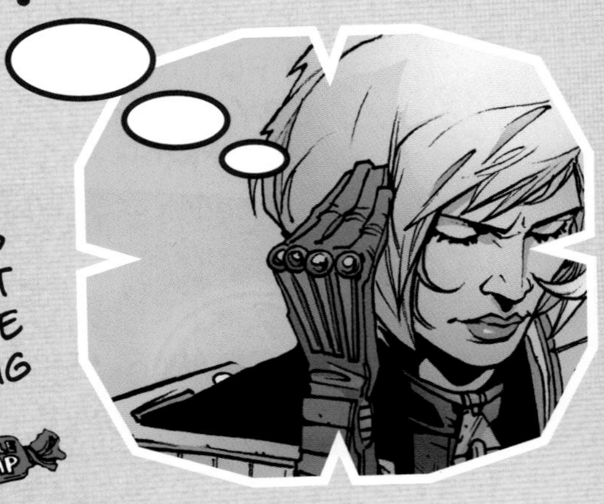

OF COURSE! UNCLE UMP'S UMPTY CANDY! A CANDY SO DELICIOUS, IT'S ILLEGAL! BUT NOW WE KNOW WHAT WE'RE LOOKING FOR, WE CAN TRACE THEIR MOVEMENTS THROUGH THE BIG MEG!

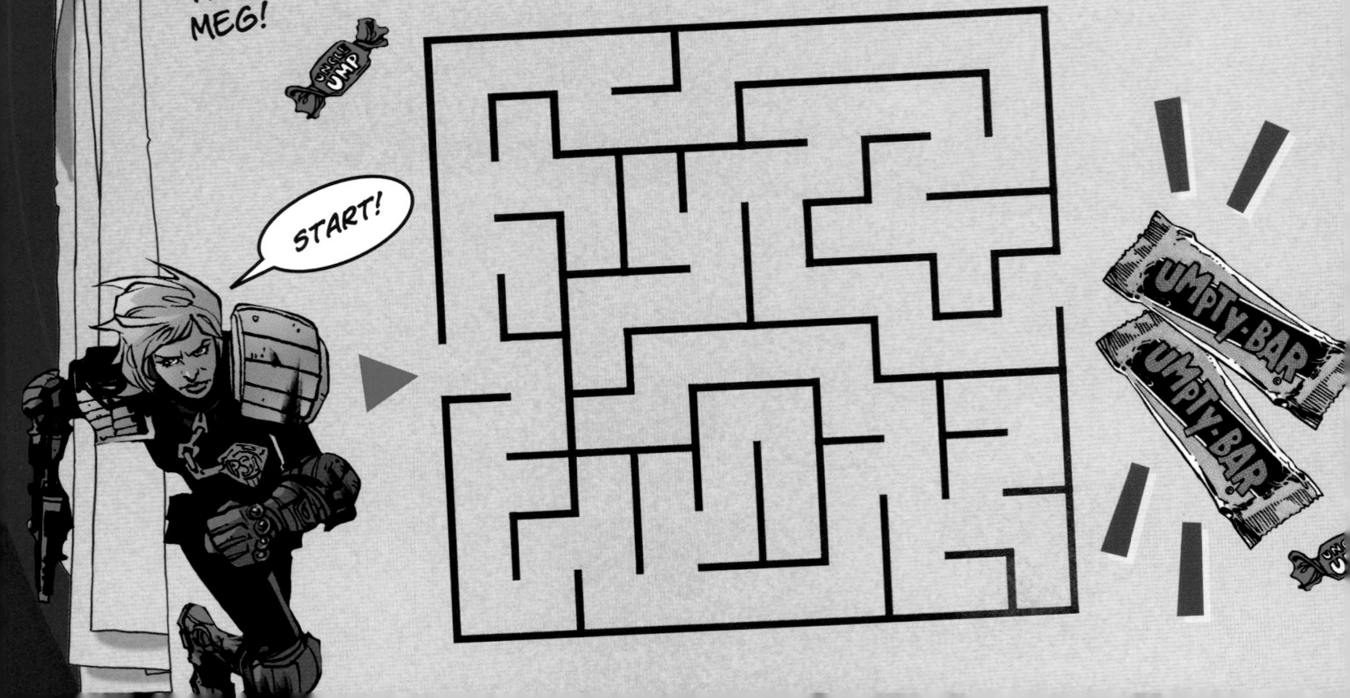
UNCLE UMP
START!
UMPTY-BAR
UMPTY-BAR

# CASE THREE

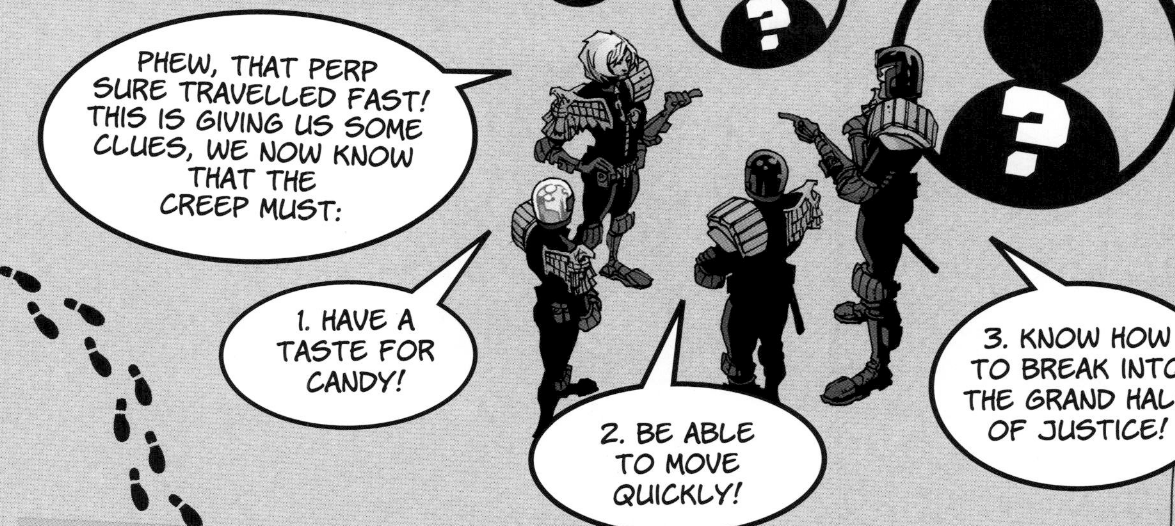
PHEW, THAT PERP SURE TRAVELLED FAST! THIS IS GIVING US SOME CLUES, WE NOW KNOW THAT THE CREEP MUST:
1. HAVE A TASTE FOR CANDY!
2. BE ABLE TO MOVE QUICKLY!
3. KNOW HOW TO BREAK INTO THE GRAND HALL OF JUSTICE!

WE'VE TRACKED THE PERP TO THE SPACEPORT! THE ONLY PROBLEM IS, EVERYONE LOVES UMP'S CANDY (*WHICH IS WHY WE BANNED IT!*). CAN YOU FIND THE ***THREE*** CITIZENS WHO HAVE BEEN THINKING ABOUT UMP'S CANDY THE MOST?

***HINT: BLUE MEANS THEY HAVEN'T THOUGHT ABOUT IT FOR A WHILE - BUT A RED CANDY BAR MEANS THEY'RE THINKING ABOUT IT RIGHT NOW!***

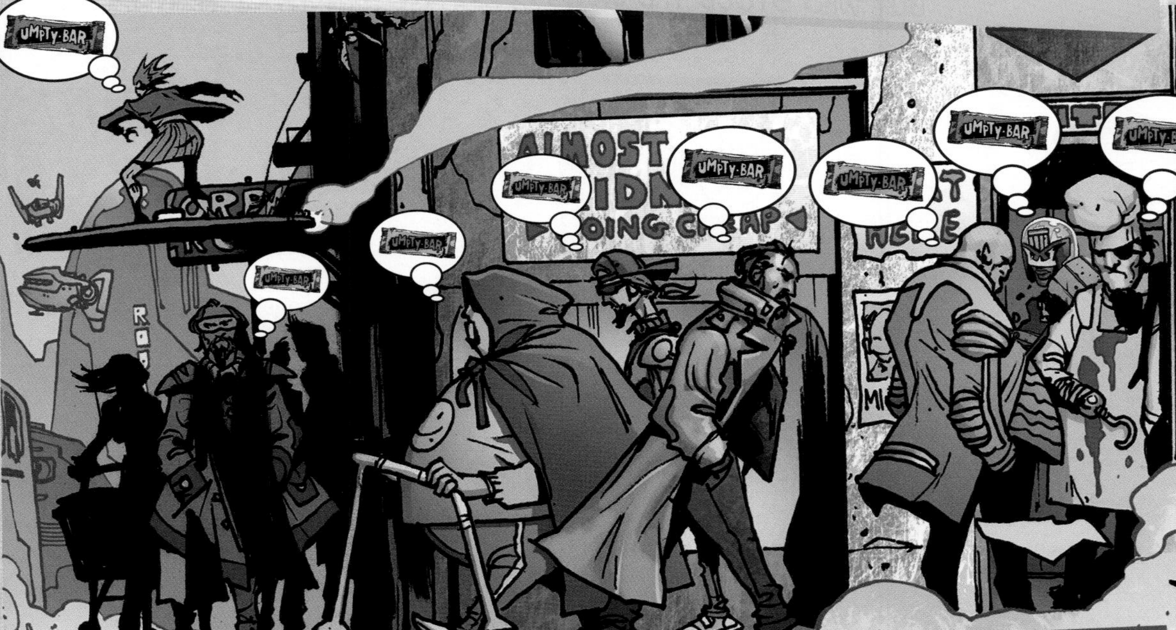
UMPTY-BAR
UMPTY-BAR
UMPTY-BAR
UMPTY-BAR
UMPTY-BAR
UMPTY-BAR
UMPTY-BAR
UMPTY-BAR

HAVE YOU FIGURED OUT WHO OUR SUSPECTS ARE?
TURN OVER AND ***SOLVE*** THE FINAL CASE!

# CASE FOUR

OK, NOW WE HAVE OUR SUSPECTS, LET'S BUILD AN EVIDENCE LOG FOR THESE THREE!

## SUSPECT ONE
**Name:** Bernard Cugsworthy
**Job:** Janitor at the Hall of Justice
**What were you doing at the spaceport?:** Taking a walk on my day off!

## SUSPECT TWO
**Name:** Joni Reeves
**Job:** Juve!
**What were you doing at the spaceport?:** Taking a flight on my hoverboard, what's it to you, Judge?

## SUSPECT THREE
**Name:** Cadet Hawkins
**Job:** Cadet Judge
**What were you doing at the spaceport?:** I came on my Lawmaster, looking for the Umpty Bar thief, same as you!

BUT WHO STOLE THE CANDY! HOLD THIS PAGE UP TO A MIRROR TO READ THEIR MINDS!

JUST MY LUCK TO BE THINKING ABOUT CANDY AT A TIME LIKE THIS! I HOPE I DON'T LOSE MY JOB!

WAIT, THEY HAD UMPTY IN THE GRAND HALL OF JUSTICE?! TOO BAD THEY'D NEVER LET A JUVE LIKE ME INSIDE!

MMM....UMPTY! I MEAN... I AM THE LAW!

WHICH SUSPECTS HAVE A TASTE FOR UMPTY?
WHICH SUSPECTS HAVE ACCESS TO A VEHICLE?
WHICH SUSPECTS KNOW HOW TO GET INTO THE GRAND HALL OF JUSTICE?

ALRIGHT THEN, WHO STOLE THE UMPTY?

THE UMPTY THIEF IS . . .

ANOTHER CASE CLOSED! THANKS, PARNER!

DID YOU GET THE RIGHT PERP? FIND OUT ON PAGE 112?

We sat down with amazing creators David Baillie and Anna Morozova to find out more about the Mega-City's Mightiest Cat Burglar!

# INTERVIEW WITH VIVA Forever

## HOW DID YOU GET INTO A LIFE OF CRIME? I MEAN, HOW DID YOU GET INTO MAKING COMICS?

**Anna:** It's not that much of a crime to me, more like the dark arts, I'd say. I mean, drawing comics and meeting deadlines is very much like spell-casting.

**David:** Oh wow - I'd totally agree with that! I totally and unironically believe that writing and drawing - creating something out of nothing - is a magical act. I suppose what I'm saying is - don't cross us!

## WHERE DID THE IDEA OF VIVA FOREVER COME FROM?

**David:** Anna and I worked on a Black Museum story together (Obsidian Ingress in Meg #423, fact fans!) and I was totally blown away by her work. I faxed Tharg (he still uses a pristine 1986 Quaxxann Quikk fax machine!) and demanded that he team us up again. Please. Joko got back in touch to say that Mega-City One needed a cat burglar character, and sent us off to do our thing.

## MEGA-CITY ONE'S A PRETTY TOUGH PLACE TO LIVE. WHICH CRIME DO YOU THINK THE JUDGES WOULD BOOK YOU FOR?

**Anna:** Used coffee cup hoarding at my desk. Fact. I've even been known to dip my ink brushes into them, which is an iso-cube worthy punishment in its own right!

**David:** Isn't reading comics illegal in MC-1? I'd be locked up for LIFE!

## HOW DO YOU THINK VIVA FOREVER HAS EVADED THE JUDGES FOR SO LONG? WHAT'S HER SECRET?

**Anna:** They say if you can make your hobby your job then you'll always be happy. In Viva's case, it's parkour and cosplay.

**David:** Yup. She's just too good!

## WHAT DO YOU THINK IS NEXT FOR VIVA FOREVER?

**Anna:** We have lots of exciting plans and trajectories of where the character could go, but the ultimate decision is in the hands of the Mighty One and the readers... we will see what the future holds.

## IF THEY WERE TO MAKE A VIVA FOREVER MOVIE, WHO WOULD PLAY HER AND WHAT CRIME WOULD IT BE ABOUT?

**Anna:** Rather than a live action movie, I'd envisaged Viva Forever more as animation. Be it 2D, 3D or a hybrid – it allows for edgy, stylised and frenetic action. As for the crime, Mega-City One offers endless possibilities...

**David:** Oh my Grud, yes! When writing Viva I kept getting flashbacks to an MTV cartoon from, I think, the 90s? Aeon Flux. Something really weird and kinetic like that would be perfect!

## IF YOU COULD BE ANY CHARACTER FROM 2000 AD, WHO WOULD IT BE AND WHY?

**Anna:** It's probably a choice between Katarina Dante the pirate queen and Halo Jones who was also on her way to becoming a pirate queen, allegedly. Can you see a theme here?

**David:** When I was a teenager I genuinely wanted to be Revere, the witch boy character John Smith created. Now I think Johnny Alpha, but just because he's effortlessly handsome and definitely benches more than I do.

## TOP TIPS FOR BECOMING AN AMAZING COMICS CREATOR?

**Anna:** I shall report back to you on this one when I know myself! On a serious note: hitting deadlines and being able to visualise anything that is asked of you. That's from an artist's perspective at least.

**David:** Oh wow - I wish I knew! I asked Alan Moore something similar when I was starting out and he said, 'Trust your own sensibilities'. So I'll go with that!

# CHARACTER FACTOIDS

# VIVA FOREVER

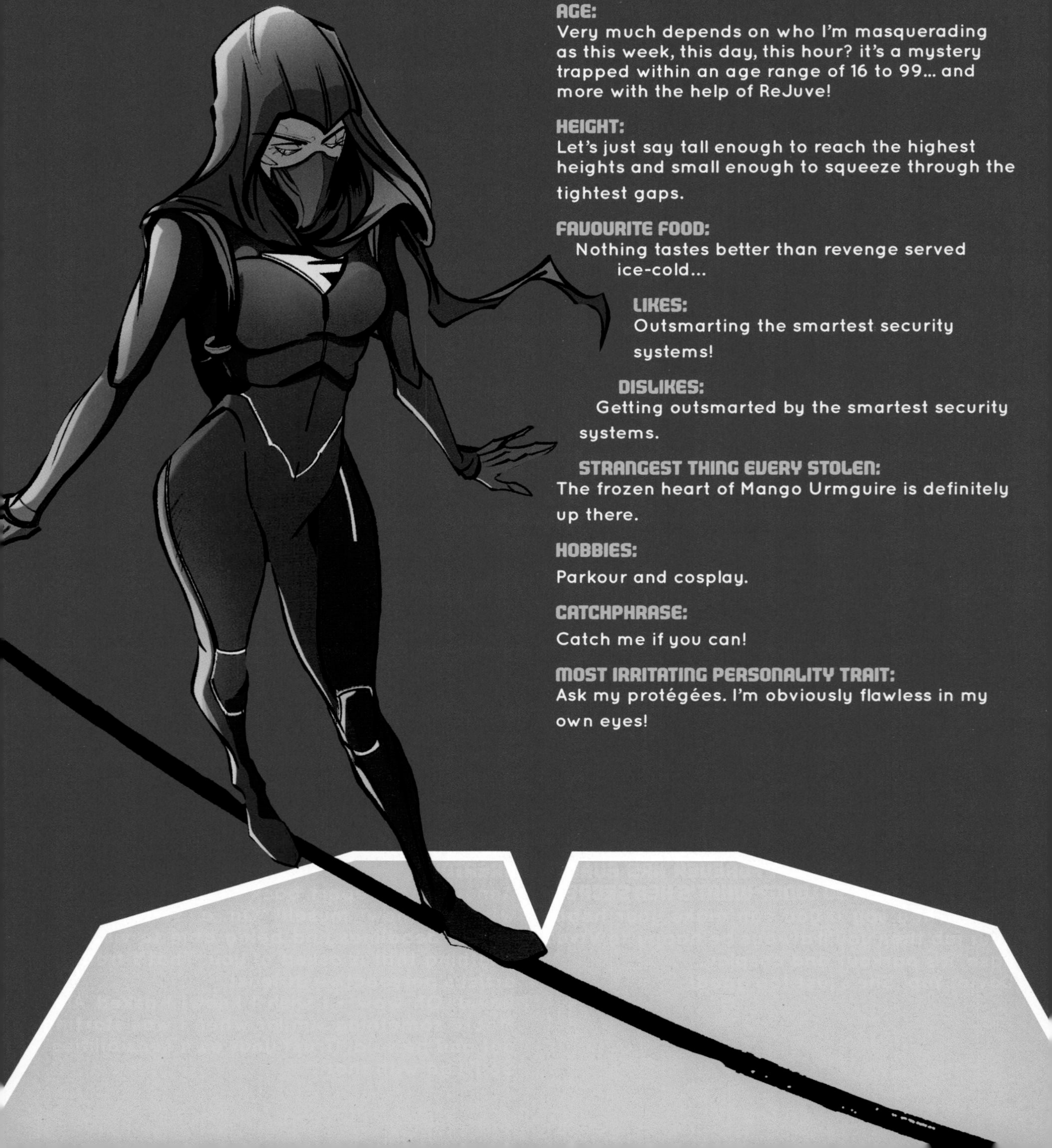

**AGE:**
Very much depends on who I'm masquerading as this week, this day, this hour? it's a mystery trapped within an age range of 16 to 99… and more with the help of ReJuve!

**HEIGHT:**
Let's just say tall enough to reach the highest heights and small enough to squeeze through the tightest gaps.

**FAVOURITE FOOD:**
Nothing tastes better than revenge served ice-cold…

**LIKES:**
Outsmarting the smartest security systems!

**DISLIKES:**
Getting outsmarted by the smartest security systems.

**STRANGEST THING EVERY STOLEN:**
The frozen heart of Mango Urmguire is definitely up there.

**HOBBIES:**
Parkour and cosplay.

**CATCHPHRASE:**
Catch me if you can!

**MOST IRRITATING PERSONALITY TRAIT:**
Ask my protégées. I'm obviously flawless in my own eyes!

# CHARACTER FACTOIDS

## GEM GIANT

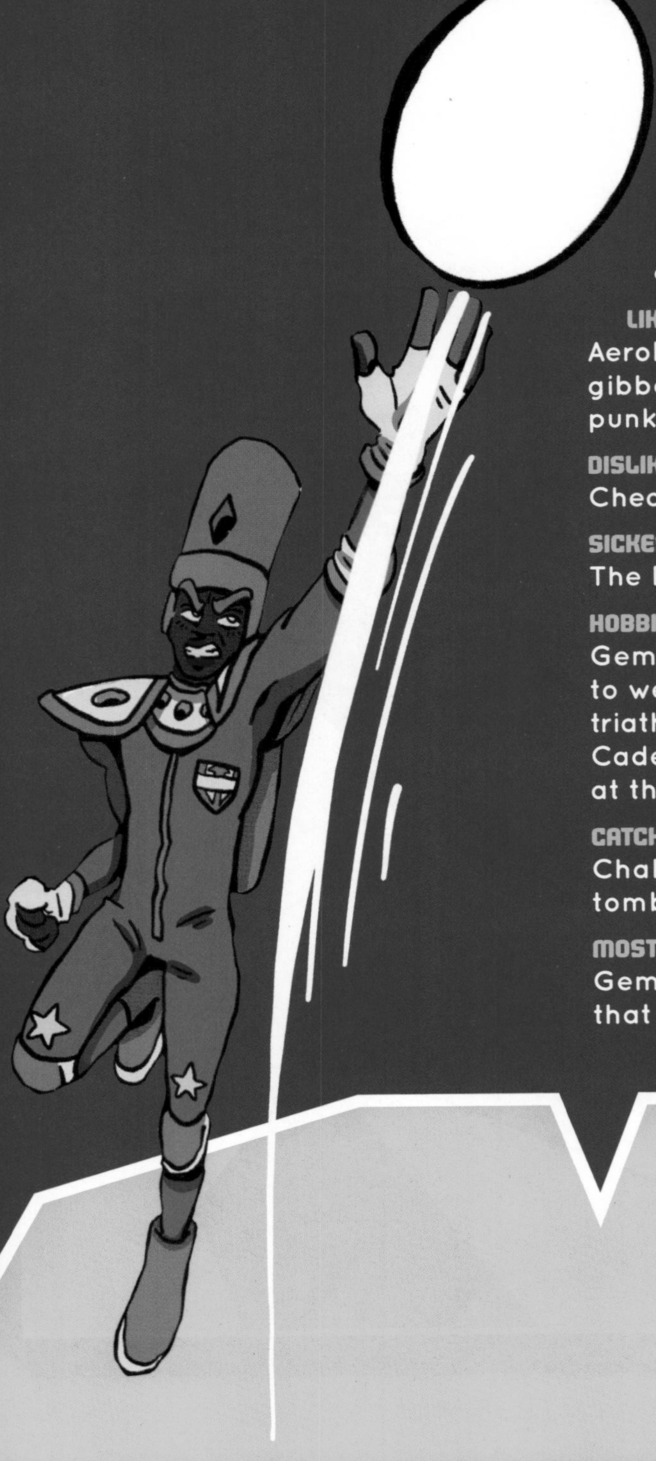

**AGE:**
18 years old

**HEIGHT:**
6 feet 1 inches (subject depending on hairstyle)

**FAVOURITE FOOD:**
Anything that doesn't come from the cadet canteen!

**LIKES:**
Aeroball, playing with 'Dave', their robot gibbon, and listening to A-Punk (African punk).

**DISLIKES:**
Cheaters and slowpokes.

**SICKEST AEROBALL MOVE:**
The Burning Knuckle Spike!

**HOBBIES:**
Gem collects customised enamel badges to wear instead of their cadet badge, does triathlons for fun (usually against their pal, Cadet Tully) and secretly likes to let loose at the Palais de Boing.

**CATCHPHRASE:**
Challenge me and your birthstone is tombstone!

**MOST IRRITATING PERSONALITY TRAIT:**
Gem turns EVERYTHING into a competition that they have to win.

# GALLERY

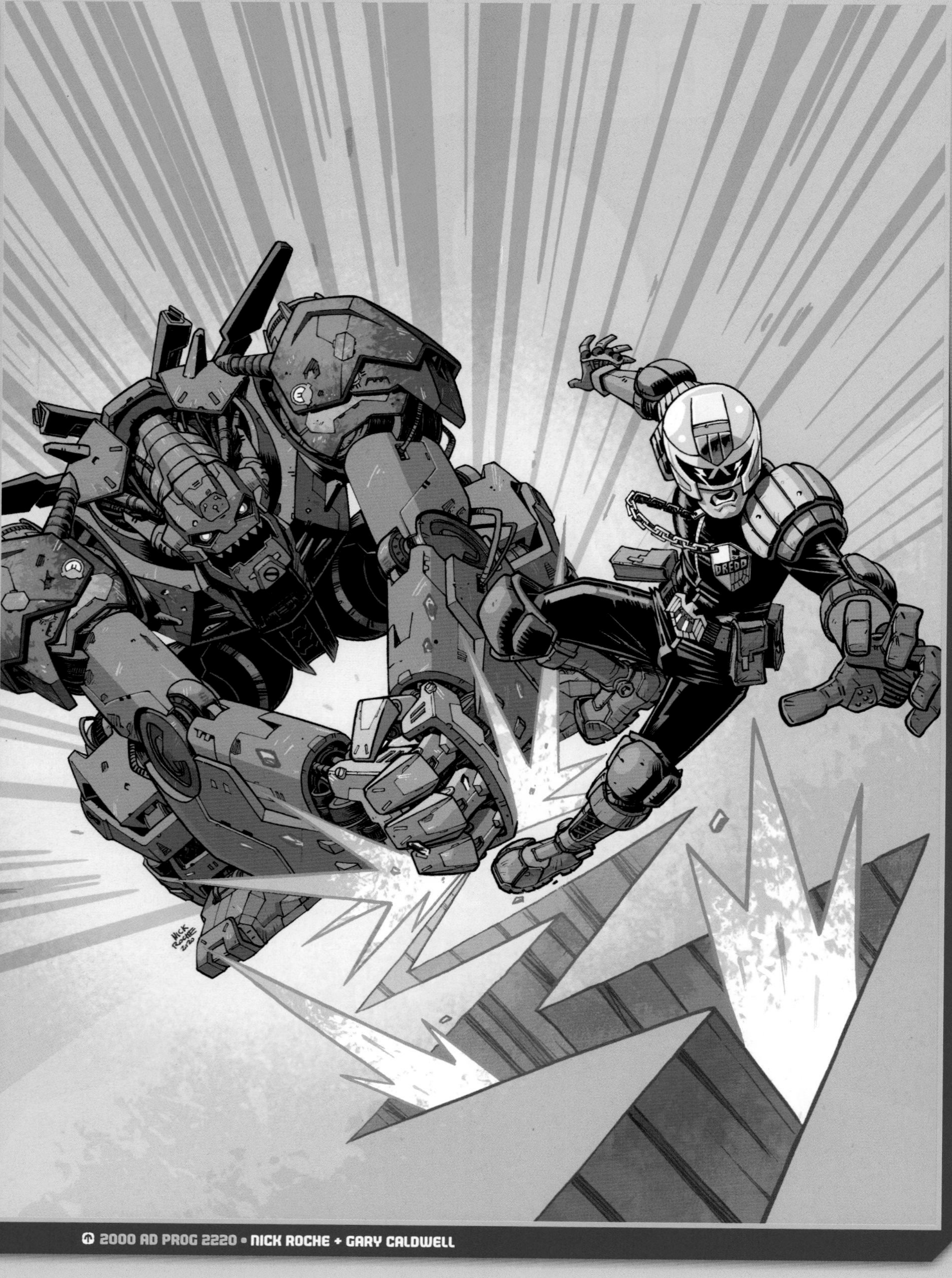

DREDD
NICK ROCHE 2020


2000 AD PROG 2220 • NICK ROCHE + GARY CALDWELL

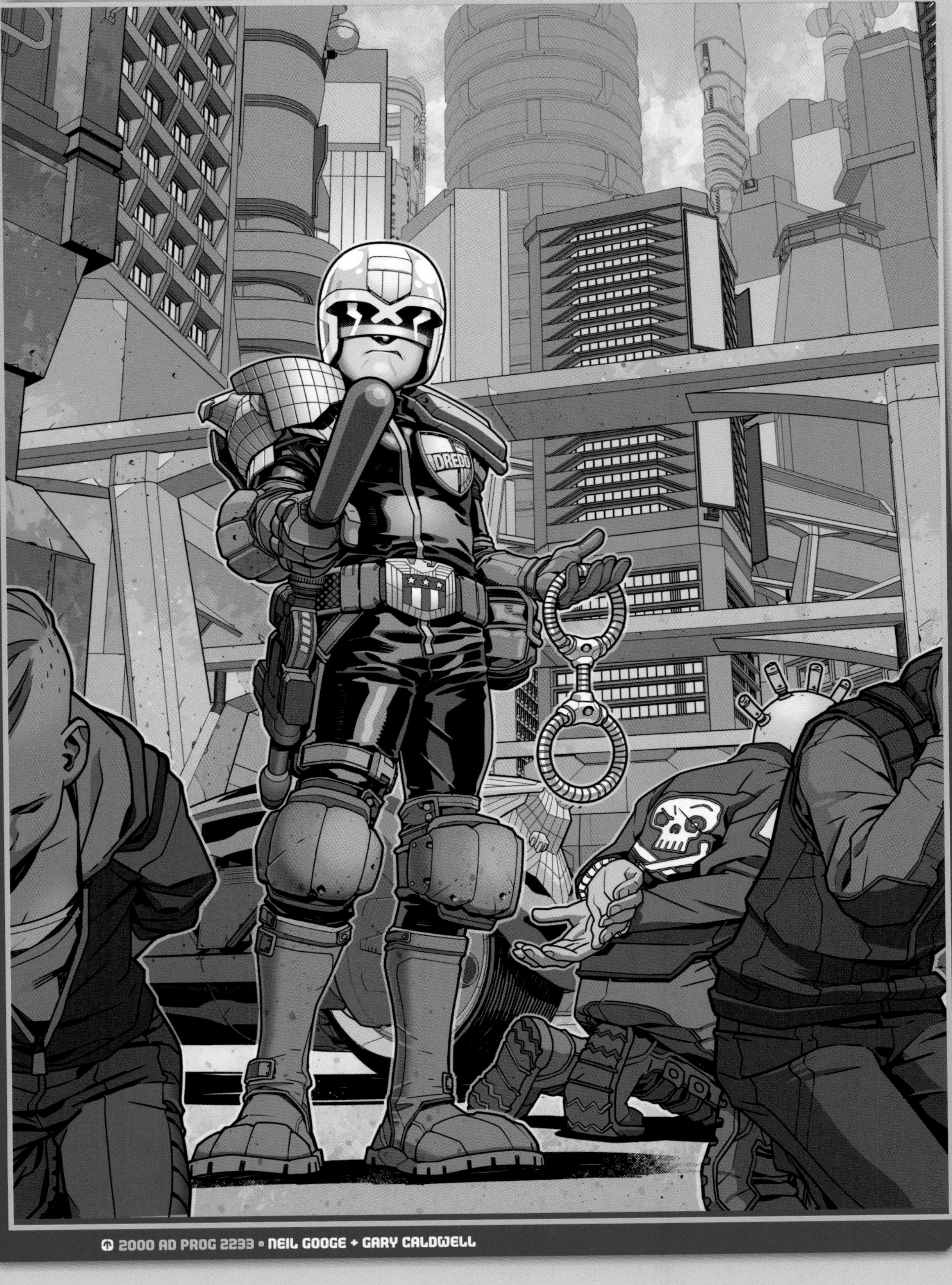
DREDD

2000 AD PROG 2233 • NEIL GOOGE + GARY CALDWELL

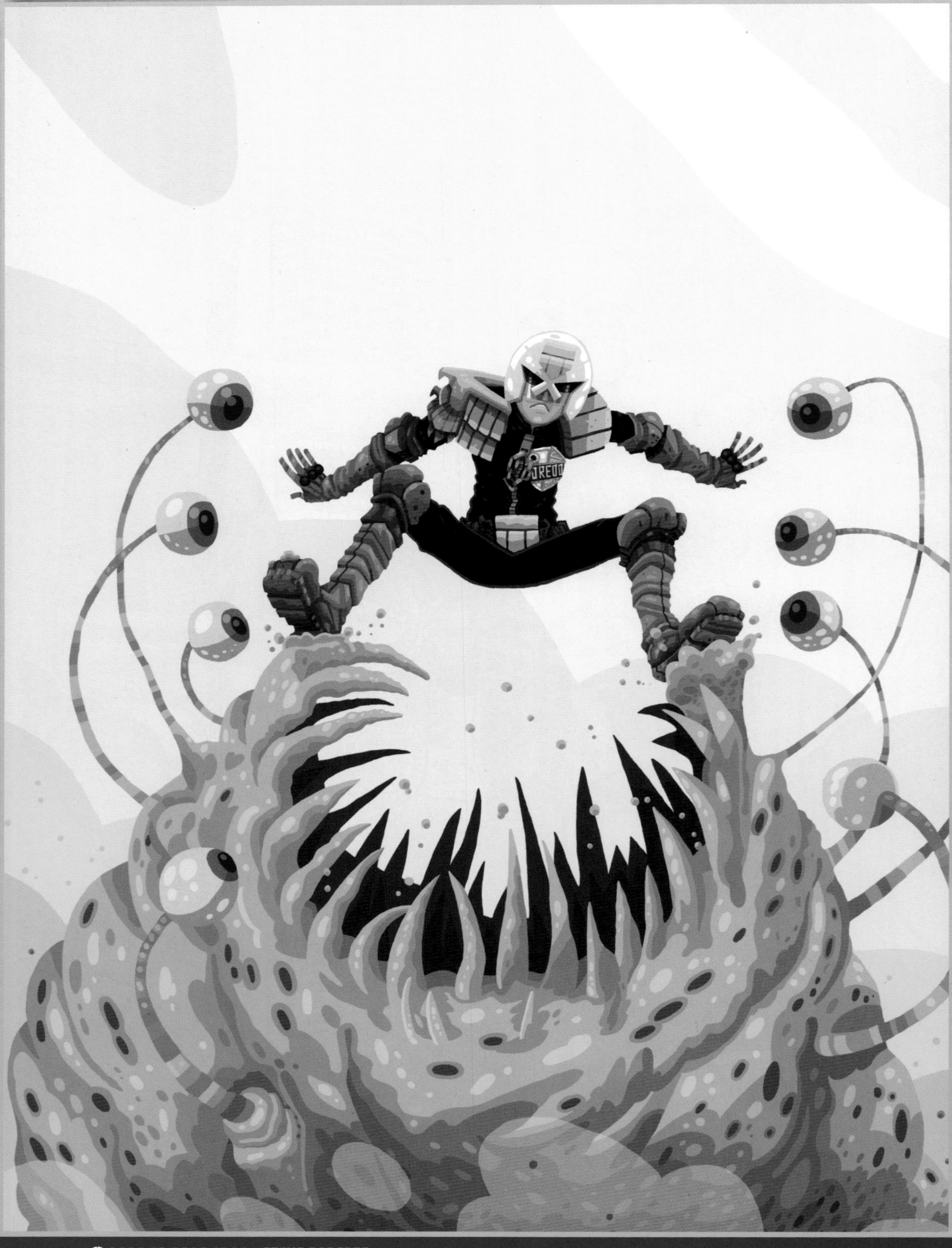

2000 AD PROG 2246 • STEVE ROBERTS

# READY FOR MORE THRILLS?

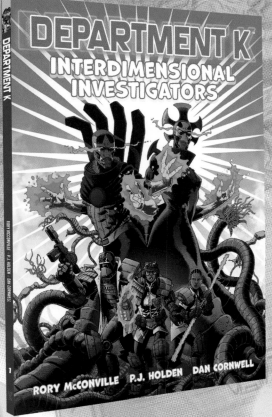

ISBN 978-1-78618-660-7

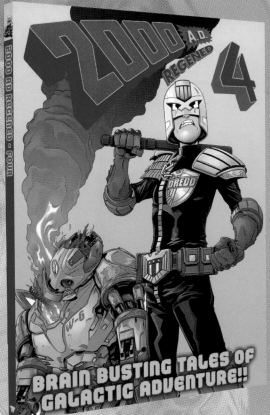

ISBN 978-1-78618-587-7

## DEPARTMENT K
### INTERDIMENSIONAL INVESTIGATORS

# COMING 2022!

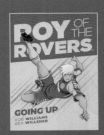
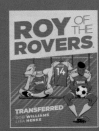

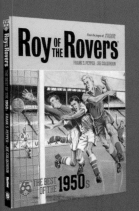
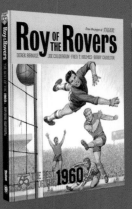
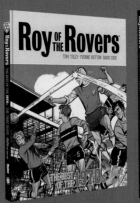

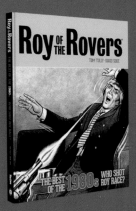

# ANSWERS

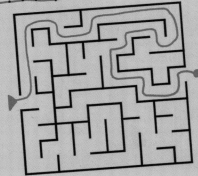

HEAD ALMOST AT *BURSTING* POINT? YOU CAME TO THE RIGHT PLACE, EARTHLET!

## ANDERSON'S BRAIN BUSTERS

THE ITEMS IN THE EVIDENCE ROOM ARE:
COMICS, LAWGIVER, COFFEE, BADGE, HELMET.

UMPTY-BAR

| | | | | | | | |
|---|---|---|---|---|---|---|---|
| ■ | ■ | C | O | M | I | C | S |
| L | A | W | G | I | V | E | R |
| C | O | F | F | E | E | ■ | ■ |
| ■ | ■ | ■ | B | A | D | G | E |
| H | E | L | M | E | T | ■ | ■ |

THE THREE SUSPECTS WHO HAVE THOUGHT ABOUT UMP'S CANDY THE MOST RECENTLY ARE: BERNARD CUGSWORTHY, JONI REEVES & CADET HAWKINS

THE SUSPECTS' THOUGHTS ARE:

JUST MY LUCK TO BE THINKING ABOUT CANDY AT A TIME LIKE THIS! I HOPE I DON'T LOSE MY JOB!

WAIT, THEY HAD UMPTY IN THE GRAND HALL OF JUSTICE?! TOO BAD THEY'D NEVER LET A JUVE LIKE ME INSIDE!

MMM.... UMPTY! I MEAN... I AM THE LAW!

WHICH SUSPECTS HAVE A TASTE FOR UMPTY?
ALL THREE - IT'S JUST A DELICIOUS CANDY BAR!
WHICH SUSPECTS HAVE ACCESS TO A VEHICLE?
JONI REEVES AND CADET HAWKINS HAVE ACCESS TO A VEHICLE.
WHICH SUSPECTS KNOW HOW TO GET INTO THE GRAND HALL OF JUSTICE?
BERNARD CUGSWORTHY AND CADET HAWKINS BOTH KNOW HOW TO GET INTO THE GRAND HALL OF JUSTICE.

| | | | | | | | | | | | | | | | | |
|---|---|---|---|---|---|---|---|---|---|---|---|---|---|---|---|---|
| X | F | U | L | L | T | I | L | T | B | O | O | G | I | E | D | V |
| A | R | O | G | U | E | T | R | O | O | P | E | R | A | D | I | E |
| C | I | C | O | F | V | I | B | L | U | B | N | A | K | U | N | N |
| T | U | A | M | I | B | A | N | D | E | R | S | O | N | O | T | U |
| I | H | D | Y | N | Z | Q | U | I | O | T | I | K | B | E | E | S |
| O | U | E | A | D | E | P | A | R | T | M | E | N | T | K | S | B |
| N | N | T | G | E | B | L | O | O | G | E | R | U | P | I | T | L |
| P | I | D | O | R | W | I | G | U | P | P | Y | T | E | G | I | U |
| A | G | R | O | G | O | A | T | E | S | I | Z | B | U | G | N | E |
| C | B | E | L | U | S | N | R | R | C | L | E | M | A | Q | A | G |
| T | A | D | I | D | E | N | K | T | I | G | R | C | A | T | U | E |
| U | T | D | A | B | E | L | A | R | D | S | N | A | Z | Z | T | N |
| T | C | E | F | R | E | P | A | R | O | D | N | A | P | A | S | E |
| Z | S | T | R | O | N | T | I | U | M | D | O | G | I | G | J | S |

THE UMPTY THIEF IS ....
CADET HAWKINS. THE ONLY SUSPECT WHO HAS ACCESS TO A VEHICLE AND KNOWS HOW TO GET INTO THE GRAND HALL OF JUSTICE. ALSO, HOW DID SHE KNOW THAT UMPTY WAS STOLEN WHEN ANDERSON WAS CALLED IN TO FIND THE MISSING OBJECT? BOOK 'EM AND COOK 'EM!

***CASE CLOSED!***

YOU ATE IT ALL AND NOW YOU HAD A SUGAR CRASH!
I'M SORRY! THOUGHT IT WOULD BE NICE TO TRY!
THERE'S YOUR PUNISHMENT, THAT'S WHY ITS ILLEGAL!
OOH...! MY HEAD... AND MY STOMACH!